THORN QUEEN

Richelle Mead

BANTAM BOOKS

LONDON • TORONTO • SYDNEY • AUCKLAND • JOHANNESBURG

TRANSWORLD PUBLISHERS
61–63 Uxbridge Road, London W5 5SA
A Random House Group Company
www.rbooks.co.uk

THORN QUEEN
A BANTAM BOOK: 9780553819878

Originally published in the United States of America by
Kensington Books
First publication in Great Britain
Bantam edition published 2009

Copyright © Richelle Mead 2009

Richelle Mead has asserted her right under the Copyright, Designs
and Patents Act 1988 to be identified as the
author of this work.

This book is a work of fiction and, except in the case of historical
fact, any resemblance to actual persons,
living or dead, is purely coincidental.

A CIP catalogue record for this book
is available from the British Library.

Addresses for Random House Group Ltd companies outside the UK
can be found at: www.randomhouse.co.uk
The Random House Group Ltd Reg. No. 954009

The Random House Group Limited supports The Forest
Stewardship Council (FSC), the leading international forest
certification organisation. All our titles that are printed on
Greenpeace approved FSC certified paper carry the FSC logo.
Our paper procurement policy can be found at
www.rbooks.co.uk/environment

Typeset in 11/13pt Sabon by
Falcon Oast Graphic Art Ltd.
Printed in the UK by CPI Cox & Wyman, Reading, RG1 8EX.

6 8 10 9 7 5

For Jen and Chad,
who understand the value of a good monster

Chapter One

Sad fact: lots of kids know how to use knives and guns.

I'd been one of them, but instead of pursuing a life of crime, I'd trained to be a shamanic mercenary. This meant that while my friends were at dances and football games, I'd been out banishing spirits and wrestling down monsters with my stepfather. On the upside, I grew up never fearing muggers or any other assailants. On the downside, an adolescence like that really screws with your social development.

It meant I'd never really been like other kids. I'd had some friends, but compared to their world, mine had been terribly stark and terribly deadly. Their dramas and concerns had seemed so petty next to mine, and I could never fully relate. As an adult now, I still couldn't really connect to kids because I had no shared experiences to draw on.

Which made my job today that much more difficult.

"Go ahead, Polly," crooned the girl's mother,

smiling with overplump lips. Too much collagen, I suspected. "Tell her about the ghost."

Polly Hall was thirteen but wore enough makeup to rival a forty-year-old whore. She sat slouched against the back of a couch in her family's perfectly decorated house, chewing gum loudly, looking everywhere but at us. The more I studied her, the more I decided she probably did have problems. I suspected they had less to do with supernatural influences and more with having a mother who had named her Polly and let her wear thongs. It was an unfortunate side effect of Polly's low-cut jeans that I could see the aforementioned thong.

After a minute of silence, Mrs. Hall sighed loudly. "Polly, dear, we've been over this. If you aren't going to help us, we can't help you."

Smiling, I knelt down in front of the couch so I could look the girl in the eyes. "It's all right," I told her, hoping I sounded sincere and not like an after-school special. "I'll believe whatever you tell me. We'll get it taken care of."

Polly sighed just as loudly as her mother had a moment ago and still refused to look at me. She reminded me of my unstable teenage half sister who was currently MIA and wanted to conquer the world. "Mom," she said, "can I go to my room now?"

"Not until you've talked to this nice lady." Glancing back to me, Mrs. Hall explained. "We hear strange noises all night: bangs, cracks, bumps. Things fall over for no reason. I've even . . ." She hesitated. "I've even seen things fly around the room. But it's always when Polly's around. Whatever this ghost is, it seems to like her . . . or be obsessed with her."

I turned my attention back to Polly, again taking in the sullen mood and thinly veiled frustration. "You got a lot on your mind, Polly?" I asked gently. "Problems at school or something? Problems around here?"

Her blue eyes flicked to me ever so briefly.

"What about any electrical issues?" This I directed to her mother. "Things shorting out? Stereos or appliances not working right?"

Mrs. Hall blinked. "How'd you know that?"

I stood up and stretched the kinks out of my body. I'd fought a wraith last night, and he hadn't been gentle.

"You don't have a ghost. You have a poltergeist."

Both of them stared at me.

"Isn't that a ghost?" asked Mrs. Hall.

"Not really. It's a manifestation of telekinetic powers, often brought on by rage and other strong emotions during teenage years." I'd evaded after-school special mode, only to slip into infomercial mode.

"I . . . wait. Are you saying Polly's causing this?"

9

"Not consciously, but yeah. In cases like this, the subject—Polly—lashes out without realizing it, venting her emotions in physical ways. She probably won't stay telekinetic. It'll fade as she gets older and settles down a bit."

Her mother still looked skeptical. "It sure seems like a ghost."

I shrugged. "Trust me. I've seen this lots of times."

"So ... isn't there anything you can do? Anything we can do?"

"Therapy," I suggested. "Maybe get a psychic to come out."

I gave Mrs. Hall the contact information for a psychic I trusted. Waiving my banishing fee, I simply charged her for the house call. Once I'd double-checked the cash she gave me— *never* took checks—I stashed it away and made moves toward the living-room door.

"Sorry I couldn't be of more help."

"No, I mean, I guess this helps. It's just so strange." She eyed her daughter with perplexity. "Are you sure it's not a ghost?"

"Positive. These are classic symp—"

An invisible force slammed into me, pushing me into the wall. I yelped, threw out a hand to keep my balance, and shot daggers at that little bitch Polly. Eyes wide, she looked just as astonished as I felt.

"Polly!" exclaimed Mrs. Hall. "You are grounded, young lady. No phone, no IM, no . . ." Her mouth dropped open as she stared at something across the room. "What's that?"

I followed her gaze to the large, pale blue shape materializing before us.

"Um, well," I said, "that's a ghost."

It swooped toward me, mouth open in a terrible screech. I yelled for the others to get down and jerked a silver-bladed athame out of my belt. A knife might seem useless against spirits, but they needed to take on a substantial form to inflict any real damage. Once solid, they were susceptible to silver.

This spirit bore a female shape—a very young female shape, actually. Long pale hair trailed in her wake like a cloak, and her eyes were large and empty. Whether it was a lack of experience or simply some inherent trait of hers, her attack proved floundering and uncoordinated. Even as she screamed at the first bites of the athame, I had my crystal-studded wand out in my other hand.

Now that I'd regained my bearings, I could do a banishing like this in my sleep. Speaking the usual words, I drew from my internal strength and sent my own spirit beyond the boundaries of this world. Touching the gates of the Underworld, I ensnared the female spirit and sent her over. Monsters and gentry I tended to send back to the Otherworld, the limbo they lived in. A ghost like this needed to move on to the land of death. She disappeared.

Mrs. Hall and Polly stared at me. Suddenly, in her first show of emotion, the girl leapt up and glared at me.

"You just killed my best friend!"

I opened my mouth to respond and decided nothing I had to say would be adequate.

"Good heavens, what are you talking about?" exclaimed her mother.

Polly's face twisted with anger, her eyes bright with tears. "Trixie. She was my best friend. We told each other everything."

"Trixie?" Mrs. Hall and I asked in unison.

"I can't believe you did that. She was so cool." Polly's voice turned a little wistful. "I just wish we could have gone shopping together, but she couldn't leave the house. So I just had to bring her *Vogue* and *Glamour*."

I turned to Mrs. Hall. "My original advice still stands. Therapy. Lots of it."

I headed home after that, wondering for the hundredth time why I'd chosen this mercenary shaman profession. Surely there were other jobs that were a lot less trouble than interacting with evil supernatural beings. Accounting. Advertising. Law. Well, maybe not that last one.

About an hour later, I arrived back home and was immediately assaulted by two medium-sized dogs when I cleared the door. They were mutts, one solid black and one solid white. Their names were Yin and Yang, but I could never remember who was who.

"Back off," I warned as they sniffed me, tails wagging frantically. The white one tried to lick my hand. Pushing past them, I entered my kitchen and nearly tripped over a tabby cat sprawled on the floor in a patch of sun. Grumbling, I tossed my bag onto the kitchen table. "Tim? Are you here?"

My housemate, Tim Warkoski, stuck his head into the kitchen. He wore a T-shirt with silhouettes of Native Americans that said *Homeland Security: Fighting Terrorism since 1492*. I appreciated the cleverness, but it lost something since Tim wasn't actually an American Indian. He merely played one on TV, or rather, he played one in local bars and tourist circles, using his tanned skin and black hair to elude his Polish heritage. It had gotten him into trouble with a lot of the local tribes.

With a garbage bag in one hand and a cat scoop in the other, he gave me a dark look. "Do you know how many fucking boxes of litter I've had to change today?"

I poured a glass of milk and sat down at the table. "Kiyo says we need one box for every cat and then an extra one."

"Yeah, I can count, Eugenie. That's six boxes. Six boxes in a house with fifteen hundred square feet. You think your deadbeat boyfriend's ever going to show back up and help out with this?"

I shifted uncomfortably. It was a good question. After three months of dating between Tucson and Phoenix, my boyfriend Kiyo had decided to take a job here to save the hour and a half commute. We'd had a long discussion and decided we were ready to have him simply move in with me. Unfortunately, with Kiyo came his menagerie: five cats and two dogs. It was one of the woes of dating a veterinarian. He couldn't help but adopt every animal he found. I couldn't remember the cats' names any better than the dogs'. Four of them were named after the Horsemen of the Apocalypse, and all I could really recall was that Famine ironically weighed about thirty pounds.

Another problem was that Kiyo was a fox—both literally and figuratively. His mother was a kitsune, a sort of Japanese fox spirit. He'd inherited all of her traits, including amazing strength and speed, as well as the ability to transform into an actual fox. As a result, he frequently got "the call of the wild," making him yearn to run around in his animal form. Since he had downtime between jobs now, he'd left me to take a kind of wild vacation. I accepted this, but after a week of not seeing him, I was starting to get restless.

"He'll be back soon," I said vaguely, not meeting Tim's eyes. "Besides, you can get out of chores if you want to start paying rent." That was our deal. Free lodging in exchange for food and housework.

He wasn't deterred. "Your choice in men is questionable. You know that, right?"

I didn't really want to ponder that too much. I abandoned him for my room, seeking the comfort of a jigsaw puzzle depicting a photograph of Zurich. It sat on my desk, as did one of the cats. I think he was Mr. Whiskers, the non-Apocalyptic one. I shooed him off the puzzle. He took about half the pieces with him.

"Fucking cat," I muttered.

Love, I decided, was a hard thing. Well aware of my grumpy mood, I knew part of my anxiety over Kiyo stemmed from the fact that he was also passing part of his sabbatical in the Otherworld, spending time with his ex-girlfriend who just happened to be a devastatingly beautiful fairy queen. Fairies, sidhe, shining ones . . . whatever you wanted to call them, they were the tall, long-lived rulers of the Otherworld. I and most shamans referred to them as gentry, an antique term. Maiwenn, Kiyo's ex, was almost nine months pregnant, and although they'd broken up, he was still a part of her life.

I sighed. Tim might have been right about my questionable taste in men.

Night wore on. I finished the puzzle while blasting Def Leppard, making me feel better. I was just shutting off the music when I heard Tim yell, "Yo, Eug. Kujo's here."

Breathless, I ran to my bedroom door and flung it open. A red fox the size of a wolf trotted down the hall toward me. Relief burned through me, and I felt my heart soar as I let him in and watched him pace around in restless circles.

"About time," I said.

He had a sleek orange-red coat and a fluffy tail tipped in white. His eyes were golden and sometimes bore a very human glint. I saw nothing like that tonight. A purely animal wariness peered out at me, and I realized it'd be a while before he changed back. He had the ability to transform to a wide range of foxes, everything from a small, normal-sized red fox to the powerful shape before me. When he spent awhile in this bigger form, turning human again took more effort and time.

Still, hoping he'd transform soon, I dumped another puzzle on my desk and worked it as I waited. Two hours later, nothing had changed. He curled up in a corner, wrapping his body in a tight ball. His eyes continued to watch me. Exhausted, I gave up on him and put on a red nightgown. Turning off the lights, I finally slipped into my bed, falling asleep instantly for a change.

As I slept, I dreamed about the Otherworld, particularly a piece of it that bore a striking resemblance to Tucson and the Sonora Desert surrounding us. Only, the Otherworldly version was better. An almost heavenly Tucson, warmed by bright sunshine and ablaze with flowering cacti. This was a common dream for me, one that often left me yearning for that land in the morning. I always tried my best to ignore the impulse.

A couple hours later, I woke up. A warm, muscled body had slid into bed with me, pressing against my back. Strong arms wrapped around my waist, and Kiyo's scent, dark and musky, washed over me. A liquid feeling burned inside of me at his touch. Roughly, he turned me toward him. His lips consumed me in a crushing kiss, blazing with intensity and need.

"Eugenie," he growled, once he'd paused long enough to remove his lips—just barely—from mine. "I've missed you. Oh God, I've missed you. I've needed you."

He kissed me again, conveying that need as his hands ravaged my body. My own hands slid along the smooth perfection of his bare skin, awakening my desire. There was no gentleness between us tonight, only a feral passion as he moved on top of me, his body pushing into mine with a need fueled as much by animal instinct as by love. He had not, I realized, completely regained his human senses, no matter his shape.

When I woke up in the morning, my bed was empty. Across the room, Kiyo pulled on jeans, meeting my eyes as though he had some sixth sense that I was awake. I rolled over on my side, the sheets gliding against my naked skin. Watching him with a lazy, satisfied languor, I admired his body and the sexy features gifted to him by Japanese and Hispanic heritage. His tanned body and black hair stood in stark contrast to the light skin and reddish hair my northern European ancestors had given me.

"Are you leaving?" I asked. My heart, having leapt at his presence last night, suddenly sank.

"I have to go back," he said, straightening out a dark green T-shirt. He ran an absent-minded hand through his chin-length hair. "You know I do."

"Yeah," I said, my voice sharper than I'd intended. "Of course you do."

His eyes narrowed. "Please don't start that," he said quietly. "I have to do this."

"Sorry. Somehow I just can't get all that excited about another woman having your baby."

There it was. The issue that always hung over us.

He sat down beside me on the bed, dark eyes serious and level. "Well, I'm excited. I'd like to think you could support me in that and be happy for me."

Troubled, I looked away. "I am happy for you. I want you to be happy . . . it's just, you know, it's hard."

"I know." He leaned over me, sliding his hand

up the back of my neck, twining his fingers in my hair.

"You've spent more time with her in the last week than with me."

"It's a necessity. It's almost time."

"I know," I repeated. I knew my jealousy was unwarranted. Petty, even. I wanted to share his happiness at having a child, but something in me prevented it.

"Eugenie, I love you. It's that simple. That's all there is to it."

"You love her too."

"Yes, but not in the way I love you."

He kissed me with a gentleness very different from the roughness of last night. I melted against him. The kiss grew stronger, filling with ardor. With great reluctance, he finally pulled away. I could see the longing in his eyes. He wanted to have sex again. That said something for my charms, I guessed.

His responsible inclinations winning out, he straightened and stood up. I stayed where I was.

"Will I see you there?" he asked, voice even and neutral.

I sighed. "Yeah. I'll be there."

He smiled. "Thank you. That means a lot to me."

I nodded.

He went to the door and looked back at me. "I

love you." The heat in his voice told me he truly meant it. I smiled back.

"I love you too."

He left, and I pulled the sheets more tightly against me and made no motions to get up. I couldn't stay in bed all day, unfortunately. Other things—like my promise to Kiyo—demanded my attention today. There was a trip to the Otherworld ahead of me, one that would take me to a kingdom I'd reluctantly inherited. You see, Maiwenn wasn't the only Otherworldly queen in Kiyo's life.

Yet, astonishingly, that wasn't the problem for me today. That was easy compared to what else lay in store for me.

I had to go to a gentry baby shower.

Chapter Two

Crossing over to the Otherworld is easier for me than most people but still requires a bit of work. Once I'd packed up what I needed, I had to drive to Saguaro National Park and hike out to a remote corner of it. Here, two very faint trails intersected in a crossroads—a common marker for gates to the Otherworld. It and the human world lie very close to each other, and certain spots between the two are thinner. Of course, even a thin spot like this wouldn't always be enough for some people to make the journey in their own bodies. They might end up going in spirit or an elemental form. But me? I bore the blood of humans and of the gentry. I could therefore travel both worlds with ease, though my gentry heritage still unnerved me. It was only a recent discovery, one I had trouble coming to terms with.

Standing at the crossroads, I closed my eyes, slipping into a trance very similar to the one I used to banish the spirit yesterday. A tattoo of a greenish snake coiled around one of my arms in tribute to Hecate, the goddess who guarded transitions and chthonic magic. Invoking her, drawing on her power, I stretched my body beyond this world. A moment later, I stood in the Otherworld. In a castle. A castle that belonged to me.

I recovered myself quickly since crossover side effects almost never bothered me anymore. The room I stood in was a small sitting room, sparsely furnished. In the center of it was a rabbit paperweight, white resin with little blue flowers. It was silly, but that rabbit was imbued with my essence, meaning when I crossed over from Saguaro National Park—or any other crossroads of my choice—my body would travel to this spot rather than to some remote place.

Footsteps sounded on the outside hallway's stone floor. A moment later, a bright-eyed young woman with long blond hair peered inside. Her face split into a wide grin when she saw me.

"Your majesty," she breathed, delighted. Turning back around, she yelled down the hall. "The queen! The queen is here!"

I winced. Man, I wished I could come here without all the hype. Bad enough I had to come here at all.

Her proclamation made, Nia ran up to me, squeezing my hand. She was one of my servants. I guess you'd call her my lady-in-waiting since she was responsible for my appearance most of the time. "Everything's ready to go to the Willow Land," she told me. "I've picked out an amazing gown for you."

I shook my head, reaching into the backpack I almost always lugged around. The gentry favored heavy brocades and other elaborateness in their fashion. I wasn't up for any of that today. "I brought my own."

She stared at the dress I produced, then looked back up at me with raised eyebrows. "You're jesting, your majesty, right?" Those blue eyes pleaded. "Right?"

I was saved from an argument when others entered the room. Still staring mournfully at the dress, Nia retreated so my senior staff could talk to me. Yeah. Senior fairy staff. Three months still wasn't enough time to get used to this.

A tall, very lovely woman with glossy black braids strode in, her movements both athletic and graceful. Her name was Shaya, and I depended on her more than anyone else around here. She was my regent, handling all the dirty work I didn't want to deal with, and I was grateful and lucky to have her.

With her was Rurik, the captain of my guard. Having guards was also something that took a lot of getting used to—particularly since they always wanted to follow me around. Rurik and I had gotten off to a bad start, probably because he'd tried to rape me the first time we met. Sporting a

23

large build and pale blond hair, he'd proven himself a capable servant, though I'd often found him fooling around with other women who worked here. I had let him know in a very pleasant voice that I'd rip him apart if I ever found out those women hadn't consented to his advances.

A few others trailed in, officials that I'd inherited with the castle when I killed its former king. I couldn't remember half their names.

"Welcome back," said Shaya, smiling. She didn't possess Nia's rapture but still seemed genuinely pleased to see me.

"Your majesty," the others intoned, bowing.

They waited for me to sit in one of the chairs, joining me a moment afterward.

"Nia says we're ready to go?" I asked, unable to hide my dismay at the upcoming trip.

"Yes," Shaya told me. "We simply await your command. At an easy pace, we should be able to do it in three hours."

I groaned. "Three hours. Do you know how crazy that is? I could do it in half that time by driving to a gateway in my own world and crossing over closer."

She regarded me indulgently, having heard this argument before. "You can't show up at Queen Maiwenn's court without your retinue."

Rurik, sprawled lazily in the chair, flashed me a grin. "It's part of your image, your majesty."

I rubbed my eyes. "All right. Whatever. Any word on Jasmine?"

His smile faded. "No. We've still got scouting parties roaming the kingdoms, but they've found nothing."

"Incredible. You guys can make trees come to life and raise stones from the earth, but you can't find one pouty teenage girl."

"We'll find your sister," Rurik said grimly. I think he'd taken this mission as a matter of personal pride. "It may take a while, but we'll find her."

I nodded because there was nothing else to do. The waiting infuriated me. Every moment that passed meant Jasmine, a mere fifteen years old, had another chance to get pregnant and give birth to a prophesied heir that would allegedly conquer the human world. I was subject to the same prophecy but was smart enough to use birth control.

"Anything else? How are things going otherwise?"

Shaya schooled her face to neutrality. "We manage, your majesty."

She kept her voice as blank as her expression, but I could see badly feigned disapproval on the others' faces. They didn't like the way I neglected my duties here. I suspected Shaya disapproved as well, but it didn't stop her from sparing me the details of the Thorn Land's day-to-day affairs. She knew I didn't really want to hear them, no matter my asking, so she didn't tell me.

I noticed then just how truly oppressive the heat was in here. Everyone was sweating.

"My God, it's hot," I said.

They all stared at me, and I immediately felt stupid. What had I expected? When I'd conquered the kingdom, it had shaped itself to my will, transforming itself into my idea of perfection: the Sonora Desert. The castle had not changed, and remained in its constant state: thick blocks of stone. Black stone. Stone that absorbed heat like crazy and had little ventilation. It was the kind of place more suited to cold, misty moors.

The land had been greener and more temperate under its last ruler, Aeson. Aeson and I had had a fair amount of friction because he'd been trying to get Jasmine pregnant and had wanted to give me a shot too, in hopes that he would be the father of that world-conquering prince. Plus, Aeson was just a total asshole. I'd killed him in battle, and when a ruler dies, the land seeks out someone else powerful. That someone else had been me. I'd claimed the land without realizing what I was doing, and that's when it had transformed to this mirror of Tucson.

It occurred to me how horrible it must be to live here. The gentry lacked most of the technology of my own world. No central air-conditioning. No electric fans. This place had to be roasting these

26

people alive, particularly after what they'd been used to before I came along.

Feeling bad for them, I reached out to the air around me with my mind. For a moment, there was nothing, and then I sensed the moisture particles hanging in the air. There weren't many, but they were there. Spreading beyond the room, I pulled in more moisture, undoubtedly turning nearby halls and rooms into ovens. In here, however, the temperature dropped and grew moist. A slight thrill ran through me, as often happened when I tapped my inherited gentry magic.

Tentatively, I then attempted to move the air itself in some sort of breeze. Nothing. I had managed that feat only once and couldn't repeat it.

Realizing what I'd done, Shaya crooked me a grin. "Thank you, your majesty."

I smiled back and stood. They all hastily followed suit, and I waved them down. "Hang out here if you want. It should stay cool for a little longer. I'm going to go do my . . . thing. Then we'll go."

I left the castle for one of its courtyards, a wide, terraced area that I loved. Saguaros and blooming prickly pears lined it. Purple-flowered smoke-thorns, the tree that had given this land its name, stood sentry, as did mesquite, filling the air with sweetness. A few hummingbirds darted here and there like bright, flying gemstones.

I sat on one of the steps that led to the upper gardens and closed my eyes. This was why I had to come back. If left to me, I would have never returned. But once the Thorn Land had bound itself to me, it was mine. It depended on me for its survival. I didn't entirely understand my connection to it, but it was unbreakable. It was the reason I dreamed about this place. There was no escaping it.

The sun beat down on me, forever reminding us we answered to nature in the end. My body relaxed, and soon, the life of the land spread into me. It always startled me at first, and then I quickly adapted, like it was the most natural thing in the world. The land was me, and I was the land. We were one, neither of us complete without the other.

When I came to, I think almost an hour had passed. I stood up, shaking off my trance. I had extracted myself from that joining with the land but knew it was still with me. It was stronger for having just made the connection. I had fulfilled my duty.

My party set out shortly thereafter. Horse riding was a skill I'd had to perfect pretty quickly since hanging out around here. There were no cars or planes.

Shaya, Rurik, and Nia were with me, as were about a dozen guards. The guards rode stoically, eyes alert and watchful as they surrounded us.

Rurik occasionally barked out an order to them, but mostly he bantered with Shaya and flirted with Nia. I wasn't too good at casual conversation and mostly just listened, more entertained by them than I wanted to admit.

It was late morning, and the sun showed us no mercy as we traveled. I fared better than the rest, wearing shorts and sunglasses. The other women at least had lightweight dresses, but the men wore full leather armor and had to suffer considerably. None of them complained, not even Rurik, but sweat poured down their faces.

So, it was something of a relief when we hit our first shift in the land. It's an oddity of the Otherworld that it folds in upon itself. Traveling is disorienting. In going in a straight line out of my kingdom, it was entirely possible to cross other kingdoms and then my own again without deviating from our course.

We crossed into the Oak Land, and suddenly it was as though the Thorn Land had never existed. You couldn't even see it behind us. One of the guards broke his rigid demeanor to emit a small cheer that made everyone laugh. A cool, almost chill breeze rushed over us. Late autumn had settled on the Oak Land, setting the trees on fire with brilliant colors. It was gorgeous—and much more comfortable—but I secretly hoped we'd pass out of it soon. I had too many disturbing memories of this place.

Sure enough, we soon crossed into the Thorn Land again, slamming into that unforgiving heat. It felt like traveling in circles, but the others assured me we stayed on course. That stint was brief, and our next shift took us to the Rowan Land. Late summer ruled here, but it was a more temperate summer than my own kingdom's. Cherry trees filled the landscape. Last I'd seen them, pink blossoms had covered almost every square inch of the branches. Now, as I looked closer, I could see bright red fruit weighing them down.

And it was then that the wights attacked.

Wights were denizens of the Otherworld, and while they weren't spirits exactly, they had the ability to turn invisible. So, my guards' vigilance had done no good. I counted seven as they swooped out of the orchards. They wore gray clothing and had long, pale faces. For the most part, they looked very much like humans and gentry. Light flared around them as they rained down bolts of power upon us. Wights were even more strongly tied to magic than the gentry, and conventional weapons had little effect on them. You had to take them down with magic. Unfortunately, the storm magic I'd inherited from my father still wasn't quite up to hardcore attacks. Neither was my guards' magic. Special magic-wielding soldiers aside, I'd learned most warriors here were weak in magic; it was why they'd chosen a more physical profession.

I still suspected the silver bullets in my Glock might hurt the wights. Only, I had a problem. My guards had closed rank around Nia—the only civilian here—and me. Getting a shot off would likely kill one of them.

"Let me out!" I yelled. "Let me fight!"

The guards ignored me and, in fact, redoubled their own shouts of "The queen! Protect the queen!"

Swearing, I managed to lean through and get a shot off that took one of the wights in the chest. It didn't kill him but clearly caused severe injury. Nearby, a cherry tree ripped itself from the earth. Infused by magic and therefore potentially lethal, it attacked the wounded wight. That was Shaya's handiwork. She had been a warrior before settling into my administration.

As we fought, I soon deduced the point of this attack. The wights wanted me—not to kill me, but for other . . . more amorous purposes. They didn't seem to have much organization save to hack through and see who could get to me. Whoever did could have me.

It sickened me, and an old, familiar fear welled up. I could handle concussions, broken bones, and the other myriad effects of my vocation. Rape was not something I could contend with. It had become a daily danger, however, since learning about my half-gentry heritage. My father, honorifically dubbed Storm King, had been a tyrannical warlord—one of the most powerful magic users the Otherworld had ever seen. He'd been intent on crossing over and conquering humanity. He'd come damned close, too, until my stepfather, Roland, had defeated him. Unfortunately, a prophecy had surfaced in Storm King's wake, a prophecy that said his daughter's son would complete his work. That was why I was such a hot commodity among Otherworldly males who believed in Storm King's vision. It was also why Jasmine wanted to get pregnant.

Giving up on the gun, I produced my jewel-studded wand and started simply casting out the wights to the Underworld. Instant death. As I did my thing and the guards did theirs, we suddenly reached a point where all grew quiet. The wights were dead or gone.

Everyone in my party immediately looked to see if I was all right, which I found ridiculous since two of the guards lay on the ground, and a number of them were bleeding.

"Forget about me," I snapped. "Check on them!"

None had died, much to my relief. Gentry were hard to kill in their own world. They were long-lived and hardy. One of the guards had some healing powers, and we spent a considerable amount of time patching the group up. When we finally set out again, Shaya glanced up at the sun's position and frowned.

"We're going to be late."

I thought about Kiyo. Then I thought about Maiwenn, who always looked like some sort of golden goddess, even with her belly ready to burst with Kiyo's son or daughter. Walking in late to her elite baby party, breaching etiquette under her cool gaze . . . Well, suddenly I wanted to ride as we'd never ridden before.

Unfortunately, our wounded couldn't do that. Frustrated, we finally split the party, and those of us who were uninjured rode on at a brisk pace, hoping to cut our time. Before long, we crossed to the Willow Land and slammed into its freezing temperatures. It was just coming out of winter, and spring thaws were in progress, but the chill proved a shock nonetheless. We rode on down the road, determined to get there. We finally made it.

But we were still late.

Maiwenn's castle staff eyed our bedraggled state but showed me to a room where I could clean up and get ready. Nia practically had a conniption as Shaya and I hastily washed ourselves off and pulled on fresh clothes. Nia's magical gifts gave her a knack for adorning others and arranging hair. Kind of a magical beautician. It killed her that I almost never utilized her services. I could see her itching to do something intricate to my hair, but I shook my head.

"No time. Make it fast. Wear it down."

Obliging—but disapproving—she used magic

and a brush to work it into gleaming, silky lengths, pulling a little of it up with a barrette and stealing a couple of small daisies from a nearby vase to tuck into the barrette. With her magic, I knew it would stay perfectly arranged for hours. I splashed on some violet perfume, hoping it would cover any sweatiness I'd missed. With that, we were off.

When Shaya and I approached the ballroom, it was obvious we were the last to arrive. The room was packed. I sighed loudly.

"It's all right," murmured Shaya. "You're a queen. You're expected to be eccentric. Don't look embarrassed."

"Is it possible," I asked, "that we could just sneak in without anyone noticing?"

Before she could answer, a herald stood in the doorway and announced in a voice designed for carrying over loud crowds: "Her Royal Majesty, Queen Eugenie Markham, called Odile Dark Swan, Daughter of Tirigan the Storm King, Protector of the Thorn Land, Beloved of the Triple Moon Goddess."

Dozens of heads swiveled toward us.

I sighed again and answered my own question. "Apparently not."

Chapter Three

Once I stopped hyperventilating from all the attention on me, I immediately realized Nia had been right about the dress.

Like always, the gentry dressed like that they were going to a Renaissance Faire that served ecstasy. Satin, velvet, silk. Even a little leather here and there. Lots of jewelry, lots of skin. The glittering array dazzled the eye, the colors shining, rich, and vivid.

I wore a sundress meant to have sort of a vintage look. Made of tan gauze scattered with a design of tiny yellow flowers, it had an empire waist and a clingy little skirt that went to my knees. The straps tied behind my neck, and most of my back stayed bare, all the better to show off my tattoos: a woman's face within a full moon on my neck and a line of violets on my lower back. The dress's color looked great with the dusky, light auburn of my hair.

Unfortunately, while the shabby-chic peasant look might be expensive and very much in vogue in the human world, dressing like a peasant in a place resembling the set from an epic medieval movie made you look like, well, a peasant.

"Oh my God," I hissed to Shaya as we walked through the room. "I look completely out of place."

"Be quiet," she snapped, in a rare display of the consternation she probably actually always held around me. "You are queen of the Thorn Land. You destroyed one of the shining ones' most powerful kings. You have the right to wear whatever you want, so act like it."

I swallowed my retort and hoped she and her tough love were right. As it was, I had to resist the urge to cling to her hand like a child. That inept social upbringing of mine made navigating this kind of attention painful. Shaya had promised to stay by my side and ensure my etiquette, though that had allayed my fears only marginally. With a great force of will, I tried to follow her advice and look haughty and unconcerned by my appearance.

"You must go to Maiwenn first," she murmured, "and then most of them will come to you for introductions. You've been a great source of curiosity, and this is your first public appearance since taking the crown."

"Got it. Maiwenn first."

The Willow Queen appeared to be surrounded by a throng of people. We headed toward them. On the way, I received an assortment of nods, curtsies, and bows. The room held a handful of monarchs, my peers, but every other noble held a rank lower than mine. A few of those we passed offered greeting. I suspected I might have met them at a ball I'd attended last spring. Most simply gave me polite murmurings of "Your majesty."

We reached Maiwenn's circle of admirers. I meant to hover on the edges, but the people parted for us, soon giving Shaya and me a front-row view.

Maiwenn sat in an ornately carved wooden throne, its whirling designs accented here and there with gold. She herself was golden, with lustrous, tanned skin and long hair that looked like spilled sunshine. A gown of teal velvet—the same color as her eyes—showed her maternal curves to great advantage. Yet, her greatest ornamentation, in my opinion, was the striking figure of Kiyo standing nearby, one hand resting on the back of her chair. He wore gentry clothing tonight, simple black slacks and a long-sleeved white silk tunic that he probably could have worn among humans without question. His eyes, warm and dark, met mine briefly before turning back to the person addressing Maiwenn. Heat flared between him and me in that moment, and electricity coursed through my body as I remembered last night.

"—best wishes for you and your child, your

majesty," the man was saying. "Truly this is a joyous occasion, and we pray to the gods for good fortune and good health."

I pondered his words, recalling Kiyo telling me this was less of a baby shower and more of a luck ceremony. The gentry did not conceive often, nor did they bear children easily. Infant mortality was high. Old superstition held that a party like this, with so many well-wishers, would imbue the child with luck and ensure prosperity.

The man finished his spiel and gestured to a servant to bring his gift. The servant handed over a small golden chest, about the size of a shoebox, which his master opened with a flourish. A few oohs sounded from those gathered, and I craned my head to see what it held. A glitter of red met my eyes.

"This is my gift to your son or daughter: the finest rubies from my land, polished and cut to perfection."

I blinked and glanced around, wondering if I was the only one who found that gift ridiculous. What the hell was an infant going to do with a crate of rubies? Choke on them? Those things definitely needed a *Not For Children Under 3* warning on them. No one else shared my view, and the group seemed to be in agreement on the gift's value. Kiyo, however, caught my eye, and I saw the faintest of smiles play over his face as he guessed what I was thinking.

The man left, and all eyes swiveled to me. We hadn't arrived first, but apparently my rank bought me cutting rights. Following Shaya's earlier instructions, I stepped forward and kissed Maiwenn's cheek. She kissed mine in return.

"Eugenie, I'm so happy to see you again."

She looked it, too. I don't know if it was faked or not, but she was one of those people who could always look happy and make you think she really cared about you. I suspected most of her kindness was sincere, but she had to have the same uneasiness around me as I did with her, given our respective relationships with Kiyo.

Glancing at his dark looks and her golden ones, I suddenly had a vivid image of them in bed together. I wondered if he'd been as wild with her as with me. I wondered if she'd liked it.

Pushing that picture out of my head, I attempted a return smile. "Thank you for inviting me. Sorry I'm late."

She waved a dismissive hand. "You didn't have to come at all. I'm just glad you're here."

I didn't have any elegant speeches, so I kept my words simple. "I'm . . . very happy for you. I hope things go great with you and the baby."

I glanced over at Shaya, who'd been holding my backpack. She handed it to me, and I noticed then that the number of watchers had increased, eyes curious as to what the half-human queen would give. The Kiyo Love Triangle was no secret; gentry gossip spread around the Otherworld faster than any human tabloid could have kept up with.

Producing a teddy bear, I handed it over to her. She took it, eyes surprised as her hands ran over its smooth, sable-brown fur. I'd paid a lot of money for it. It was some kind of designer brand I'd been told was much coveted among upper-class suburban moms.

"It's, um, a toy," I explained, immediately feeling idiotic. The gentry weren't technologically advanced, but even they could figure that one out.

"It's lovely," she said, touching the seams. "We can't match this kind of workmanship. Thank you."

"Oh, and well . . . I honestly didn't think there was anything else I could give that the baby wouldn't already have. So, instead, I made a donation in its name to a children's charity. Or rather, once we know its name, I'll finalize the donation."

Forgetting the teddy bear, she looked up at me, clearly perplexed. "I don't understand." Those gathered apparently didn't either, judging from the curious expressions.

"I, um, well, gave money to a group that helps sick kids. They'll use that money to take care of them, and it'll be . . ." I grasped for something gentry-friendly. ". . . it'll be done in your baby's honor."

A supreme look of delight flooded her gorgeous

face, and I knew without a doubt she wasn't faking it. She understood, and she liked the gift.

"It's very generous," Kiyo explained to her. The smoldering message his eyes gave me indicated he had a few ideas of how to express his gratitude for the present.

She put her arms around the teddy bear, holding it to her ample chest while her eyes gazed off with thought. "Acts of such kindness . . . done in the baby's name . . ." She turned that radiance back to me. "Acts like that cannot help but generate good will from the gods. Thank you, Eugenie."

A murmur of considering whispers stirred behind us. She and I exchanged a few more remarks, and then I yielded the floor to the next well-wisher.

"Was that okay?" I asked Shaya as we walked away.

"Extremely." A wry note hung in her voice. "I doubted your gift, but now I think you understand this custom better than we do." She switched to a lower tone. "Ah, this is Katrice, the Rowan Queen, coming toward us."

I looked up with interest, having passed through the Rowan Land so many times during my Otherworldly journey. Katrice looked about fifty or so in human years, which meant she could boast a few centuries. Only a little silver laced her thick black hair, and her dark eyes glittered with a keen intellect. A dress of red and white satin covered her stout figure.

"Oh, oh, oh! This is her at last! The Thorn Queen. My dear child, you have been too absent from our gatherings." She put her arms around me and kissed my cheek. It was a bit more slobbery than Maiwenn's kiss. A little overwhelmed by her presence, I returned the gesture. She smelled like roses.

"It . . . it's nice to meet you."

"You are so lovely! Look at her, Marlin. Isn't she lovely?"

She grabbed the arm of a man who looked about twice her age, his wispy gray hair barely covering his head. His eyes indicated he wasn't really at the party right now.

"What?" he asked.

Katrice raised her voice. "Lovely. Isn't she LOVELY?"

"Loverly," he muttered, staring off to my left.

"Duke Marlin, the queen's consort," Shaya whispered.

"Look at you, look at you!" Katrice continued, still bubbling over. "How could a little thing like you have killed Aeson? Hmm? Old Tirigan Storm King would be so proud."

I jerked with surprise, taken aback by the callous reference to both my slaying of Aeson and my father's name. Not noticing my reaction, she gestured frantically to a young man passing

42

nearby. He had slim good looks and raven-black hair tied back in a ponytail. He too wore red and white, and I remembered once seeing the Rowan Land's flag, a rowan tree bordered in red and white. Apparently, they were a patriotic group.

"Darling, darling! Come meet the Thorn Queen." Smiling, he hastened to her side and gave me a courteous nod. "This is my son, Leith. Leith, Queen Eugenie."

He took my hand and kissed it very properly, as was the custom. "A pleasure, your majesty."

"Likewise."

I studied him, curious at seeing a gentry prince. With all the gentry reproductive issues, none of the other monarchs I'd met—aside from Maiwenn—had any children. They tended to be solitary rulers.

He looked so nice and friendly—and like he wasn't currently make plans to get in my pants—that I wanted to make conversation, but I was never very good at initiating that kind of thing. Katrice took the dilemma out of my hands.

"Isn't she beautiful, Leith? I was just saying how I can scarce believe she killed old Aeson. Can you believe that? What was it that I heard, my dear? That you drowned him?"

I cleared my throat uncomfortably. "Um, no, not exactly. I sort of summoned all the water out of his body and blew him apart."

"Oh!" She clapped her hands together as

though it were the most wonderful thing she'd ever heard. "Oh! Oh! Isn't that fascinating? And so clever!"

Apparently noting my discomfort, Leith hastily said, "Mother, I'm sure the Thorn Queen would prefer to discuss more pleasant topics. This is hardly the place to talk about death."

I flashed him a grateful smile. We did indeed move to more mundane topics, and I found he managed a conversation far more effectively than his mother did. "I saw your expression over the rubies," he teased. "You don't think the baby will appreciate those?"

I made a face. "Maybe if they can decorate a crib with them. Or maybe make a mobile. Are those kinds of gifts normal?"

"I'm afraid so," he said, still smiling. "As I heard you say, there isn't much this baby won't get from Maiwenn. Most of these nobles are more interested in making the queen happy, not the baby—hence all the useless gifts."

"Why, Leith," scolded his mother. "That's ridiculous. I'm sure Maiwenn's child will absolutely love the crystal dinnerware we brought."

When I finally excused us, Leith kissed my hand again and spoke in a voice too low for Katrice to hear.

"I'm sorry about her. She doesn't always think before she speaks."

I laughed. "It's okay," I murmured back. "She's a queen. That's her job."

More loudly and properly, he said, "I hope you'll come visit us. Mother's been dying to receive you at our court."

"Sure," I agreed. "One of those days." I tried to reciprocate the politeness. "You should come visit us too. I'm not around much, but you're welcome whenever."

He brightened, as did Katrice who actually stayed silent for a change. "Thank you, Your Majesty. I'd love to. I've heard amazing things about your land. They say it's very fierce. Fierce, but beautiful."

Shaya laughed softly as we departed. "Oh, you don't know what you've done."

I stared at her. "What do you mean? I think I handled that well, considering that woman's endless chattering."

"Don't let her surface fool you. She's shrewder than you think. And powerful. Unfortunately, her son is not."

"Leith? What do you mean? Magically?"

She nodded. "His magic is almost nonexistent. He won't be able to inherit her kingdom."

"Whoa . . ." Considering how long gentry lived, I'd never thought much about inheritance issues. "But he seemed pretty competent. Very intelligent."

"He is. Extremely so. He's an inventor of sorts.

He's created things that have revolutionized their kingdom—and the others, slowly. He most recently created tools to print text in books the way your people do. It'll save a fortune in scribes."

"Like a printing press? Wow." Who knew? Leith was like a fairy version of Gutenberg. Cool. Maybe the Otherworld was well on its way to the Industrial Revolution. "And that doesn't count for anything with ruling?"

"No." Shaya didn't sound sympathetic in the least. Magical strength was the greatest measure of a gentry's worth, which is why my bastard father had been held in such high regard. Those who believed I would match him one day regarded me similarly. "Ingenuity alone is not enough to inherit the throne or bind the land. However, his odds might improve if he had a powerful consort."

I suddenly tripped on my own feet when I caught her meaning. "What, you mean me?"

"By their estimation, you're a good match. Powerful, already ruling a kingdom. Your human blood and ability to conceive makes you extremely attractive, your role in the prophecy doubly so."

"Christ. You people are nuts."

She seemed to be enjoying my dismay. "Like I said, Katrice is shrewd. She wasn't lying when she said she wanted to meet you. She's probably planned this for a while. You inviting Leith to visi fulfilled her dreams. Just wait, he'll come soon."

"How come you guys have no concept of 'just friends' around here? Why is every guy I meet a potential mate? Leith was nice enough and cute, but I mean . . . come on."

I supposed I shouldn't have been surprised, really. The gentry had much looser sexual mores than humans—as a few couples in the room's corners were currently demonstrating—so they probably treated everything as a possible romantic encounter. Considering the wights' less-than-romantic bid for my affections earlier, I should have been grateful for Leith's more civilized courtship. Still, I found it all wearying.

Shaya introduced me to a number of other nobles that afternoon. Most blurred together. I simply smiled and nodded a lot, fantasizing about being home in bed with Kiyo. Near the end of the party, one new person actually caught my attention.

The first interesting thing was just how dark his skin was—a rarity in the otherwise Caucasian gentry of this portion of the Otherworld. His black hair hung around his face in a shower of tiny braids, perfectly setting off the burgundy satin cloak around him. He bowed low over my hand, sweeping his cloak away with a flourish.

"Your majesty," he said with a faint French accent. "It is an honor and a privilege. The stories of your beauty do not do you justice. I am Girard de la Colline."

I accepted his hand kiss with astonishment. "You must be from very far away."

The Otherworld mirrored my own world in geography. The residents here, near Arizona, spoke variations of American English. I wondered idly if those who ruled now had supplanted an American Indian version of the gentry.

"Such a journey is well worth it to be in your presence, but sometime, if you like, I would be honored to tell you stories of my homeland. Its beauty is enough to make a man weep, though I'm given to understand that the terrible beauty of your own kingdom can make men weep as well— for different reasons."

I laughed. "I suppose so. Those who respect it can survive it; those who don't . . . well, don't."

"It sounds just like its queen." He inclined his head. "I also have a small talent with metalwork, if you would ever like anything crafted. I live in the Rowan Land now but would happily take a commission if you require one."

I thanked him for the offer and said I'd think about it. When we left him, I turned to Shaya. "I liked him. But let me guess—he wants to woo me and father my child, too?"

"Oh, he wouldn't be opposed to it, but that's not his short-term goal. He really is quite a gifted artisan—he's even got a little human blood in his ancestry, which lets him somewhat touch iron. But a man like him . . . well, he's a courtier. He hangs around nobility and tries to find connections that might help him rule a kingdom of his own one day."

"Which, my dear Shaya, is a very kind way of saying he is a schmoozing bottom-feeder who will do anything to further his own political aspirations. I will agree with you on his artistic talents, however. Why, we should have him make our good friend the Thorn Queen here a proper crown and solidify her title."

That smooth, laconic voice sliced my heart in two, and I froze. Turning around slowly, I met a pair of long-lashed green eyes flecked with gold and hazel, all framed by a sweep of long, fiery hair that rivaled the trees of autumn in his kingdom.

Dorian, King of the Oak Land.

"Your majesty," exclaimed Shaya happily, giving him a low curtsey. "How are you? How is your domain?"

Dorian smiled and lightly chucked her chin. "Are you afraid my household has fallen apart without you? I confess, it does run a bit less smoothly than before, but we endure what we must. I have no doubts your new mistress has more need of your services than I, so I shall suffer longer for her sake."

He gave me a pointed look. I said nothing. Shaya glanced between the two of us, her happy mien turning nervous. "If you'll excuse me, your majesties, I'm going to find some refreshment. I'll return momentarily."

I sincerely doubted that, but she departed too quickly for me to protest. I wanted to follow her but was now trapped.

A bit of his showmanship dimmed, but the wit and lazy amusement that constantly cloaked Dorian remained. He always behaved as though he were on a stage, both in his mannerisms and his melodramatic—and often wry—commentary. I guess as a king he kind of was on stage during his life.

"Well, Eugenie, here we are." Dorian carelessly smoothed down the black velvet of his robe. Gold and red patterns danced around the hems. "You are a vision of sublime beauty, as always."

"Oh come on," I exclaimed. "Not from you, of all people. I'm the most shoddily dressed person in this room."

"No. I saw a scullery maid dressed nearly as badly. A crown really would go a long way to establish your standing. But, barring that, your dress is actually lovely and well-made, even if plain. Wait and watch: you'll see women wearing copies of it soon. The fact that you can still draw eyes while wearing it is a testament to your beauty and presence. You achieve what most of these trumped-up, painted women cannot, no matter how many layers of heavy, rich fabric cover them up."

I gestured toward his robe. "You're covered up in a fair amount of heavy, rich fabric yourself."

The edges of his lips curled up. "If they bother you, I can remove as many of these layers as you like."

I rolled my eyes, but the damage was done. With those few words, I once again saw his naked body, smooth and perfect in the moonlight, hovering over mine as I lay bound to his bed. It had been one night, one night only, but it was a night I'd had little luck in forgetting for the last three months. Seeing Dorian stirred it all up again, filling me with confusion over the way my body had responded to such domination.

Long before that night, Dorian had been one of my first allies in the Otherworld. He'd supported Storm King—and would have loved to knock me up—but had stood firm against any notion of rape. He'd wanted me of my own free will. In the end, he'd helped me defeat Aeson and had shown me the fundamentals of using magic.

"Did you give Maiwenn something?" I asked abruptly, steering us elsewhere.

He scrutinized me a moment before answering. "Yes, of course. What was it? Ah. Yes. Bolts of lovely cloth that I'm sure she can do . . . something . . . lovely with. My steward picked it out. A paltry present compared to yours, or so I hear." His eyes tracked across the room to where Maiwenn and Kiyo laughed with some woman I didn't

51

recognize. "Look at them. Their child will be something to see, don't you think? They make a very striking couple. I should commission a painter to do a family portrait once the baby arrives. Something they can all treasure for years to come."

I stiffened. "That's why you wanted to talk to me, huh? You haven't changed, Dorian, and I'm not going to stay here and play if you're just going to try to bait me. I didn't want to talk to you anyway."

Dorian gave a long-suffering sigh. "You always think so little of me, Eugenie. I wished to speak with you because I wanted to know how you've been. I've missed you. How do you like being a queen? Your land hasn't perished . . . yet . . . so I'm taking that as a good sign."

Still irked by the Kiyo jibe, I fixed him with a glare. "I didn't want to be a queen at all. It's *your* fault I've gotten into this. If you hadn't tricked me into claiming the land, I'd be in Tucson right now and away from all of this." The sting of what he'd done, binding me to the Thorn Land, still itched within me. I wasn't sure if I could ever forgive him for that.

"Not true. You'd still be here, moping around while your lover receives gifts for his child, just as you are right now. And men like the young Rowan prince would still solicit you because whatever other titles come and go, you will always be Storm King's daughter."

"I don't really want to be that either."

He spread his hands out, palms up, in a gesture of helplessness. "That I cannot change. All I can do with that is help you to develop the powers you inherited, but you've already refused my aid there."

I looked away. "I don't need your help." Aside from the grudge I held against him, I couldn't shake the feeling that more of his "help" would result in me in his bed again.

He took a step toward me. "Have you been teaching yourself?"

I didn't answer.

"You have been, haven't you? Or trying to, at least. Odd, considering I distinctly recall you saying you were satisfied with the level of magic you'd reached through my training." He smiled. "How is that going? Perhaps you'd like my help again?"

I jerked my head back toward him. Too much at this party had ground me down already, and his serpent's tongue was the point that threatened to break me. "No. I don't need your help. I don't need anyone's help, okay? I'm happy with what I'm teaching myself. If I advance, fine. If I don't, fine. It doesn't matter to me."

He laughed, a soft and deadly sound that poured over me like honey. "Eugenie, Eugenie. You may lie to other people, you may lie to your kitsune, and you may even lie to yourself. But *do not* lie to me. I was the one who first taught you to control your magic. I've seen how you crave it, how you glow with the rush of that power. I know how it makes you feel because I've felt it too. I can see in those lovely violet eyes of yours how passionately you want to tap more of that magic. It's consuming you."

"As usual," I said in a low voice that matched his own, "you're imaging more than is actually there."

"And you, as usual, are denying what *is* there, not to mention your own nature. You are what you are, Eugenie, and the sooner you accept that, the sooner you can begin doing great things."

"This conversation is done," I snapped, turning away.

Dorian's hand closed around my wrist, and he pulled me toward him with an unexpected harshness. I don't think he'd meant to do it quite so hard. I let out a small gasp as those fingers tightened against my skin. I wasn't trapped by any stretch of the imagination, but for half a moment, I could believe I was. The painful restraint on my wrist sent shockwaves of heat through my body, and the scent of cinnamon drifted around me, standing this close to him. My breathing had grown heavy, and I willed it to slow down.

He hadn't expected that reaction. A slight widening of his eyes showed rarely expressed surprise. Leaning his face toward mine, his thumb stroked the skin on my arm while the rest of the fingers maintained their hold.

"Just like old times, hmm? It seems you haven't entirely lost your taste for restraint. Yet, like everything else, I'm sure you deny yourself that as well."

"You think so?" I asked nastily. "You should try fucking Kiyo. Lots of restraint there."

Amusement lit his face, contrasting with the dark desire in his eyes. "Since I'm presuming you don't mean you finally bought him a leash, let me say simply that there is a big difference between allowing an animal to ravage you and allowing yourself to be ravaged. One is common. The other is art. It is planned. Crafted, even. Only capable of being done by a master." His next words came out so conversationally, we might as well have been discussing the weather. "As it is, I've been planning out what I'd like to do the next time we make love. I think I want you to lie on your stomach, with your hands bound to the front of the bed. We'll have to shift your hips up a bit, put you on your knees just a little, but otherwise you'll stay prostrate, almost like you're bowing in humble obeisance as I kneel behind you and take you." He paused. "Unless you have other suggestions?"

I broke from his grasp and backed up, surprised to find I was shaking.

This was Dorian. The same dangerous,

presumptuous, and scheming Dorian I'd first met months ago, no matter the sweetness and charm that poured off of him. He had no right to speak to me like that, not after I'd parted ways over his trick with the Thorn Land, not after I'd told him I wanted to stay with Kiyo.

And yet, he had once been my friend and my teacher and my ally in battle . . . and my lover. And as I stood there staring at I him, I could imagine everything he'd just described. I could feel it. And, God help me, I wanted it. My whole body tingled with the arousal his words wrought.

"I have to go," I said. It took two tries for my dry mouth to get the words out. "I have to find Shaya."

He inclined his head politely. "Of course."

I turned and walked away, but not before I heard him call after me.

"Eugenie? Don't forget, if you change your mind, my offer still stands. For all things."

I bit my lip so as not to retort and was so focused on maintaining control that I nearly ran into a woman heading in the direction I'd just come from. She was gorgeous, with red hair that stood out like bright flames against her fair skin. She wore a puff-sleeved dress that matched the sky blue of her long-lashed eyes and reminded me a little of Cinderella's ball gown. Of course, Disney would have never allowed that much cleavage. The woman stepped gracefully aside, just barely avoiding a collision. And then, to my complete and total shock, she sidled up to Dorian and wrapped herself around him, pressing her lips to his cheeks.

"Ah, there you are," he said happily. He returned the kiss—except, well, it was on her lips. And lasted awhile. With tongue.

I stood there, frozen, urging myself to ignore them and keep moving. Yet, I couldn't. Dorian, seeing me still there, gave me one of his grander smiles. "Queen Eugenie, a moment. Have you met my charming young friend yet?"

That, of course, was one of Dorian's more annoying habits. He knew perfectly well I'd never met her but enjoyed playing the innocent.

"I haven't," I said stiffly, crossing my arms over my chest.

"Queen Eugenie, may I present Ysabel, one of my subjects here in the Oak Land. She's been spending some time . . . here in the castle." I took the subtext to mean that said time was specifically being spent in his bed.

Ysabel bowed, giving me a polite "Your majesty." Yet, when she straightened up, I saw the look in her eyes was anything but polite. There was a distinct hostility there, and it was directed at me. I was a bit taken aback until I realized what it was. Jealousy. This woman was insanely, adamantly jealous of me. She pressed herself closer to Dorian, almost possessively, her hands roaming over his body in the way that was so commonplace among their kind.

"A pleasure," I replied. I turned around to leave again, having no desire to watch Ysabel grope Dorian. If she wanted to make me jealous, she was wasting her efforts. Dorian and I were finished. There was nothing more between us, nor would there ever be again.

"Dorian's latest lover," Shaya explained later.

"Yeah, I kind of figured that out."

"My understanding is that he went an astonishingly long time without a consort ever since . . ." She didn't finish. She was referring to when Dorian and I had been involved.

"How long is a long time?" I asked.

"Mmm . . . a couple of weeks."

"A couple of weeks after we broke up? That's a long time?"

"For King Dorian? Yes. I believe she's his fourth since then, but she bears a distinct resemblance to all the others." Shaya looked at me meaningfully.

"So?" I asked, not getting the point.

"Always fair skinned. Always redheads. Violet eyes are harder to find, though, so he's settled on blue."

It took me a few moments more to catch on. "Wait. Are you saying Dorian's been taking lovers that look like *me*?"

"It could just be a coincidence," she said diplomatically.

"Jesus Christ," I said, suddenly freaked out. Had I really made that big of an impression on him?

Shaya paused a moment, face thoughtful. "I don't think Ysabel likes you very much."

"I kind of figured that out too. She was trying to make me jealous." Then, in case there was any question, I added, "But I'm not."

"As you say," replied Shaya, voice and face perfectly pleasant.

I couldn't tell if she believed me or not, but it didn't matter. I knew the truth. I really wasn't jealous of Ysabel and Dorian.

Well, not much, anyway.

Chapter Four

We left as soon as etiquette said we could. I tried using Shaya's argument about eccentric queens doing whatever they wanted, but it didn't work on her. She said if we didn't stay a certain amount of time, I'd appear intimidated by Maiwenn. So, we stuck around a bit longer than I liked before finally making formal farewells to the others. Kiyo was preoccupied with a group of well-wishers, but he looked up at my departure and smiled. He mouthed the word *soon*.

My group rode back in a subdued mood. The urgency was gone, and I think my glum attitude threw a cloud over everyone. Seeing Maiwenn and Kiyo had bothered me more than I liked to admit, and Dorian . . . well, that was another story. For now, I wanted nothing more than to cross over to my own world, throw on pajamas, and watch mindless TV. Possibly while eating ice cream.

And as our journey continued, ice cream sounded more and more appealing once we crossed back into the Thorn Land. The sun was sinking, but heat still radiated off the sand and rocks. It wouldn't dissipate for another couple hours, and even at midnight, the temperature probably wouldn't drop below seventy. I'd changed back to my shorts and sunglasses before leaving Maiwenn's, so again, the heat didn't bother me as much as it did the others. Dorian had claimed my sundress would catch on as a fashion trend; I wondered if shorts would as well.

"There's a village ahead," murmured Rurik.

I snapped out of my daydreams and followed his gesture. Sure enough, a small cluster of buildings darkened the horizon. Like my castle, it was something more suited to a medieval British landscape than the desert. Considering how infrequently I visited my kingdom, this was the first settlement I'd seen outside of the castle. It unnerved me a little, my discomfort growing when I saw that our road went straight through the town. Damned twisting Otherworld. This village hadn't been here on our earlier trip.

And for that reason, I knew better than to suggest we go around it. With the way this world worked, a slight deviation could toss us into the Rowan Land or add hours onto our trip. Steeling myself, I tightened my grip on the reins, deciding that this place looked small and wouldn't take long to clear.

When we entered its outskirts, though, I discovered something that made me lose my resolve.

The road was lined with people. It was like everyone in the town had come out to see us pass through. They stood along the sides, staring at my party and again looking like extras from some medieval movie. Except, it must have been a low-budget movie. The people's clothes were ragged and dirty, their faces gaunt. Everyone seemed too skinny, even the children and babies held in parental arms.

My discomfort grew as we rode deeper into the heart of the village. I hated crowds and having eyes upon me. There was something particularly discomfiting about this group in particular. Their expressions were either completely blank or . . . well, terrified. Everything was dead silent.

"What are they scared of?" I whispered to Rurik.

He gave me an amused glance. "You, of course."

"Me?" I squeaked. Glancing at my attire, I tried to imagine how out of place I looked here. Was my foreignness that frightening?

"You're their queen. Everyone knows how you slaughtered Aeson—and that isn't a particularly heartwarming tale. Likewise, Storm King's legacy of terror lives on after all these years. You've inherited it."

"So, what, they see me as some kind of tyrant?"

He shrugged. "You're their queen," he repeated, as though that explained everything.

My discomfort grew. I'd never wanted to be queen. I certainly didn't want to be seen as some kind of despot queen either. I didn't want these eyes upon me, these eyes that all seemed to be filled with apathy, judgment, and a kind of weary defeat. I breathed a sigh of relief when we reached what looked to be the half-way point. All of a sudden, a man stepped in front of us, bringing us to a halt.

He was an older gentry, tall and gray-haired. He was skinny and clothed only a little better than the rest, though there was an air of dignity and authority that made him stand out. When he saw he had our attention, he swept me a bow so low, his face nearly touched the dusty road.

"To Eugenie, great queen of the Thorn Land, I offer the most humble greetings of your servant, Davros."

At least, that's what I think he said. He was bent so low that his words came out muffled. I glanced uneasily at the others in my group, unsure what to do. They all remained silent and looked at *me* expectantly. Oh, sure. They were full of advice back at Maiwenn's, but when it came to peasants groveling in the road? That was apparently all me.

"Please, um, stand up," I managed at last. "Um, Davros."

He rose, clasping his hands in front of him, looking totally overwhelmed that I'd used his name.

"Thank you, your majesty. I am the mayor of this village. Words cannot express what an honor it is to have you among us."

Considering what Rurik had just told me about my reputation here, I wasn't entirely sure I believed Davros' words. I forced a smile.

"Thanks. We're just passing through on our way back to the castle."

Davros spread his hands wide. "I hope, then, that you'll consider resting and taking a brief refreshment in my home."

"Oh, well, that's really nice, but—"

Shaya cleared her throat loudly. I glanced over at her. She gave me a pointed look that gave no question to what she wanted me to do. Grimacing, I glanced back down at poor, groveling Davros. Damn. I wanted nothing more than to get out of the Otherworld right now. I didn't want to stop for teatime. My expression must have looked scary because Davros blanched and lowered his head meekly.

I sighed. "We'd love to."

Mayor or not, Davros didn't have a very big house. Only Shaya, Rurik, and I joined him inside, while the rest of my party milled around outdoors. From the village, Davros had invited a few other important officials, as well as his wife and two grown sons. We sat at a round oak table while his wife served us red wine and something that reminded me of baklava. I sipped only a little of the wine, not wanting to risk dehydration in this weather.

I wasn't much better at making conversation

here than at Maiwenn's, but fortunately, there was no need for me to do anything. Davros and his associates kept the talking going, most of the conversation centering on how glad they were that I had come by, what an honor it was to meet me, how they hoped I'd call on them if I needed anything, et cetera, et cetera.

Which was why it was a bit shocking when Davros' wife suddenly asked, "But if you would, your majesty, please tell us what it is we've done to displease you. We'll do anything at all to make amends and gain your favor once more. Anything."

I almost choked on the honey cake. "What do you mean . . . displease me?"

The villagers exchanged glances. "Well . . ." said Davros at last. "There must be something. You've placed a blight on the land, stripping us of our water and food. Surely we've done something to warrant your most righteous displeasure."

"You need only let us know what it is," piped in someone else. "We will do anything you require to lift this curse from us."

This was the most astonishing thing to happen to me all day—which was saying something. I looked at Shaya and Rurik for help, having no clue how to respond to this. For a moment, I thought they would once again make me fend for myself, until Shaya finally spoke.

"The residents had built their lives around the

shape of the land when Aeson ruled it, when it was the Alder Land. When it transformed itself to you, their old ways no longer worked. Their crops don't grow in this weather. The wells have run dry."

I stared at her in shock. Never, never had this occurred to me—but then, it wasn't like I'd spent a whole lot of time thinking about the Thorn Land. Most of my energy had been spent on figuring out how to avoid it. Studying Shaya, I wondered how long she'd known about this. I somehow doubted there was much that went on around here that she didn't know about. From the looks of Rurik's averted gaze, it appeared as though he'd known about this problem as well. Both knew how upset I got when forced to deal with any sort of queenly issues. So both had spared me the details while these people suffered.

I turned back to Davros. "It's not a curse . . . it's, I don't know, it's just the way the land is. The way I wanted it to be."

Astonished looks met me, and I could only imagine what a freak I sounded like. When Aeson had ruled, this land had been green and lush, filled with forests and fertile farmland. Who in their right mind would turn it into a desert? Davros confirmed as much.

"But this land . . . this land is impossible to survive in," he said.

"Not where I come from," I told him. "This is

like the land I grew up in. People live and flourish there."

People also had modern ways of bringing in water and shopping for whatever other stuff they might need. And that wasn't even taking air-conditioning into account.

"How?" he asked.

I didn't know how to readily answer. I didn't really understand the intimate details of my world's infrastructure. I turned a faucet and water came out. I went to the grocery store and bought milk and Pop-Tarts. Desperately, I racked my brain and tried to pull out elementary school lessons about Arizona's history.

"Irrigation," I said lamely. "Squash, I think. And, um, corn." Had the natives grown corn? Or was I getting confused by stereotypes? Shit. I was so ignorant. The only thing I felt confident of was that Pop-Tarts were not cultivated natively in Arizona. The looks the others gave me told me I wasn't helping this situation any.

I glanced at Shaya and Rurik, but this time, no help came. The full weight of what I'd done started to sink in. Maybe I hadn't wanted this land. Maybe I hadn't intentionally turned it into a mirror of wild Tucson. The point was: it was done. The Thorn Land was as it was, and taking in these ragged and starving people, I realized it was all my fault. Only, I had no clue how to fix it. I was too much a product of modern innovation. There was nothing I could do.

Scratch that. There was one thing I could do.

I abruptly stood from the table, catching everyone by surprise. As custom dictated, they all hastily scrambled up and rose as well. Without explaining myself, I headed outside, back out into the village. Behind me, I could hear Davros babbling something, apparently thinking they'd again caused offense. They probably thought I was about to send lightning bolts from the sky.

As it was, that might not have been a bad idea—if I actually had that power. These people could certainly use rain. But one rainstorm wouldn't fix things, and I could hardly do it day after day. Instead, I walked out to the middle of the street and came to a halt. My guards straightened up, awaiting my orders, and other residents stopped to see what was happening. Those from Davros' gathering soon poured out of the house and joined everyone else.

I closed my eyes, opening myself to the world around me. I smelled the clean, fresh scent of the desert and the faint, faint breeze blowing through it. The setting sun warmed my skin. Then, I pushed deeper, reaching out to that which the magic within me instinctively bonded to. I felt the minuscule water vapor in the air, but that wasn't what I wanted. I had to go further. I sent my magical senses into the ground, seeking water throughout the village. None. I remembered what

Shaya had said about wells drying up, which meant the surface wasn't going to yield anything. That meant I'd have to go deeper still.

There. Back in the direction we'd entered town, I felt a hit. I opened my eyes and strode toward it, the water calling to me. I was vaguely aware of a crowd following me, but I paid them no attention. Only the water was my goal. When I reached the spot, I found that it was just on the town's outer edge. A mesquite tree grew nearby, which should have been a tip-off. They had deep feelers that penetrated the earth in search of moisture.

I too sent my power into the ground, trying to summon the water up. There was a lot of dirt between me and it, and I realized it wouldn't do these people any good in the long term to just suck it to the surface right now. I turned around and found Davros right behind me, face anxious. I pointed to the ground.

"You guys need to dig here. Right now. There's water here."

He stared at me, mouth agape. A moment later, he snapped out of it and turned to those nearest him. "You heard the queen! Fetch shovels immediately. And find anyone who can work with the earth."

Earth magic. A smart idea. Gentry didn't have bulldozers or drills, but they did have people who could throw around huge piles of dirt, which was pretty sweet for this kind of thing. Dorian—who was probably the strongest earth user in the

Otherworld—could cause earthquakes and level buildings.

In minutes, a group had assembled. I tried to take a shovel and help, but that nearly caused Shaya and Davros to have a heart attack. Queens didn't do that kind of work. Instead, I stepped back, watching as the other villagers used magic and manual labor to dig where I'd indicated. When the hole grew too deep for shovels, the village's two earth-magic users took over. Even combined, they were nowhere near Dorian in strength, but they definitely sped the process along, kicking up towers of dirt along the sides. Finally, I heard a great cheer. I and everyone else crowded to the hole's sides, peering down. It was deep in the ground, but muddy water was slowly filling up the bottom.

I looked at Davros. "Can you guys turn this into a well?" I certainly hoped so because I sure as hell had no idea how to do it. I imagined it involved stones and a bucket, but maybe that was just my naïve fairy-tale images.

His head bobbed eagerly. "Yes, yes, your majesty. Thank you, your majesty."

After that, it was nearly impossible to leave. I was regarded as a miracle worker. I was no longer the tyrant queen. I was their savior, the generous and wonderful monarch who had brought life to their land. I declined their pleas to stay and celebrate but told them I'd be back with other ways to save their town. Admittedly, I had no idea what that would entail, but mentioning such a minor detail would have seriously brought down everyone's mood.

When we were finally mounted up and able to head out, I suddenly felt a tug on my shoe. Surprised, I looked down and saw a middle-aged man gazing up at me. A similarly aged woman stood close beside him.

"How dare you touch the queen!" gasped Davros. From his face, it looked like he was seriously afraid I might level the town.

I waved him off. "It's okay."

The man who'd pulled my leg regarded me pleadingly. "Please, your majesty. My wife and I have a boon to ask of you!"

"That's a favor or a request," said Rurik helpfully.

"I know what a boon is," I snapped. I looked back down at the couple, unwilling to make any promises yet. "What is it?"

The man put his arm around the woman. "We've heard that you're both a great warrior and a great magic user."

"And clearly kind and compassionate," added his wife.

"And?" I asked.

"And very beautiful and—"

"No," I exclaimed. "I mean, what's your boon?"

"Our daughter has been taken," the woman

said, eyes filling with tears. "We beg you to help us get her back."

"Whoa. That might be a little beyond my reach," I told them. "When you say taken, do you mean, like, kidnapped?"

They both nodded, and I was swept by a strange sense of déjà vu. I'd first stumbled into this Otherworldly mess when I'd been hired in the human world to also find a missing girl. The girl had turned out to be Jasmine, though I'd had no clue at the time that she was half-gentry, let alone my sister. Was my life destined to be filled with missing girls?

Davros stepped forward, looking upset and embarrassed. "Your majesty, please ignore them for troubling you with something so meaningless. Their daughter was not taken by anyone. She ran off to Highmore with her lover from a neighboring village."

I glanced at Shaya and Rurik. "What's Highmore?"

"Really?" asked Rurik dryly. "I thought you already knew everything."

I glared at him.

"It's a city," said Shaya. "The largest in this kingdom."

"Wait, what? I have cities?" I asked, feeling my eyes go wide. The distraught couple interrupted my new revelation.

"Davros is wrong," the woman said. "Our

72

daughter did not run off. She was taken by the bandits who live in the passes."

"Everyone knows they're there," added the man. He eyed Davros. "Them and their beasts. Even you won't deny their existence. They've been there for years, and she isn't the first girl to disappear."

I turned to Davros. "Is that true?"

He shifted uncomfortably under my gaze. "Well, yes, your majesty, but such brigands are nothing you need to concern yourself about, just as King Aeson did not."

"Wait. Aeson knew there were bandits going after you guys and didn't do anything?"

"Such petty concerns were beneath him," said Davros. To my astonishment, he seemed to believe that.

"I don't know," I said slowly. "If a monarch doesn't take care of that kind of thing, I'm not really sure what they're supposed to do."

Truthfully, I didn't want to deal with this any more than I wanted any other Thorn Land responsibilities. But the mention of Aeson had stirred my blood. Aeson had been a self-serving asshole, and it pissed me off that he would have left these people to fend for themselves. The only thing I wanted less than to be a ruler was to be a ruler like him.

Furthermore, the same fury that Jasmine's abduction had stirred in me flared up. Maybe it was my own experience with always being chased down by aggressive men, but I hated the thought of any girl facing rape or abduction. It didn't matter that these were gentry girls and not humans. The principle was the same. Brigands and thieves taking advantage of young girls, of preying on those weaker, had to be stopped.

"I'll send people to take care of these bandits," I said finally. Behind me, Rurik made a strange sound. "But I can't make any guarantees about your daughter."

The couple's faces lit up, and they fell to the ground in gratitude. "Thank you, your majesty!" the woman cried.

Her husband chimed in. "Truly you are generous and magnanimous and—"

"Yeah, okay, there's no need for that," I said hastily. "Or to kneel. You're going to get all dirty."

We had just started to ride away when Shaya leaned toward me. "You've made a lot of promises today."

I thought about it. She was right. I'd promised to help them get food, rebuild their infrastructure, and rid themselves of those who preyed upon them. "Yeah. I guess I did."

She gave me a bemused look. "And how are you going to accomplish all of this?"

I glanced around us, noting that the faces watching us leave town were no longer blank and afraid. They were grateful and adoring. I sighed.

"That," I told her, "is an excellent question."

Chapter Five

I fully intended to make good on my promises, and in Tucson the next day, I began acquiring an odd assortment of goods that I hoped might improve the Thorn Land's situation. Admittedly, they were kind of lame, but I figured I had to start somewhere and was rather proud of my attempts when I finished.

I was sitting down in front of the TV with an early dinner that night when Kiyo walked in, clad in his white vet's coat. Naturally, all the animals lifted their heads or actually walked over to him in greeting. If I hadn't been balancing a plate of ravioli on my lap, I would have leapt up and run into his arms. Instead, I gave him a dazzling smile, one that grew larger when I saw he carried a bouquet of flowers.

"I would have been here sooner," he said, tossing the coat onto a chair. "But I had an afternoon shift."

"Hey, I'm just happy to see you at all. I figured you'd still be busy with baby stuff."

"Nope." He sat down in a chair opposite me and laid the bouquet down on the coffee table. "You were amazing there, you know."

"If by amazing, you mean shoddily dressed and leading on gentry princes—then, yes. Yes, I was. What are those for?" I gestured with my fork to the flowers—an arrangement of brightly colored gerbera daisies.

"Do I need a reason? Aside from you being awesome?"

I swallowed the piece of ravioli I'd just chewed. "Of course there's a reason. There's always a reason. We've talked about this before."

He gave me a lazy, dangerous smile, propping his head up on his elbow as his dark eyes assessed me. "Right. Standard practices in courtship and mating. Gifts given as subtle suggestions. 'Here, take these plant sex organs.' Hint, hint." It was an old joke between us.

"Fortunately, in your case, you don't need to be that subtle. I already know you want sex."

"True, but I wanted to clear up any doubts. Besides, you've been so great lately . . . I don't know. I just wanted to do something nice. Figured we could have a fun night—although, you're dashing my dreams of taking you out to dinner with the way you're inhaling that ravioli."

"Sorry," I said through a mouth full of food. "I've got a job tonight, so I had to eat early."

His eyebrows rose. "What kind of raw deal is

this? I get off work so I can take you out on the town, and you've got to go into work now? Why can't you have Lara schedule you day jobs?"

"Because I was busy today with Thorn Land business."

Kiyo gave me a wary look.

"Hey, don't judge me," I warned. "I wasn't actually over there. But I kind of found out recently that people are starving and going without water."

"Yeah. I've heard that."

Now I was the one with the incredulous look. "You knew and didn't tell me?"

"Don't jump all over me! I figured you had people to deal with it. And probably those people had people."

"Yeah, well, all of those people are having a little trouble. In fact, I've got to go back tomorrow to help round up some brigands."

"Did you just say 'brigands'? That's very . . . I don't know. Very 1683."

"Well, whatever they are, they're a pain in the ass and possibly abducting girls." I gave him a quick recap. "You want to go with me and help?"

He shook his head ruefully. "You know, I came here hoping to spend time with you. Instead, I find out you've got a job tonight and are playing sheriff tomorrow."

"Would it help if I wore a cowgirl outfit?"

"It might." He came over to sit beside me and

kissed my cheek. "And yes, I'll go tomorrow. I'll even go tonight, if you want the company."

"You see? We are spending quality time together."

"I just hope there's some quality time in bed later to help make up for it all."

"Well," I said haughtily, setting my plate on the table, "that depends on you, huh? I have no doubts about my quality."

He put a hand on my thigh and brushed his lips against my neck. "Oh, Eugenie. Don't push your luck here," he growled, "or you might be late for work."

I grinned and answered by way of a long, deep kiss that probably would have turned into more if my appointment hadn't been so close. That, and we also heard Tim coming in the back door. He never took it very well when he found Kiyo and me in a compromising position.

The two of us drove over near the university, to a quiet residential neighborhood that was split evenly between single-family residences and crowded houses shared by students. As we pulled up in front of a narrow two-story home in need of a new paint job, Kiyo frowned.

"That microbus looks really familiar," he said, eyeing the driveway.

"Really?" I asked innocently.

We got out of the car and approached the house. When we'd cleared the microbus, Kiyo paused to look at its slew of bumper stickers. *Question Authority* and *Roswell or Bust!* were only a few. He gave me a sharp, accusing look.

"Eugenie, did Wil Delaney move?"

"Nooo," I said slowly. "But this is a friend of his."

Kiyo groaned. "If I'd known this, I would have stayed home. That guy is insane. And wait—did you just say he actually has a friend?"

"A friend with a legitimate problem. And you can always go wait in the car."

Kiyo said nothing, merely steeling himself as we approached the door. Wil Delaney was a former client of mine. He was a conspiracy theorist who almost never left his home and whose sole income depended on a blog he ran that furthered his ideas on the government, aliens, mind control, genetic manipulation, and a whole host of other wacky premises. He was quite possibly the most paranoid person I'd ever met.

He was also Jasmine's half-brother. It was how we'd met. He'd been the one to hire me to go find her in the Otherworld, long before I'd known anything about Storm King and the prophecy. Apparently, Wil and Jasmine's mother hadn't been so virtuous and had cheated on Mr. Delaney a lot—even with gentry warlords.

About a dozen locks unclicked before we were allowed into the house, which was almost as many as Wil had at his own home. The person who greeted us was a woman, a very young one. She was short with plump cheeks, cropped brown hair, and pink cat-eye glasses. "Is this her?" she asked.

A moment later, Wil's head peered around the doorway's side. He looked the same as last time: pale blond hair in need of cutting, glasses, and skin that never saw the sun. "Yup."

"Who's the guy?" asked the woman suspiciously.

"Her boyfriend. He's cool. Cairo."

"Kiyo," I corrected. I held out my hand to her. "You must be Trisha."

"I prefer to be called Ladyxmara72," she said. "Because really, we're all just anonymous faces in this society, as far as the government is concerned. Plus, Ladyxmara72 is one of my World of Warcraft character names. Ironic that a virtual society like that can be more honest and egalitarian than our own. Or maybe . . ." She paused dramatically. "It's *not* so ironic."

Wil stared at her adoringly. Beside me, Kiyo made some sort of strangled noise.

They led us inside a home nearly as dark as Wil kept his. I guessed Trisha—I refused to call her Lady-whatever—worried about the same issues with radiation that he did. Her home was neater, however, and bore slightly more feminine touches, like furniture that matched and a few scented candles. The candles appeared to be homemade, undoubtedly so they wouldn't poison the air with artificial scents or be laced with trackers that the government could use to listen in on Trisha's conversation.

"So," said Trisha as we entered the living room. An episode of *The X-Files* was paused on the TV. "You're here to take care of the alien problem."

"I'm here to—what did you say?" I looked back and forth between Wil and her.

"Aliens," she said. "My house is infested with them."

I peered around, half-expecting to see E.T. hanging out on the love seat. All was empty and still. "I don't really understand. Didn't Wil tell you what I do?"

"We don't know for sure that they're aliens," he said hastily. "But there is something here."

"Of course they are!" she exclaimed. He cowered a little under her glare. "I've seen them looking in the windows—just like on that documentary."

Immediately, his chagrin turned to outrage. "Oh, come on! You know that's a hoax. The evidence is overwhelming."

"The hell it is! There's no way anyone could fake that kind of—"

"Um, hey, you guys?" I said. "Can we just get this taken care of? Tell me more about the ali— whatever. Have you both seen them?"

They nodded. "They're short with big eyes," Trisha said triumphantly.

"But they wear paisley suit coats," added Wil. "And they do chores at night."

"Doesn't sound so bad to me," murmured Kiyo. "Why get rid of them?"

"Kobolds," I said after a moment's thought. "You've got kobolds."

"There is no known planet by that name," argued Trisha.

I sighed. "Just take me to your basement."

Trisha led us through the house, and Wil drifted over beside me. "Isn't she amazing?" I swear he was on the verge of swooning.

"Your first girlfriend?" I asked.

"How'd you know?"

"Instinct." Engaging Wil in conversation was always dangerous, but seeing as he never left the house or had much social interaction, I just had to ask the next question. "How'd you guys meet?"

"On a forum. We were both in this thread and kept arguing about whether there was a government connection between the overdoses of Marilyn Monroe and Heath Ledger, and then we—"

"Okay," I said, grimacing. "That's enough. Really."

We reached the basement door, and Trisha started to go down. "Don't," I warned. "You guys need to stay up here." I gave Wil a stern look. "Don't let her down there until we're done. You of all people know I'm not fucking around."

Wil blanched further—if that was possible—and gave a hasty nod. Wil had traveled with me to

82

the Otherworld and fully understood the perils of my job. I could hear Trisha arguing with him as Kiyo and I descended the stairs, yet somehow, Wil managed to do his job and keep her away.

"I never thought it was possible," said Kiyo, once we were out of earshot. "He's found and fallen in love with someone exactly like him." I guess there really is someone for everyone."

"She's a little more assertive than he is, I think."

"Good. He needs it."

"On the bright side, this'll be cake. Kobolds aren't an issue."

Kiyo nodded his agreement but wrinkled his nose when we reached the bottom of the steps. "They're bad-smelling ones, though."

The basement wasn't finished and bore the usual clutter one found in such places. Lots of hiding spots for kobolds. I pulled on a hanging chain, and a bare bulb offered meager illumination. Taking out my wand, I extended my arm and swept the whole basement.

"By the earth and fire you serve, I command you to reveal yourselves."

Shamanic magic tingled from me, through the wand and its gems, and into the room. A moment later, three forms materialized. They were about three-feet high, male, and hardly resembled the big-eyed aliens popular in modern culture. These guys were wizened, with patchy yellow hair. Wil's comment about the paisley coats wasn't entirely accurate either. One wore plaid.

"Why did you call us out?" the one in plaid demanded in a high-pitched voice. "We haven't done anything to you. We haven't done anything to anyone."

"You guys, you can't stay here," I said. "Not in this house. It's not yours. This world isn't yours." I was a stickler for world ownership.

"We're helping," argued one of the paisley ones. "Do you know how messy these people are? Books and paper everywhere."

If Trisha's house had resembled Wil's before the kobolds arrived, I could well imagine it. Kobolds were kind of like benign goblins, originating in northern Europe and rarely given to maliciousness unless provoked. My hope was that they could simply be talked into leaving.

"That's really nice and all, but I mean it: you can't stay here. I've got to send you back to the Otherworld. Give me a hard time about it, and I'll make it the Underworld."

The plaid one scowled. "You're as cruel as they say, Eugenie Thorn Queen. We've done nothing to deserve this."

I tried not to scowl right back. Before learning about my gentry blood, I'd often conducted shamanic business under the pseudonym Odile Dark Swan. It was what Otherworld denizens had known and feared me as. I wasn't thrilled to know that no part of my identity was a secret anymore.

"You guys, I am *not* screwing around. You know who I am. You know what I can do, so stop wasting time." Wand still in hand, I began to channel an opening to the Otherworld. "You can't take on both of us, let alone one."

"No," agreed the other paisley one. "But *he* can."

"He—*ahh*!"

Furry hands reached around from behind me just seconds after Kiyo exclaimed, "Eugenie!"

Kiyo was normally on high alert but had been as cocky as me about dealing with the kobolds. His attention had been on them, and he hadn't sensed the other threat lurking in the basement. Well, that wasn't entirely true. Kiyo had scented this creature, if the odor emanating from its hands and arms was any indication. He just hadn't made the connection.

I still didn't have a good look at my furry-armed captor, seeing as I was still struggling to break free of its grasp. Kiyo was on it in a flash, needing no weapons save his own brute strength. His hands closed around the creature's arms, and he managed to pull them loose enough for me to slip out of its grip. Once free, I was able to get a good look. It was a . . .

Huh.

I wasn't really sure. It was furry, brown, and tall, with rounded ears like a mouse or bear and hooves like a deer and a whole other assortment of random animal parts. It gave a strangled roar of displeasure, and I braced for it to turn back on me. Usually, that was how it worked. Creatures who came after me usually had one of two goals: either rape me on the spot or kill me to prevent me from fulfilling the prophecy.

But Smokey the Bear or whatever it was was going after Kiyo, ignoring me while the kobolds watched gleefully. Kiyo socked the creature hard in the chest, and I noticed a faint ripple of light spread through it that faded quickly. Smokey then returned with a punch that took Kiyo hard in the face and sent him toward the wall. It was hard, too—that punch had been meant to kill. Kiyo's reflexes were too fast, though, and he caught himself before his skull could smash against the solid concrete.

I leapt into the fight then, pulling out my Glock. I'd loaded it with silver bullets earlier and was glad I'd done so. I got off a couple of shots into the monster. Each time, I saw its form ripple, but it still didn't come after me. It was too intent on killing Kiyo. The two grappled further, and I continued firing, knowing I had to be weakening it. Nonetheless, one lucky blow knocked Kiyo off his feet and onto his back. The kobolds cheered when he remained still.

Me, I screamed in rage, taking my wand in my other hand and facing the furry monstrosity head-on. It attempted no killing blows on me and merely kept trying to get a hold of me as I fired and began the banishing words. Suddenly, Kiyo was on his feet again, thrusting himself between us.

"Stay the hell away from her!" he snarled. I saw all the muscles in his body tense and had a feeling he was on the verge of shape-shifting.

Smokey looked angry and turned into full assault mode again. "Get out of the way," I said. "I've got him."

"I'm not letting him lay a hand on you," retorted Kiyo, eyes fixed on his foe. A flash of gold glimmered in Kiyo's eyes. Gold like a fox's.

"He's not trying to kill or rape me," I argued, as Kiyo dodged another crushing blow. "He wants to subdue me—*you* he wants to kill."

But Kiyo was dead set on protecting me, and I finally decided he'd be safest if I hurried up and just finished the banishing rather than attempt to protect him. Firmly channeling my power into the wand, I again began opening a gate to the Otherworld. As I did, though, I kept thinking about those ripples I saw when I'd attacked the beast, like it couldn't quite stay together. An idea struck me, and rather than direct the banishing magic into ripping open the fabric of this world, I directed it toward Smokey—or, rather, toward the Otherworldly magic holding Smokey together. Kiyo sprang away from the fight, realizing what I was going to do.

Sure enough. A spiderweb of light suddenly covered the monster, fragmenting his form. With the wand, I destroyed the magical bonds, and suddenly—he exploded.

But not like Aeson had exploded. It was more like he fell apart. Gone was the large, hulking, furry form. Instead, scuttling on the ground was a swarm of woodland creatures: mice, rabbits, a deer, and a couple of ducks. The mice and rabbits immediately scurried into whatever nooks and crannies they could find. The ducks looked confused. The deer ran up the stairs.

With the banishing magic already started, it was easy to complete the actual opening to the Otherworld and send the kobolds through. Just before they vanished, Kiyo leaned toward them—keeping out of the magic's way—and fixed them with a dark, angry expression. The blood on his face from the fight only added to his fearsome appearance.

"Tell whoever sent you here to leave her the hell alone, or I will come after him myself and rip him apart limb by limb. And I'll do the same to you guys while I'm at it. *None* of you are ever going to lay a hand on her again," he growled.

The kobolds' faces reflected true fear as they disappeared from this world. Silence fell, aside from the quiet and confused quacking of the ducks who still didn't know what to do with themselves.

"Well," I gasped. "That was one of the more

convoluted schemes I've seen yet." Would-be rapists often did attempt to distract me with a seemingly ordinary banishing and then would swoop in unexpectedly. This person had sent the kobolds to lure me out and then that woodland conglomeration to actually subdue me and bring me back as a war prize. Kiyo, as an obstacle to that plan, had had to be eliminated first. I took in his ripped shirt and blood. "Are you okay?"

"Fine, fine," he said, wiping his face. "It's superficial. What the hell was that?"

"Some monster that a gentry put together with magic. Bound all those animals into one stronger form and ordered it after me."

"Will it come back together?"

"No. I broke the bonds, and they're all spreading apart anyway."

"Um, Eugenie?" Wil's voice suddenly rang down the stairs. "Is everything okay down there? A deer just ran through the living room . . ."

Kiyo and I both decided later that it was a good thing Smokey had disbanded like he had. Otherwise, if they'd seen his full form, Trisha and Wil would have had enough Bigfoot material for their forums to last until the next century. Goodness only knew what kind of threads and rumors this event alone would start.

Trisha paid me in cash once we frisked the deer out of the house, and I told her she was on her own for the other animals in the basement. As we were leaving, Wil briefly caught me alone, his goofy, paranoid expression replaced by a much grimmer one. "Have you found Jasmine yet?" he asked in a very soft voice.

I bit my lip. No matter how absurd I thought Wil was, whenever I saw how much Jasmine's disappearance grieved him, it broke my heart. I'd never told him the truth of her heritage. The only information I'd given him was that she was on the run and hadn't been kidnapped. I thought he'd take comfort in knowing she wasn't being held against her will, but it hurt him to think she didn't want to be with him. He truly loved his sister, no matter how much she despised the human world. It was really quite sad.

"No, I'm sorry. I really am."

His face fell further, and he gave a weak nod. "Yeah. I figured. I know you'll keep looking, though. And you'll let me know if you find her?"

I tried to give him a reassuring smile. "Sure."

The truth was, I didn't know if I would tell him. It all depended on what state I found her in. If I found her pregnant and bent on conquering the worlds . . . well, I wasn't entirely sure what I'd do then, but one thing I felt certain of was that there was no way I was ever going to let her return to this world.

Chapter Six

Kiyo always healed quickly, and when we got home that night, he was in fine condition to see who could put on the highest-quality performance in bed. Consequently, he woke in a very cheerful mood the next day, though he still couldn't help a little grumbling about following along yet again. I knew it was all gruffness, though. He liked knowing I was safe, and that warmed something up inside of me.

"You tricked me," he remarked once we'd crossed over to the Otherworld that morning. I was hoping these bandits would be as easy to dispatch as the kobolds, unnatural hybrids of small animals aside. "After that thing you did in bed . . ." He sighed happily at the memory of a particularly skillful feat my mouth had performed last night. "Well, you know I'd agree to do anything now."

"Come on," I said, still feeling a bit proud. "It has nothing to do with that. Don't you want to see justice served to those who dare torment my subjects?"

"Careful there. People might think you're acting like a real queen."

I glanced down at my torn jeans and Poison T-shirt. "Well, let's not get carried away. Maybe it'd help if I got a crown like Dorian said."

To my astonishment, Kiyo's teasing expression immediately hardened. "No. That's the last thing you should do."

I stared in surprise. "Why not? Too Miss America?"

"It'll make you seem more . . . official."

I gestured around at the tapestry-draped castle room we'd appeared in. "We're in a fucking castle, Kiyo. I don't really see how it can get any more official."

"You don't understand. I mean, you're a queen, yeah, and they all know it . . . but a lot just see you as this warrior stand-in. Like a regent. Get a crown . . . start appearing before lots of people in it, and I don't know. It makes you legitimate. It makes it real. It'll be harder for you to get out of this than it already is."

I thought about how often I'd wished I hadn't been saddled with this land and how often I'd tried to avoid it—yet still kept coming back. "I don't think it can get any harder."

We found Shaya before heading out on our raid. I'd brought some things that I hoped would help with the Thorn Land's drought and famine. When I gave the first one to her, she could only stare in silence for several moments.

"Your majesty . . . what is this?"

"It's a children's place mat I got from Joe's Tex-Mex restaurant." Along with Joe's kid's menu, the place mat also depicted a map of Arizona that kids could color while waiting for their food. I pointed to the assorted symbols on the map. "See, this shows Arizona's natural resources. The stuff that grows and can be found there. Cotton. Copper."

"What's this?" she asked, pointing to something that resembled a glass of liquid.

I frowned. It certainly wasn't water, that was for damned sure. "I think it's some kind of citrus product. Orange. Grapefruit." I shrugged. "I think you can grow either in this weather. And that's the point. This land mirrors Tucson, so all the things there should be the same here. There should be copper deposits that you guys can find. That's valuable in trade, right?" Copper was one of the few metals gentry could handle. Iron was right out, being the harbinger of technology. That's what made it one of my most lethal weapons. "And the rest should grow here, if you can find seeds. Someone must have them somewhere, even in this world."

"They still need water," she pointed out.

"Right. That's what this is for." I handed her my next prize: a book. "It's a history of the engineering of wells and aqueducts from ancient and medieval Europe. It should help in moving water around." She still looked stunned, so I tried to think of something comforting. "I'll help find more water sources too." I then handed her another book about Southwest architecture, adobe and stucco homes.

She took the books and flipped through them, taking in the dense chapters and diagrams. "I don't think I'm the right person to do this. I don't have the mind for it."

"Maybe not. But I'm sure you can delegate to someone who can." I patted her encouragingly on the arm. The truth was, I was as baffled by the book as she was. I could put together jigsaw puzzles in record time. Reading engineering diagrams? Not so much. "Just be careful with them—those are library books."

I had to go then and felt a little bad about leaving her. Yet, despite her confusion now, I knew she would find people and ways to implement this. She was just that competent. Maybe I should have had more of a hand in this, but hey, I'd been the one who had to choke down Joe's crap Tex-Mex food in order to score the place mat. That had to count for something.

If I'd had my way, I would have just taken Kiyo and gone out to hunt down these bandits ourselves. I had to imagine they were just riffraff and not much of an obstacle to us. Kiyo was a pretty fierce fighter, as last night had shown, and between my weapons and magic, I was his equal.

Rurik had protested this plan, however, insisting that he and almost two dozen guards come along. I didn't think this gave us much in the way of stealth, but he'd told me we'd dismount and go on foot once we reached the passes the bandits lived in.

Before we left, I decided we might as well add one more person to our entourage. I stepped into a darkened corner, far from the light of candles in the room, and took out my wand. Immediately, the guards moved away from me. They knew what I was going to do and didn't like it. When something magical made gentry uneasy, you knew it was bad.

I spoke the words of summoning and felt magic move through me. It wasn't the storm magic I'd inherited, the pull to water and air. This was a learned human magic, a way of reaching out to the worlds beyond. The temperature in the room dropped, a sudden shock compared to the dry heat we'd just been in. Then, the cold lifted, and Volusian stood before me.

Volusian was my minion, for lack of a better word. He was a damned soul, cursed to wander without rest for all eternity after committing atrocious acts in life. I'd fought and bound him to me, forcing him to serve me. Volusian wasn't very happy about this and frequently liked to remind me of how he would destroy me if he ever broke free of my control. After hearing stuff like that over and over, it almost took on a familiar feel, kind of like how a pop song heard often enough will work its way into your heart. While Otherworldly spirits often had insubstantial forms in the human world, the shape Volusian had now looked exactly the same as it would if I summoned him back home: a short, imp-like creature with black skin, pointed ears, and red eyes.

"My mistress calls," he said in a flat voice. "And I answer. Regretfully."

"Oh, Volusian," I said cheerfully. "Always a joy to have you around. You're such a ray of sunshine on a dreary day."

Volusian merely stared.

I turned to the others, hoping I sounded queenly and authoritative. "Alright. Let's go kick some outlaws out of town."

I still wasn't used to having an entourage of guards. So much of my life had been solitary, so much of it spent fighting on my own ... well, I didn't really know what to do with so many people at my back. As we headed toward our destination, I found it was a lot easier to deal with the guards if I just focused on Kiyo and pretended we were alone.

"I can't believe you gave Shaya a place mat and now expect her to revolutionize this place's total infrastructure," he noted.

"What else am I supposed to do?" I asked.

"You were just complaining about me getting too involved in this place. Handing off a place mat is about as uninvolved as I can get—unless you're saying I *should* take a more active role now?"

"No," he answered swiftly, face darkening a little. "Believe me, if there were an easy way for you to give up this place, I'd make you do it."

I cut him a glance. "You'd make me, huh?"

"Encourage," he amended. "Unfortunately, it's a moot point. The only way to lose a kingdom is if your power drops or . . . well, if you're killed."

"I'm sure Volusian would love to help with that."

My minion walked near me, needing no horse to move swiftly. Upon hearing his name, he said, "I would perform the deed with great relish and much suffering on your part, mistress."

"You can't put a price on that kind of loyalty," I told Kiyo solemnly. "No crown even required."

Kiyo grunted noncommittally. There was a lot of tension between him and Dorian, but the one thing they both agreed on was that Volusian was trouble. Both had encouraged me to get rid of him. I didn't have the power to completely banish him to the Underworld, but it probably could be managed with another magic user. Still, dangerous or no, I continued to retain the spirit's services.

"Are you going to stick around when we're done here?" I asked. That was my subtle way of asking if Kiyo was going to see Maiwenn.

His dark eyes were on the road ahead, thoughtful. "No. I was hoping to go back to Tucson and see if I could get this hot chick I know to go out with me. I hear she's in demand, though. She keeps putting me off each time I try to plan something romantic."

"Yeah, well, maybe if you come up with a good itinerary, you could lure her out."

"I was thinking dinner at Joe's."

I made a face. "If that's the case, maybe you'd better brace yourself for rejection."

"Red Pepper Bistro?"

"Okay. Now you're in the zone."

"Followed by a long massage in the sauna."

"That's pretty good too."

"And then indecent things in the sauna."

"I hope you mean you'll be doing the indecent things—because I more than did my share last night."

Kiyo glanced over at me with a mischievous grin. "Who says I'm talking about you?"

I would have swatted him if he'd been in reach. Instead, I grinned back, my mood happy and light. Bantering with him like this was just like the old days, back before Maiwenn and this baby business was an issue. I felt like his girlfriend again. And despite just having had sex last night, I couldn't deny the truth. Thinking about having sex with him in the sauna was doing uncomfortable—pleasantly uncomfortable—things to my body, particularly with my legs spread like they were. Our gazes met, and I felt an answering heat in his eyes. I remembered how fierce he'd been while throwing himself in front of me last night and could perfectly envision that same fierceness translated into passion in bed. The lines and muscles of his body suddenly seemed that much stronger, and I could imagine his hands all over me . . .

Rurik trotted up beside me and interrupted my pornographic thoughts. "We need to go on foot now. We're getting close."

We stopped on the edge of a "forest" comprised of saguaro cactuses and scraggly trees. They spread on ahead of us, up toward some sharp rises in the land that turned into sandy red cliffs studded with rocks. While tethering the horses, Kiyo decided he'd go ahead and scout in fox form.

"If you can't change back, that's going to seriously interfere with our date," I told him.

He ran a hand along my bare arm, making every part of me tingle. "Nah, nothing's interfering with that. I'll go in small fox form—they'll never see me."

He slowly shape-shifted, his large, muscled frame growing smaller, then elongating into a red fox about as big as a medium-sized dog. He brushed against my leg and then disappeared into the vegetation ahead. I watched him go. Some part of me would always worry about those I loved, but overall, I had confidence in Kiyo when it came to dangerous situations.

The rest of us milled around in the midday heat, passing water around. About twenty minutes later, Kiyo returned. With each approaching step, he transformed from a cuddly furry critter into the man I loved. Not that I didn't love him as a fox too.

"They're over there, just like we thought," Kiyo said. There was kind of a lope as he walked, a left-over from the fox form. It was both cute and sexy at the same time. "Looks like they're camped out and resting for the day."

"Any lookouts?" asked Rurik.

Kiyo grinned. "Not anymore."

I rolled my eyes. "Did you see any girls?"

His smile faded. "No. Just the bandits. They've got a few less people than we do."

"Well, that's good," I said, frowning. No girls. What did that mean? Had the couple in the village been wrong? Maybe their daughter really had run off with her boyfriend. Still, if this group was harassing people, getting rid of them would certainly be a good deed.

Kiyo and Rurik plotted strategy on how to sneak up on the camp, and our group set off, planning to fan out around the brigands. With no lookouts, the gang had no one to warn them of our approach and seemed totally unaware when we got our first glimpse of them. They were mostly men, with a few women. The women clearly weren't captured girls, though. They were older and hardened from harsh living. The whole group looked like it had seen hard times, actually. There was a toughness about them that suggested they'd fight tooth and nail.

Based on an earlier discussion, I'd thought our whole group would just swoop down at once. Instead, one of my guards suddenly stepped out and shouted, "Surrender in the name of the queen!"

Oh God, I thought. *He did* not *just say that.*

There was no time to ponder it further as my party charged forward. "Remember," I hissed to Volusian. "Subdue. Don't kill."

He didn't look happy about this. Of course, he never looked happy. The rest of my guards had orders to avoid killing if they could but not to hesitate if it was their life or a bandit's. I wanted prisoners we could question later and didn't really like the idea of furthering my tyrannical image if I could help it.

As I'd expected, the bandits fought back. No surrender here. They had conventional gentry weapons, as well as some weak fighting magic. It became clear early on that taking prisoners was a little harder than killing. Killing was fast. Taking someone down and tying them up was a little more complicated. It exposed you to attacks from others. Nonetheless, I saw my guards handily bind two of the bandits right away. A couple other bandits got killed shortly thereafter, but they'd had knives at my men's throats and left us no alternative. Kiyo and I were working together to tie a flailing man up when I suddenly felt a surge of magic in the air.

I stopped what I was doing. It wasn't gentry magic. In fact, none of the others noticed it right away. As a shaman, I'd developed a sensitivity to creatures and powers from the different worlds. This power made my skin prickle and had a slimy, oily feel to it. It wasn't from the human world or even the Otherworld. There were Underworld creatures here.

"Demons," I said, just as they materialized within the camp. "There are fucking demons here."

Chapter Seven

There were five of them, to be precise, each standing about seven feet tall. Their skin reminded me of a salamander's, smooth with a slightly moist appearance. It was mottled red and black, like marble. They had fangs like saber-toothed tigers, and flames glowed in the hollows of their eyes.

"Fire demons," I amended. Not that the type mattered too much. I'd fought other creatures from the Underworld, but full-fledged demons? Those were bad. The type was irrelevant. These guys made last night's fight with Rocky Raccoon seem like a warm-up stretch.

Immediately, those bandits that weren't actively engaged with us began retreating behind the demons. Those we were fighting struggled to break away, knowing the demons would cover them. One of my men bravely charged a demon. The demon put its hands together, and a huge orb of fire appeared. The demon then threw it at the guy, instantly turning him into a screaming, living torch.

"Shit!" I yelled.

Without even thinking, I pulled all the moisture from the air and hurled it toward the guard. Water materialized around him, drenching him in a tidal wave. It turned the rest of the air oppressively dry, and a few trees withered and collapsed. I'd sucked out their water to make the wave as well. Nonetheless, the flames dissipated, and the guy dropped into wet, smoldering unconsciousness. At least, I hoped he was unconscious and not dead.

My guards attacked in groups and fared a little better that way, able to distract the demons' attention. Volusian fought well too, but it was quickly becoming apparent that this was not going to end well for us. Picking the demon who appeared to be putting up the best fight, I took out my wand and focused my energy. I sent my will out toward the demon, grabbing hold of him with my mind and letting my senses spread beyond me and this world. The black and white butterfly tattoo on my arm began to burn. It was the symbol of Persephone, goddess of the Underworld, and I used its power to open the gates to that domain.

Down the slope, the demon suddenly looked in my direction, sensing the binding wrap around it. He was powerful, and banishing him from this world into the next was taking more of my strength and power than I expected. Ignoring the attacking guards, he hurled a huge ball of fire at me. Immediately, I dropped my connection to the Underworld and pulled as much water as I could to me. Aside from my companions—whom I was careful to avoid—only the vegetation provided a quick source of water. Plants and cacti crumpled and died in a wide arc around us, but it was what I needed. A wall of water appeared before me, blocking the fireball.

"Damn it, Eugenie," cried Kiyo. "You can't keep doing that."

"I can banish them," I said. "Just distract them."

Kiyo grimaced and then transformed into that "superfox" form, a huge beast of primordial strength and power, the Otherworldly ancestor of all foxes. He leapt on the demon who'd attacked me, and I once more attempted my binding. Volusian joined him. Between those two and the guards, the demon couldn't block me this time. Speaking words of banishment, I pushed him out of this world and into the next, careful to keep myself from getting sucked in along the way. The demon exploded in sparks that quickly dimmed and disappeared.

I nearly fell over. The exertion to do that had been excruciating, and I was pretty sure I couldn't do it again. We had to get out of there and pray the demons didn't follow us. "Rurik," I yelled, hoping the big warrior would hear me. "We need to retreat!"

He gave a quick nod, eyes on the demon he attacked. Between magic and swords, his group was doing a good job of fighting it, but the battle was far from over. He barked out some orders. My group began falling back, fighting our way through the retreat. To my relief, two men picked up the guy who had been burned earlier and helped drag him out. Kiyo and Volusian stayed to cover our retreat, and I tried once again to banish a demon. No luck. So, relying on an old standby, I took out the Glock and began firing silver bullets. They hit the mark, weakening some of the demons and allowing our escape. When we'd reached a certain point, I saw that they were no longer following us. They were based around the camp, as I'd suspected. Demons like those had to be summoned, and they would stay close to their summoner.

We eventually cleared the area and made it back to our horses. Not long afterward, Kiyo—still as a fox—and Volusian joined us. I glanced at Kiyo with a sigh, relieved he was okay and frustrated that it would be awhile now before he could become human again. I wanted to discuss this with him. Instead, I turned to Rurik as we rode away.

"What the hell was that?"

"Fire demons," he replied.

"I know that! What were they doing here?"

"They were summoned." He frowned. "Which is unexpected for ruffians like that. Someone who can wield that sort of magic would have no need to live that kind of life."

My adrenaline-charged heart rate had slowed down, allowing me to get a good look at our group now. We'd managed to cart off two prisoners—a few of the others had been freed by their friends in the demon chaos—which meant we could do some questioning later. For now, they weren't my chief concern. The guards were. Many of them were burned and wounded, though none as badly as the guy I'd saved. Some of the injured rode on their own; others required help.

"They need healers," I told Rurik anxiously. He was singed and cut but had emerged unscathed for the most part. It had taken almost an hour to get to the spot we had tethered the horses, and I didn't want the injured waiting that long.

Rurik didn't answer right away. He annoyed me and wasn't as socially graceful as he could be, but he knew military matters and was a good strategist. At last he said, "If we veer west, we can be in Westoria in fifteen minutes."

"Westoria?"

"The village we passed through yesterday."

"How is that—" I didn't finish the question. I would never understand how the Otherworld folded upon itself, how yesterday Westoria had been an hour and a half from the castle and now it was right around the corner. I also didn't understand how everyone but me seemed to always know what direction to go.

Rurik assured me they'd have healers in the

107

village, so I followed his lead. As soon as we turned, we found ourselves in the Rowan Land. Ten minutes later, we were back in the Thorn Land, and another five brought us to Westoria.

"Un-fucking-believable," I muttered. I really never would learn this land's layout. Only Kiyo the fox was close enough to hear my profanity, and I didn't know if he understood or not.

Our approach was noticed just like before, and I paused before entering the village in order to say the words that would send Volusian away for now. I didn't want to terrifying the townspeople more than I already did.

Of course, when we'd left last time, their terror had been replaced by hope and faith. Today, once we told our tale, that optimism faded to disappointment and fear of a different kind—fear that their queen couldn't defend them. If they couldn't look to their wonderful new monarch for protection, what hope did they have? I tried to ignore those disillusioned faces as best I could. Otherwise, I thought I might snap back that fire demons were hardly an everyday occurrence for a king or queen. I doubted Dorian or Maiwenn would have done much better.

Instead, I directed my attention to those who had fought for me and been injured for it. The burned man was still alive but in very bad shape. Davros, the mayor, assured me they had a healer who could bring the guard back to a stable condition. The healing took awhile, so I accepted Davros' invitation to sit and have a drink in his home once again. They'd already gotten my well up and working, and he seemed very pleased to be able to offer me water.

"There were no girls there," I told him. I sat in a plain wooden chair. Kiyo lay on the floor at my feet, his furry body pressed up to my leg.

Davros snorted. "Of course not, your majesty. I told you that girl ran off. It's easier on her parents to believe otherwise. We certainly appreciate your, uh, efforts to clean out those villains, however."

I grimaced. "Yeah, well, the fire demons were kind of unexpected."

"There have been rumors for some time, your majesty, that there were some very strong fire users among them. It's part of what's made their raiding so problematic."

I widened my eyes. "Oh? That might have been useful information earlier."

He cowered at the tone in my voice. "Begging your pardon, your majesty. None of us could have imagined their power was *that* great."

I questioned him further on where the bandits might go now and if he'd heard any other stories about their magic users. If we faced these guys again, I didn't want any more surprises. We spoke until Rurik came to get me, telling me that most of the wounded were in traveling shape but that the severely injured man would stay behind for further recovery. There seemed no point in remaining after that, so we set out for the castle.

The ride back wasn't too different from our last ride from Westoria. There was a dark mood over the group, and I was probably the worst. We'd set off counting on an easy victory and had more or less gotten our asses kicked.

It was late when we finally arrived, the sun having set and cooled the weather to a comfortable eighty degrees. Time in Tucson tended to run a little later than here, which meant it was well into the night back home. So much for the date with Kiyo. That saddened me further, and I wandered out to a stretch of garden—by which I meant rocks and cacti—that extended beyond the castle. I settled down on a patch of grass that Shaya had been painstakingly trying to grow. As someone who controlled and spoke to plant life, I think this barren landscape killed her sometimes.

I'd been sitting there and ruminating for about an hour when Kiyo joined me. His fox form had finally lifted.

"Don't take it so hard," he said, putting an arm around me and guessing what had me worried. "There was nothing you could have done differently."

"I suppose. I just feel bad now. Like, I still don't want this place. Not at all. But here it is, and then I feel horrible and guilty because even if I try, I can't do anything for it. I pushed the thinking off on Shaya, and then I failed at the fighting part—the one thing I can usually do. Argh." I buried my face in my hands. "It's so confusing. I never wanted to deal with this."

Kiyo pulled me close, and I rested my head against his chest. "It's okay," he said. "We'll get through this."

"We? You've got enough to worry about without this." I was in one of those glum moods where everything seemed hopeless. How could he possibly have time for me with a new baby on the way?

"*We*," he said firmly. "And as much as I hate to say it . . . you just being here is going to help the land."

"How?"

"It's tied to your life, right? You affect it, strengthen it just with your presence. It's why that meditation you do soothes it."

"Maybe. But I've been meditating for months, and there have still been droughts and famines."

"You're still helping it, whether you know it or not. Your thoughts, moods . . . it's all connected."

"Wonderful. It must be doing just great tonight then," I muttered.

In the moonlight, I saw him gesture around us. The sky was clear, and there was no breeze. There was a dry, stagnant feel to the air. It seemed unhealthy. Like you could feel the energy being sapped from everything.

I sighed and lay back on the grass. "If I stay the night, will it help?"

"Probably." He lay beside me. "No Joe's then."

"Yeah. And I was so looking forward to their Salmonella Burrito Special. I guess there's always tomorrow."

"Mmm, well . . ."

I turned toward him. "Oh, I don't like that."

"I promised Maiwenn . . ." He couldn't finish.

"It's fine. I understand." I did. I just didn't like it. Were we ever going to have some semblance of a normal dating life?

"Oh, Eugenie." Kiyo wrapped himself against me and brushed the hair from my face. "You're the only one. You know that, right? The only one I want in this world." He paused. "Or any other world."

I laughed, but it was smothered when he pressed his lips to mine. There was almost never warm-up with Kiyo's passion. He always came on hungry and strong, and to my surprise, I always responded right away with equal intensity. I opened my mouth to his, feeling the thrust of his tongue and brush of his teeth against my lips.

He slid a hand up my T-shirt, squeezing my breast through the thin lace of my bra. His other hand slid along my hip and down the back of my ass, shoving me closer to him, so that we were pressed hip to hip as we lay on our sides. My own hands were tangled in his hair, keeping our faces close as we kissed. Then, growing impatient, I reached down to the edge of his shirt and tugged it up over his head. It broke our kiss momentarily, but it was worth it to have the warm, wonderful skin of his chest exposed. I ran my hands over it, wanting to kiss every part of it, but he had other ideas and took off my shirt in return. I saw it land on a prickly pear when he tossed it away.

His hands moved just as quickly to my jeans, and I leaned back, extending my legs straight out while he pulled them and my underwear off in one motion. I was grateful then for the grass beneath me that Shaya had grown. Gravelly sand would have been a bit harsh on bare skin.

Nonetheless, he was the one I pushed down, forcing him to keep his back flat on the ground. Straddling him and still wearing my lace bra, I undid his belt and tugged his jeans and boxers halfway down, just enough to expose what I needed. I leaned over him, pressing us and our naked skin together, rubbing my hips provocatively without taking him into me. I kissed him as I did, and his hands reached around to unfasten my bra and remove the last of my clothing, leaving me completely naked. In that unforgiving heat, though, I barely noticed.

He was hard underneath me, and I continued writhing my hips, taunting and teasing him more while I grew wetter. The lust in his eyes burned into me, laced with the remnants of the animal he'd been earlier. His hands were still all over my breasts, rubbing and squeezing them. Each touch sent shockwaves through my body. Occasionally, he'd draw me forward so that he could take one breast into his mouth, suckling and stroking the nipple with his tongue.

As he did, I moved one of my own hands down between my thighs and began touching myself, wanting to reach my own climax before he took me—and I knew he would soon. I could see the desire and impatience all over him. Drawing sex out was not in his nature. I much preferred it when a man touched my clit—there was nothing like it in the world—but I had a feeling I'd have to literally take matters into my own hands with the way he looked tonight. Besides, I knew my body well enough to know I could get myself off pretty quickly.

Not quickly enough. Kiyo's hands gripped my hips, sitting me up slightly and then roughly pulling my body down. I got my hand out of the way just as he shoved into me, penetrating with a strength I hadn't expected since I was the one on top. I tried to pull off, but his grip on me was firm as he began bucking his hips upward.

"Too soon," I said, even as my body reveled in the feel of his inside me.

"Never too soon," he growled back.

I managed to shift myself away, and he slipped out of me. I grinned triumphantly, loving how I could prolong this and torment him. His erection was harder and bigger after being inside me, wet and slick from my body as my hand gripped him hard and began stroking back and forth. He groaned, arching his body up to reclaim what I'd taken away.

He seized me again, this time rolling me over onto my back so that I'd now have to fight the full strength of him. "You are so sexy," he gasped, lowering his body to mine. The rough ground scratched my skin. "All day, I just think about fucking you."

He thrust into me again, and I cried out so loudly, I wondered if someone from the castle would hear me and come running. If so, it probably wouldn't be a big deal to them. With nothing to hold him back, Kiyo gave me his full force, pumping into me and driving deeper and deeper with each thrust. I was still burning and wet from where I'd touched myself, and with each stroke, he managed to heighten that pleasure, driving me increasingly wild.

The muscles in his body were strong and hard, working without rest as he moved furiously, his eyes burning into mine as he took me deeply and forcefully, letting the animal in him do what it wanted. I cried out again, exulting in the harshness mixed with ecstasy as I felt myself grow closer and closer to orgasm. I could see the clench of his jaw and tension within him as he tried to hold back.

"God, I want to come . . ." he managed through labored breathing. "Want to come in you so badly . . ." He was waiting, trying to hold out for me to come first.

I clenched my hands against his back, digging my nails into his skin. "Do it," I hissed. "Come in me. Now . . . let me feel it . . ."

It was all he needed to tip him over. His mouth opened in something that was half-moan and half-roar. He still managed to keep moving in and out of me, but the movements were slower, more punctuated as he came and his body found release. At last, he shuddered and pulled out, only to then collapse on top of me. I wrapped my arms around him. Even without an orgasm, my body felt renewed and alive, burning with pleasure at the intensity of what we had just put our bodies through.

He rested his head on my chest, and I continued holding him, neither of us saying a word. At some point, I drifted to sleep like that, only to be woken up about an hour later. It took me a moment to figure out what had happened, until I felt a wet drop hit my face. Then another. Then another. I squirmed and sat up, wiping water out of my eyes.

"What's wrong?" murmured Kiyo drowsily, stirring slightly.

I looked up into the sky, scattered with both stars and much-needed clouds.

"It's raining."

Chapter Eight

Kiyo was gone the next morning, as I'd suspected he would be. We'd stumbled inside to my little-used bedroom once it started raining, and his side of the bed was cold, telling me he'd left some time ago. I sighed, trying not to let the knowledge of him being with Maiwenn get me down, and headed out to see what was going on in Queen Eugenie's domain.

The first thing I picked up on was that everyone was really excited that it had rained. We'd returned to normal sunny conditions this morning, but last night's rain had brought the land to life. Cacti bloomed. The trees seemed stronger. And while there were no ostensible signs of excess water, I could sense it in the ground and even slightly in the air.

Had having sex caused it? Maybe. Maybe not. Regardless, I was pleased with my good deed. I made motions to leave, but Rurik stopped me.

"Don't you want to question the prisoners?"

I paused. What I wanted was to go home,

shower, and change into clean clothes. "Can't you do that?" I asked.

He frowned. "Well, certainly, but . . ."

But it should be my job. That was the unspoken message. I suspected Aeson would have never done such a thing. He would have left it to thugs. I knew if I delegated it to Rurik, he'd do it without (much) complaint. There was something in his eyes, though, that told me he expected more of me than an ordinary monarch. I'd never expected to gain such regard from him—or to feel so uneasy about it. Rurik had pissed me off to no end in the past, but suddenly, I didn't want to disappoint him.

"Okay," I said. "Let's do it."

I'd interrogated plenty of monsters, gentry, and even humans in my day. But there was something weird about interrogating *prisoners*. It was strange enough to learn that I actually had a dungeon in the castle. There were even shackles on the wall, but thankfully, our two prisoners weren't bound. They were a man and a woman, both ragged and sullen. He looked my age; she looked older.

I entered the bronze-barred cell, Rurik and another guard behind me. I crossed my arms over my chest and swallowed my misgivings. I was Eugenie Markham, badass shaman and slayer of Otherworldly miscreants. This was no different from any of my other jobs.

"Okay," I told the prisoners, my voice harsh. "We can make this easy or hard. Answer my questions, and it'll go a lot faster and smoother for all of us."

The woman glared at me. "We don't answer to you."

"That's the funny thing," I said. "You do. You're in my land. You're under my rule, my jurisdiction."

She spat on the ground. "You're a usurper. You stole the land from Aeson."

Considering the way power was always shifting in the Otherworld, I found that statement ludicrous. "Everyone's a usurper here. And in case you haven't heard, I didn't steal the land from him so much as blow him up."

Her face remained hard, but I saw the slightest flicker of fear in the guy's face. I turned to him. "What about you? You going to be reasonable? Are you going to tell me where the girls you kidnapped are?"

He nervously glanced at his companion. She gave him a hard look, its message easily interpretable: *Don't talk.*

I sighed. I didn't want to resort to torture. All-powerful ruler or not, it was just an ugly thing I didn't want to dirty my hands with. I had a feeling my iron athame pointed at their throats would go a long way to get them to communicate. Instead, I opted for another solution.

Producing my wand, I stepped away from the others and spoke the words to summon Volusian. The momentary cold descended upon us, and then the spirit stood before me. Rurik and the guard were growing accustomed to this, but the prisoners gasped.

"Volusian," I said. "Got a task for you."

"As my mistress commands."

I gestured to the prisoners. "I need you to put muscle on them. Get them to talk."

Volusian's red eyes widened slightly, the closest he ever came to looking happy.

"But you can't kill them," I added hastily. "Or hurt them—much."

The pseudo-happiness disappeared.

"Start with the guy," I said.

Volusian sidled across the cell and was only reaching his hand out when the guy cracked. "All right! All right! I'll talk," he cried.

"Stop, Volusian."

The spirit stepped back, his glum expression growing.

"I don't know anything about girls disappearing," the man said. "We aren't taking them."

"You've been preying on people," I pointed out. "And girls have been vanishing near your base of operation. Seems kind of suspicious."

He shook his head frantically, eyeing Volusian warily. "No, it's not us."

"Have you heard of them disappearing?"

"Yes. But it's not us." His words were adamant.

"Yeah, well, I find it hard to believe they're all running off. If it's not you, then who is it?"

"You're a fool," the woman snapped. "What would we do with a group of girls?"

"The same thing men usually use girls for," I replied.

"We can barely feed our own people! Why would we take on more mouths to feed?"

That was kind of a good question. "Well, you still haven't really given me another explanation."

"We heard a monster's doing it," the man blurted out.

"A monster," I repeated flatly. I looked over to Rurik who simply shrugged. I turned back to the prisoners. "Any details on this monster?"

Neither responded. It was strange, particularly considering how some prejudiced part of me still regarded most gentry as dishonest, but I believed them about not taking the girls. I thought the monster explanation was bullshit, but they might honestly have believed it to be true. Volusian took a step forward without my command, and the guy hastily spoke.

"The monster lives in our land. In the Ald— Thorn Land, that is."

"How do you know that?" I asked.

"Because only girls from the Thorn Land have disappeared," the woman said. "Westoria borders the Rowan Land, and two of their villages are very close. Skye and Ley. But they've had no one go missing."

"You guys seem to know a lot about this for allegedly not being involved."

"We don't need to be involved. We raid both sides of the border—word gets around." She spoke of her raiding as a matter of pride, and I tried not to roll my eyes.

"Okay. Let's put the girls on hold. Where did the fire demons come from?"

No answer.

I sighed again. "Volusian."

Volusian swiftly moved forward again and wrapped his hand around the guy's throat. Most spirits had little substance, but with his power, Volusian was as solid as any of us, his touch cold and deadly. The man screamed and crumpled to the ground.

"Stop! Stop!" yelled the woman. "I'll tell you."

I halted Volusian and looked at her expectantly. The man remained on the floor, rubbing his throat and moaning. The skin on his neck bore bright red marks. The woman looked angrier than ever.

"It's our leader who summons them. Cowan."

"You expect me to believe some vagrant has that kind of power?" I asked. "Why isn't he off working for a noble?"

"He was a noble, one of Aeson's advisors. He

preferred to live a rough life, rather than work for someone like you."

"Aeson did have a noble named Cowan," Rurik said. "Her story isn't implausible."

I suddenly felt weary. None of these were the answers I wanted. No leads on the girls, and now I had a rogue noble who could summon demons. "Okay," I said. "That's all I've got for now."

"What are you going to do with us?" the woman demanded.

"Another excellent question," I murmured.

"Aeson would have killed them," said Rurik.

"And you know I'm not Aeson."

Would setting them free accomplish anything? Much of what they'd done had been from hunger and desperation, not that that justified robbing and potentially killing and kidnapping. If I freed them out of guilt, I doubted they'd learn their lessons and go on to become upright citizens. I certainly wasn't going to kill them, though. I didn't even want to hold them in this cell much longer.

The guard who'd accompanied Rurik cleared his throat. "Your majesty, you could sentence them to a work detail."

"A work detail?"

"There are others like them, other criminals, who serve a term doing labor as punishment for their deeds."

"Like digging your aque . . . whatever," said Rurik.

That didn't sound so bad. And hey, it might actually be useful. I gave the order and was assured the two prisoners would be transported to their work site. The whole thing felt a little strange. Here I was judge, jury, and—if I chose—executioner. No one argued with my decision. No one questioned the time I set—six months. Although, Rurik's arched eyebrow made me think he would have sentenced them to life.

"Okay," I said when we'd emerged out of the lower levels of the castle and I'd sent away Volusian. "*Now* I'm going home."

Shaya suddenly rounded the corner. "There you are," she said anxiously. "I've been looking for you."

"I'm leaving."

Her face turned confused. "But Prince Leith is here to see you."

"Who . . . oh." The image came back to me. The moderately cute guy from the party. The Rowan Queen's son, who hadn't been all that annoying. "Why is he here?"

"After your last visit, I dispatched those with any affinity for metal out to search for copper. They found a lot of it—thought it's been difficult to extract—and I sent out word that we'd be in a position to set up trade for it soon. Leith is here to negotiate on behalf of his mother."

"Man," I said. "You guys move fast."

Her looked turned wry. "Well, yes, but there's

also the fact that you invited him to visit some-time. He's taking you up on the offer. In fact, I suspect seeing you is more important than the trade negotiations."

"Good thing. Because I'm not so good in the way of negotiations." I never wore a watch and had left my cell phone back in Tucson. I had no idea what time it was, only that I was spending more and more time in the Otherworld. Seeing Leith was only going to delay me further. "I'll see him. But it's going to be fast."

Shaya looked relieved. I think she'd worried I would bolt, which was a very good fear to have. As we walked to the chamber Leith was waiting in, she gave me a curious look. "Perhaps you'd . . . like to change and clean up first?"

I looked at my clothes. They were pretty badly wrinkled, and I didn't doubt that I had grass in my hair from last night.

"No," I said. "The less appealing he finds me, the better."

Unfortunately, that proved impossible. When we entered the room, Leith leapt up, face aglow with delight. "Your majesty! It's so wonderful to see you again." He swept me a half-bow and kissed my hand. "You look amazing." He was apparently into the grunge look. "I hope you don't mind me arriving like this. When my mother heard the news of your find, she wanted to make sure we could get in on it as soon as possible."

"Sure," I said, taking my hand back. "No problem."

The room was a comfortable parlor that still bore the signs of Aeson's tastes in decorating. Tapestries, lots of velvet, and dark colors. Everyone waited for me to sit on one of the plush sofas and then followed suit. I made a point of kind of sprawling on mine. It wouldn't have been out of the range of gentry etiquette for Leith to come snuggle up beside me. As it was, he was still beaming at me and seemed a bit put out when Shaya jumped right in.

"So, your highness. We'd like to discuss trading our copper for your wheat."

As they began to talk, I had a sudden flashback to that god-awful board game my mother used to make me play, Pit. I let my mind wander as the two of them hashed out the finer details of matters I didn't entirely understand. My thoughts drifted to some upcoming jobs I had, the mystery of the demons and the missing girls, and of course, Kiyo. Always Kiyo.

Leith and Shaya wrapped up their negotiations fairly quickly. From the happy look on her face, I took it our team had come out ahead. With a polite bow in my direction, Shaya rose, holding some papers to her chest. "If you'll excuse me, I'm going to have these written up and formalized so that the prince can sign them before he leaves."

I took this as my cue to entertain him, but

nothing readily came to mind. I couldn't really talk to him about reality TV or American politics. Finally, lamely, I said, "Thanks for your help. I mean, with the trade and everything."

He grinned. "We're getting as much out of it as you. Maybe more."

"Shaya didn't seem to think so," I said, speaking without thinking.

This made him laugh. "She's a good negotiator. You're lucky to have her." He leaned forward. "Especially since I'm guessing this really isn't your . . . well, let's just say it's not one of your normal pastimes."

The frankness caught me by surprise. I'd expected him to remain star-struck and silly, like most of the guys around here who wanted to hit on me. Leith's current expression wasn't lecherous or adoring now, just knowing and sympathetic.

"No, it's really not. This is a kind of a big life change."

"And yet, you knew you'd be taking this on when you defeated Aeson."

I hesitated. Both Shaya and Rurik had hinted to me on a number of occasions that I really shouldn't elaborate on the totally unexpected—and unwanted—nature of my queenship. Even if I hadn't fought Aeson with the specific intent of supplanting him, the point remained now that I was stuck with this. Coming across as weak and whiny to those outside my inner circle could create more problems.

"Well, yeah," I said brightly. "We just didn't anticipate this many problems when the land changed."

"But this is how your world is?"

"The part I live in. But we've had a long time to get to used to it and figure out ways to survive and get water in. I gave Shaya books on how to construct some of that stuff, so hopefully she'll find someone to do it."

His brow furrowed. "Is there any way I could take a look? I might able to help."

For a moment, I wondered if this was his new ploy to schmooze me—until I recalled what Shaya had said about him having a brilliant mind for technology—inasmuch as the gentry could. If he could parse diagrams and whatnot, it might be worth getting closer to him.

"Sure," I said. "We could certainly use it."

He smiled again, and as it lit up his face, even I could acknowledge he was pretty good-looking. Not like Kiyo, of course. Or even . . . well, like Dorian. But pretty cute.

"I'll set to it as soon as I can. If there's anything else I can do to make this easier for you, I'll do it." There was an enraptured look on his face. Yeah, he definitely had a crush, but he didn't irritate me in the way so many other more obnoxious suitors did. An odd thought occurred to me.

"Leith . . . here's something you might be able to help with. Have you ever heard of girls disappearing from the Rowan Land? In the areas that border my land?"

The look on his face showed that this was the last question he'd expected from me. "I . . . beg your pardon?"

"Girls have been disappearing from my land, right near your borders." What were those names? "Skye and Ley. But the people I talked to say nothing's happening to your girls. Do you know anything about this?"

He shook his head, utterly confused. "No . . . I'm afraid I don't know very much about the lives of those people."

Leith's words weren't contemptuous by any means, but there was an implication that villagers and peasants just weren't people he associated with. It reminded me of Rurik's comments about how Aeson would have never troubled himself to investigate bandits or missing girls unless they directly affected him. Leith wasn't as much of an asshole as Aeson, but he and his mother were likely just as out of touch as any other noble.

I think a fair amount of disappointment must have shown on my face because he suddenly grew eager to make me feel better. "But I swear, I'll look into this when I return. I'll ask Mother, and we'll send messengers out to report back. I'll find out everything I can for you."

I smiled at his enthusiasm. "Thanks, Leith. It's really great of you to help."

"Helping a pretty queen is no trouble at all. By the way, have you ever thought about getting a crown?"

We talked a little longer, and I found he actually was a really nice guy, given to moments of humor and intelligence. It wasn't enough for me to jump into bed with him, but I appreciated finding someone else to connect with in the Otherworld. Shaya returned at last with the paperwork—hand-printed on scrolls, of course—and while Leith signed, we got a hold of the engineering books for him. His eyes widened with delight, and I swear, he probably could have sat down and started reading then and there on the floor. Instead, he took the hint that I had other things to do, and after many more compliments and hand kisses, he took his leave.

"You've given him another open invitation," Shaya pointed out.

"Yeah, I know. But he's harmless. I like him."

"None of them are harmless, your majesty." I couldn't entirely tell if she was joking or not.

"Well, it'll be worth the hassle if he can solve our water problem and help with the girls."

"The girls?"

I gave her a quick recap of my interrogation with the prisoners. Her face turned thoughtful as she processed my words.

"Skye and Ley . . ."

"Do you know those towns?"

She nodded. "They and Westoria are configured in a way that places them equidistant from a gateway. A crossroads."

"What, to my world?" She nodded again. "Huh. I wonder if that's a coincidence. I wonder . . . I wonder if it's possible that . . ." One of my crazier ideas came to me. "Do you think those girls could be leaving and going to my world?"

"I don't know. Shining ones do often cross over. It's not unheard of."

"Yeah, I know. To cause trouble. Or to steal women." I had to fight a scowl on that one. My own mother had been one such woman, abducted and forced to be my father's mistress. "You think these girls are going to go kidnap guys so they can have kids?" The easy ability to conceive was why so many humans got kidnapped. Usually, it was gentry men taking human women.

Shaya's smile turned wry. "I somehow doubt it would come to that. Women have been known to cross over, spend time in your world, and return pregnant. They don't need to bring the men back."

Fair point. Well, this was certainly a weird development. I'd have to wait and see what Leith reported back, but I supposed if these girls weren't actually being abducted . . . well, there was little for me to do. Admittedly, I'd always fought adamantly against gentry sneaking to the human

131

world, but I wasn't sure where the right and wrong of this situation lay.

"I guess that'd be easier to deal with than a monster taking them. Still leaves that stupid demon problem." I sighed. "Well, one issue at a time, I guess."

"Are you leaving now?"

"Yes. Finally. Thanks for handling this today."

"Of course," she said. She actually sounded like she meant it. Her pleased expression turned momentarily hesitant. "Although . . . there's something you should know. Someone else responded right away to the trade offer."

"That's good news."

"It's Dorian."

"Oh." Of course Dorian would respond. How could he stay away from an opportunity to put me at his mercy? "You can deal with it, though, right?"

"Well, that's just it. He's specifically requested that you talk to him. At his home."

"What?" I stared. "He . . . he can't do that."

That wry smile of hers returned. "He's a king. He can do anything he wishes."

"Yeah, but Leith came *here*! Dorian just wants me to go to him so that he can taunt me." And no doubt flaunt Ysabel in front of me.

"Leith's kingdom needs copper more than Dorian's. I suspect Dorian is doing this as a personal favor to you."

"That's not exactly how I'd put it."

She shook her head, the amusement now warring with exasperation. "I know there's tension between you, but I suspect if you could be nice to King Dorian, he might make us a very generous deal. One that could help us immensely."

A generous deal. The Oak Land was flourishing. I didn't doubt they had all sorts of food and other items we could use. I thought about those poor people in Westoria and even about my prisoners who'd spoken of having too many mouths to feed. I sighed.

"Fine. I'll talk to him. And I'll even be nice." I started to turn away, needing more than ever to get back to my own home. Then I glanced back behind me. "But Shaya? Just to be safe, you might want to keep looking for more trade partners."

Chapter Nine

Returning home was great. I was exhausted mentally and physically and didn't even mind the onslaught of dogs and cats that greeted me. Tim stood in the kitchen, mixing up some kind of batter. He also wore a full Native American feather headdress that went all the way down his back.

"Isn't that a Sioux thing?" I asked. "Er, Lakota?"

"I keep getting in trouble when I pretend to be one of the local tribes," he explained. "So, I figure if I claim to be from out of town, no one can push for details. Besides, you're one to judge appearance. Did you sleep out in the rain or something?"

Ironically, I had, but I wasn't about to tell him that. "It's been a long day. Days. Whatever."

"Lara called like eighty times. She's got a real attitude, you know."

"That's why she makes the big bucks," I said with a yawn. "I'm going to go take a nap. Wake me if she calls."

"You going to go hear me perform tonight?" he called as I headed down the hall.

I froze. "Oh, um, gee. I've got plans . . ."

"You do not!"

"I do." I turned around. "I'm going to my mom's."

"The reading's late," he said. "Doesn't start until nine. You'll be done by then."

I had long since accepted Tim's fake American Indian gig, but accepting it and witnessing it— aside from when he stood in full regalia in my kitchen—were two entirely different things.

"I've even written new material," he added when he saw that he wasn't making much progress.

"I'm not sure that's a selling point."

He held up the bowl of brownie mix. "I'll make them with walnuts."

I sighed and turned back toward my bedroom. "You don't play fair."

He whooped with joy. "You'll love it, Eug. I promise."

I fell asleep pretty easily and woke to two pleasant surprises. One was the scent of freshly baked brownies wafting in the air. The other was Kiyo sitting in a chair in my room, eating one of the aforementioned brownies. With the way he'd been in and out lately, I never really knew when to expect him.

"Nice surprise," I said, sitting up.

"Likewise," he said, eyeing my bare legs. I'd gone to sleep in a T-shirt.

"Anything new in the Otherworld?"

"Not much. Maiwenn's getting nervous about the delivery, but I kind of figured that would happen."

"She's got good healers," I said, wanting to reassure him in spite of all the troubled feelings Maiwenn generated in me. I noticed then that he wore his white coat. "You going into work?"

"Just got out." Damn. It was later than I'd realized if he'd hung out with Maiwenn and pulled a shift at work.

"Do you want to go see my parents with me?"

Kiyo made a face. "Roland hates me."

"Hate is a strong word."

But it wasn't an entirely inaccurate one. Roland, my shaman stepfather, made no secret of the fact that he didn't like me spending as much time as I did in the Otherworld. Bringing home an Otherworldly boyfriend hadn't earned his approval either, even though Kiyo was half-human like me. Still, Roland was always more or less polite. My mother, who didn't know about Kiyo's heritage, couldn't gush over him enough. I think she'd nearly given up on me ever dating anyone, so me landing a veterinarian was quite a coup as far as she was concerned. She was a fantastic cook, and so even though Roland made him uneasy, Kiyo still consented to go.

"Are you sure you got enough to eat?" she asked after we finished dinner with them later that night. She operated under the assumption that I was on the verge of malnutrition and that Kiyo was incapable of feeding himself if someone else didn't cook for him. In truth, Kiyo was a much better cook than me.

"It was great," he assured her. "Believe me, I had more than enough."

"Well, don't be afraid to go back for more. Or take home leftovers."

"Geez, Mom. He had three helpings. Are you fattening him up for the kill?" I asked.

"There are worse fates," mused Kiyo good-naturedly.

My mom beamed. I thought she was exceptionally pretty, but maybe I was just biased. People said we had similar looks, and we did as far as build and facial features went. It was the coloring we differed in. Her eyes were just plain blue, and her dark hair was graying. My reddish hair and violet-blue eyes were Storm King's legacy.

After dinner, I stole Roland away to the den to talk shop and left Kiyo to entertain my mother. She knew what it was we did, but after her own experiences in the Otherworld, she preferred to avoid our shamanic discussions.

"Still with him, huh?" asked Roland, relaxing back in an easy chair.

"He's nice, and you know it. He's the same as me."

Roland scratched his head thoughtfully. His hair had gone gray, and he seemed to have new wrinkles every year. He was still more than a match for most Otherworldly foes (even though he'd ostensibly retired), and the crosses, whorls, fish, and other Christian tattoos on his arms could summon the same power my goddess-based ones could.

"He is like you," he agreed. "He's not entirely Otherworldly—but he's tied to it. He's spent more of his life there than you, let it become more a part of him. And you being with someone like that means that you'll just be that much more tied to it in return. With everything that's going on over there, it's really better if you stay away."

"Everything," of course, meant the prophecy about me bearing the Otherworld's savior. While I usually recapped a lot of my shamanic business to Roland, I had neglected to mention a few of my recent activities—say, like inadvertently conquering a kingdom and becoming a queen. Call me crazy, but I just had to think our relationship would be better if he remained in ignorance about that.

"Well, I've kind of gotten involved with something over there. And don't give me that look," I warned, seeing his frown. "I'm helping out some people who need it, and it's too late to back out. But the other day, I saw fire demons."

That got his attention. "You do mean in the Otherworld, right?"

"God, yes." Demons in our world would be pretty horrible. "There were five of them."

He let out a low whistle. "That's substantial even for them. It'd take a powerful summoner to do that."

"I was with, uh, some others, and they managed to do some damage, but for the most part, we were useless. I banished one, and that just about wiped me out."

"Yeah, it can be done, but it's not easy. You could do it with a couple of other shamans, but on your own . . ." He shook his head. "I *really* don't like you getting involved with that."

"I know, I know, but like I said, it's too late. Do you know how to get rid of them? Aside from assembling a shaman posse?"

"The easiest way—and I use that term loosely—would be to find a gentry who could summon water demons. Put them with fire demons, and they'll all turn on each other."

"Somehow I'm not optimistic about finding someone like that." Yet, even as I said that, I wondered if *I* could do it. As far as I know, that wasn't part of my storm magic. I could summon water and had once controlled air, bending those forces to my will. Summoning elemental creatures was out of my range. Storm King had allegedly been able to do it. Jasmine had commanded water creatures as well, though I didn't know if that would include demons. It irked me that I couldn't do what the rest of my family could.

"True," Roland agreed. "In that case, brute force may be the only way to go. Let them assemble their own forces to get rid of the demons. It's not your problem. It's the gentry's and their leaders' responsibility."

"Right," I said uneasily. "Well, we'll see what happens." The look he gave me showed that he didn't believe I'd leave this alone. It also said he knew nothing he could say would convince me. "I've got another question. Ever heard of Otherworldly towns called Ley and Skye?" Shamans generally avoided crossing over to that world, but Roland had been there many times and knew a lot about the land.

"Ley sounds familiar . . . it's in the Alder Land, isn't it? Or is it Rowan?" In addition to not knowing about my queenly status, Roland also didn't know there'd been a complete upheaval in the Alder Land.

"Rowan," I said. "But very close to, um, Alder. There's supposedly a crossroads near there. Do you know where it comes out?"

"No . . . nowhere around here, I'm sure."

"Any way you could find out?"

"Is this tied into the demons?"

I hesitated a moment and opted for the truth.

"No, it's something else. A different thing I'm helping them out with."

"Eugenie!" Roland rarely lost his temper, but I could see the anger in his eyes now. "What are you doing? You can't do this. You can't get entangled in their affairs. Your job is to protect *this* world, to keep them and the other monsters and ghosts out of here."

"They're not all bad," I said, surprised as the words came out of my mouth.

"Do I need to remind you about your mother's abduction and the assorted attempts to rape you?"

Hearing him say those words stung, but I held my ground. "I'm dealing with that. It's not an issue."

"It's *always* going to be an issue," he argued. "And I'm not going to help you keep getting into more trouble with them."

"What, are you threatening to cut me off from information?" I exclaimed.

"Maybe. If it'll keep you safe."

"Well, it won't. The only thing you'll do is put me in more danger if I keep going there uninformed!"

His eyes narrowed. "So now you're the one threatening me?"

"What's going on?"

My mother stuck her head in the den's doorway, concern on her face. "Is everything okay? I thought I heard shouting."

I stood up. "Roland's just getting hard of hearing, so I was helping him out."

I followed her back to the other room, where Kiyo watched me curiously. Even in human form, he had a fox's hearing, and I wouldn't have found it surprising if he'd heard the whole argument.

"We have to take off," I said. "We're going to hear Tim recite some poetry."

Kiyo's raised eyebrow was his only sign of surprise at our evening plans. I'd neglected to tell him earlier because I was pretty sure he would have never left the house with me. He smiled politely at my mom. "Thanks for dinner. It was great."

My mom was sad to see us go. "Well, you should come back next weekend. I'll make lasagna. And cherry pie."

I kissed her cheek. "You don't have to bribe us to come over."

"No, but it doesn't hurt."

Mad or not, I gave Roland a hug too. In that brief moment, he murmured in my ear, "I'll talk to Bill."

He sounded weary and defeated, and I hugged him closer. "Thank you." Bill was a shaman friend of his in Flagstaff.

Once we were finally able to leave, Kiyo didn't waste any time in getting to the point. "Trouble on the home front?"

"Like you don't know," I said.

"Told you he hates me."

"I think he hates me making all these trips to the Otherworld more."

"But he still thinks I'm a bad influence."

"You *are* a bad influence."

We drove in silence for a few moments. Then Kiyo noticed that I wasn't heading toward my house. We were going downtown. "No," he groaned. "We are *not* actually going to hear Tim, are we? I thought that was just an excuse to leave."

I shook my head. "Sorry. I promised."

Kiyo sighed but took it like a man.

We went to one of Tim's regular venues, a place called the Fox Den. I thought Kiyo would think that was funny, but he didn't. When we walked in, there was a girl on the stage reciting poetry about the bleakness of existence and litter on the side of the highway. Kiyo looked around, taking in the patrons and tables—and then realized we were in a coffee shop, not a bar.

"They don't serve alcohol here? There's no way I can do this without hard liquor."

"Oh, just hush," I said, trying to hide my smile. We found a small round table in the middle of the crowded café, and I left him there while I went to get hot chocolate. I would have loved coffee but had enough trouble sleeping without the addition of caffeine this late at night. When I returned, I saw three visitors had pulled chairs up to our table.

"Hey, guys," I said.

"Nice to see you again, Eugenie."

The speaker was named Barbara. She was an elderly woman, belonging to the Pascua Yaqui tribe. Their religious beliefs, while having some similarities to the nature-oriented views of neighboring tribes, had picked up a lot of Christian influences over the years. Indeed, she wore a cross around her neck but was also still regarded by many as a type of holy woman. She had no problem with me calling myself a shaman, as those of other Indian tribes sometimes did. Her grandsons, Felix and Dan, were with her tonight, and they didn't have a problem with me either. Tim, however, was a different story.

"Please tell me your asshole roommate isn't performing tonight," said Felix.

"Watch your language," said Barbara in a very grandmotherly way.

I shifted uncomfortably. "Well . . . he might be up there tonight . . ."

"Jesus Christ," said Dan, munching on biscotti. He looked apologetically at Barbara before turning to me. "We've told him a hundred times not to do that."

"Come on, guys. Don't start something again—it took forever for that last black eye to go away," I reminded him.

Felix shook his head. "Look, impersonating us wouldn't be so bad—and it *is* bad—if his poetry wasn't such shit."

"Felix!" warned Barbara.

He turned sheepish. "Sorry, Grandma. But you know I'm right."

"It's the only thing he knows how to do," I said lamely. "Besides, he's going Lakota tonight—if that helps."

"I don't think it'll improve the poetry," noted Kiyo, stretching back in the chair.

"Agreed," said Felix. "His poetry's crappiness transcends all cultures." He looked smugly at his grandmother, pleased that he hadn't sworn this time.

She turned to me, ignoring him. "How's business?"

"Good," I said. "Weird."

While she had no issues with me being a shaman, she was sometimes troubled by the thought of me fighting Otherworldly creatures. She seemed undecided about whether they were holy or not, though she had seen her fair share of evil ones and knew what I did was sometimes necessary. She was about to ask me more when Tim suddenly walked onto the stage. He had on the feather headdress, no shirt, and leather chaps.

"Oh God. No," groaned Felix.

Tim held up his hands to silence the scattered applause. "Thank you, friends," he said in a deep, flat voice. "The Great Spirit welcomes you and your joining of our holy circle tonight."

"I am not even joking," said Dan. "I am this

145

close to walking up there and dragging him out back."

"Please," I hissed. "Not tonight."

"For my first poem," continued Tim, "I would like to read you something I was inspired to write while sitting outside and considering the way the beating of a butterfly's wings are just like the beating of our hearts in this transient world." Spreading his hands wide, he recited.

"Sister Butterfly upon the wind
Wings so yellow
Let us fly with you into the sky so blue
Our souls soaring in the clouds so white
As we look down on those who dream to fly
But are too afraid
And must stay earthbound
Like Brother Beetle so brown."

"I'm going to help Dan," said Kiyo as the audience applauded. "I'm going to help him drag Tim off."

"Seriously?" said Dan, excited.

"No," said Barbara and I in unison.

Tim's next poem was about a mythological woman named Oniata, a girl of divine beauty and youth who came to Earth and caused men everywhere to fight over her. The story was interesting, but like all of his poems, the verses were pretty bad and filled with horrible metaphors.

"That's a real story," I challenged my companions. "I've heard it before."

"Yeah, but it's not Lakota," said Felix. "I think it's Iroquois or something."

"Honestly, I don't think it matters at this point," said Dan, looking weary. "Besides, everyone's got some story about unearthly beautiful women."

Kiyo linked his hand with mine and murmured, "And fortunately, I've got my own."

"Sly man," I said back. "Sly as a fox."

When the poetry reading wrapped up, Tim sold his self-published poetry books. I think this was the most remarkable part of all—he always sold a bunch. And the women . . . the women loved him. A number were cozying up to him already, no doubt wanting to go out later. Watching the women, Dan declared that he was going to quit his job as a computer-support technician and start up on Tim's gig, causing us all to laugh.

"Say what you want," I said to Kiyo, watching Tim and his admirers. "This all means Tim probably isn't coming home tonight."

"What are you saying exactly?"

"That the sauna is all ours."

Not that anyone else could have really fit into it, though. My wet sauna wasn't that big, which just meant that when Kiyo and I got home, we had to be that much closer to each other. Neither of us really minded.

We shed our clothes in the hallway, and he pulled me to him, hands running over my waist and lips grazing my neck. "You owe me big for making me endure that poetry," he growled in my ear.

"Whatever. That was practically foreplay. Are you saying Tim's poem about Brother Wood-pecker *plunging* his beak into the tree didn't turn you on? You know that was a total metaphor."

Kiyo's only response was a smothering kiss that ended any other witty commentary I might make, his lips hot and hard as his tongue sought mine. Without breaking the kiss, we somehow managed to open the door to the sauna and stumble inside. Immediately, heat and steam surrounded us. Everyone always praised Arizona's heat for being dry, but I loved humidity and the way it enveloped my body.

I also loved the way the moisture dampened Kiyo's dark hair, making it curl up even more against his neck. Still holding on to that kiss, he pressed me against the sauna's wooden wall, his hands gripping my hips. In only a short time, the heat had us both slick and sweating. I tangled my fingers in his hair and then ran them down his arms and chest. The oil and sweat made my hands glide effortlessly across his skin. I paused to run circles around his nipples, slowly increasing the pressure and squeezing them in the way he so often did to mine.

He gave a small grunt of surprise and pleasure and then moved his lips to my neck. I tipped it back, giving him greater access. His kisses were hard, like he was trying to consume me with his mouth alone, and there were even a few teeth involved. With as fair as my skin was, he actually left me with the occasional hickey after sex. It always made me feel like I was sixteen and foolish the next day, but in the moment? It seemed totally worth it.

His lips moved from my neck to my shoulder while his hands slid up from my hips to my breasts, again moving easily with all that sweat and moisture. He rubbed them and cupped them, his fingers slipping back and forth against my wet skin and occasionally pausing to stroke my nipples in a way that sent waves of need throughout my entire body. Driven to impatience by my own desire, I slid my hands down his stomach, down to the erection pressing against me. I grabbed a hold of him and started to bring him into me.

Unexpectedly, he turned me around, still keeping me pressed against the wall. I held my hands against it for support while his strong fingers rubbed my back, massaging the muscles that always seemed sore lately. I gasped, finding the massage almost as arousing as the rest. It was fleeting, however. His hands soon moved to my hips again, tipping me out slightly so that I was bent over, rather than pressed flat against the wall.

A moment later, he pushed against my body, and I felt him enter me. My own wetness made the thrust almost as effortless as our hands had been on each other's flesh. I cried out at the feel of him filling me up, pushing harder and harder into me. I rested my check against the sauna's wall, bracing myself and allowing him to take me more deeply.

He gripped my breasts as he continued moving in and out of me, and I moaned as his touch sent shockwaves through my skin. I was overloaded with sensation as he seemed to take control of every part of my body, both inside and out. His thrusts grew more urgent and fierce; his hold on my breasts became tighter. Having him inside me built a heat between my thighs that radiated out to the rest of my body, rivaling the heat of the air around us. That bliss grew and grew to unbearable heights, until at last the orgasm burst within me, making my legs go weak and nearly give out underneath me. Every part of me tingled and burned, and the feel of him still slamming into my body was almost too much for my flooded senses. Yet, even as I thought I couldn't handle any more, I still felt that intense pleasure building within me once more and knew that it would take only a little more of this for me to come yet again.

By then, Kiyo's hands had moved back to my hips, steadying himself so that he could push even harder. With all that force, it was a struggle to continue bending and not simply get pressed flat against the wall. Then, I felt his body grow tense and knew he was about to come. He made a guttural, primal sound, his thrusts growing long and deep as he came and let his own orgasm explode within me. He pressed his face against my shoulder, his motions gradually slowing down as his body sated itself.

When he was done, he slid his hands from my hips to my shoulders, turning me around and pulling me toward him. We wrapped our arms around each other, gasping as we leaned against the wall. He said nothing but gently kissed my cheek. I smiled, pushing closer to him and drowning in the scent of his sweat and skin.

"Worth enduring the poetry reading?" I asked.

"Yes," he said. "Definitely."

The phone woke me up the next morning. Kiyo dozed naked beside me in bed, and I had to practically crawl over him to reach my cell. It was Roland.

"I found out about your crossroads. It crosses over to a town in Texas called Yellow River."

"Texas, huh?" That was unexpected.

"Yep. And there are two shamans who live there already to keep an eye on it."

"Two?" There weren't really that many in our profession. We were spread thin, so more than one in a region (aside from a father-and-daughter team like Roland and me) was surprising.

"It's apparently a big gate. Doesn't take much power or effort to cross through it, so it needs a lot of attention."

Interesting. Crossroads varied in accessibility. Most required more power than the average human or even gentry could use, fortunately. On certain days of the year—like Beltane and Samhain—areas between our worlds grew thin, making it easier for crossings. Those were dangerous times that kept Roland and me busy. A gateway that was usable the rest of the year was even more dangerous.

But, if it was easily accessible, then it wouldn't be too difficult for these girls to cross and seek out humans to father their children. The whole thought made me squirm. A generation of half-Texan, half-gentry kids. God help us all.

"Eugenie?" asked Roland warily. "What are you thinking?"

"I'm thinking I need the names of those shamans."

He still seemed troubled at my involvement, but I think he felt better about me getting in touch with others—particularly others who were human. He pushed me a little about what was going on, but I still refused to talk about it. After much thanks on my part for the information, we finally disconnected.

Kiyo had climbed out of bed during the call and was in the shower. As I waited for him, I wondered how I should proceed. Presumably, I should contact these shamans and see if they'd noticed a recent influx of gentry girls. If I could confirm that, it'd ease my worry about bandits (or monsters) kidnapping them, even though it still left the moral dilemma of whether I should be kicking those girls back to their own world.

A drop in temperature and a prickling of my skin signaled Volusian's sudden arrival. He materialized in the darkest corner of my room, expression as sullen and malevolent as usual.

"Well, this is a treat," I said. "I do so love seeing your cheery face in the morning. What's up?" When I'd left the Otherworld last time, I'd kept Volusian on standing orders to ferry any messages over to me. My joking aside, I wasn't overly thrilled to see him because I knew it meant there was something I had to deal with.

"The hulking imbecile who commands my mistress's guards has requested your presence," said Volusian.

"Do you mean Rurik?"

"Yes, unless my mistress has appointed another hulking imbecile to command her guards."

"Did he say why?" If it had been more trade business, Shaya would have been the one to ask for me.

"He wished to tell you that one of the missing girls returned."

"What?"

I sprang out of bed and hastily threw on some clothes. Kiyo returned to the room, astonishingly sexy with wet hair, and gave me a surprised look. "What's up?"

"I got a lead on one of the girls. You want to come with me?"

He shook his head. He held up his white coat. "Can't. I've got to work."

I was disappointed. I would have liked to have him with me, but that petty part inside of me felt better about him working than hanging out with Maiwenn again. So, we made our good byes, parting with a long kiss—a really long kiss. When we finally dragged ourselves away from each other, Volusian looked as though he wouldn't have minded being smote out of existence.

I sent him on ahead of me and then crossed over shortly thereafter. Nia as usual fell all over herself, but I had to politely dismiss her in my eagerness to find Rurik. He was sitting with Shaya in the parlor adjacent to her room, deep in conversation. Both sprang up when they saw me.

"Your majesty," intoned Shaya politely.

"Where is she?" I exclaimed. "The girl. I want to talk to her and get this settled."

Rurik grimaced. "Ah. About that."

"What's wrong? Volusian said you found her."

"Well, we did, in a manner of speaking. It was the girl from Westoria—the one whose parents spoke to you. She surfaced last night in the village, hysterical and going on and on about how she escaped and how horrible it all was."

"There really was a monster?" I said, surprised. "Or did she escape from the bandits?" I still hadn't ruled out their involvement.

He shook his head. "Nobody knows. She wasn't making any sense, and mostly, her parents wanted to calm her down. In the meantime, they sent word to us because they knew you'd want to talk to her, and . . . well, that's when the problem started."

"Like the rest of this isn't already a problem?"

"When the girl heard you were coming, she became even more hysterical."

"More hysterical over me than a monster or whatever?"

Rurik shrugged. "As we've learned, your reputation is a bit . . . alarming to some."

"Good God. Didn't she hear I got my ass kicked by fire demons?" I sighed. "What happened."

"She ran away. For real this time."

I groaned and sank back into a chair.

"We sent out a search party as soon as we heard," he added somewhat hopefully.

"Well, that's something, I guess. It's one girl . . . she can't be that hard to find, right?"

Rurik and Shaya exchanged doubtful looks. I groaned again. With the way the land was around here, it was likely anyone who wanted to disappear could. I'd had parties out looking for

Jasmine for the last three months and found no clue to her whereabouts.

"We need to start putting faces on milk cartons," I muttered.

"I beg your pardon?" asked Shaya.

"Never mind. Anything else I should know about? Any word from Leith?" I figured I'd go do my meditation and connection with the land and then head back to Tucson.

"Nothing yet," said Shaya. "However . . . we did hear from Dorian."

Right. Another of my problems. She seemed a little nervous about going on.

"He sent a message wondering why you hadn't contacted him yet about trade. And . . ."

I rolled my eyes. "Go on. I expect the worst."

She looked embarrassed. "He said if you can't be troubled to come in a timely manner, then he's going to rescind his offer."

"That might not be horrible," I pointed out. "I mean, you've told other people, right? We've got other kingdoms wanting to buy the copper, don't we?"

Her look of discomfort grew. "Well, not so many."

"How many is not so many?"

"Aside from the Rowan Land? None."

"Son of a bitch." Honestly? I wouldn't have put it past Dorian to influence others *not* to trade with me just so he could play these games. I steeled myself and met Shaya's pleading gaze. "I don't suppose he specified what a 'timely manner' is?"

"He did, actually," said Shaya. Rurik was smiling, which I took as a bad sign. "Today."

Chapter Ten

I set out to Dorian with a sense of foreboding, made worse by the fact that I wore a skirt with a slit all the way up to my hip. Both Shaya and Nia had wanted me to go see him in a dress, arguing it befitted my station *and* would endear me to Dorian. I'd argued that I wouldn't be able to ride in a dress, and this slit thing had been their solution. And like always, I had a handful of guards in tow. Their constant presence still continued to make me feel like a child. In this case, a kind of slutty child.

In keeping with the Otherworld's bizarre geography, we passed through another village. My visit was brief, just long enough to see how they were doing. Their situation wasn't too different from Westoria's, though they had a woman who was pretty adept at finding water sources. Her technique, the way she wove magic, was more skilled than mine, though she didn't possess my strength. After observing her, I mimicked what she did and managed to find a spot ripe for well-digging. The dress kept me from getting out there and shoveling along with them, but it didn't matter. I left regarded as a savior yet again.

Reaching Dorian's took less time than it had taken to get to Maiwenn's. Unlike that journey, much of our trip today passed primarily through my own land, with no respite in one of the more temperate kingdoms. The heat beat down on us, and I sweated profusely into the violet silk of my dress. I would have given anything for a breeze, anything to stir that stagnant air. My own Tucson was often windy; I didn't get why the Otherworldly version wasn't.

My father had been able to control all things connected with storms: water, air, charged particles, temperature, et cetera. So far, I only had a hold of water, but every once in a while I could *feel* the air with the same senses that could touch and control water. Reaching out now, I had that same experience: I could sense the air. It hummed to me. It called. But when I called back, nothing happened. Over and over I tried, attempting the same technique I used with water, urging it to bend and stir and cool me off. Nothing. I finally gave up when Dorian's castle came into sight. It was stone like mine and somehow managed to be both imposing and graceful.

Where once I had been greeted with hostility and suspicion, I was now welcomed with respect and a fair amount of groveling. And, yeah, some wariness too. My guards were led away, and Dorian's servants fell all over me, offering me any refreshment I wanted. I declined. I simply wanted to get these negotiations done with.

A servant led me to an opulently decorated chamber and announced me, titles and all. Dorian sat there, casual in a long-sleeved, cream-colored shirt, leaning over a chessboard. An old man with a beard that went all the way to the floor sat opposite him. Dorian's green-gold eyes lifted at my name, and he broke out into a dazzling smile. Honestly. The man was too good-looking sometimes, and he knew it. A moment later, Dorian turned a disapproving glance toward his chess partner.

"By the gods, Kasper. Have you no manners at all? The Thorn Queen is here. Show some respected before I have you flogged."

I started to protest as the old man rose. The hunched-over posture he'd held in the chair appeared to be permanent, and it took him forever to actually get up. He managed something that passed for a bow—really, it was hard to tell the difference between that and his normal stance— and gave me a gravel "Your majesty."

And as the old man's back was to the board, Dorian leaned over and moved some of the pieces around.

I opened my mouth, more in shock than to make any sort of protest. Dorian raised one finger to his lips in a shushing motion. I swallowed my comments and smiled at Kasper. "Thank you. Please sit down again."

"And you, my dear," said Dorian. "Come join us."

The servant who'd led me in hastily pulled a velvet-cushioned chair over to the chess table. I thanked him and sat down, crossing my legs out of habit. When I saw half the skirt spill over and reveal nearly the whole length of my leg, I hastily uncrossed them. Dorian saw the leg, of course. He always saw everything.

Kasper's eyes, underneath his bushy gray brows, were fixed on the board. He made a play, capturing one of Dorian's pieces. Dorian frowned briefly, then put his smile back on as he turned to me.

"You are radiant as always," he said. "That dress is particularly lovely. Kasper, look at her. Do you see the way that shade matches her eyes?"

Kasper looked like he wanted to study the board, but he turned to me obediently and gave a quick bob of the head. "Yes, your majesty. Most becoming." Dorian quickly swapped a few more pieces and then put on a look of deep pondering when Kasper turned back around.

With a sigh, Dorian moved his bishop. "Not my greatest play, but it'll have to do." He seized one of Kasper's pieces.

The move clearly took Kasper by surprise, not

all that astonishing considering the pieces weren't where they'd been the last time he looked. He studied the board for almost a minute and then moved a knight, though it didn't yield a capture.

"Eugenie, you look as though you've been stranded in a desert," mused Dorian. "But then, I suppose that's the case, isn't it? Such a shame, all those towns suffering and starving, towns like Songwood."

The old man looked up sharply, eyes wide as he stared at me. "Songwood?"

"Songwood?" I asked in equal confusion. Dorian covertly moved more pieces.

"I was born in Songwood," said Kasper. "People are starving there?"

"Oh, wait," said Dorian. "Songwood's in the Willow Land, isn't it? Sorry for the scare. I was thinking it had been part of Aeson's kingdom. I'm sure Songwood's perfectly fine." He studied the board for a moment and then deftly moved his queen. "Checkmate."

Kasper gaped. "That's not . . ." His eyes roved over the board, no doubt looking for any possible way to counter Dorian's move.

"You can't fight against the queen," said Dorian glibly. "Once she's decided to take the king, you might as well give in and enjoy it." I rolled my eyes. Kasper sighed.

"Excellent game, your majesty."

Dorian gave him a comforting pat as the old

man stood up. "Don't take it so hard. You played pretty decently yourself. Sloppy here and there, but who knows? There's always next time."

Kasper gave another wizened bow and then left us alone. I gave Dorian a censuring look.

"You're a bad man. You should be ashamed of yourself."

"Hardly," he said. "That man's the grand chess champion of seven kingdoms. A little humbling will do him good. And speaking of humbling, shall we get on to our business?"

He stood up and extended a hand to me. I didn't take it and simply followed as he walked over to the far side of the room. He sank down onto an ivory satin couch while I chose a velvet love seat the same color as my dress. I felt adrift in a sea of purple. Dorian produced a stack of parchment from a nearby table.

"There you are. Just sign, and we can get this out of the way."

I flipped through the papers, astonished. I didn't understand most of it. It detailed amounts and shipments of assorted goods, listed interest rates, and laid out some sort of schedule. I gave Dorian an incredulous look.

"What happened to negotiating?"

He poured two glasses of white wine from a carafe that sat on the table to his other side. "Oh, come now. You don't want to actually do that. *I* don't want to do that. So why waste our time? I assure you, the terms are very, very generous. Probably more generous than you deserve, considering the way you toy with my affections. Your people will be getting a lot of goods on faith for copper that has yet to materialize."

"Then why did you make me come here?"

"Do you have to ask?"

"No," I grumbled, signing my name with a quill. A quill. Honestly. "You're a bad man."

"I try. Wine?" He gestured to the glass he'd poured for me.

I shook my head. "Wouldn't want you to run out. So, I guess me sitting here is part of the price I pay for my kingdom's food. What do you want to do now?"

His eyes held mine over the top of his wine-glass. "I could make up a list of things to do longer than that contract."

Yeah. I'd set myself up for that one. "Okay, then. What would you like to talk about?"

"You," he said. "And why you never come see me."

"You know why. Because you used me and stuck me with that kingdom."

"You sure do hold a grudge. Is that a human trait?"

"It's a Eugenie trait."

He smiled. "Of course. You know, Rurik tried to rape you, yet now you welcome him with open arms."

164

"That's not exactly how I'd put it."

"You know what I mean. How can you forgive him and not me?"

I looked down at my lap and played with the dress's fabric. I didn't have a good answer for that. Rurik had really been a total asshole when we'd met, yet now I took him as a normal fixture around my household. Why did I hold such animosity for Dorian? Because things hadn't started as hostile between us, I realized. Sure, I hadn't trusted him initially, but he'd never done me any true harm.

I had grown to like him—care about him, even—which made what he'd done hurt that much more. Dorian was the one who'd guided me through claiming the Thorn Land after we'd killed Aeson in a pretty horrific battle. I'd simply followed Dorian's direction, having no clue what I was doing until it was too late. Once I realized what I'd been stuck with, I'd felt like every inter-action with Dorian had been one big setup. It had seemed like his endgame the whole time had been to oust Aeson and give me that land so that Dorian could eventually control it. That was why I resented him.

Are you sure that's it? a sneaky voice inside me wanted to know. No, there might be more. Even I could admit that to myself. The truth was I'd developed physical and emotional attachments to Dorian, and I didn't want them. I didn't want to be bound to someone like him, someone who was full-blooded gentry—and had the annoying tendency to make me lose control. Slamming up walls of animosity between us was a way to protect myself.

"What are you thinking?" Dorian asked, sparing me from his other question.

"I was wondering if I just blindly signed my name to sexual favors in that contract."

"Damn," he said. "I wish I'd considered that." From the tone of his voice, I think he meant it. "Oh, well. Perhaps next time since I'm sure this will be the first of many dealings between our kingdoms."

"I hope not."

For a moment, he almost looked hurt. "Is it that painful coming here?"

I felt bad. "No, I'm sorry. I didn't mean it like that. I mean . . . I hope I don't need any more help. I hope things will just work themselves out in the Thorn Land."

His easy smile returned as he finished off his wine. He reached for my untouched glass. "Well, according to rumor, things are on the mend, thanks to the omnibenevolent Thorn Queen. Why, I heard the other day that you were out digging ditches and feeding orphans. It's a wonder you have the time for that, what with your hypocritical job of battling your own subjects in the human world."

"My subjects don't cross into the human

world," I said loftily. Of course, the irony was that might not be true, not if the evidence surrounding those girls was any indication. "And I never did any of that other stuff. I just found water."

He tsked, eyes sparkling with delight. "Yes, which is a hundred times more than most monarchs do. You're out with your people, maybe not working beside them exactly, but it's close enough. They think you're some kind of messiah. I guess that sets a good precedent for your son, hmm?"

I made a face. "Don't even go down that road. And anyway, I'm not trying to be a messiah. I'm just trying to help."

"Good gods," he said, downing the glass in one gulp. "The frightening thing is that you're actually serious. Were you helping them before you arrived here today?"

"Er, well, a little. We stopped in a village and helped find some water."

"I can tell. When you use your magic, it wreaths you like some sort of afterglow. It's very . . . becoming."

Something about the way he spoke and looked at me made me want to cross my arms and legs protectively—until I remembered crossing my legs wouldn't do me any favors. Fucking dress.

"I daresay your control of water is becoming very useful," he added. "Too bad you didn't continue your lessons with it."

"I don't need your help anymore. I've practiced on my own—I've gotten a lot stronger."

"Hmm. I see. And what about the rest of your inherited powers? Have you been practicing with, say, air?"

For half a second, I thought he'd been spying on me. No, that wasn't his style. He'd guessed I would attempt air magic because . . . well, he knew me. And because he was Dorian and canny about such things.

"As a matter of fact, I have," I said loftily. There. Take that.

His lips twitched. "I see. And have you been successful?"

I wasn't fast enough with my answer. He laughed and moved to sit beside me. I tried to scoot over, but there wasn't much room.

"Eugenie, Eugenie. When are you going to stop fighting this—stop fighting me? You're only going to create more trouble down the road if you don't learn to fully harness your abilities."

"Right," I said, trying not to notice the apple and cinnamon scent that always surrounded him. Why couldn't I shake this attraction when I found him so annoying half the time? "It's for my benefit, right? Not because of your desire to rule the Otherworld *and* see the prophecy fulfilled?"

"Of course it's for those reasons," he scoffed. One thing you had to love about Dorian was his unflinching honesty. "But that doesn't mean you can't benefit too. You don't think it'd be useful to control air? You don't think that would aid you in helping those poor suffering souls under your control?"

"Damn it. Don't involve them."

"They're already involved. Learn to control storms, and there'll never be a drought again." His voice was low, filled with promise and temptation.

I thought about the things I'd seen, the fields gone barren and hungry faces. I shook my head. "I'm not going to let you teach me again."

"What if I got you another teacher?"

"What?" I shifted so that we could look at each other eye to eye. "What do you mean?"

"Exactly what I sound like. As hard as it is to believe, I'm not the only one who knows how to use magic around here. True, I'm the most stunningly attractive and dazzlingly intelligent, but if you're dead set against my help, there are others whom you could benefit from."

I turned away and stared off across the room. The water finder I'd worked with today had certainly been useful. She was actually the first gentry I'd met who had any sort of magic compatible enough to mine to teach me anything. Dorian's magic was actually completely different from my own, but he was skilled enough to still transfer the basic principles. But what if I had someone else to tutor me? Someone more in sync with my powers—who wasn't always trying to get me into bed?

No. Self-chastisement instantly arose. Magic was dangerous. It made you crave more of it, and the more I used, the more I embraced my gentry side and lost some of my humanity. Kiyo had advised against it over and over, and I didn't even want to think about what Roland would say.

And yet . . .

"You've actually got someone in mind?" I asked, turning back to Dorian.

He nodded. "She's not an exact fit for your powers—honestly, no one is—but she's close and is an excellent instructor."

She. That was promising. No one who'd want to father a child on me.

He seized on my hesitation. "Eugenie, why resist this? It's obvious you want to learn more, no matter how haughty you pretend to be about dirtying your hands in the affairs of the shining ones. Stop your pandering and accept this as a gift."

"What do I have to do in return for this gift?" I asked warily.

"Nothing except learn. If you take my tutor back with you to the Thorn Land, I just want you to promise me you'll give her a fair chance."

"That's it?"

"Yes. You already know all my other motivations for doing this, so there's no trick there. The rest is on you."

True. He had been up-front about his larger designs on me and his megalomania. "Okay . . ." Kiyo was going to freak out. "I'll give her a chance."

"You promise?"

"I promise."

Somehow, every time I agreed to something with Dorian, I always felt like I was signing my soul away.

"Excellent," he said. "We'll make an all-powerful queen out of you yet." He reached his hand over and smoothed out where some of my dress's fabric had wrinkled up near the slit. His motion actually covered up more of my leg with the skirt, though it did involve his fingers brushing against my skin. For a brief, dangerous instant, I kind of wished he'd move his fingers underneath the dress. Instead, he simply left his hand on my thigh.

"Dorian," I said warningly.

"Hmm?"

I looked pointedly down.

He followed my gaze. "Oh, look at that. It seemed so natural, I hardly noticed," he said cheerfully, removing the guilty hand. I almost felt . . . disappointed. "Let me fetch your new teacher since I'm guessing you won't be lured into staying for dinner."

"You guessed right. You really are dazzlingly intelligent," I said wryly.

He stood up and flashed me a grin. "And stunningly attractive?"

"Just go get her."

He left the room, and I watched the way his long, lean build moved and how the sunlight streaming through a window turned his hair every shade of red, orange, and gold. Dorian was trouble. Yes, I suspected I really had made a deal with the devil.

Particularly when I saw who his instructor was.

"*Her?*" I exclaimed.

I shot up from my chair. Dorian had just entered the room, and standing beside him was Ysabel—the Eugenie-clone strumpet from the party. Her blue eyes widened when she saw me. Apparently I wasn't the only one who had been caught by surprise.

"What is this?" she demanded. "You said you wanted me to instruct someone."

"I do," he said calmly. "You're going to pack your things and return with the Thorn Queen. You will teach her to use her magic to the best of her ability."

"No," she said icily. "I will not."

His pleasant demeanor dropped. "Yes, you *will*. This isn't a request. You're my subject, ergo you follow my commands. And I am *commanding* you to go with her. Unless you're openly defying me?"

I couldn't help a shiver. I'd occasionally seen this hard side of Dorian, and it always unnerved me. It was such an abrupt change from his usual laconic self, the self who bantered and tried to feel me up . . . and I found the change kind of terrifying.

"Dorian," I said uneasily. "Don't make her do anything she doesn't want to do."

She glared at me. "I don't need your assistance here."

"What she wants is irrelevant," said Dorian. I was a bit surprised at how casually he was able to order her about and objectify her. I'd assumed whomever he was sleeping with at any given time would be someone he had feelings for. Who knew? Maybe he cared about her a lot but was still able to treat her as a subject. Or maybe he just cared about me more.

"Yeah, well, I don't want *her*," I retorted.

"Also irrelevant," he replied, eyes still fixed on Ysabel. "You made a promise to give your teacher a fair chance—unless you're going to be human and go back on your word?"

"This isn't quite what I expected!"

"It doesn't matter. You're either going to keep your promise or you won't. And you," he said to Ysabel, "are either going to obey or not."

Ysabel's eyes were ablaze with rage, and her breathing was heavy. I had the feeling she wanted to burst forth with a million expletives, but she bit her lip as though physically forcing them back. At last, she swallowed and took a deep breath. When she spoke, her words were to Dorian, but her gaze was on me. I hadn't seen malevolence like that in quite some time—no, wait. That wasn't entirely true. Her look was a lot like the one Volusian often gave me.

"Of course, I will obey, your majesty. With great pleasure."

Chapter Eleven

Along with Ysabel, Dorian sent me back with some shipments of food on credit. I almost would have thought he was trying to soften the blow of me being stuck with her, except Dorian was the type who would actually enjoy the thought of us having an uncomfortable trip. He would get a kick out of knowing how irritated I was and probably regretted he couldn't be there to witness our interactions. Nonetheless, I mitigated the discomfort by riding at the head of my group, sticking Ysabel all the way in the back behind my guards and Dorian's servants.

Shaya was understandably surprised when we arrived back. I left her to distribute the food and deal with Ysabel. "Put her somewhere. Anywhere," I said. "It doesn't matter to me."

"But why . . . why is she even here? That's Dorian's mistress."

"Oh, yes," I said, watching as a scowling Ysabel stepped aside for the rest of the entourage spilling into my castle. I kind of took offense at the sneer she gave my residence, despite the fact that I knew it was in disarray compared to those of other monarchs. "Believe me, I know she is."

Shaya seemed mollified and distracted enough by Dorian's gifts that I was able to slip away without too much argument. I made the crossing back to my world, not even bothering to change clothes before I went. When I finally got back to my own house, I had the pleasant surprise of finding Kiyo lying on the couch. Three cats slept on the couch's back while one rested on its arm. The fifth lay sprawled across Kiyo's stomach.

"That," he said, "is a great dress. Smells a little like horse, though."

I glanced down at the purple silk dress, which was holding up remarkably well considering all the dust and sweat it had been subjected to today. "It was part of a diplomatic outreach."

"Dorian, huh?"

"What was your first clue?"

"The slit."

I headed across the living room, toward the hall that led to the other side of the house. "I'm hitting the shower. You want to go to Texas with me afterward?"

Kiyo straightened up, spooking a couple of the cats. "Is that like a new restaurant? Or do you mean the state?"

"State. I have to go talk to those two shamans that Roland told me about." I glanced at a clock. "We'd probably have to stay overnight."

He considered. "If we can be back by noon tomorrow, I'll do it."

I assured him we could and then left to shower away the day's dirt. Miraculously—and a little disappointingly—Kiyo didn't come harass me while I cleaned up. He had a tendency to show up while I was showering and offer to "help" clean me off.

Conscious of our time, he let me be, and a half-hour later, we were ready to hit the road. Yellow River was just over the Texas border, making it about a four-hour drive if we kept a little over the speed limit. Kiyo liked to drive—I think it was some manly instinct—so I let him. We stuck to casual topics, which allowed my mind to wander to the Otherworldly affairs on my plate.

The whole stress of running and caring for a kingdom still weighed upon me, but I had the comfort of knowing I'd done what I could and that Shaya would manage the rest. That was her job. We both knew it, and she would perform her duties excellently. I needed to stop stressing about that. The missing girls . . . well, those were my problem. At least, I'd made them my problem. Meet with these shamans in Yellow River would hopefully shed light on that situation, so until I saw them, there was no point in worrying about that either.

Ysabel . . . yes, well, that was something worth worrying about. I'd just let a viper into my household and took some comfort in realizing that my reluctance to stay the night in my castle would probably save me from being smothered in my sleep. If I'd had my way, I would package her up and send her straight back to the Oak Land. My stupid promise bound me. Maybe she did have something useful to teach me, but I had no evidence that she'd actually try to be helpful. She'd probably just glare the whole time, no doubt paranoid I wanted to move in on Dorian . . .

Dorian.

I sighed. He was a problem, one I kept thinking would go away but didn't. I needed him, and we both knew it. So long as I did, he was going to use that as leverage to keep seeing me and taunting me. For the most part, that annoyed me. I hated being part of his games. Yet, at the same time, there was always something irresistible about Dorian, something that made me laugh in spite of the exasperation he so often caused.

And, yeah . . . I hated to admit it, but no matter how much I loved Kiyo, and no matter how much I'd washed my hands of the romance between Dorian and me, there was still a part of me that would probably always be attracted to him. Our night together still haunted my dreams. His hand on me earlier today had woken a lot of those feelings up, and I couldn't help but imagine again how easy it would have been for him to slide that hand up my leg . . .

"Eugenie?"

"Huh?" Kiyo's voice startled me out of my indecent thoughts.

"What are you thinking about? You have the weirdest look on your face."

"Oh, well, I . . ." I was totally astonished when the next words burst out of my mouth. "How come we never have any foreplay?"

Kiyo's hold on the steering wheel momentarily faltered, and I feared we'd run off into the shoulder. He quickly regained control. "What are you talking about? Of course we have foreplay. Remember that thing I did with the honey last week?"

"Yeah, I guess. But that's more the exception than the norm. We always just kind of jump right into it."

"You never really seem to mind."

He had a point. "No . . . I mean, it's always good. It'd just be nice to . . . I don't know. Expand our horizons."

"I'm okay with that," he said after several thoughtful moments. "I'm up for anything. It's just my . . . well, instincts, I guess, that tend to drive me right toward the main attraction."

I knew what he meant. The problem with spending part of your life as an animal was that you picked up some of their traits. Foxes in the wild didn't really devote a lot of time to foreplay.

"I don't really mind. I'm just saying that I'd like to shake it up."

He fell silent for a while. Finally, he asked, "Does this have anything to do with Dorian?"

"Why do you say that?" I asked blandly.

"I don't know. More instinct." His dark eyes narrowed as they focused on the road. "I'm not stupid, you know. I know you slept with him."

I jerked my head in surprise, unable to attempt any sort of denial. I'd never technically lied to Kiyo about what had happened with Dorian, but seeing as we'd been broken up at the time, I'd never really felt the need to go into detail.

"How do you . . ." I couldn't finish the question.

Kiyo gave me a rueful smile. "Dorian used to watch you like a starving man who wants meat. Now he looks at you like he wants seconds."

I didn't say anything. No response came to mind.

"It's okay," continued Kiyo almost amiably. "I know it happened when we were apart. What's past is past—so long as it doesn't mess with our present."

It was rather magnanimous of him, and I felt both grateful and guilty. "It's in the past," I agreed. "It has nothing to do with anything anymore."

The first shaman Roland had directed us to was a guy named Art. Like Roland and me, Art lived in his own piece of suburbia, in a large house that hardly looked like it belonged to someone who battled spirits and gentry. The sides were painted a sunny yellow, and the yard—which bore the signs of daily tending—was even ringed with a white picket fence. I could hear children playing down the street.

In fact, Art himself was out in the yard, weeding flower beds as the afternoon light turned orange. I pegged his age around thirty or so. A red snake tattoo coiled around one of his arms while a stylized raven showed on the other. No doubt there were more under his shirt. He glanced up and smiled when we stopped beside him on the house's sidewalk.

"You must be Eugenie," he said, standing up. He brushed dirt off his gloves and looked apologetic. "I'd shake hands, but . . ."

I smiled back. "No problem. This is Kiyo."

The two men exchanged nods of greeting, and Art directed us around the side of the house. "Roland said you wanted to chat, right? How about we sit down in the back? Let me clean up, and I'll go get us something to drink."

Kiyo and I followed his direction and found ourselves sitting at a cute, umbrella-covered table in a backyard even more lush than the front. Though a bit more humid, Yellow River's climate wasn't that far off from Tucson's, so I could only imagine the amount of water and labor it took to maintain this greenery. A funny thought came to me, and I couldn't help but laugh.

"What?" asked Kiyo. He'd been watching a hummingbird dance around a red-flowered bush that flanked the house.

"I was thinking I need Art to come do landscaping in the Thorn Land."

"I think that might blow your cover."

"Likely. I don't even know if he crosses over very much."

"If he does, it's probably only a matter of time before he finds out and tells Roland. Actually, it's only a matter of time before *anyone* does that."

I made a face. Roland knew a lot of shamans, all around the country. "Yeah, I know."

Art stepped out through the back patio, gloves gone and a new shirt on. He set down a small cooler, carefully sliding the glass and its screen shut again. The drapes hanging on the other side of the patio were blue and purple watercolors laced with silvery threads that I envied after my own had been ripped up by a storm I'd inadvertently caused. Between his excellent décor and yard, I was feeling like a lame homeowner.

He opened the cooler. "I didn't know what you wanted, so I brought some options."

The cooler revealed an assortment of pop and beer. Kiyo opted for the latter; I took the former. The hot summer afternoon had cooled down to a pleasant temperature, and the shadows cast by the trees helped too. The memory of the hot journey to Dorian's was still with me, though, and I drank my Coke gratefully.

"This is a great yard," I said. "Wish I had the patience. Mine's kind of a rock garden."

Art grinned, crinkling up the lines around his eyes. They were an azure blue that stood out against his sun-weathered skin. "But that's fashionable up there, isn't it?"

"Yeah, kind of. But there's a fine line between a fashionable arrangement of sand and rocks, and, well . . . just a pile of sand and rocks."

He laughed again. "Well, I'm sure you have better things to do. Roland tells me you're keeping busy now that he's retired."

" 'Retired' is a dubious term. It's hard for him to sit still, knowing I'm out there doing business by myself."

"And I hear you've got some business questions to ask me?"

Right to the point. I liked that. "You've got a big crossroads here."

"I do," he agreed. "Keeps me busy."

"You get a lot of gentry crossing over?"

He took a long sip of his beer and considered. "Well, there are always gentry crossing over."

"Has there been an unusual amount lately? Girls in particular?"

His eyebrows rose in surprise. "Not that I've noticed. Why do you ask?"

"Following up on a job," I said vaguely.

"Women cross over all the time, of course," he mused. "But men outnumber them. Seeing a surge would be noticeable. Most of my time lately has been spent on exorcisms."

I nodded. Until gentry and Otherworldly creatures had decided they wanted to father my child, spirits had made up the bulk of my business too. That was a normal shaman workload.

"Sorry I can't be of more help," added Art kindly. I must have looked disappointed. "You should check with Abigail, though."

"She's the other one here, right?"

"Yup. We work together sometimes. Maybe she's noticed something I haven't."

I thanked Art for the info, and we spent the next hour or so chatting about assorted things. Art asked questions about Kiyo's background. Roland could sense Kiyo's Otherworldly nature, but Art's blandly polite style made me suspect it wasn't a talent he possessed. Art also wanted to know about my jobs, no doubt curious about my interest in gentry girls. I kept my answers vague, in no way coming close to the fact that I was protecting my subjects.

After making our good byes, we headed off to the second address Roland had given me. Abigail lived in an apartment in downtown Yellow River, very different from Art's homey location. The downtown area was actually more thriving than I would have expected. Yellow River was a small town at the end of the day, but it still had an assortment of interesting shops and restaurants. Abigail's apartment was above an antiques store, and we climbed two flights of rickety stairs to get to her. The mysterious, dusty nature of it all was much more in line with stereotypical shaman images.

Indeed, when she answered the door, I suspected she would have met most people's visions of a shaman. She was an older woman, gray hair styled into a long braid down her back. Her loose peasant blouse was patterned in mauve and yellow flowers, and crystal beads hung around her neck. She broke into a beatific smile when she saw us.

"Eugenie! So nice to finally meet you."

She ushered us inside, and I introduced Kiyo. The apartment was beautifully constructed and nicer than its outside suggested—but cluttered with candles and assorted statuary. It made me feel better after Art's immaculate home. The apartment was also filled with cats. I counted at least seven, and all of them looked up at Kiyo's entrance. Four of them got up and rubbed against his legs.

"You've certainly got a way with animals," noted Abigail.

"I'm a vet," he explained, giving her a winning smile that tended to make women weak in the knees.

Like Art, Abigail sat us down and forced beverages on us, this time in the form of herbal tea. We started with the usual small talk. Abigail was a big fan of Roland and couldn't say enough nice things about the work he did. I couldn't help feeling a little bit of stepdaughterly pride. When we finally got to the issue of gentry girls, though, Abigail didn't have much more to offer than Art had.

"Most of my work is actually along the lines of healing and spirit retrievals," she explained. Spirit retrieval was itself a form of healing, often done when some entity was plaguing a human in a possession sort of way. I'd done it a few times but was no expert. "I don't do much in the way of casting out. That's Art's specialty, but that cross-roads is so big that he sometimes gets more than he can handle. So, I help out every once in a while."

"But you haven't noticed a surge of gentry girls?"

Abigail shook her head, making the crystal beads click together. "No, but like I said, I'm not out in the field enough to say for sure. And gentry usually aren't so difficult to cast out . . . Art tends to handle those on his own and call me in for the entities that are harder for him to get rid of." She gave me a rueful grin. "Neither of us is as strong as you or Roland."

I played with my tea bag, wondering how to

parse this new information. Was my theory about gentry girls sneaking over here a total bust? Or were they being crafty enough to avoid detection? I usually ended up casting out gentry because they did something troubling that put them on my radar. Gentry girls slipping in among humans wouldn't necessarily attract a lot of attention.

We thanked Abigail when we finished our tea and left for our hotel. I'd booked one that sat just on the edge of town. As we walked toward where we'd parked my car on the street, Kiyo declared that he wanted to take it over to a gas station on the corner for both gas and air for the tires. I told him I would walk down there and meet him. I wanted to browse a few of the shops before we called it a night.

Poking my head in the little stores gave me a chance to get my mind off the gentry girls and today's disappointing intel. Most of the shops were what you'd expect for a small town. Antiques. Vintage clothing. Crafts. One, however, was a sex-toy shop, and I couldn't help but raise my eyebrows at that. It was surprising in this town. Equally surprising was that I went in and bought something.

I met Kiyo at the gas station shortly thereafter. "Not much in the way of information," he said as we drove out to the hotel.

"Yeah. I want to check out the crossroads in the morning before we go." That was the main reason

I'd chosen to actually come out to Yellow River in person, rather than simply call with my questions. "If that doesn't yield anything, we might just have to give this theory up."

Kiyo shook his head, a small smile curling his lovely lips. "I don't know what to think of you sometimes. You're so annoyed about this whole queen thing, yet here you are, going to a lot of trouble to help these girls." We reached the hotel and found a parking spot. He turned off the car.

"And let me guess. You want me to stay away from it all?"

"Only inasmuch as it'll keep you safe. But truthfully? What you're doing is great."

The look he gave me showed just how great he thought it was—and how great he thought I was. There was admiration there in his eyes, underscored with something heated and dangerous and wonderful. I might make jokes about his animal intensity, but when channeled into sex and passion . . . well, there was nothing to laugh about. My whole body felt the heat of his gaze, every nerve coming to life.

"Let's go inside," I said softly.

"Yeah," he agreed. "No place I'd rather be."

His hands were on me as soon as we cleared the hotel room's door, reminding me of the first night we'd spent together. He pushed me onto the bed, tearing off my clothes as he did. I wanted to sprawl right there and let him take me—but just barely had enough presence of mind to wriggle away.

"Did you mean what you said earlier?" I asked, my breathing hard.

His dark eyes were hungry and impatient. "If it gets the rest of your clothes off right now, then yes, I stand by whatever I said earlier."

"About expanding our horizons?"

This gave him pause. "What did you have in mind?"

I slipped away from him—no small feat—and produced my purse and the purchase I'd hidden in it: the bag from the sex-toy store. I pulled out a pair of handcuffs.

"Are you serious?" Kiyo asked, not sounding particularly opposed so much as curious.

"That headboard's got a nice spot to lock your wrists in." I might dream of Dorian restraining me, but right now, it was the thought of me being Kiyo's captor that aroused me.

"Me?" This was a surprise to him too. He hesitated only a moment, though. There was desire and lust radiating from him, and while he might have preferred simply jumping in and having his way with me like usual, the bottom line was that he wanted me, period. One way or another. "Okay."

He pulled off the rest of his clothes and lay back against the bed's covers, hands stretched up. I paused to admire his body, filled with such strength and power. After removing my own clothing, I leaned over him and fastened one wrist to the headboard. I heard his breath catch as I did, my breasts only a few inches from his face. His other hand immediately went out to my hip and ran up along the side of my body. I pulled away, out of reach.

"Not allowed," I warned. "You don't get to call the shots here."

He gave me a saucy grin. Being tied down wasn't in his nature, but he felt bolder with only one hand bound. He was still able to feel in control.

"I've got another hand and two feet," he pointed out.

I smiled sweetly and reached back into the bag. I pulled out three more pairs of handcuffs. His smile faded to astonishment.

"Don't worry," I said. "I've got it covered."

I made sure all his hands and feet were locked into place, putting him at my mercy and ensuring he wouldn't do anything I didn't want him to. And as I lowered my hips down near his face, spreading my thighs so that the warmth of his mouth and tongue had no choice but to lick and suck as long as I wanted, I felt smug satisfaction in knowing for certain that I would be the one who got off first tonight.

Chapter Twelve

Kiyo took off as soon as we got back to Tucson, saying he had to go to work. He also added that I shouldn't expect him later that night since he'd promised Maiwenn he'd come visit. Normally, that would have set my mood plummeting—and I won't lie, I wasn't thrilled as it was—but after last night, I felt superior and confident in my position with him at the moment. Somehow, I doubted he'd be looking at Maiwenn with the same awe he kept regarding me after I'd ridden him to exhaustion last night. If the crossroads in Yellow River—which we'd visited before heading out of town—had only yielded some answers this morning, I would have considered the trip a resounding success.

"Nice of you to spend some time around here," Tim told me when I emerged from the shower. As usual, he appeared to be cooking something.

"What's that?" I asked, watching him roll out dough.

"Cinnamon rolls," he replied. "The second

batch I've had to make, thanks to *someone* raiding the kitchen while they cooled." He shot a glare over in the direction of one of the dogs—Yang, I thought—lying under the table. Yang looked extremely pleased with himself.

"Sorry," I said, even though it wasn't exactly my fault.

Tim finished rolling out the dough and sprinkled the surface with a mixture of cinnamon and brown sugar. "And don't think you're going to change the subject about never being around."

I found a Coke in the refrigerator and sat down, a little irritated over the scolding. "Well, sorry you miss my company, but I don't really see how it matters. Our deal is you live here rent-free in exchange for cooking and cleaning. Me not being here means you have less work. Besides, I've had things to do."

He scowled. "Yeah, I suppose. But do your 'things' actually involve your job—the one that gets the mortgage paid? Your secretary called last night and said you missed an appointment. And you know, dealing with her isn't part of my rental agreement."

Despite having never met, Tim and my receptionist, Lara, had an antagonistic relationship over the phone. I had no time to give to their drama today, though. The other news was too startling. "I did what?"

I took out my phone, which also doubled as my

192

planner. In addition to two missed calls from Lara, I discovered I had indeed missed an appointment for a banishing last night. I'd been so fixated on my quest in Yellow River that I'd totally forgotten I had it.

"Shit," I muttered, dialing Lara's number. As keen as I was on these missing girls, Tim had a point—my human jobs paid the bills. Not the gentry ones.

"What happened?" demanded Lara as soon as she answered. No hello.

"I got distracted by something else," I said. "I'm really sorry. You think we can reschedule? Give them a discount or something?"

"Probably," she conceded. "I mean, it's not like they've got many other options to get rid of a ghost. In the meantime, though, I've got some other pending clients."

I hesitated. Normally, I wouldn't think twice about accepting as many jobs as I could. It was good for my bank account and a good deed for the world. With as much as the Otherworld was preoccupying me, however, I couldn't afford losing the time right now—or possibly missing another appointment.

"Reschedule the one I missed and book only one of the others. Tell the rest we have to wait-list them."

Lara was silent for several seconds. "Are you serious?"

"Afraid so."

She sighed. "Okay. You can still pay my salary, though, right?"

"Yes," I laughed. "I haven't gone bankrupt yet."

"Okay then." She sounded only moderately pacified. "But for the record? Your roommate needs to learn some manners. He was a total asshole when I called last night."

Before we disconnected, Lara made sure to remind me about two jobs I had later that day. She wouldn't get off the phone until I repeated the times and places back to her. I was just as eager to take care of them as she was, as sort of a mental retribution for the missed one from last night. I'd never forgotten a job before. My career might be an unusual one, but I still considered myself a professional and didn't want to start falling into bad habits as a result of all this Thorn Queen business.

And yet . . . as soon as I finished those jobs, I had to send myself back to the Otherworld. I only intended it to be a quick visit, though. I simply needed to check Shaya's progress and find out if the runaway girl had been located. Questioning her would make this whole search and rescue a lot easier and let me get on with my human life.

The news wasn't good, however.

"No sign," said Rurik, once I hunted him down in the castle. I'd found him in a compromising position with one of the cooks. "We've got people scouring the area but haven't had any luck. We did, however, find where those bandits have relocated. Do you want us to go after them?"

I hesitated. I did want to round them up, both to take the pressure off the villages and see if they knew anything about the girls that my prisoners hadn't. In the end, I shook my head. If they still had that fire demon summoner, I didn't want to go after them until we had an overwhelming show of strength.

"No. Not yet. Just keep looking for the runaway." I gave a sidelong glance toward the kitchen, into which the woman whose skirt he'd just had his hand up had disappeared. "You know, if it's not too much of an inconvenience."

At least the news from Shaya was good. The supplies Dorian had sent me home with had been shipped out, and apparently Leith had contacted her to say that after going through the irrigation book, he had some ideas for us. Naturally, he wanted to meet with me again. I suspected an ulterior motive, but, it was something I'd happily endure to keep the food coming. I at least felt like Leith's intentions were easier to understand than Dorian's—and that I was a lot less likely to yield to temptation along the way. I sent the young prince a message back, saying I'd love to meet with him. On impulse, I also asked if he had anyone who might be capable of summoning water demons. Once that chore was done, I made motions to go back to Tucson.

"Well? Are we going to get this done with or not?"

I turned around, surprised to see Ysabel standing there in the hallway, hands on her hips. I'd been heading out toward the courtyard to do a little communion with the land before returning home. The heat was sweltering, as usual, and most of the women around here had taken to wearing light, gauzy gowns, often with short or no sleeves—not unlike the dress I'd worn to Maiwenn's party. Ysabel had made no such concessions and stood clothed in a green velvet gown, complete with long bell sleeves. The color looked stunning with her hair, but I knew she had to be miserable.

"Get what done with?"

She threw up her hands in exasperation. "This . . . tutorial. Or whatever it is my lord sent me here to do."

Oh, right. I hadn't forgotten Ysabel, exactly. I'd just kind of tried to pretend she didn't exist, in a feeble (and futile) hope that she might just disappear. No such luck.

"Sorry," I said, returning her hard look. "I don't really have time."

"You promised Dorian," warned Ysabel. "And until you do this, I can't leave this godsforsaken place. I want to go home."

I shrugged and turned away. "We can't always get what we want. Kind of like that song. God knows I haven't."

I'd barely taken one step when a huge gust of wind shot toward my back, whipping my hair in front of me and rustling the tapestries on the wall. I immediately came to a halt and looked back at her. Her expression was both smug and hostile.

"What's the matter? Afraid you can't keep up with me?"

Charming. The old baiting tactic. She was hoping to get her way by playing on my pride. It was like the lamest trick in the book . . . except, well, it was kind of working. Okay, it was more than just my pride here. I was succumbing to temptation. With hardly any effort, Ysabel had just nearly knocked me over. It was more than I could do—much more—and her power nowhere near matched mine. If I had that kind of mastery, I could create hurricanes and blow apart buildings. Being in full possession of my magic would make me a god.

That shouldn't have mattered. I shouldn't have wanted that . . . but some secret part of me did. Well, not the god part. But certainly the rest. Power like that could help my people, I tried to convince myself.

"Okay. Let's get this over with then." I acted like getting rid of her was my only concern—not that that wasn't a huge motivating factor.

This castle, I was finding, was filled with rooms—most of which didn't seem to have much use. Most of the servants and guards had their own quarters, still leaving a ton of rooms unoccupied and gathering dust. I really only had need of my meeting room and parlor when I was there, and the rest had thus far stayed unused.

The parlor was apparently being cleaned, so on impulse, I led Ysabel to one of the abandoned rooms. It had a river-rock fireplace that wasn't going to see use anytime soon, but the striped brocade furniture hadn't accrued too much dust. I flounced down onto a chair, arms crossed and posture defensive.

"Okay. Make this fast."

Ysabel examined her sofa carefully before easing down and spreading her voluminous skirts around her. She crossed her hands on her lap, and if not for the expression on her face that said she wanted to rip me apart, I would have said she looked dainty and ladylike.

"Dorian says I'm to teach you to improve your power with air."

"Something like that."

She eyed me critically. "Before we begin, I want it made abundantly clear that I am *not* doing this by choice."

"Really? I hadn't noticed."

Her lips curled into a sneer at my sarcasm. "I don't know what Dorian sees in you. You think you're so clever and witty when really, you're just a plain, uncouth human."

"Half-human," I corrected. "And plain or not,

your boyfriend—and, like, every other guy around here—would give up his right arm to get me into bed." I really shouldn't have provoked her like that. Not only was it mean, it was also going to make this whole magic lesson probably even more unbearable.

"Believe me, it's through no charm of your own. It's only the prophecy and your alleged breeding ability, and once that's run its course . . . well . . ." She demurely smoothed the wrinkles out of her skirt, not that there really were any. "It's only your child anyone will have interest in, not you."

"Sorry to disappoint you, but there isn't going to be a child." Not as long as my doctor kept prescribing me birth control pills.

Ysabel looked up, face filled with skepticism. "Oh? Then why are you with the . . . kitsune." She said *kitsune* like it was a dirty word. Dorian often did too, though he did it mostly to irritate me. I think Ysabel legitimately looked down on Kiyo. "If you really are a queen . . ." She looked skeptical over this as well. ". . . then why lower yourself by taking him as a consort? The only reason you would have is in the hopes of him fathering a child on you, just as he did Maiwenn. Clearly, he's proven his virility . . . which might be of particular concern to you. You claim you're trying *not* to conceive, but perhaps that's a lie to hide the fact that you *can't*."

"What? That's insane!"

"Whereas I . . ." She ran her hands proudly along the sides of her hips. ". . . have already born two children."

Whoa. That was startling—and a point of pride for her, no doubt, considering the gentry fertility issue. "To whom?" For some reason, the thought that it might be Dorian bothered me.

"My husband. He was killed years ago in battle." She frowned slightly, the first sign of true emotion I'd seen on her. In a flash, her normal bitchy expression returned. "They live with my parents right now and are healthy and strong. My lord Dorian knows I can undoubtedly have more. That's why he cast you aside for me, forcing you to turn to the kitsune for your fleeting chances of offspring."

"That's not what Dorian and I—never mind. Look, for the last time, I'm not with Kiyo to get pregnant, okay? I'm with him because I love him."

She sniffed. "I find that unlikely. If you just wanted a lover for pleasure, you would pine for my lord. No other man can match his skills in the bedroom. When he binds my hands in ropes or paints my flesh, I find no greater ecstasy than—"

"Whoa, just stop," I said, holding up both hands. This entire conversation was grating on my last nerve. "I do *not* want to hear any details about your sex life with Dorian, okay? That is not part of this deal. No part at all. I don't want to— wait. Did you say something about painting?"

A sly smile lit her features. "My lord has a great

appreciation for art. Often, before we make love, I'll lie naked before him and let him use my body as a canvas. He will spend hours adorning my flesh with color and design, often using the paintbrush as a means to pleasure me and—"

"Okay, okay. I'm sorry I asked."

As the words left my lips, though, it shocked me that I could envision what she was describing perfectly. Dorian's magic lessons had often involved tying me up—the necessity of which I was never 100 percent certain of—and he would spend a large amount of that time weaving the silken cords that bound me. He'd arrange them in interesting patterns and color formations, consumed by the process itself. Somehow, I imagined him being the same with paint. I could see his face lost in thought as he painted flowers or suns or whatever, his clever, sensual hands taking their time as they lightly touched my body . . .

No, not my body. Ysabel's. I had no part of this.

"Let's get this done with," I said gruffly, hoping she wouldn't guess my thoughts. "Then we can both go home."

"Very well then. So, you need my help because you're weak."

"That's not entirely true." Jesus Christ. It was all going to be like this, wasn't it? "I have a lot of power. I know how to control and use water magic—though I guess I could be better. Everyone assumes I must have inherited wind magic too, but

201

so far . . . well, I've only been able to use it once."

"You may simply be deficient," she said lightly. Her eyes flicked to my chest. "Like in so many other ways. But we shall see."

It kind of went on like that for a while. Every other sentence of hers was a barb. Yet, a lot of what she explained to me sounded similar to what Dorian had said, which at least gave me some confidence that she wasn't bullshitting me. In particular, she kept trying to describe how I could reach out and feel different types of air—just as Dorian used to encourage me to do with water. Unfortunately, it had taken a very long time to do that with water, and I felt a little pessimistic about history repeating itself.

"There are different types," she kept saying. "Don't try to sense them all. Focus small."

"What do you mean different types of air?" About an hour had gone by at that point, and I was growing weary and longing for Tucson. "Air is air," I argued.

"Spoken like a savage," she remarked. "Perhaps we should just end this and tell my lord we fulfilled our promise to try."

I gritted my teeth. "Just explain it one more time."

She shrugged. "There are different types of air."

When she offered no more, I began to agree with her. It might be best to abandon this after all. A few moments later, though, she elaborated.

"There is different air around plants. Different air after we exhale. Different air when the land is foggy. Not that you'd understand that in this wretched place."

My eyes widened. "Gas. Molecules. That's what you mean."

Now she was the one wearing the confused expression.

"The different types of air," I continued, excited in spite of myself. "You're saying the magic depends on feeling each kind . . . oxygen, hydrogen, carbon dioxide . . ."

I was speaking a foreign language. Ysabel seemed as confused as ever, but by this point, I was running away without her. It made sense. Dorian's entire teaching method had been built on baby steps. It had started with me sensing a bucket of water and culminated in me using the water in Aeson's body to blow him apart. Starting at the molecular level with air seemed daunting, but the human in me clung to the science.

And as I sat there, I began to expand my mind out, much as I did when preparing to use water magic. Air had always remained blank and untouchable, yet as I began to simply focus on a tiny part of it, it became more manageable. I thought about Ysabel's breathing—oxygen in, carbon dioxide out. The world slowed down to a heartbeat, one breath at a time . . .

I'm not sure how long I sat like that. I lost track

of where I was or even if she said anything else to me. Only her breathing mattered. At last, I could sense the differences, the changes in the air coming in and coming out. As she exhaled, my mind scooped up the air—the carbon dioxide—leaving her lips and flung it as I would a ball. My control was imprecise; I had no real target. The air brushed past her shoulder, ruffling her hair.

"You . . . you touched it," she said grudgingly, clearly surprised.

I was alive and burning with energy now, too consumed by what I was doing to answer her. Using magic always set my senses ablaze, made the world seem more vibrant and real. I wanted to do the trick again but decided to see if I could work it the opposite way and exert control over a different type of air—oxygen. I waited again to get a feel for her breathing, letting my mind actually sense the different particles in the air. When I felt certain I could grasp the oxygen, I did—just as she was about to inhale.

Ysabel began to cough, her hands going to her throat as she tried to draw breath. Sucking the oxygen away meant, well, that she couldn't inhale it. I froze in my surprise at the obvious yet not entirely unreasonable consequences—so much so that I couldn't stop what I did. I was just . . . stunned. I was controlling air. The magic burned through me, and her oxygen just kept flowing away and away. It obeyed my commands, and I didn't have the coherent reasoning to cut it off.

After several seconds that felt like years, the realization of what I was doing suddenly penetrated my higher reasoning. I finally cut off the magic, letting go of my hold on her oxygen. By then, Ysabel had fallen to her knees in a desperate attempt to get air—and probably because she was starting to lose consciousness too. At last, free of the magic, she drew a large, shaking breath, face pale and terrified. A few moments later, when she'd recovered herself, she looked at me accusingly.

"You—you tried to suffocate me!"

"No!" I exclaimed, aghast. "I . . . I didn't. I'm sorry. I wasn't thinking. I was just trying to control the air . . ."

She stood up, and where once her face had been pale, it was now flushed with anger. She was shaking. "You deceived Dorian. You already know how to use this kind of magic. This is all part of some elaborate plot."

"No, no," I said, standing as well. "I've never used it before—except once and only for a few seconds."

"I don't believe you. What you just did . . . you couldn't have done that if you were as inexperienced as you pretended to be!"

What I'd done—aside from the fact it could have killed her—didn't seem like it was that big a deal. I'd sensed air and moved it. It was hardly a hurricane, and it had taken a lot of concentration—so much so that I didn't think I could repeat it anytime soon. I hardly had the effortless control she exerted over the wind.

"I'm sorry . . . I really am. I didn't mean to hurt you. It was an accident."

Ysabel's only answer was a scowl, just before she stormed out of the room. As she passed me, I thought I saw both fear and tears in her eyes. Despite her bravado, I realized that what had seemed more like anger in her was actually terror. She was in the home of someone she saw as a rival, someone with a reputation as a warrior and a tyrant—*and* someone who had just tried to kill her. She was trapped here by Dorian's orders.

"A terrifying feat, your majesty," a voice near the doorway said.

I took a few steps forward and saw Shaya standing just outside in the hall, her pretty face grim.

"It was an accident," I said, surprised at the trembling in my voice. "I don't like her, but I don't want to hurt her."

"I know." Shaya's expression turned both gentle and sad. "But her fear isn't unfounded. You learned that too quickly and too well."

"It was easy! It's the same as moving water around or any other type of air."

"From what I understand, stealing someone's breath—denying them air—is harder than simply creating breezes. You're fighting against life itself. Those who suffocate others in this way usually require great strength and stamina. For you to be able to do it already . . . well, it's a testament to your power—and that's nearly as frightening as the act itself."

The full impact hit me. "Wait . . . there are people who do that on purpose? Steal someone's air so they can't breathe?"

She shrugged. "Well, to those with the skill, suffocation's an effective weapon."

"It's sick . . . it's an inhumane way to die."

"I agree. And most people don't have that kind of strength, so it's not an issue. Among those who do have the strength, most would never consider doing it to another person, enemy or no."

I groaned. "Well, if that's true, then she has to understand that I wouldn't purposely do it to her either. She has to believe that it was an accident."

"I don't think you're going to have a lot of luck with that."

"Why not?"

"Because while most consider such torture unusually cruel, there was one person who enjoyed denying someone their breath—and who frequently used it as a form of execution and entertainment." Shaya's look was meaningful. "Tirigan Storm King."

Chapter Thirteen

Ysabel couldn't be coaxed out of her room, no matter how hard I tried. I even sent Shaya to do it, seeing as she tended to be a bit more personable than I was. No luck. Ysabel remained firmly entrenched and would only ramble over and over about how she was going to tell her lord about me and escape of this accursed place.

Evening wore on, and I couldn't drag myself back to Tucson. My feelings were in turmoil. I'd never expected to feel guilty about anything pertaining to Ysabel, but there it was. And as more time passed, I didn't just feel bad about inadvertently suffocating her. As soon as I'd realized what I had done, I knew I had to cease practicing this kind of magic immediately. Storm King had used it to kill his enemies in horrible ways. Kiyo had warned that delving further and further into my powers would put me on a path I might not be able to turn away from.

And yet . . . that was the problem. I knew I had to stop . . . but I didn't want to.

Sure, I didn't want to learn air magic to kill. But after touching that power . . . I couldn't stop thinking about it. I found my mind spinning, analyzing the air around me and how easy it would be to manipulate it. What had started as a seemingly small lesson from Ysabel was quickly moving into larger and larger implications as I grasped more of air's patterns and how it worked. It was like I didn't even need a teacher. My own nature and pull toward magic was running away and creating its own lessons.

My conflicted ruminations were interrupted when a letter arrived via the Otherworld's equivalent of the Pony Express. It was from Leith. As I'd suspected, he'd devoured the engineering books. What I hadn't expected was that he'd already developed a plan for how to implement some of the irrigation systems and was going to accompany some workers out to Westoria in the morning to get started—unless I had any objections, of course. If I didn't, then he would be honored if I would come out to meet them.

He also added in his letter that he had investigated the towns near the Yellow River crossroads. None of them had any reports of missing girls. It figured, I thought. I either had enough bad luck to be the only monarch with runaway girls—or I possibly had an enemy specifically targeting me. Considering the number of gentry who resented my rule, the latter wouldn't have surprised me.

Regardless, I decided I had to go out to see Leith tomorrow. Even if it was just an elaborate attempt to woo me, he was still going to an awful lot of trouble with this. Plus, I hoped that if I spent the night here, Ysabel might finally emerge.

So, I stayed over, giving me the opportunity to meditate with the land. While I noticed no ostensible difference in the morning, there was a strange, intangible feel to it . . . It seemed healthier. Like always, I couldn't exactly articulate why. Perhaps most disturbing of all, I found that staying over wasn't quite the agonizing ordeal it used to be.

I was preparing to head out to see Leith when a guard announced that a rider was approaching. I wondered if it was a messenger—or possibly Leith himself. Instead, it was someone quite unexpected.

Dorian.

The castle servants fell all over themselves to welcome the Oak King, and he swept inside as though perfectly entitled to it. Which, I guessed, he was. Nonetheless, I had no time for his antics today and greeted him with hands on my hips.

"Not today, Dorian. I have things to do."

"As do I," he said. He had that typically laconic tone to his voice, but there was an oddly serious—and impatient—look in his eyes. It was not an expression I'd seen very often. "I've come to see my subject. I knew you wouldn't welcome her with open arms, but honestly, my dear, your attempts at murder shock even me—no small feat."

My jaw nearly dropped to the floor, both because of his assumption and the fact that she'd somehow gotten a message out to him. "Wha—? Dorian, it's not true! It was an accident. I didn't realize what I was doing."

"May I see her?" he asked, not acknowledging my plea.

I could hardly deny him that, and he hurried off to her room without another word. She admitted him—no surprise there—and I found myself pacing the entire time they were together. It had been bad enough that Ysabel had thought me capable of assault. But somehow . . . the idea of Dorian thinking badly of me? Well, it struck me harder. I shouldn't have cared what he thought—God knew I was mad at him more often than not. Yet, I realized that deep inside I wanted his good opinion. I felt sick to my stomach that I might have lost it.

When he emerged, his face was still serious. "I believe I have convinced her that your intentions weren't murderous."

I sagged in relief—more, I think, because *he* appeared to believe me. "Thank you."

"The question now is: do you want her to stay?"

"Will she?" I asked, startled.

"She obeys me," he said simply. "She'll stay and continue to teach if I tell her to."

"I don't want anyone here against their will . . ."

"I've assured her of her safety. She won't live in—much—fear of you. So, that's no longer the issue. The issue instead is if you want to continue with her teachings."

"I can't—not after . . ." I stopped, realizing I was unsure of the words leaving my lips. I didn't want to be like Storm King. I didn't want a natural affinity for learning ways to kill people. And yet . . . I couldn't stop thinking about the way I'd felt wielding that kind of power. Controlling water had given me a rush; air had doubled it.

Dorian's gold-green eyes were watching me very carefully. "I see," he said. "Then I'll tell her she'll be staying a little longer."

I started to protest but couldn't. He returned to her, stayed a few more minutes, and then joined me in my parlor where I had resumed pacing.

"Well, then," he said briskly, "that is that." The grim set to his face was gone, and I found myself grateful to see the return of his usual mien. "I noticed you were about to leave. Off to free humans from your subjects?"

"Off to free my subjects from me."

I explained my task, and his features lit up with interest. "How convenient that I'll be traveling in the same direction. Unless you'd like me to wait here until you return?"

No, the last thing I wanted was to encourage Dorian to make himself at home in my castle. So, I grudgingly conceded that he could go with me, partly because I still felt guilty and grateful over his intervention in the Ysabel incident. One bright side to him being with me was that Rurik decided I didn't need an entire retinue for the trip. He alone accompanied us, and I wondered idly how Dorian managed to go wherever he wanted without an entourage. I didn't like to think he was a more authoritative ruler than me.

"Don't give me a hard time about this air thing," I warned. "I don't want any spiels about how I'm embracing my heritage and approaching my destiny."

Dorian smiled, eyes on the road ahead of us. "I don't need to tell you things you already know."

"Of course . . . I suppose if I did get a better grip on my magic, I might be able to get rid of those fucking fire demons."

"You see? I told you I don't need to say anything. You're finding ways to rationalize your use of magic all on your own."

"Hey, this is a serious threat. You can't tell me you'd be all casual if you had demons running loose in your kingdom." I frowned. "Or would you? I got the impression a lot of rulers don't bother themselves with that kind of thing."

Dorian's eyes took on that serious glint again, despite the small smile on his face. "Aeson didn't bother. Don't generalize to all of us. You know better. If I had demons in my land, I'd lead a group out myself to obliterate them."

I wondered if Dorian could. My potential power might be greater than his, but at the moment, his control and skill made him a more dangerous force than me. A ruler in the Otherworld had to be powerful, or else the land wouldn't accept them. It was a wonder I'd been found worthy.

"Do you want me to help you?" he asked when I remained silent. "I'll go with you the next time you strike."

"What would that cost me?" I asked with an eye roll.

"Why do you assume everything I do has an ulterior motive? Isn't it enough I'd want to help you?"

"I don't know," I said, not liking how his words made me feel bad. Was I attributing more insidious motives to him than he deserved? "I don't trust anyone around here." Westoria was looming in the distance. "I don't even trust Leith's engineering generosity. He's not doing this for the sake of trade."

Dorian's eyes lifted to the approaching village. "That," he said, "we can both agree on. No matter how much you beat yourself up over those demons, you have more than enough strength to bind the land to you." I hated his uncanny ability to guess my thoughts. "When Katrice dies, the Rowan Land will either pass in entirety to someone with the power to control it, or it will divide itself and be subsumed into other kingdoms."

"Shaya said the same thing—and that Leith thinks being hooked up with me would help keep it in the family." I shook my head. "One land's bad enough. I don't have the power to control two."

"You'd be surprised," he said ominously.

Our arrival was greeted with the same wonder and awe I'd had before the demon incident. Apparently, yesterday's food shipments and Leith's presence today had re-established my awesome reputation. Dorian seemed to have an effect as well. As we dismounted and walked through the village, the residents' eyes followed both of us, filled with admiration and wonder. Glancing at Dorian, I could understand their feelings. He strode through the dusty town just as he had my castle, confident and majestic, even after a hot and wearying ride. He looked like, well, a king, and even I couldn't help but admire his good looks. Beside him, I felt frumpy and insignificant.

Then, I tried to pull back out of my glum thoughts and imagine what we must look like to these people, both of us tall and red-haired. We looked good together, I knew. I was in jeans, but I'd cleaned up this morning, and my hair was down. Out of the corner of my eye, I could see where the sun lit it up, giving the red a golden hue that complemented Dorian's truer red. My tank top was blue, a good color for me, and I had on my usual gemstone jewelry. Perhaps most importantly, we carried our titles as king and queen, and to these people, I realized we were probably the equivalent of a Hollywood couple on the red carpet.

"Your majesty! I'm so glad you could—" Leith had come running up to us and came to a total standstill when he saw Dorian. After a few stunned moments, he made a polite bow to the Oak King. "Your majesty. Also a pleasure."

I could tell Dorian was delighted to have ruined Leith's plans for a romantic interlude. "Well, I hated to part from Eugenie this morning, so I thought I'd come along and see what's new."

I had to restrain myself from elbowing him. His wording implied that we'd woken up together. Our former relationship was no secret, and Dorian had pitched his words loudly, so that some of the gathered villagers would hear. No doubt this would be all over the Otherworld by tonight. Leith looked even more dismayed than before, and I tried to smooth things over.

"Why don't you show us the project?" I asked him. "I don't think I can thank you enough for what you've done."

Leith brightened and eagerly led us forward. As we walked, Dorian murmured in my ear, "Believe me, he's more than sure you *could* thank him enough."

"How come you can allegedly do things for me without ulterior motives but no one else can?" I hissed back.

Dorian only grinned as Leith headed toward the village's edge and showed us his handiwork. There was little to see of his irrigation system at this point. Mostly people were digging and laying out the foundation. Leith did his best to explain what it would develop into and even showed us blueprints—quaintly written on parchment. I followed them a little but could tell they were gibberish to Dorian, despite his polite and confident smile.

Zealous or not, a prince of the Rowan Land was not about to do manual labor, and once the tour was done, he sat down with Dorian and me at the mayor's house. Davros seemed only too happy to keep offering his home as my hangout and eagerly served us wine before leaving his esteemed guests to discuss whatever it was royalty talked about.

"This is only the beginning of what we can do," Leith said, positioning himself so that Dorian wasn't in his line of sight. "I'd love to come visit and discuss more ways to work through this. I've got some ideas on how to construct buildings that will reflect light better. Have you ever considering redesigning your castle?"

"Yikes," I said. "No. That'd be a big feat."

"Not as big as you think. Not with the right help."

I shook my head with a smile. "Let's just focus on the people first."

Leith smiled back. "Sure. But I will come by some day to show you some palace ideas—just in case you change your mind. Or, better yet, you should come visit us. Mother would love to show you the hospitality of the Rowan Land."

"Or, better yet, you should throw the Thorn Queen a party," said Dorian, deadpan. "I'm sure she would love it."

This time, I did elbow Dorian. Leith didn't notice. Dorian knew perfectly well I dreaded Otherworldly social events—particularly when the focus was on me.

"Really," I began. "That's not—"

"Of course!" said Leith. "We haven't had a grand ball in quite awhile. We could invite hundreds of people . . ."

I decided then that elbowing wasn't severe enough. It was with great restraint that I didn't actually kick Dorian. He placed his own elbow on the table, resting his chin in his hand, appearing quite entertained.

"You'd have to outdo Maiwenn's party, to truly show Eugenie honor," said Dorian. "That's going to be hard to do. Of course, Maiwenn has an unfair advantage with her maternal glow, eh? Eugenie was just telling me on the way here how all this baby talk is kindling longings of her own."

I choked on my wine.

"I love children too," Leith told me. "I can't wait to have some—once I find the right woman."

I was spared more of this when one of Leith's workers came in, anxious over some mishap. Leith looked devastated at the thought of abandoning me—and also embarrassed over me witnessing a flaw in his grand plans. "I'm sorry," he said. "I hate to leave you. I'm sure this will only take a moment."

"Actually," I said, rising. "We should probably get going as well."

"Must you?" he asked, face falling further.

"I'm sure I'll see you soon."

"Yes," agreed Dorian. "You should get moving on that ball. Or maybe I should just throw one for her . . ."

Leith totally fell for the baiting. "No, no. I would be more than honored to." He swept me a bow, and I let him kiss my hand. "I'll have news for you soon, I promise."

I smiled and expressed my thanks and allowed him to kiss my hand *again* when he insisted. As soon as he was gone, I turned on Dorian. "Are you trying to push me into his arms or away?"

"Ironically, doing one causes the other." He

stretched and stifled a yawn. "Were you telling the truth? Are you ready to leave?"

"Yeah, I think so—"

"Your majesty?"

Davros stuck his head into the room, wearing his usual apologetic look. His eyes flicked nervously from Dorian and then to me. "I'm so sorry to bother you . . . I know you must be busy and . . ."

"What is it?"

"She's been found, your majesty. The missing girl? Her parents tracked her down last night but were afraid to tell you . . . she seemed so distraught. I only just found out myself. I told them you'd want to know—"

"Of course, I do." I was already moving toward the door, Dorian fast on my heels. "Where are they?"

Still bobbing his head in obeisance, Davros hastily led us to a small home on the opposite side from Leith's construction. He beat impatiently on the door. "Open up! The queen is here."

Almost a minute passed before the door opened. The woman who had accosted me on my first visit peered out, eyes wide. "Your majesty," she said humbly, inclining her head. She didn't seem to recognize Dorian. "We—we didn't know you were here."

"I want to see her," I said impatiently. "Let me talk to her."

220

The woman hesitated, fearful of me but also fearful of something else, apparently. Davros was undeterred. "This is the Thorn Queen! Let her in."

With a gulp, the woman stepped aside. I found myself in a small but clean cottage, dimly lit thanks to all the curtains being drawn, though all the windows were open to allow a breeze. The woman's husband met us as we walked through the kitchen, his face pale and afraid.

"Your majesty . . . forgive us. We were afraid to tell you. We were afraid she'd run away again."

"I'm not going to hurt her. I just want to talk to her." It was a bit depressing, between Ysabel and this family, knowing everyone was terrified of me. Ironically, before I'd known about my gentry heritage, I'd been proud of the fear I inflicted on Otherworldly inhabitants. "Please take me to her."

I felt Dorian's hand on my shoulder and his breath warm against my ear as he whispered, "You do *not* need to say please."

With a quick exchange of looks, the couple led us to the back of the cottage, into a tiny bedroom. It too was darkened, and I could make out a slim girl lying on a bed. There was a washcloth on her forehead that fell off when she sat upright at our approach. She cringed against the wall.

"Who is it? I told you I didn't want to see anyone . . ."

"It's all right, Moria," said her mother. "This is

the queen. She's come to talk to you. She's not going to hurt you."

The girl wilted even more, blond hair covering half of her face. "No, no . . . She's come with the others, come with her human blood to bind us and kill us and—"

"Moria," I said gently, holding my hands out as one would under a white flag. "She's right. I'm not going to hurt you. I just want to talk to you. It won't take long."

"They all say that," Moria said, eyes wide with tears. "They all say they won't hurt you . . . all the humans . . . you're no different . . . they all say they aren't . . ." She lapsed into muttering too low for me to hear, her hands clinging to the covers.

"I think," Dorian murmured to me, "that her experience has left her . . . ah, a little touched. I doubt you'll get anything useful from her. There's a healer at Maiwenn's court who's particularly good with sickness of the mind. You should send for her."

I had a feeling he was right but had to make one more attempt. "I just want to know where you've been. Who took you. I want to make sure it doesn't happen again. Tell me who it is, and I'll stop them."

"No," she breathed. "You're the same . . . the same as him . . . the Red Snake Man."

"Red Snake . . ." I still had demons on the brain, and an image of their red and black mottled skin came to mind. Were they snake-like? "Moria, were you taken by demons? Or some kind of . . ." Hell, in the Otherworld, any monster you could imagine pretty much existed, as Smokey had shown us. ". . . um, snake monster?"

She shook her head frantically. "Our own kind don't hurt us. It's only yours . . . you're all the same . . . the human blood . . . all marked the same . . ." Her eyes left my face and lowered. For a disorienting moment, I thought she was staring at my chest until I realized her gaze was on my arm. I absent-mindedly touched the spot. It was where my snake tattoo coiled around my arm. Moria squeezed her eyes shut. "All the same . . ."

I stiffened. "Did he . . . are you saying the person who took you had a tattoo like this on his arm?"

"The Red Snake Man," she whispered, still refusing to open her eyes.

"Did he banish you? Did he force you to this world? Or did you come back on your own?"

"Iron . . . iron everywhere . . ."

I stared off at nothing for several seconds. "I'm done," I said, turning to her parents. "She can rest now."

I left the house as swiftly as I'd come in, Dorian matching my pace. "What's going on? That meant something to you."

I nodded, heading toward where Rurik stood with our horses. "I think I know who took her—and maybe the others. Not bandits or a monster. It was a human."

"How do you know that?"

"Because of the tattoo." *The Red Snake Man.* I'd seen a red snake tattoo just the other day—on Art. He'd had that on one arm and a raven on the other. "It's another shaman, one who lives very close to where the crossroads around here opens up in my world." He was also the shaman who had told me to my face he knew nothing about gentry girls. I came to a halt by the horses and absentmindedly stroked the side of mine. She looked back and sniffed me. "But why? Why would he take a gentry girl? Or more than one? His job is to get them out of our world. I could see him banishing them out of the human world. . . .That might traumatize her, but that doesn't sound like what happened. She disappeared from *this* world. She made it sound like she didn't want to be in the human world."

Dorian snorted. "Eugenie, where in your jaded existence did you pick up this naïveté? If a human took one of our girls, it'd be for the same reason we'd take one of theirs. For the same reason any man would abduct a girl."

I blanched at his implications. "But more than one?"

"He wouldn't be the first man to prefer—ah, how shall we say it? Variety."

I couldn't see it of Art, not the Art who happily

tended his garden and offered us beer and pop. He'd known Roland for years. They'd worked together. Was Art truly a kidnapper and rapist? Or was the girl just traumatized from being banished? It could be a pretty horrific experience.

I grimaced, feeling a sharp twisting in my stomach. I'd come too close to rape already in my life to treat even a hypothetical situation lightly. Was Moria a victim? Were there others like her out there? Maybe it wasn't truly Art . . . and yet, her words had dark implications. The human blood. A mark like mine. The Red Snake Man. The crossroads to Yellow River. He had to be involved; I just didn't know how.

I gave the horse one last pat and then mounted. "I have to get home," I said, tuning back to Dorian and Rurik. There was some mistake here, some mix-up. Art wasn't involved in this. He couldn't be, at least not in the way Dorian had suggested. "I have to talk to someone. Immediately."

I waited for the requisite Dorian joke, but none came as he mounted his own horse. "Then we go different ways. Be careful, Eugenie." For some reason, frankness and concern from Dorian was more disconcerting than his usual banter.

"If I'm right about this, then it's a human matter. Should be a cakewalk compared to what I deal with around here."

Dorian shook his head. "I'd have to disagree.

Give me demons and restless spirits any day over human deceit. But if you need help, I'm here. Just ask."

Again, there should have been a joke here. I glanced away, troubled by the way he looked at me. "Thanks. Hopefully it'll be a simple matter." How exactly? That I didn't know. I wasn't sure that roughing Art up would really accomplish anything—if he truly was at fault here. "See you later, Dorian."

He nodded by way of a farewell. Then: "And of course, my dear, you may kill as many humans as you like, but please try not to harm any more of my subjects. If you can help it." There it was, at last. The joke.

"Noted," I said. I attempted a glare, but there was a smile on my lips as I did.

I set a hard pace back to my castle and the gateway that would bring me back to my own world. Crossing over at the Yellow River one would have been faster, but I needed to go to my home in Tucson and prepare myself before facing Art. Rurik matched my pace easily and mercifully stayed silent. He'd watched me and Dorian together the way a child watches his or her divorced parents, in the hopes that mommy and daddy might make amends someday.

My whirling thoughts made the trip go fast—as did the land's quick route today—and we were greeted with a commotion when we reached the castle's outer borders. A group of guards came tearing toward us, and my heart seized. What now? A siege? Demons? Kiyo? Yet as they got closer, I could see that the guards almost looked . . . enthusiastic.

"Your Majesty! My lord! We found her."

Rurik and I drew our horses to a halt and climbed down. I felt my legs scream and knew I'd be sore later. I wasn't so practiced a rider that I could ride like that without consequences. I ignored the pain and turned to the guards.

"Who?" I demanded.

"We have her. The girl. The runaway girl from Westoria," said the guard, clearly pleased at his success. Rurik and I exchanged puzzled glances.

"That's impossible. We already saw her."

The guard shrugged. "We found her out near the steppes, by the Rowan Land border. She matches the description and was clearly afraid of us. She tried to run away."

"Take me to her," I said helplessly. Had my guards found another of these kidnapped girls? It would certainly provide more information.

He led us inside toward one of the little-used rooms, explaining that they hadn't wanted to put her in the dungeon—although her fear and desire to escape had required a guard. His expression turned uncomfortable.

"We, um, also had to bind her in iron. She kept

attempting magic. They're still not able to fully stop her."

A guard like this could never handle iron shackles without causing himself intense pain. Sometimes, though, prisoners would be bound in bronze cuffs with a tiny bit of iron affixed to them. It required delicate handling by the captors but was usually enough to stunt the prisoner's magic.

We reached the room, and the men on duty stepped aside for us to enter. There, across the room, a slim young woman had her back to us. Long blond hair cascaded down her back, and I had a weird, disorienting sense for a moment as my brain grappled with the possibility that Moria had somehow made it here before us. Then, as the girl slowly turned around, the torchlight began bringing out glints of red in the golden hair that little Moria hadn't had. I realized what was happening even before I fully saw my prisoner's face.

"You have *got* to be kidding me," I said.

It was Jasmine.

Chapter Fourteen

"**Y**ou!"

Even with her hands bound, Jasmine didn't hesitate to attack me. She came tearing across the room, face filled with fury. I'm not sure if her intent was to kick me or simply throw herself at me, but she never even got close. My guards were on her in a flash, hauling her back. Magic started to flare around her, but one of the guards countered it with some weak nullifying magic. Her iron cuffs made magic hard to use, but the human in her gave her greater resistance. I turned on all of them incredulously.

"That's not the missing girl. That's my sister! How could you not know that? She was Aeson's mistress!"

It was Rurik who answered. "A lot of the guard has changed since Aeson's time. Many here came as a gift from King Dorian." It was true. Dorian had warned that even though I'd won the Thorn Land fair and square, many of those who had served Aeson would have a hard time shaking that loyalty. Rurik had consequently sifted through the servants and guards, getting rid of those he didn't think could be trusted.

"Still," I said. "Someone should have known. Where the hell is Shaya?"

"She is away, tending to administrative errands," said the guard who'd been so excited initially. Now he seemed deeply embarrassed and upset.

Jasmine, meanwhile, hadn't ceased in her struggles to break free of the guards. Without her magic, she wasn't much of a threat and seemed to realize using it was futile right now. She stood average height for a girl her age, but her build was slim, and she always seemed a little too skinny. Maybe that just ran in our family. Her eyes were large and blue-gray, reminiscent of storm clouds.

"You can't hold me here, Eugenie!" she screamed. "I'm going to break free and kill you. Then *I* will be the one to bear our father's heir!"

"Jesus Christ," I muttered. "The song remains the same."

To be honest, I was actually kind of surprised Jasmine wasn't already pregnant and took it as a positive sign that she was still referring to it as a future event. The prophecy that loomed over both of us said that Storm King's daughter's son would be the one to lead the battle to conquer humanity. It hadn't specified which daughter, and apparently, Jasmine was still hell-bent on beating me to it.

"It's going to happen," Jasmine continued. "You can't stop it."

"Are you out of your mind?" I demanded. "You're fifteen! You have no business even talking about getting pregnant, let alone conquering the human world. You were raised there, for God's sake. Do you know how much Wil misses you?"

"I hate them," she spat. With the angry look in her eyes, I expected to hear thunder rumbling somewhere. "I hate them all. Even him. I never belonged there. *This* is my world."

"Not if I pack you up and send you to Catholic boarding school somewhere," I mused, rather entertained by the idea.

"They'd never be able to hold me."

"I was joking. Geez, doesn't sarcasm run in the family?"

"You'll never be able to hold me either. Your men got lucky, and you know it. I've been dodging them for weeks, each time they thought they had me."

I rolled my eyes at her smug attitude, secretly wondering what the hell I was going to do with her now. I'd spent all this time hunting her and had almost gotten used to the idea that she was gone for good. Now that we had her, I was at a bit of a loss. Never would I have guessed that my guards would inadvertently stumble across her while looking for Moria. In the midst of my puzzling, Jasmine's words suddenly replayed through my mind.

"My guys have never found you before," I said. "Believe me, we've been looking."

Jasmine stared at me like I was crazy, which was something, considering that she was the one who needed to be on medication. "They almost got me last week. Maybe they were just too embarrassed about how I nearly drowned them with a tidal wave to tell you."

I shot a questioning look to Rurik, who shook his head. I turned back to her. "Those weren't my guys." A strange thought suddenly occurred to me. "Were they human?"

"No, of course not."

"Are you sure?"

Jasmine gave me a narrow-eyed look. "I know the difference between humans and shining ones. *You're* the one who's in denial, trying to act like you're all-human."

I doubted she would say that if she had any idea what I'd been contending with here lately. Her obnoxious adolescent attitude aside, I was thinking again about what she'd said. She'd spoken of nearly being caught . . . by whom? I thought back to my meeting with Moria and her babbling about the Red Snake Man. I'd made a huge leap about Art being responsible for kidnapping her and the others.

Again, I slowed down my racing mind to think of other options. It was possible that Moria's red snake was something entirely different. Or, maybe she'd just run into him here. Like all shamans, he probably crossed over every now and then. Maybe she'd seen the tattoo then. Or, perhaps most likely, was my earlier notion that Art had simply banished her back. All of that seemed more plausible. Yet was it enough to cause Moria such terror? That was the repeated question with no answer.

And now here was Jasmine, also talking about abduction. It seemed too much of a coincidence that that would happen while other young girls were disappearing.

"Were they brigands?" I asked Jasmine. "Like . . . sort of rough and dirty types?"

"They were guards or some other kind of fighter," she said. "Stop trying to act like you had nothing to do with it. I know the difference between a bunch of gross beggars and trained soldiers."

"Yeah, yeah, you're a freaking genius," I muttered.

"That's not hard, compared to you."

"Oh, look at that. Sarcasm is in the genes." When I was younger, I'd hated being an only child and had longed for siblings. I'd never in my wildest dreams imagined this was what I'd end up with. "What did these guys look like? Were they in uniform?" My guards' uniforms were mismatched. They all had leather armor, but Dorian's recruits wore the green of his army while mine had blue left over from Aeson. Some just wore whatever color tunics they wanted.

"I'm not telling you anything else," she said. "Now let me go!"

There was almost a whine to her command, making her seem very much her age and less like someone literally set on world domination. Of course, there was no way I was letting her out of this place, not when she was clearly willing to spread her legs for anyone who might help fulfill our deranged father's grand plans.

Then, staring at her young face, a new thought occurred to me. I was always so concerned about her wanting to get pregnant that I never paid much attention to the idea of her facing the same risks I did. My queenly status had given me some reprieve, but there were still plenty of Otherworldly guys not above raping me. Jasmine had to be facing the same thing, the target of anyone who wanted to be the father of Storm King's heir. These soldiers she was talking about might have had no connection at all to Moria's abductors—if she had been abducted. Fuck. This was all hurting my brain. I needed to talk to Roland and Art before jumping to any more conclusions.

And in the meantime, this was all good reason to keep Jasmine under lock and key.

"Sorry," I told her. "You aren't going anywhere. You'll be lucky if I don't break out the Depo-Provera and fill your cell full of abstinence propaganda."

"Cell? You are *not* locking me in any cell." Her lips were puffed into a pout. Again, she seemed so much like any ordinary surly teen that I nearly laughed. She looked more like a girl who'd been grounded from texting than one who aspired to be an all-powerful fairy queen.

When I didn't respond, the impact seemed to truly hit her.

"You can't . . . you can't do that! Do you know who I am? I'm a princess. I'm Storm King's daughter! My son is going to rule the worlds."

I shook my head. "No, you're a self-absorbed brat in serious need of discipline and counseling."

"You can't do that!"

"I can . . . or did you forget who *I* am? I'm the big sister who rules a kingdom and isn't going to let you jump all over this prophecy."

"You can't lock me up forever," she warned.

"She's right," a voice behind me said.

I turned and saw Ysabel hovering near the doorway. She didn't look terrified of me anymore, but she no longer bore that cocky arrogance. She looked cool and aloof.

"You can't lock her up forever," continued Ysabel. "You should kill her."

"What?" Both Jasmine and I spoke at the same time. Ysabel seemed perfectly blasé about it all.

"She's your greatest rival to bearing Storm King's grandson. So long as she lives, she always

235

will be an obstacle. The only way you'll be free and retain your power is if she's gone."

I started to protest that I didn't want to beat Jasmine to the prophecy. Then, I realized that part didn't matter. It was Jasmine's own desire for getting pregnant that was the problem, and Ysabel was right to a certain extent. As long as Jasmine was around, I wouldn't have any peace.

I slowly shook my head. "I'm not killing my own sister. But I am double-binding her. Somebody get another set of iron cuffs."

I saw a few guards flinch. Even with as little iron as the cuffs had, that was still more than most gentry could comfortably handle. Doubling it would stunt her magic even more, but that human blood was still going to give us trouble.

"I want her cell guarded at all times," I told Rurik. "With more than you usually would post. And make sure you've got as many guards that can actually use magic." Someone had returned with the second set of cuffs by then, causing Jasmine to start up a new round of shrieks and protests.

Rurik gave me a nod and then said in a low voice, "If I could speak to your majesty in private?"

I arched an eyebrow. Rurik always obeyed me but rarely bothered with formalities or respect, which didn't bother me. In public, though, he always used my titles, and I wondered what was on his mind. We stepped out of the room, past a disapproving Ysabel, and came to a halt a little ways down the hall.

"Keeping the girl locked and under guard might not be the best idea," he said.

I groaned. "Don't tell me you think I should kill her too."

He shrugged. "Dorian would tell you to. But if you insist on keeping her here, then get that demon of yours to guard her."

For a moment, I thought of the fire demons. Then, I realized he was using a more generalized term. "You mean Volusian?"

"I'm not saying they'd do it . . ." Rurik hesitated. "But I'm not saying they wouldn't either. A lot of those guards might be tempted by the thought of fathering the heir, and if she offered . . ."

"Good God. She's fifteen."

"Old enough. It didn't stop Aeson, and if she convinced one of the guards, her age wouldn't matter. I'm guessing your, uh, friend wouldn't be so easily swayed."

Volusian swayed by sex? Hardly. Particularly if he was under my commands.

"Fine. I'll summon him." Volusian would also stop any magic she could muster.

"You might also consider finding a potion master to create a tincture of nightshade."

"A what?"

"It's a drink that will inhibit her from using her magic."

"Isn't nightshade poisonous?"

"Not to shining ones. Not if mixed with the right ingredients. With her human blood, it will, ah, leave her a little . . . disoriented. But it won't kill her."

"I'm not going to keep her in a drugged stupor." I started to return to the room and then paused to give Rurik a canny look. "Why warn me? I remember a time when *you* wanted to father the heir. Why not take your own shot?"

"With her?" Rurik snorted. "I still wouldn't hesitate to beget Storm King's grandson—but she's not the one. The heir's mother should be a warrior, and unfortunately, that only leaves you."

"You're never getting near my bed, Rurik."

"Yes, I've deduced as much. But I would still support Storm King's grandson and would be nearly as happy for my lord the Oak King to father him."

"Dorian? That's the only other alternative as far as you're concerned?"

Rurik's expression seemed to wonder that there could be any question. "Who else?"

I shook my head and left him, off to order the imprisonment of my sister.

Before setting Volusian on permanent guard duty, I had one brief task for him. He wasn't very happy about it, not that that came as any real surprise.

"My mistress, as usual, is intent on furthering my eternal torment."

"I don't really see how watching a teenage girl is that bad—for you, anyway. It's going to be a lot harder on her."

"I am a being of considerable power. I cannot die. If you insist on enslaving me, you should use my abilities to bring nations to their knees." Volusian's red eyes narrowed ever so slightly. "Instead, my mistress dispatches me to supervise children and deliver love notes."

"It's not a love note! Just ask him, okay?"

Volusian blinked once and then vanished.

While he couldn't teleport, exactly, he could travel much faster than human or gentry. After Jasmine's capture and Moria implicating Art, I wanted nothing more than to sit down with Kiyo. I needed to talk this out. I wasn't used to this sort of turmoil and indecision in my life. I longed for the days when my job had simply been to go out, find the monster, and get rid of it. It had been a lot easier than this sort of deliberation.

Kiyo, to my knowledge, was with Maiwenn, and I'd dispatched Volusian to see if Kiyo would come to me later. It was the closest I could get to making a phone call in the Otherworld—but still far from it, seeing as that took Volusian about twenty minutes to get back to me.

"You see?" I said when he appeared in my bedroom. "That wasn't so bad."

"The kitsune says he will come to you in two hours," Volusian said in his flat voice, not deigning to acknowledge my comment.

Two hours. Well, it was better than nothing. I sighed. "Okay. Thanks."

Volusian simply stared. My gratitude meant nothing to him.

"All right. Go watch Jasmine then. Don't let her escape, and for God's sake, don't let her get pregnant."

"For how long?"

"Until I say so," I snapped.

The malice radiated off Volusian, but my mastery of him would not let him disobey. Demeaning task or not, he had no choice. He vanished.

Once alone, I lay back on my bed, hoping two hours would go by quickly. Like everything else among gentry royalty, the bed I'd inherited was plush and luxurious, with a thick down mattress. The covers were heavy brocade and almost never needed in this weather—but they felt great to lie against. It wasn't quite sunset outside, but the light was fading, casting long shadows onto the room's heavy stone walls. I'd need to light torches soon.

A knock at the door forced me upright. "Yeah?"

It was Nia. She gave a polite curtsey. "Your majesty, you have a guest."

For a glorious moment, I thought it was Kiyo.

Then: no. It was too soon. And Nia wouldn't have announced him. Everyone around here knew enough to let him in by now. "Who?"

"Prince Leith of the Rowan Land."

"Leith?" I said, certain I'd misheard. "I just saw him, like, six hours ago."

Nia shook her head helplessly. "He's here, that's all I know."

I swung my legs over the bed's edge and stood up, slipping my socked feet into short leather boots. Leith? What was he doing here? A flash of panic went through me. Had something gone wrong in Westoria? If so, wouldn't my own people have told me?

They'd taken him to my parlor, where he sat on the edge of one of the satin-lined chairs. He sprang up at my approach, hurrying over to catch my hands in his. He leaned down and kissed them.

"Your majesty. Thank you for seeing me so unexpectedly. I'm sure I'm interrupting all sorts of important things."

"Not so much," I said, withdrawing my hands. "And you should really just call me Eugenie now. What's up? Is there a problem?" Around here, who knew what could go wrong? Famine, flood, locusts . . .

"A problem with—oh, no. Everything in Westoria is great. We made amazing progress today."

I relaxed. "Good. I was worried."

Leith shook his head, eager to reassure me. "No, no problems there. I just . . . well, I know this is strange, but I just had to come see you. That is, I had to ask you something. I feel like an idiot, though."

I frowned. "You can ask me anything. What's going on? Are *you* okay?"

"Oh, yes." His embarrassment grew. "But after today . . . I just had to hear something from you."

"Okay, ask."

"Are you involved with the Oak King?"

"Involved with . . . what, you mean romantically? With Dorian? No!"

Leith's face shone like the sun. "You mean it? When I saw you together today. The way he spoke . . . and the way you two interacted . . . well, I thought for sure the rumors were true."

"What rumors?" I asked warily.

"That you were still lovers."

"Where are you hearing these rumors?"

"Pretty much everywhere."

"Well, the answer is no. Absolutely not."

"Really?"

"Really."

Leith exhaled with palpable relief. He reached for my hand, and I stepped back, putting space between us. The rapture on his face made me uneasy. "Then there's still a chance."

"A chance for what?" I asked.

"You and me."

"You and—oh, Leith, no." It was just like everyone had said. "I like you—you're really great—but there isn't going to be anything happening with you and me."

"But . . ." He moved forward again, and again, I moved away. "But you keep wanting to see me and have asked me to be a part of your kingdom I just assumed . . ."

"No, no . . . Leith, I'm involved with someone already . . . you know, Kiyo? The kitsune? We're together."

He frowned and was still too close to my personal space. "I didn't think it was a serious romance. I thought he was just a . . ."

"Fling?" I suggested.

"Yes. I mean, someone like you couldn't take him as a true consort."

I sighed. "Why does everyone say that? I love Kiyo. We're together. We're going to be together for a very long time."

Leith's earlier joy was rapidly giving way to distress. "But . . . I mean, with my background and the way we get along, we're a perfect match. Admit it: you *are* usually happy to see me."

"Of course I am. But that's because I want to be your friend, not encourage you romantically. I like you—like hanging out with you. But that's it. I'm sorry. I'm sorry if I led you on."

"It has to be more than friendship. I know it is for me." He sighed. "I've never been able to talk to someone so easily. It feels natural."

"That's because you guys always make everything so . . . exaggerated. There are probably a dozen girls you could sit down with and have great conversations with if you just got rid of the formality."

"No." The grief on his face was killing me. "It's something about *you*. I just can't help it. I'm falling more and more in love with you every day."

"You barely know me! You can't love me."

"I do," he said in a low voice, and some of that glowing passion returned. "From the moment I saw you. Mother had said you'd be a suitable match politically, but even if that weren't true, I'd still love you. I've never met anyone like you, Eugenie. So brave and beautiful . . . I'd want to be with you even if we weren't ruling a kingdom together."

"Leith," I said, trying hard to make my voice stern. Goddammit. Why couldn't he have been an annoying jerk like most of my other would-be suitors? Why did he have to be a nice guy? With great effort, I tried to let him down easy instead of in my usual harsh way. "I meant it: I like you. But that's it. I value your help and your friendship, but I'm not leaving Kiyo."

"But I love you." It was weak and plaintive.

I shook my head. "I'm sorry."

His face fell, and he turned away, wrapped in

despair. He started to walk toward the door and then abruptly turned, eyes alight once more. "If things end between you and the kitsune . . . then I'd be next in line, right?"

"Next in line? Er, well . . ." Why couldn't I just lie and say yes? Or why not use a "I don't want to ruin our friendship" kind of crap line? "I don't think so, Leith. I just don't think I could ever feel that way about you."

Leith stared at me wide-eyed for several moments, and then at last, his features tightened. "I see. I'm sorry to have taken your time, your majesty. Your workers in Westoria understand my task and should no longer require my help." He gave a small, polite bow and then hurried out the door.

"Leith . . ." I took a few steps forward, my stomach sinking. I felt horrible. I knew he'd had a crush on me, but I hadn't thought it was much more than the usual Otherworldly attractions I experienced. His face at the end there had broken my heart. I hadn't wanted to hurt him, particularly after all he'd done for me.

Dejected, I returned to my bedroom and ordered wine sent up. It arrived in a jewel-encrusted pitcher, complete with a heavy golden goblet. Had to love gentry room service. I declined any requests to see anyone until Kiyo arrived. I sat down on the floor, leaning against the bed and wondering how much of the wine I could get through before he arrived.

To my surprise, all of it.

I had no clock there but was pretty sure more than two hours had passed. I'd drunk goblet after goblet, thinking about Jasmine, Leith, and Art—and finding no resolution for any of them. I was staring at the bottom of the empty pitcher, pondering the time, when I heard a soft knock at my door. Finally!

I stood up and felt the world sway around me. I gripped the bed for support. "Kiyo?" But it wasn't him. It was Shaya.

Like Rurik, she'd dropped a lot of formalities and didn't bother with a curtsey. Her face was troubled, and I saw her clever eyes assess me and my drunkenness in a matter of seconds. "I'm sorry to bother you . . . but a messenger just arrived from the Willow Land."

The anger I'd been kindling against Kiyo's tardiness ran cold. "Oh my God. Is he okay?"

Shaya hesitated and then gave a swift nod. "As far as I know, he's fine. It's Queen Maiwenn everyone's concerned about . . . she's gone into labor."

Chapter Fifteen

I stood there for several long seconds, staring at Shaya but not really seeing her.

"Thank you," I said at last, my voice unnaturally flat even to me.

She hesitated, eyes worried. "Is there . . . is there anything I can get for you?"

More wine, I thought. But I shook my head. Wine suddenly didn't seem strong enough. I wanted to go home just then and raid my liquor cabinet, seeking solace in my own home and its bed, not this godforsaken Dark Ages fortress. The wine was going to make transitioning between the worlds harder, though. It wasn't impossible but would hardly be as smooth as usual. No, it seemed I might be stuck here for a while.

"I need to see Volusian," I said.

She stepped aside for me, and though I didn't ask for it, she followed me solicitously as I headed downstairs, down to the keep's dungeon. It seemed darker and drearier than it had last time, but maybe that was the wine. Jasmine's cell was easy to spot because four guards stood in the hall outside it. I reached it, and through the bars, I saw Volusian standing in one corner, perfectly still, with his arms crossed over his chest. Jasmine sat as absolutely far from him as she could, her face equal parts fear and sullenness.

"What do you want now?" she snapped. I didn't even look at her.

"Volusian," I said. "I have an errand for you. I'll watch Jasmine while you're gone."

Volusian walked forward, passing through the bars and coming to stand in front of me. "No doubt my mistress has a more urgent task."

"Moderately. I want you to go back to Tucson and bring me the bottle of tequila I keep in my liquor cabinet. And *don't* scare Tim."

Volusian remained motionless in that way of his. "My mistress grows increasingly creative in her ways to torment me."

"I thought you'd appreciate it."

"Only in so much as it inspires me to equally creative means to rip you apart when I am able to break free of these bonds and finally destroy you."

"You see? There's a silver lining to everything. Now hurry up."

Volusian vanished. With him gone, Jasmine grew bolder. She hurried to the front of the cell, holding the bronze bars as best she could with her bound hands. "When are you going to let me go?"

I sat down against the hall's wall, opposite her. I wondered if she'd try any of her stunted magic with me around. "When are you going to stop asking?"

"You're a real bitch, you know that?"

"Look, little girl," I growled. "You do *not* want to mess with me tonight. I'm not in a good mood."

Jasmine was undeterred. "I can't believe you're keeping me in here with that . . . that thing! That's just cruel and sadistic."

"Wow, sadistic's kind of a big word. I didn't think you'd stayed in school long enough to learn that kind of vocabulary."

Her glower darkened. "When I get out, I'm going to kill you."

"Then you and 'that thing' should get along beautifully, seeing as he spends all his time plotting my grisly death too."

She nodded down to her bound hands. "I can barely feed myself, you know."

"Barely isn't the same as can't." But I did feel a little bad about that. Was I really going to keep her in cuffs forever? Yet, how could I not? Maybe I should investigate that potion Rurik had told me about. No . . . that wasn't right either. I sighed, and spent the next half-hour listening to her alternate between insults and whining. It was better than thinking about Kiyo, though. All the while, I was sobering up, so when Volusian finally appeared and handed me over a full bottle of Jose

Cuervo, I gave silent thanks that I'd purchased an extra-large bottle.

"Thanks," I said, rising to my feet. I pointed to Jasmine's cell. "Now—back to guard duty."

I turned around without a second glance, Jasmine's cries of outrage echoing behind me. Shaya, who had waited silently the whole time, fell in step with me as I walked back upstairs.

"Are you sure there isn't anything I can do for you?"

I eyed the bottle. "See if you can find some little glasses about this big." I held my fingers out to the size of a shot glass. "And bring enough for . . . I don't know. You, Rurik . . . hell, anyone who wants to get drunk with me. Even Ysabel." I was feeling magnanimous tonight. Or, well, at least in a misery-loves-company mood.

Shaya's face looked more troubled than ever, but I paid it little concern as I walked outside to a small circular courtyard in the castle's center. This seemed to be a fixture in most gentry holdings. Dorian had a couple. I'd been told that this one had been green in Aeson's time, filled with lilies and lilacs. Now, it was sandy and gravelly, lined with cacti, mesquite, and even some of the thorn trees that had given the land its name. At least the mesquite scented the air, and I decided one perk of the Otherworld was that those trees always seemed to be in bloom.

I sat down cross-legged in the middle of the

courtyard, noticing that someone had started to set stone tiles into it to create a kind of patio area. It hadn't been there last time, and I wondered if it was Shaya's doing, just like the patches of grass she kept trying to grow around here. Not waiting for shot glasses, I uncapped the tequila and took a long swig, the strong liquor burning my throat.

Shaya returned shortly, Rurik following. His face was uncharacteristically serious. After a brief moment of exchanged looks, they joined me on the tiled ground. Shaya set down some tiny cups made of engraved silver. Not quite shot glasses, but they would do. I took the bottle and filled three of them up.

"To the Willow Queen and her child," I said, holding my cup in the air. I downed it one gulp. "Damn. Wish I had some salt and lime."

Shaya and Rurik exchanged glances once more—did they honestly think I didn't notice each time?—and then followed my lead with the tequila. Rurik took his down stoically, but Shaya choked on hers.

"What . . . what is this?" she asked, once she was able to speak.

"God's favorite liquor. I should have had Volusian run to the grocery store and get some margarita mix while he was out." I paused, laughing at the thought. I poured another shot. "It's made from a kind of cactus, you know."

Shaya eyed the bottle askance. "Truly?"

"Yup. Huh. I wonder if we could manufacture this stuff. I've seen agave around. I bet we could set up some serious trade with it."

"I'm not so certain," she said.

Rurik was pouring another glass. "I don't know. It might appeal to some."

"Ah, Rurik. I knew we were kindred spirits." I held up my empty shot glass, studying the way the half-moon's light shone on it. My head was regaining its pleasant buzz again. "Do you think Maiwenn's going to have a boy or a girl?"

"I don't know," said Shaya after several moments of silence. "There are those who can magically determine such things. But I haven't heard of the Willow Queen doing that."

"Probably not." Kiyo would have told me. Or would he have? Maybe he would have held on to that news, keeping it as a special secret between him and Maiwenn. I poured another shot but didn't drink it yet. Shitfaced was one thing; sick was another. "Back in my world, they would have known its gender a long time ago. They also would have been able to tell all sorts of things—its size, if it had any diseases, even if it was twins or triplets. There's this machine we've got. You run a paddle over the mother's stomach, and then you can see the baby up on this screen. Or, sometimes, even earlier, they can take a needle and suck up amniotic fluid to find out the same things."

Rurik and Shaya were staring at me wide-eyed.

It was a common expression amongst Other-worldly denizens whenever I began talking about human technology.

"I wonder sometimes if there's any mystery or wonder left in your world at all."

I glanced over and saw Ysabel's form silhouetted in the doorway to the castle.

"Oh, sure. Plenty of it." I gestured her over. "Come have a drink. I'm pretty sure I'm too drunk to kill anyone tonight."

Ysabel hesitated a few seconds and then slowly walked over, sitting near Rurik and Shaya, as far from me as she could respectfully go. She grimaced slightly at the tiles as she tucked her flowing silk skirts underneath her. No doubt being on the ground went against her fastidious nature. Rurik cheerfully handed her a tequila shot. She sniffed it, and her scowl returned.

My mind was still on babies. "Seems like ultra-sounds would be useful to you guys. I mean, what with the trouble you have having kids."

There was a good chance, I knew, that Maiwenn might not even survive the delivery. Or that her child wouldn't. It was common among the gentry, sort of the cost for their long and healthy lives. I didn't know how I felt about that. I didn't wish death on either of them . . . and yet, how much simpler would things be if there was no Maiwenn and no baby? Even now, I could picture Kiyo by her side, holding her hand. His handsome face would be lined with worry as he spoke words of encouragement. Surely, with his human blood, their baby would be healthy and strong. And Maiwenn was a healer . . . would that be useful to herself? Maybe. Everything would go well, I was certain, and they'd undoubtedly have a beautiful baby, one that would create a bond between them forever, a bond I could never be a part of . . .

I drank my next shot and noticed that Ysabel had manfully downed hers. "Nice work," I said. "You want another?"

She shook her head. "I don't consider it ladylike to drown oneself in excess, losing hold of inhibitions and all sense of decorum."

"Of course you don't," I said.

"I believe," she added primly, "that the Willow Queen shares my views."

I smiled, spinning my cup on the ground, watching in fascination as it turned in smaller and smaller circles before coming to a stop. With Maiwenn's baby consuming my thoughts, Ysabel's baiting seemed insignificant tonight.

We continued on for a while, Rurik keeping up with me in shots, with Shaya only occasionally indulging. Ysabel seemed to have lost her fear of me and continued her running commentary of barbed remarks. I think knowing I was in a fragile state over Maiwenn's labor had emboldened her. In fact, she was in the middle of some anecdote about how Kiyo and Maiwenn had first gotten involved when her words came to a halt, and her features lit up with surprise.

"My lord!" she cried, springing up just as one of my servants began announcing, "His royal majesty, King Dorian, of the House of Arkady, caller of earth—"

Dorian strode forward into the courtyard without waiting for his titles to finish. Ysabel fell to her knees before him, face radiant. "My lord!"

He gave her a brief nod of acknowledgment and then swept on past her toward me. I don't think anyone except me saw the devastation that filled her face over the slight. Shaya and Rurik began to rise out of courtesy, but Dorian quickly motioned them down. Unfastening his cloak—it appeared to be navy in the moonlight—he spread it on the ground and sat beside me.

"Well, well, a party, and no one invited me."

"It was kind of impromptu," I said, reaching over to pour him a shot. My hand trembled as I held the bottle.

Dorian took it from me and finished pouring. He eyed me carefully. "And yet, it appears to have been going on for some time."

"Yes. We're toasting the birth of the next king or queen of the Willow Land."

"So I've heard, which is why I came to see how the news was received here." Dorian tossed back the tequila. His eyebrows rose in surprise at the taste, but it didn't stop him from pouring another. "And don't presume her child will inherit. It all depends on strength and power."

His words reminded me distantly of Leith's own inheritance problems, which then reminded me of Leith's declaration of love. Ugh. I'd probably killed our one chance at engineering help. Well, that was a concern for another day. "How'd you get here so fast?" I asked Dorian.

"Not that fast. I heard hours ago."

Hours ago. Dorian had found out before I had. Probably everyone had. Who was I, after all? Certainly no one who was connected to this birth. I was just another monarch who'd be expected to send jewels or tapestries when the baby was born. I poured another shot, but Shaya reached for it.

"May I have another?" She wasn't a fan of this stuff, but I had a feeling she wanted to stop me from drinking any more. Oh, well. There appeared to be about one more shot in the bottle—though Dorian beat me to that one too.

"You'll make yourself sick," I warned, reaching for the bottle. Only a few drops poured into my cup.

"I'll take my chances. This is a fascinating substance."

"It comes from cacti," I said helpfully, hoping it might deter him from that last shot. It didn't.

"Intriguing," he said after downing it. "You should try producing it here. I'm certain a number of people would trade for it."

I couldn't be certain in the near-darkness, but it looked like Shaya rolled her eyes.

Part of me resented Dorian's presence, though I had to admit that he did a good job in keeping the subject away from Maiwenn and Kiyo. That didn't stop me from thinking about them, of course, but I couldn't help but smile as he entertained the others. Whether it was part of being a king or just something inherently Dorian, he had a powerful charisma about him that could make everyone laugh and stay captivated. With my social reticence, his were skills I admired—and occasionally envied.

As the night wore on, though, I could feel the tequila's effects lessening a little. That wasn't to say I still wasn't drunk as hell; I'd taken down half that bottle myself. But, I wanted to go to bed while I was still in that delirious haze. It didn't stop me from feeling down over Kiyo, but I had to imagine being sober would be worse.

Everyone stood up when I did, and I felt my legs struggle for balance. "Let me assist you," said Shaya, reaching toward me. Dorian intervened before she could help.

"No, no. Allow me to guide the Thorn Queen to her room. I'd like a few words." Ysabel's face darkened at this, and he gave her a chastising look. "Oh, stop it. I'll come to you shortly— provided Eugenie will allow me to stay overnight in her castle."

"Sure, sure," I said. "Come on over. Make yourself at home. Pick out curtains."

He extended his arm to me, and I decided the indignity of letting Dorian guide me was less than that of me falling over in front of my servants. Ysabel's eyes followed us furiously, and I couldn't blame her. If my boyfriend were taking a drunk woman to her bedroom, I'd be pissed too.

"It was very high-handed of you to think I needed your moral support," I told him once we were out of earshot of the others.

"Right. You only need the moral support of a bottle," he teased. "Be honest, Eugenie. Your lover's at the side of a former lover, eagerly awaiting the birth of their child. I'd be distressed as well."

"Nothing distresses you," I grumbled. We reached my room, and he followed me in without invitation.

"Plenty of things do," he said. He frowned, ever so slightly, and it occurred to me he was none too sober himself.

I let go of his arm and walked over to the full-length mirror that stood on one side of the room, edged in gold. I'd pinned up my hair earlier and let it down now, wondering if I wanted to bother with sending Nia for a nightgown or if I'd just sleep in my clothes. Standing there, I stared at my body, thinking again of my mother's claims that I was too skinny. I always argued it was an athletic build. Running my hands over the sides of my stomach and down to my hips, I studied my figure. Whatever you wanted to call it, it was slim.

"I can never do that for him," I said in a small voice. "I can never give him a baby like she can."

Dorian strolled over and stood behind me, meeting my eyes in the mirror. "Do you want to?"

"I don't know. Kids were never on my radar . . . it was always a 'maybe someday' kind of thing. But now . . . knowing I can't . . ." My hips and stomach suddenly seemed as unhealthily skinny as my mother had always said. They would remain untouched and infertile, never filling out with the kind of life Maiwenn's had. I would never share that with Kiyo.

I flinched as Dorian reached from behind and placed his hands on the narrowest part of my waist. He rested his head on my shoulder, and I was too weary to shoo him away.

"You speak like someone who's been condemned with infertility or like you've passed your prime."

"I might as well be."

"That's not true. You're young. You radiate health and fertility. You could have a dozen children."

I shook my head slowly. "I can't," I said sadly. "I *won't*. You know I won't, no matter how much you and every other Otherworldly creature want me to."

"Maybe you'd have a daughter."

"I can't take the risk." I knew I'd never be confiding in him sober. "And what if Kiyo decides he doesn't want that—to be with someone who's always going to be childless? What if he wants more kids? Maybe this baby . . . Maybe he'll go back to Maiwenn. Maybe . . . maybe he'll leave me . . ." I could feel tears forming in my eyes and hated myself for the weakness.

Dorian tightened his grip on my waist. "He'd be a fool. And you'd be a fool to mourn him if he did. You're more than a childbearing vessel."

"Not the way everyone talks. Not the way you talk."

To my shock, Dorian spun me around. Still gripping me, he pressed his forehead to mine so that only an inch was between us. I could smell the tequila on his breath, no doubt mirroring my own.

"Eugenie, you're a woman without equal, and no matter how much you annoy the hell out of me and no matter how much I try to get you out of my head—and believe me, both occur regularly— I can't stay away from you. Even if you were barren, I'd take you as my consort in an instant and spend the rest of my life with you—childless, so long as it meant you'd be by my side. I would gladly bring you to my bed with no other thoughts than taking joy from your body. It would be enough."

I swallowed. "But you're with . . . I mean, what

about . . . what about Ysabel? She can have kids . . ."

"Ysabel," he said dismissively, "is nothing. A pale imitation of you—and not even a good one at that."

That was harsh of him, but it filled me with something warm and loved and special. I realized then that no matter the bantering, sexual tension, and many schemes, Dorian really was my friend. I also realized that I wanted so badly then for him to kiss me, to crush his body against mine and run his hands along my bare skin. I wanted to have sex with him against the wall, on the bed, on the floor . . . it honestly didn't matter, so long as our bodies were joined, and I could feel him in me . . .

Whoa. I jerked away, my heart racing, barely stopping myself from doing something I'd regret. Deciding he was my friend was one thing; jumping into bed was another. I knew it was the tequila and my worry over Kiyo causing this. I didn't want to be with Dorian again; I couldn't be. Even if he claimed it would be for love and pleasure, I knew it could never be that simple. There would always be politics and schemes . . .

And so, I did the most unsexy thing I could. I summoned Volusian.

The icy, dark presence of my minion caught even Dorian by surprise, and he took a step back. It was the Otherworldly equivalent of a cold shower. Volusian's eyes flicked to him and then turned back to me.

"My mistress requires more intoxication," he said.

"No." My magical hold on him trembled ever so slightly. It was nowhere near enough for me to lose control, but the alcohol messed with my power a bit. "I wanted you to go to the Willow Land and see if there's any news."

"More romantic errands."

"Just go," I snapped, trying to sound as harsh and commanding as I could.

As soon as Volusian was gone, Dorian strode angrily to me, all traces of sensuality gone. "That was stupid, Eugenie. You shouldn't have summoned him after drinking so much."

I turned away from him. "I need to find out what's going on."

"You need to banish him. You're going to regret keeping him someday."

"He's useful," I protested. "I don't need any lectures. You should go to Ysabel now. I don't need any more declarations of love today."

"Oh?" His light tone returned. "Had a few of those today?"

"Leith," I admitted. "He came by tonight to profess his undying devotion and see if he had a chance with me."

Dorian's green eyes watched me carefully. "And?"

"And, of course not. I had to tell him no a few times before he finally got it."

Dorian didn't bother hiding his satisfaction. "You've broken the poor boy's heart. And his mother's, no doubt. There'll be no ball now. Would you like me to throw one instead?"

"No." My sadness was turning into irritability. "I want you to leave. Go to Ysabel and paint her or tie her up or whatever it is you do together. I'm tired and want to go to bed. Alone."

To my surprise, Dorian didn't protest. Much. "As you wish. If you need me, you know where I'll be."

"It would take a lot for me to interrupt you," I said dryly.

Dorian gave me one of his knowing, sly smiles and then left without another word. The thought of him going to Ysabel's bed troubled me more than I would have liked. He'd barely been gone a few minutes when Volusian returned.

"Well?" I asked. My stomach was queasy. I didn't know what I wanted to hear.

If it was in Volusian's nature to smile, I swear, he would have. "The servants of the Willow Land report joyfully that their queen has given birth to a daughter. All are healthy and well."

My body went perfect still, and for a moment, I saw nothing in the room except those glowing red eyes. Finally, I snapped back to myself. "Thank you, Volusian."

"Does my mistress require me to learn anything else about this joyous occasion?" There was a sneer in his voice.

"No. Go back to Jasmine. *Now.*"

He obeyed, leaving me alone. I sat on the bed for several minutes, thinking of everything and nothing. I felt numb. I felt every emotion in the world. And when I suddenly ripped the air from the room and used it to smash a vase against the wall, I couldn't say if it was because of Dorian or Kiyo.

Chapter Sixteen

I tossed and turned that night, surprised I didn't lapse into the alcohol-induced coma I'd kind of hoped for. I finally woke up with the sunrise and decided to leave before too many people noticed. Only a few servants were up and around, for which I was grateful. I didn't want to see Shaya's concerned look or listen to Dorian and Ysabel flirt over breakfast. I didn't want to think about what the two of them had done last night—or why it bothered me so much. I was Dorian's friend. That was enough.

Before leaving, I stuck my head downstairs in the prison. The night shift of guards was still awake and alert, and Volusian kept his emotionless watch in the cell's corner. Jasmine was curled up in a ball, fast asleep, thought I could see dried tears on her cheeks. Unguarded in sleep, she seemed very young.

I transitioned back to Tucson, bearing one of the worst hangovers of my life. Despite the fact that it was later in the morning there, my house was as still as the castle had been. Considering the way the cats and dogs watched me expectantly, I had to assume Tim hadn't gotten up to feed them yet. I let the dogs out in the backyard and told the cats they'd have to wait. As for me, I downed two glasses of water and half a bottle of aspirin practically, before collapsing in my room. My own bed provided the comfort the castle's couldn't, and I slept heavily for two hours.

I felt a lot better when I got up, and a shower improved things further. The smells of French toast wafted out to me, and my tormented stomach welcomed the thought of food. I headed out to the kitchen to tell Tim to serve up a double helping and found that he wasn't alone. A girl in her twenties sat at the table, giggling and wearing his *Homeland Security* T-shirt. Tim stood at the stove with the aforementioned French toast, bare-chested in sweatpants and several beaded necklaces.

"Oh, hi," squeaked the girl.

"Eug! What are you—er, greetings of the morning, Sister Eugenie." Tim held up his palm. "I did not realize you were home."

I rolled my eyes, having no patience for his routine this morning. I poured myself a cup of coffee. "I hope you've got real maple syrup."

He handed me over a plate of French toast, fresh off the stove. I think it had been intended for his lady friend, but he knew better. I found the maple syrup in the refrigerator, doused the toast liberally, and then headed back out to the living room without another word to either of them. A few minutes later, Tim scurried in, looking sheepish.

"You know you aren't supposed to bring them home," I said.

"Yeah, I know. It's just . . . well, I didn't actually think you'd be home with the way things have been lately."

"Not unreasonable," I conceded. "But that doesn't change the rules. You stay at their places."

He nodded. "Can she at least finish breakfast before I kick her out?"

I chewed my own food, thinking about what I had to do today. I swallowed and sighed. "You can let her stay all morning. I'm leaving soon anyway . . . I'll probably be gone most of the day."

Tim brightened with unexpected pleasure. "Really? Oh, sweet. Thanks, Eug. You're the best—"

I handed him my empty plate. "Just get me a refill, and we'll call it even."

Since telling Lara to keep my schedule open, I now had days with no plans—which proved terribly convenient today. I was going to drive out to Yellow River again to talk to Abigail and Art and try to make some sense of this red snake business. There were too many questions and loose ends surrounding it all, and I needed to start tying some of it up so that I could get on with my life.

The downside of a drive like that was that it gave me lots of time to think. Lots and lots of time. It was a clear day, and there were no major cities along the way. It was just me, my mind, and the open road. I kept thinking about how Kiyo and I had last driven this trek together and the sex that had followed at the hotel. I thought about him and Maiwenn now, celebrating the birth of their daughter. I thought about my breakdown with Dorian and my fears that Kiyo wouldn't want me anymore.

I'd brought my cellphone with me and had it sitting on the passenger seat, volume up high. I didn't want to miss a call from Kiyo . . . because surely he'd call to tell me about his daughter as soon as he could, right? If I hadn't heard anything, it meant he was still in the Otherworld, which—as one might imagine—didn't have the greatest cell coverage.

We'd visited Art first last time, but when I got off the highway, I found I was closer to Abigail's. So, I drove through Yellow River's modest downtown—past the sex-toy store—and parked outside her building. It was afternoon by now, and people were out and about, with tourists in particular poking their heads into the antiques store beneath Abigail's apartment. I found the little doorway by the store's entrance and headed upstairs, wondering if I'd be overrun with cats.

But I wasn't—largely because I never made it into the apartment. I knocked several times and even called Abigail's name once. When that didn't pan out, I dialed the number Roland had given me. I got her voice mail but nothing more.

"So much for that," I muttered. Maybe it was just as well. Art was the one who held most of my attention anyway, what with his tattoo and all. He was the one who needed to be questioned.

So, I left the town for the suburbs, and in full day I could really take in how cute Art's neighborhood was. The houses were large and new like his, and his neighbors appeared to love their lawns just as much. I didn't see Art outside, but a large red SUV in the driveway boded well for him being around.

I knocked twice on the door, and for a moment, I thought he too must be out and about. Just as I nearly rang the doorbell, he finally opened the door. His hair was damp, like he'd just come out of the shower, and he held a pair of hedge clippers in one hand.

"Eugenie!" His face split into a grin. "This is a surprise." The smile momentarily faltered. "Is everything okay? Roland . . . ?"

"Fine, fine," I assured him. "I just wanted to ask you some more questions."

"You drove a long way for that," he mused, stepping outside and shutting the door behind him.

People had an easier time lying over the phone, but I could hardly tell him that. "I had the time and thought it would make things simpler."

"Sure. I'm happy for the company . . . so long as you don't mind hanging out with me while I get a little work done?" He waved the clippers by way of explanation.

"No problem."

He offered me something to drink first, but I was still holding on to coffee I'd bought at a gas station and declined. I sat down on his front step while he began trimming some of the thick shrubs flanking the front of the house. They were thick and heavy-leaved, filled with pretty yellow blossoms. They seemed to want to consume the house, and I was reminded of Sleeping Beauty's castle, and the thorns that had surrounded it. He didn't cut their overall height but mostly seemed concerned with making them look neat.

"I stopped by Abigail's on my way here, but she didn't seem to be home."

"I think she's in El Paso for a few days," Art said. The muscles in his arms bulged, raising his T-shirt's sleeve and showing me the coiled red snake. "Her sister lives there. They're close, which is good, but I sure could have used her help with a banishing the other day. You should have come by then. It was a gentry girl, actually—you were looking for those right?"

"Yes," I said, startled. "I take it you managed to send her back on your own?"

"Yeah. She wasn't that tough. More scared than anything else."

I sipped my coffee, trying to make sense of this new development. I may have very well indeed jumped to conclusions about Art's kidnapping role. Maybe Moria had just been banished after wandering here. "Do your jobs ever actually take you to the Otherworld?" I asked.

He gave a gruff laugh. "Not if I can help it. Those transitions are a bitch, even with that crossroads. I haven't actually been over in . . . I don't know. Years."

"Huh," I said.

Art paused in his clipping, giving me a puzzled look. "Why do you ask?"

"I've heard stories . . . that is, gentry rumors about some human over there who kind of sounds like you."

"Like me?" His confusion grew. "That's a little weird."

"It was a human with a red snake tattoo." I didn't mean to sound accusatory, but a tiny bit of it slipped into my tone.

"Why on earth would I lie about crossing over?" he asked. He wasn't angry, exactly, but some of that friendly demeanor had cooled a little.

"Whoa, hey. I didn't say you did." I tried not to sound too defensive. "It was just weird that there were sightings of someone who looked like you near where your crossroads lets out."

"The gentry I've banished are probably getting confused and thinking I was in their world when I kicked them out of this one . . . it's honestly hard to understand how any of them think. And you know how disorienting banishing is."

"Yeah, I know. I'm just saying the story I heard was weird." Art said he'd kicked a gentry girl out, but Moria sure had sounded like she'd escaped.

If I thought his attitude was cool earlier, it was frigid now. "I find it equally weird that a shaman is chummy enough with gentry to be listening to their stories—and concerned about them. Why does it matter to you if humans are over there anyway?"

"Because those humans might be harming gentry."

"And?"

"And it's not right."

He snorted and returned to his trimming. "They're gentry, Eugenie. They're not like us. And from what I hear, you're not all that gentle with them anyway."

"When they're in *this* world, yeah."

"Any world, Eugenie. They're literally not human. Why do you care so much?"

"None of your business." The harsh words were out before I could stop them. Art paused again and this time turned to fully face me.

"And it's none of your business where I go and what I do—in either world."

My heart lurched in my chest. "What, are you saying it is you? That you have been over in the Otherworld recently?"

"I'm saying I'm done with this discussion. You're not welcome here if you're just going to toss around ridiculous accusations—accusations that don't even matter."

"It matters to them."

"I think you're asking the wrong questions here. You need to examine your motives and figure out why you're so eager to defend those who have no regard for us—and why you're picking fights with your own kind."

I shot up, careful of the coffee. "I'm not picking a fight."

"Then get out of here before there is one."

We stood there, locked in antagonism, and I wondered if it would come to a fight. I was armed, and he wasn't, though he was bigger and better-muscled. No, that was stupid. Why would he fight? He hadn't confessed to anything, only grown hostile at what he read as me accusing him of things he didn't consider crimes. That didn't make him guilty—but it didn't make him innocent either. Something just didn't feel right here.

"Fine," I said, backing off. "I didn't mean to upset you. I'm just trying to figure things out and make sure no one's being wronged."

He smiled, but it was a far cry from the easy grin that had greeted me. "What in God's name would you do if someone was? Come on, Eugenie. Don't overinflate your sense of obligation—or importance. There's no shaman police. You don't have any jurisdiction or right to dictate what I or anyone else around here—or anywhere—does."

"Noted," I said, heading toward my car. I was afraid if I stayed, I was going to say something I'd regret. Regardless if he had a role in all this, I didn't like the callous way he treated gentry—particularly since it was similar to the attitude I'd once had. "I'll send your regards to Roland."

"Make sure you do," called Art. "And maybe you should have a talk with him about some of these ideas while you're at it. Roland knows what's right."

I bit my lip and got in the car without further comment. So. No real answers here, but something felt wrong about Art. He was too guarded and hostile, and despite his claims about not having been to the Otherworld recently, the rest of his comments made it seem very plausible that he could be lying.

Yet, I realized what also bothered me as much as his reticence was his attitude toward the gentry. Roland's was similar, albeit not as harsh, and he'd warned me away plenty of times. Kiyo also wanted me to keep out of gentry affairs—inasmuch as I could—which was rather hypocritical, considering his involvement. I was enmeshed, whether I liked it or not, and had accepted that my views on the gentry had changed. They were odd, and I didn't always approve of them, but in their hearts, I knew they were people not all that different from me, full of the same feelings and hopes. I couldn't understand how Art or anyone else could think girls disappearing was unimportant—even if they were gentry.

It occurred to me as I drove away that Art hadn't invited me inside either time. Coincidence? His meticulous yard certainly suggested he spent as much time outdoors as within. And yet . . . would I have found some evidence in there to shed more light on his activities? Damn. There was nothing to be done for it now, not with Art still there and suspicious of me.

As I drove back through town toward the highway, a backup plan came to me. What had Art said? That Abigail was out of town for a few days? As of yet, I had no evidence whatsoever to suggest that she was involved with any of this Otherworldly intrigue, but she was an associate of Art's. Maybe there was something to be unearthed at her place.

So, I parked outside her apartment once more and slipped in past the antiques store. My athame, wand, and gun were my usual tools of the trade, but I did carry a few little-used ones, such as a quartz crystal for reading energy. I also had a small lock-picking kit I kept in my bag. Imps, trolls, and other creatures of that ilk sometimes tried to lock themselves away from me. If Abigail's lock wasn't particularly state of the art, I should be able to get in.

It wasn't, and judging from the lack of beeping, there was no alarm system within either. The closest she had was her herd of cats. They swarmed around me in a furry, slithering mass, less hostile apparently hungry. I wondered who fed them when she was gone. Uneasily, I decided to make this search quick, lest an unsuspecting pet sitter come trolling around.

Searching wasn't easy since the place was still cluttered with books, incense, and candles. My task was made more difficult by the fact that I had no clue what I was looking for. I lifted and moved things as best I could, hoping the place wouldn't look ransacked. In spite of the mess, I was again struck by how nice the apartment was, how it had been expensively restored. The floors were true hardwoods—no laminate here—and all the molding and crownwork was elaborate and beautiful. This place couldn't be cheap, and it seemed a shame she'd let her pack-rat habits get the best of it. Not that I was one to talk.

I concluded my search with a quick scan of the bedroom. It was less messy and hence had less to browse. Her duvet was a patchwork of brightly colored silks, and the closet was filled with scarves and gauzy dresses. A jewelry box on her dresser displayed a stunning collection of necklaces and rings, and beside it was—so help me—a pair of handcuffs. I almost laughed, trying to imagine New Agey Abigail into something kinky. Maybe I hadn't been the only one to visit the sex-toy shop. Of course, whereas mine had been cheap and lightweight, these were industrial-strength steel ones, like cops would use. If she was into kinky stuff, then it was pretty hardcore.

I drove back to Tucson after that, arriving in early evening. My autopilot sense of direction started to take me home, and then, at the last moment, I called Tim.

"Has Kiyo called or stopped by?"

"Nope. But one of his cats threw up on the living-room floor."

"That's not quite the same."

We disconnected, and I checked my cellphone for the hundredth time. Nope. No missed calls there either. With a sigh, I turned toward Saguaro National Park and its easy-access crossroads. If Kiyo couldn't emerge from the Otherworld and into this one, then perhaps he'd sent some sort of message to the Thorn Land. I felt stupid and desperate, like a girl waiting by the phone. But what else could I do?

Unfortunately, the Otherworldly news was no better.

"No, your majesty," said Nia. Her voice was anxious and apologetic, as though she herself was personally to blame. "There's been no word."

I thanked her and figured that if I'd gone to the trouble to come here, I should find Shaya and get some sort of update. When I went searching, however, it was a most unexpected visitor I found instead: Girard, the dark-skinned courtier and metalsmith from Maiwenn's party.

"Your majesty," he said with a bow, as flamboyant as ever. "I was hoping I'd see you before I had to leave."

"Before you had to . . . what are you doing here?" I asked, more perplexed than displeased by his presence.

"I've come to bring you this."

Like a magician producing a rabbit from under his cape, Girard held out a stunning necklace. The chain was made of exquisite, swirling links that rippled like water, and a pear-shaped sapphire ringed in pearls hung from it.

"Oh my God," I gasped, taking it from him. "This is incredible. Did you make this?"

"Yes, your majesty." His voice was modest, but he was clearly pleased by my regard.

"Who's it from?"

Recalling the comments others had made about his political aspirations, I half-expected it to be a gift from him. Then, suddenly and hopefully, I wondered if Kiyo had sent it as a token of affection since he had to spend so much time away from me. I wouldn't have put it past Dorian either, but he would have presented it himself.

"It's from Prince Leith of the Rowan Land."

Of course. I should have known. Leith accepting his fate last night had been too good to be true.

"His highness adds that he'll also have me make a crown to match if you would like. He sends this with his greatest love and devotion."

"I'm sure he does." I sighed and handed the necklace back. "Well, a crown is definitely out of the question, I'm afraid. And actually . . . I'm really sorry, Girard, but I can't even keep this. I hate for your work to go to waste."

He took the necklace and deftly slipped it into one of his many pockets. "It's no trouble at all. I understand how romantic affairs go—or rather, how they don't go. His highness will be sad, but I enjoyed the chance to work on something new for a change, so it was worth it, even if it won't grace your neck."

I recalled how he lived at Katrice's court. "What do you usually work on?"

He made a small face. "Her majesty Queen Katrice is partial to animals and collects figurines, jewelry . . . anything depicting them. Last week, I made a crystal squirrel. It was lovely, of course, but it's the fifth squirrel I've made this year."

I couldn't help but laugh. "Well, I guess I'm

glad for this, then. Maybe . . ." An idea suddenly came to me. "Maybe I can give you another project away from her menagerie. Do you have the time?"

Girard bowed low. "Of course."

"I heard you can work with iron to a certain extent. Here's what I need . . ." I described my problem with Jasmine and how I needed more flexible restraints that contained as much iron as he could handle. Theoretically, I could have brought over human handcuffs, but I wanted special ones not only for mobility but because I needed bronze or copper somewhere on them so that my guards could touch them if need be.

Girard listened thoughtfully, nodding as I spoke. "Yes, of course I can do this. I can have them for you tomorrow."

"Whoa, I didn't expect—"

He threw back his head and laughed. "Your majesty, you forget that we don't forge and work metal like humans do. I order the metal to bend, and it does. The rest is in skill and patience."

I supposed he had a point. I thanked him profusely, telling him that Shaya would settle the price with him later. Once he left, I then set out to find Shaya myself, still needing a report.

Before I could, I was intercepted again—this time by Ysabel. She was alone, which I took to mean Dorian had returned to the Oak Land. That was something, at least. I didn't want him camping out around here—particularly after my teary-eyed weakness last night.

She came to a halt before me, arms crossed. Whatever fear she'd had from our last lesson seemed to have completely vanished. Maybe Dorian's visit had reassured her. Or maybe she figured she had little to fear from someone who'd spent all of last night moping and drinking away her sorrows.

"My lord says I *still* cannot leave until we've worked together at least one more time."

"Bummer," I said and started to pass her. "I've got to find Shaya."

She blocked my way again. It was déjà vu of the last time she'd accosted me about this. "Shaya's gone right now. The sooner we get this over with, the better. I know you have nothing else to do with your time right now either. You're simply waiting for your kitsune to throw you some sort of bone."

All right, now she'd pissed me off, largely because she was right. "That's not true. I have plenty of things to do. Besides, I don't know if I really need your help anymore. I think at this point it's all just practicing on my own."

With my mind, I reached out, feeling the different types of air around us. I stayed well away from her but pulled together several groups. Now that I understood their individual natures, it wasn't that hard to combine them into larger gusts. I blasted the air through the hall, creating a gust of wind that rivaled the one she'd smugly showed me that first day. Her expression showed disdain, but I swear, there was fear in her eyes again. I remembered what Shaya had said, that I was learning too quickly and too well.

"That is . . . acceptable," Ysabel said at last. "But it was clumsy. And you can't combine it with water yet to truly control the weather."

She was right on that, but I felt I had a good enough understanding of both to just keep practicing. "It'll come with time. I'll be fine on my own."

"My lord said one more time . . ." That scornful expression faded now, replaced by uncertainty. "There is something else . . . something . . . well, you haven't even come close to it yet."

"I inherited storm magic. Water and air. What else is there?"

"Follow me, and I'll show you—if you can handle it." There it was, the old attitude. It was almost comforting.

She took me back out to the courtyard we'd been in last night. A servant I'd seen around the castle was painstakingly setting more tiles into the ground, expanding the patio area. We stood well away from him, and Ysabel continued keeping her arms crossed over her chest, posture still rigid and defensive.

"I'll be glad when this is over and I can return to the Oak Land. It's obvious my lord misses me."

Her eyes glinted wickedly. "He made love to me last night with a passion I've never seen before. It left me screaming and aching in ecstasy."

I rolled my eyes and stopped myself from saying, *Yeah, because he was thinking of me.* "Let's just get this over with so you can leave and get all the screaming and aching you want. What else was there I needed to know?"

"There's something else in the air," she said. She bit her lip in thought, trying to articulate her meaning. "I can feel it, but I'm unable to touch it. Probably you can't either."

"Can you be a little more specific?"

"It's always there . . . it's like the pieces of the air are . . . prickly. Sharp to the touch. There are more of them, though, before a storm."

I stared stupidly for a moment, and then the human part of me put it together. "Lightning . . . you're talking about making lightning," I breathed. What was the scientific term? "Those are charged particles."

The term meant nothing to her, but she'd nodded when I mentioned lightning. Eagerness flared up in me, and I immediately felt out around me. Sensing all the air molecules was easy now. The only two I could name were oxygen and carbon dioxide. All the others had their own unique feel, but I couldn't say if they were nitrogen or hydrogen or what. After a few minutes of groping with my mind, I shook my head.

"I don't feel anything like that."

Ysabel seemed pleased by this. "Like I said, you likely aren't strong enough."

"It's a clear day," I pointed out. "There probably aren't any around."

"No, they're always there. There aren't many today, but I can feel them."

I set my lips into a hard line, trying again. It was just like the old days with Dorian: endless waiting, save that he would have tied me up. Ysabel probably would have too if I'd let her, if only to use the chance to slit my throat.

Air, air, air. Every particle unique, yet none of it had the sharp, prickly feel she was describing. Distantly, I remembered the one time I had summoned a storm. I'd been caught by an elemental gentry, on the verge of being raped while my mother lay injured. In my crazy desperation and panic, I'd summoned a storm that nearly leveled my house. I had little memory of how I'd done it, though. The whole thing was a blur, like some kind of dream that—

All the hairs on my arms suddenly stood up. There. There, mixed in with other air above us was something . . . well, to put it bluntly, electric. It felt prickly, just as she'd described. I reached for it, trying to control it as I had the other particles, but it was slippery. It was like oil running through my fingers, and I understood now why she couldn't do it. It was a very different phenomenon.

Steeling myself, I tried again, and for one heartbeat, I drew them together into a knot. The smell of ozone filled the air, and then I lost my grip. No flash of light, no thunder.

But Ysabel's face was aghast. "You . . . you did it. You shouldn't have been able to . . ."

"I didn't really do anything."

"You shouldn't have been able to do that . . . not yet . . . *I* can't even touch them."

Too fast and too easily. Just like my father.

"I'm nowhere near to being there yet." I hoped I sounded reassuring. "This is going to be harder." I couldn't say how I knew; it was just something I felt. Wielding air, creating wind . . . that would come with practice. Lightning was a different beast. But when I did . . .

I suddenly shivered and was astonished at the exultation that ran through me. If I could learn to create and control lightning . . . Jesus Christ. That kind of power was unimaginable. It was a large part of what had made Storm King so feared. Being able to do that would be unbelievable. Amazing. Exquisite. Being like a god . . .

I snapped myself out of those thoughts, aghast at what I'd been thinking—again. Talk about megalomania. I was no god. Craving that kind of power was wrong; everyone said so. Well, those from the human world, at least. Yet, if I could summon lightning, I could blow a fair number of those fucking demons out of existence. Surely that was a good use of my power. Unfortunately, what I'd said to Ysabel was true. It was going to take awhile, and until I developed some other amazing weapon, those demons were going to keep coming back and—

I froze, suddenly forgetting about the phenomenal power I'd just touched. I had a weapon right in front of me, something that might seriously get rid of those demons once and for all. Unfortunately, it was not an easy one to use.

"Son of a bitch," I said. "Jasmine."

Chapter Seventeen

Jasmine nearly leapt ten feet in the air when I came tearing through the hall that led to her cell.

"You!" I exclaimed. "You can summon water demons."

She widened her eyes, speechless for a change. It appeared as though I'd interrupted her doing . . . well, nothing. In a fit of guilt, I'd sent some books down to her to pass the time, but reports from the guards said she did little but sulk. Well, that and try to cajole them to let her out. I guess she figured she'd deal with Volusian after she got one of the guards to crack.

Recovering herself a moment later, she adopted a sneer reminiscent of Ysabel's. Considering their mutual hatred of me, maybe I should have sent her down here to entertain Jasmine.

"Maybe," Jasmine conceded. "Why? Afraid I'll use them to break out?"

"No," I said. "But I need them to get rid of some fire demons."

Roland had told me the best way to oust the

demons would be by summoning their opposites. I'd dismissed the idea then, knowing it was beyond my capability. At the same time, I'd considered the possibility that Jasmine could do it . . . though it had seemed a useless sentiment considering I'd had no clue to her whereabouts or any reason to think she'd help me.

But now? Well, things were different.

Art's attitude had left me feeling helpless and ineffectual. Now, I suddenly felt as though I had the means to take control and actually right some wrongs in this kingdom.

"So?" Jasmine asked, not seeming startled in the least. "That's got nothing to do with me."

"Not true. You're going to help me. We're going to face them and their master, and you're going to summon water creatures to take down those demons."

Jasmine's expression was almost comic in its disbelief. "Why would I help you?"

I tried good cop first. "Because it's the right thing to do. They're hurting innocent people."

"So? Like I said, that doesn't affect me."

"Spoken like the selfish child you are." She flushed. Considering her obsession with having a baby and ruling over both worlds, she didn't like having her age or capabilities mocked. "I thought you wanted to be the queen of this land once."

She glowered. "Yes. And I would have been if you hadn't stolen it!"

"Why? Why be queen if you have no intention of doing anything? Did you just want to wear a crown and have people grovel?"

She didn't acknowledge that and instead replied stonily, "I'm not helping you."

I stepped toward the bars, smiling sweetly, even though I was about to enter bad-cop mode. "Oh, you are. Whether you like it or not."

"What, you're going to force me or something?"

In a matter of seconds, I had my Glock out and pointing straight at her. She paled and backed up against the wall, looking very much like she wanted to melt into it. Behind me, I heard a slight shuffling among the guards. Guns were a very human weapon, made of steel and alloys and other substances that were anathema to the gentry. They were equally deadly to humans—or, in Jasmine's case, half-humans.

"You're crazy," she said.

I shrugged. "I've got a job to do, and you're key to getting it done. You can co-operate, and maybe I'll improve your living arrangements. Give you a room instead of a cell."

I could see thoughts and schemes spinning behind her eyes. Jasmine was young, in-experienced, and self-centered . . . but she wasn't stupid. I had to think somewhat cheerfully that that too was a family trait.

"And if I don't do it, you're going to shoot me?"

"Well, everyone says I should kill you anyway."

My voice was calm, my face hard. I didn't know if she would believe me or not. Hell, I didn't know if I believed myself. She knew I had little love for her after everything she'd done, and I'd long had a reputation as a ruthless fighter and—as many gentry saw it—murderer. Jasmine swallowed. She was trying to look calm too, but her eyes betrayed her.

"How do you know I won't summon them and have them turn on you once my cuffs are off? You know I can't wear them and still have that kind of power."

I released the safety on the gun, which was still pointed at her. "Because I'll have this on the back of your head the entire time."

Long silence fell. Volusian was so still that I'd nearly forgotten he was there.

Finally, Jasmine said, "I hate you."

"So . . . that's a yes?"

I took her silence as a confirmation and put the gun away, putting the safety back on and feeling a bit surprised at the pounding of my own heart. Had I really just pointed a gun at a fifteen-year-old girl? Roland and Kiyo both believed dealing with magic could change the kind of person you were. Was messing with lightning and air turning me into someone who could easily threaten others to get my way? No, I decided. This had nothing to do with the magic. This was necessity. I needed to oust those fire demons, and this was the way to do it.

"Eugenie?"

A soft voice pulled me from my churning emotions. "Kiyo!"

He stood there in the hall, and I wondered how much he'd overheard. It didn't matter. I was just so insanely happy to see him. The heaviness in my heart lightened, and if there hadn't been so many witnesses, I would have run into his arms. He looked amazing, dressed in human garb: jeans and a plain gray T-shirt that hugged his muscles perfectly. The silken black hair curled around his chin, and his skin looked like caramel.

But his eyes . . . his eyes were hard.

I gave Jasmine a warning look. "We'll talk later."

"Fuck you, Eugenie," she called.

I caught hold of Kiyo's hand and walked back upstairs with him. Seeing him released all the nervous tension in me that had been building up since last night. I'd been so wound up, so worried and afraid. Now, it was like all was right in the world once again. The news about the baby was hard on me, but I still wanted to congratulate him. The words were on my lips as soon as we were alone, but he spoke first.

"Really, Eugenie? This is what it's come to?"

My head was still giddy over seeing him. "What do you mean?"

He pointed back toward the dungeon door from which we'd just emerged. "That! I never expected to find you with a gun to a teen girl's head."

"It wasn't exactly to her head," I said. "And she *can* help us get rid of those demons. Even if she can't summon true water demons herself, we both know she can call other water creatures." Kiyo and I had fought off some such creatures— including one that had caught us in a compromising position in his car and nearly killed both of us. "Those could give us the edge."

"And if she doesn't, you really are going to kill her?"

I sighed and stopped walking, leaning against one of the tapestry-covered walls so I could face him. "Do you really think I'd do that?"

"She seemed to think you would, and to tell you the truth, I kind of did too. I don't think you realize how scary you can be." He stood in front of me, with little distance between us, and there was an odd mix of sexual chemistry and antagonism in the air. "There's a strange feel to you ... Have you been practicing magic?"

I didn't answer immediately, which was as good as an admission of guilt. The look he gave me was almost more horrified than when he'd thought I was going to shoot Jasmine. "A little."

"A little! Eugenie," he hissed, leaning close. "There's no in-between with this stuff. You keep doing it, and you're just going to fall further and further down the rabbit hole."

I laughed and threw my arms up, gesturing to

the castle. "I fell into Wonderland a long time ago."

"You know what I mean. I thought you weren't going to do it anymore. I thought we agreed it was bad."

"You agreed," I corrected, feeling my own temper start to rise. "I had a chance to learn more, and I decided to take it. And like I said, it's only been a little."

"Learn from who?" he asked suspiciously.

"A woman from Dorian's kingdom. She has some ability with controlling air and has been showing me how to use it. I might be on the verge of calling lightning too." In front of his furious gaze, there was an instinct to be sheepish . . . and yet, I felt kind of proud at what I'd accomplished.

"Of course. Dorian. Somehow, I'm not surprised."

"Hey, Dorian's been nice to me lately." My defense of the gentry king surprised me—as did the truth of it. With so much in chaos recently, I'd found Dorian's presence almost comforting.

Kiyo rolled his yes. "Yes, and I'm sure he'd love to be nicer still. Look, you start putting all those magical elements together, and you're going to have some serious power on your hands. You're going to be like—"

"Do *not* say like Storm King!" I cried. "I wish everyone would just stop assuming that's inevitable. Plenty of gentry use magic without becoming tyrannical warlords. Give me some credit here."

"I'm just worried about you," he growled.

"And do you know what I'm worried about? I'm worried about people starving here, about people not getting enough water. I'm worried about brigands and demons preying on innocents. I'm worried about girls disappearing and possibly being abducted by those who face no accountability. And all of this is on top of trying to still live my human life and keep every goddamned Otherworldly guy out of my pants. So don't come here and start dictating to me. You're never around. You have no idea what I'm going through!"

I was shouting, and it was a wonder none of the servants had come scurrying to see what was wrong. My breathing was heavy, and I'd clenched my fists without even realizing it in my anger.

"Why *are* you here anyway?" I demanded.

Kiyo's dark eyes were hard to read, but I could see some of his earlier fury had cooled. I wasn't sure if he'd reconsidered his accusations or simply decided I wasn't worth arguing with. "I came to see if you wanted to visit the baby."

"Oh."

For whatever reason, it was like a bucket of cold water on the rest of my anger. I sighed. "Kiyo . . . I'm sorry. I shouldn't have yelled at you—"

He raked a hand through his dark hair. "And I shouldn't have jumped all over you." A sly grin turned up the edges of his lips. "Well, not that way at least. But you're right—I haven't been around. You're going through a lot that I've missed, and I don't know fully what's going on. I mean, that doesn't change how I feel about Jasmine and magic—"

I held up a hand. "Enough. We can fight about those later. Tell me about the baby."

And like that, Kiyo's face completely transformed. Joy and wonder of such purity filled his features that it was amazing to behold. I'd hardly ever seen him look like that—no, scratch that. I might have never seen him look like that.

"Oh, Eugenie. She's so beautiful. So perfect. I never . . . she's like nothing I ever could have imagined."

Something sank in the pit of my stomach, something cold and leaden. I almost wished he'd get angry again so that my own fury would return. Anger was warmer than sadness.

Forcing a smile, I reached for his hand. "I'm so happy for you," I said. "I'd love to see her. What's her name?"

"Luisa."

He said the name like a prayer, like a magic word that could fix all the world's ills. I'd heard him say my name like that too, often in the midst of sex. Obviously, his attitudes toward the two of us were a bit different, but the intensity of his love was similar.

"It's a pretty name," I said, still trying to smile. A moment of uneasy silence fell. "Ready to go?"

I was growing better at convincing Rurik to let me leave without an escort, and Kiyo and I were able to make good time to the Willow Land. I rode on horseback, and he ran alongside in fox form, able to easily match my pace. While this wasn't an official state visit, I'd grumblingly put on a gentry dress in recognition of my queenly status. It was a simple one, pale blue with cap sleeves and light material. It actually had kind of a Jane Austen feel. The worst part was that since I refused to ride side-saddle or anything ridiculous like that, the skirt rode up on my legs. With only Kiyo to see me, it didn't matter too much, and he certainly didn't mind.

Along the way, we passed another village in my kingdom, one I had yet to visit. I recognized it from Shaya's descriptions. I was pretty sure it was one of the ones with copper ore. Near its outskirts, I could see people working and digging. I made a mental note to stop on the way back—if the Otherworld didn't decide to send me through a different route.

Kiyo's fox form meant we didn't have to make any conversation. Spring was progressing rapidly in the Willow Land when we arrived. In fact, it had come much more quickly than I would have expected based on my last visit. There was no snow, and buds were bursting on the trees. The air was warm and picnic-perfect, with crocuses, daffodils, and other spring bulbs sprouting in brightly colored clusters. I was startled at the change until I remembered how the Otherworldly kingdoms were tied to their monarchs. I could pour my energy into the land and help heal it. Dorian kept the Oak Land in a perpetual state of autumn because it brought on memories of his youth that made him feel good and strong. If Maiwenn had just given birth, wouldn't her land reflect that burst of new life?

Kiyo shifted back to human shape as we approached the castle's main gates. Those guarding it gave me curious looks but welcomed him with cheers and genuine affection. Indeed, the happy energy was palpable as we walked the halls. Everyone in Maiwenn's hold acted as though they were on their way to a party. Smiles shone on everyone's faces.

Kiyo required no escort or guide as he led us swiftly through the halls, up a few flights of stairs, and into Maiwenn's bedroom. As soon as we entered, I decided I might need to have a talk with Shaya about redecorating. The bedroom I'd inherited from Aeson was that of a medieval warlord, with blocky furniture, few windows, and everything—from the thick stone walls to the bedding—in dark, somber colors. Maiwenn's room was light and airy, ringed in windows and filled with exquisite, delicate-looking birch furniture. The sheets on her bed were lavender silk, and gauzy material hung from the canopy. It looked like a room befitting a fairy princess—er, queen.

"Eugenie," she said, smiling. She was sitting in bed with pillows propped behind her. "I was hoping you'd come."

Were you? I wondered. A day after having a baby, she looked as gorgeous as usual, her golden hair cascading over a soft pink nightgown. A delicate crown of pearls, even in bed, adorned that luxurious hair, and I pettily thought again about my alleged need for a crown. Kiyo claimed it would send the wrong message, but I suddenly kind of wanted one. A small bundle was in Maiwenn's arms, but mostly all I could see of Luisa was a lacy white cap and a shock of black hair.

I smiled back and approached tentatively. Had I treated this visit too casually? Should I have dressed up even more than I had and come bearing gold and frankincense? "Congratulations. You must be so happy."

Maiwenn's smile became even more radiant. She met Kiyo's eyes, and something passed between them—not romantic, exactly, but a strong emotion I wasn't privy to. Maiwenn carefully lifted her blanket-wrapped bundle, and he took it from her with equal gentleness.

"See?" he said, coming to stand beside me. "Isn't she beautiful?"

Beautiful wasn't quite the word I would have used, though Luisa was definitely cute—which was a relief. I'd met people with ugly babies, and in those situations, you almost always had to lie and say the baby was cute. No need for lies now. Luisa was adorable—which was no surprise with her parentage—and indeed, it was obvious whose genes she'd gotten the bulk of. With her black hair and tanned skin, Luisa was clearly her father's daughter.

"Here," he said, handing her to me before I could stop him.

I hadn't held many babies before, and I took her awkwardly, one arm supporting the length of her body while the other supported her head. She was warm, nearly round with all those blankets, and shifted ever so slightly as she slept. Everything about her was tiny—tiny nose, tiny fingers, tiny eyelashes. A weird feeling built up at the back of my throat, and I remembered my conversation with Dorian. My hips would forever stay slim. My body would never create anything like this. When Luisa briefly opened her eyes to look at me—they were dark blue, no doubt to become brown—I handed her back to her father.

Kiyo took her happily, still wearing that wondrous look on his face, and sat on the edge of the bed. He placed Luisa in Maiwenn's arms, and while there was no more touching than such an act required, I again had that sense of connection between them all. An intangible bond that would keep them together forever.

I wanted to leave after that. I wanted to run from this place and never come back. But, I had to stay because Kiyo wanted me to be a part of this and because it was the polite thing to do for Maiwenn. So I kept that smile frozen on my face and made small talk that I barely heard, like whether Luisa would inherit any kitsune abilities and when Maiwenn should host the celebration of her birth.

At long last, Kiyo said we had to go, and I could tell he only did so for my sake. If he'd had his way, he would have stayed all night. I told Maiwenn congratulations again and assured her of my happiness and the baby's cuteness and a dozen other things new mothers like to hear. Kiyo was full of smiles too, but as soon as we left the room, his faded.

"Was it really that awful?" he asked.

I did a double take. "What are you talking about? Did I say something wrong?"

"No, Eugenie. You were perfect. Everything was perfect. I don't think Maiwenn noticed a thing—but then, she's pretty distracted." He sighed. "But I know you. I can see you're upset. Are you really still that worried about Maiwenn and me getting back together?"

Maiwenn and him? How could I explain that what I felt went beyond simple jealousy? It wasn't just that I feared the birth of this baby might bring them together—and that was a legitimate fear of mine—but Luisa's birth impacted me in so many other ways too. I thought about Kiyo and how much I loved him and wanted as strong a relationship as we could have—but that no matter what happened with us, we could never have a family like that. I worried again if he might cast me aside for my inadequacies. And while I was still a long way from being baby crazy or hearing my biological clock, how awful was it going to be if someday I did want a baby and couldn't have one? Or what if—God help me—I did have a baby through some accident? I could never love it, not with that prophecy hanging over my head . . .

"It's complicated," I said, realizing Kiyo was waiting for an answer.

"Eugenie," he said wearily. "I love you. I love you so much. This isn't going to change that. Maiwenn and I are through as lovers. I will always care about her, and we're going to work together to make sure Luisa's raised with all the love and attention she needs. But *you're* the woman I love, the woman who's my partner and who I want to be with forever."

His words were sweet, and they did warm part of me up. But he still didn't get the whole picture, didn't understand the tangle of emotions this birth had stirred up in me. It was so hit or miss with Kiyo lately. Some days, I felt like he knew me better than I knew myself. Other days, when it came to the issue of babies—or magic or ruling a kingdom—it was like he didn't get me at all.

"I know," I said, laying my hand on his. I certainly wasn't going to fight or debate this in the middle of Maiwenn's castle. "Look, it's okay. We'll talk about this later. Right now . . . well, I can tell you don't really want to go."

He shook his head. "No, no. I'm coming with you—"

"Kiyo," I said, unable to help a small smile, "I know you. I saw your face up there. You want to be with Luisa more. And you should. Stay awhile, and I'll just go back myself."

"Eugenie . . ." But I could tell I was right.

"It's fine. And I'll be fine. I'm the big bad Thorn Queen, remember? Besides, I want to visit that village we passed."

He was silent for several seconds. "Where will you be tomorrow? I want to find you."

"I'm not sure. In the morning I have to be back in Tucson for a job—and to talk to Roland—but after that . . ." So much kept happening lately that I was always shuffling one problem around for another. I hadn't had the chance to talk to Roland about Art and the Yellow River connection, nor did Kiyo know about the recent developments around that either. Before I could start to explain, Kiyo turned us in an unexpected direction.

"Do you want to go hunting fire demons?"

I regarded him with surprise. "Really?"

"Well, if you've got Jasmine and your new

tricks, you've got more of a fighting chance, so I figure you might as well make it a slam dunk and bring me along. You've been wanting to get rid of them, right?"

We'd come to a stop in the hall, and the scenario was eerily parallel to when we'd been in my castle earlier. There was no chastisement or echoes of that argument now, and I was grateful. "Thank you," I said, leaning toward him. I placed a light kiss on his lips—or at least, I tried to make it light. His hand reached out and grabbed my shoulder, bringing me closer still and intensifying the kiss.

I pulled back, wondering just how weird it would be for a servant to see the father of their queen's child making out with someone else. Of course, among the gentry, that kind of thing was probably pretty typical.

"Go," I said, stepping back before I was tempted to kiss him again. "Go see your beautiful daughter. We'll talk tomorrow."

"Thanks, Eugenie." His face split into one of those wonderful grins. "And thank you for . . . I don't know. You understand me. I don't think anyone else does."

I smiled back and then watched him turn around. A few moments later, I turned as well. As I stepped outside into the balmy spring air, I wondered if anyone truly understood me.

Chapter Eighteen

The village I'd passed earlier was called Marmant, and I had to get directions from Maiwenn's guards to make sure I didn't accidentally take some twisted Otherworldly path in my attempt to return. I rode there with troubled feelings, still replaying the events with Kiyo and trying to decide if our assorted arguments today had qualified as true fights. I soothed myself a little by reaching out and manipulating the air, creating gusts and eddies and attempting to see how big a blast I could make. At one point, I made a scrubby tree bend pretty far, but it tired me out. I had to practice more to sustain true gale-force winds, and lightning still remained out of my grasp.

The people of Marmant greeted me with that same mix of fear and awe I had come to expect. Word of the changes being wrought in the land was getting around, so they were grateful and allowing themselves optimism at last. Yet, my fearsome reputation always lurked on the horizon, so they spoke gingerly around me, fearful of enraging the dangerous monarch who had forced this dangerous land upon them.

"How is everything?" I asked, hoping I seemed concerned and nonthreatening. Rather than a mayor, this town had a council of five that made decisions, and they'd invited me inside for a private meeting. They were ordinary-looking men and women—still with that peasant feel so common in the Otherworld—but there was an air of competence around them. "You've got water and food now?"

"Yes, your majesty," said a middle-aged woman who seemed to be the speaker of the group. "Thank you, your majesty."

"Good. I'm sorry it's been so hard on you. Things should be better now." There was a brief silence in the group, one heavy with unspoken meaning. I looked from face to face. "What?"

"We don't want to trouble your majesty . . ."

"Trouble away. It's what I'm here for."

This got another round of exchanged looks. It was still apparently an odd concept for these people.

"Well," began the woman, "near the outskirts of our town's boundaries, there have been some attacks."

"What kind?"

"Bandits, your majesty."

"Son of a bitch," I said. We'd known the group

had moved, but they'd been quiet thus far, allowing me to hope I could take Kiyo up on his offer and deal with them before they caused more trouble.

"We actually have many fighters and strong magic users," she said with some pride. "But we could not stand against their monsters."

"You mean demons."

She gave a nervous nod.

"Son of a bitch," I said again. This *had* to be dealt with, and at this point, I really was willing to be a bastard and hold a gun to Jasmine's head. "Don't worry. They're going to be taken care of. Soon. Very soon."

The woman looked startled at the menacing tone in my voice, but her words were grateful. "Thank you, your majesty."

"Anything else I should know about?"

This time, it was a man who spoke up. "We don't want to trouble you . . ."

I groaned. "Just tell me what it is."

"We heard your majesty has been seeking missing girls."

I straightened up. "Yes. What about it?"

"One of ours disappeared two days ago. My neighbor's daughter, Markelle." A small, wry smile crossed his lips. "She's a wild one, often wandering off where she shouldn't. But she hasn't come back . . . and she always does . . ."

I felt my fists clenching and forcibly relaxed

them. I didn't need to scare these people any further. "Aside from the bandits, have you seen anyone else lurking around? Humans, maybe?"

He seemed even more afraid to discuss this topic. "We see humans sometimes, your majesty." I think he thought mentioning my own kind would anger me. "It's not uncommon. Often there are humans who . . . ah, give chase to some of the denizens of this world." Shamans like me, he meant. "Usually, they leave us alone once they've found their quarry."

I thought back to Jasmine. "Any soldiers or warriors of the gent—shining ones?"

"Occasionally. I presume they're deserters from King Aeson." Not a bad theory, actually. "But we see none of them regularly. There's no one in particular who keeps returning."

I leaned forward, some part of me feeling like everything was about to fall together. "But there is a human you keep seeing, isn't there? Especially since the girls began disappearing?"

He nodded.

It was here. Everything was here. "A man, right? A man with a red snake tattoo?"

"No, your majesty."

"I—what?" I froze for a moment. "Then who?"

"A woman, your majesty. A woman with graying hair that she wears in a long braid."

I stared at him for several seconds, and then I

laughed. This seemed to scare them all more than if I had burst into a rage.

"Abigail," I said at last, more to myself than them.

"Your majesty?"

I waved a hand at them. "Never mind."

Abigail. Fucking Abigail *and* Art. Working together to . . . what? Abduct gentry girls? But why? I'd toyed with the idea of Art as some kind of sick rapist, but where did Abigail fit in with this? Surely that would hold no interest for her. With a sigh, I pushed the questions to a small box in my mind, needing to wrap this up and get back to the human world. I needed to have that talk with Roland.

"Anything else going on I need to know about? You've got copper nearby, right?" Finding water and food was naturally essential, but it was copper that was going to truly change things in the Thorn Land. It was what all our trade agreements were being based on. "How's the extraction going?"

"Slowly until today, your majesty," the woman admitted. "Our magic users are skilled in many things, but we have few who can work with metal. Much of our labor has been manual."

I frowned. "Why did things change today?"

"Why," she said in surprise, "because you sent the Oak King to us."

"The Oak—wait. You mean Dorian?" I exclaimed. "He's not here now, is he?"

They were all clearly surprised at my surprise. "Yes, your majesty," said the guy who'd spoken earlier. "He's out with the workers now. I thought you knew."

I stood up, still full of shock. "I have to see him. Excuse me."

They all murmured polite farewells and nearly knocked each other over with bows. I didn't stick around to return the formality. Instead, I headed back out into the bright afternoon sun, lightly jogging to where I'd seen the workers on the far side of the village. At first, I saw no indication of Dorian. Men and a few women were digging diligently, sweat rolling down their faces.

Then, suddenly, I heard a slight rumbling, and the ground trembled. Huge chunks of rock rose from the earth, a few of them glinting in the sunlight. They lifted in a cluster and then slowly drifted off to the side of the work site, gently coming to rest on a pile of similar stones. Turning, I looked to the opposite side of the area and finally found Dorian, his hands moving in the air as he guided the ore. His clothes were simple today, but that hair burned and rippled in the sunshine like liquid fire.

His face was filled with concentration as he watched the rocks, but once they'd come to a halt, he broke into a smile as he strode forward. "My lady Thorn Queen, what a delight."

I let him kiss my hand for the sake of

appearances—seriously, why were the gentry so into that?—and then pulled him out of earshot of the others. "What the hell are you doing here?" I exclaimed.

"Why, retrieving my copper."

"That's not what I mean!" He shrugged and wiped sweat off his brow. His devil-may-care expression aside, it was clear he was tired. I grabbed hold of his arm and led him back toward the town. "Come on, get something to drink before you get dehydrated. And start explaining."

"I heard there was some difficulty with your copper, and I decided to come help, seeing as it benefits me too. My sword is in need of replacement, you know—and that's not a metaphor. The metaphorical one is just fine. Besides, you don't honestly think I can let you take all the glory as being the most helpful monarch around, do you? You're making us all look bad."

"Dorian," I groaned. Because there was really no other response.

If people had fallen all over me when I arrived, the two of us together created quite the stir. Again, I was reminded of some celebrity tabloid couple. We returned to the council hall, at which point I used my queenly authority to get some privacy and some refreshment. It was a bit startling to see how quickly my orders were obeyed.

Once we were alone and Dorian was sprawled in a chair, I truly got a good look at just how exhausted he was. "How long have you been out there doing this?" I asked, pouring him water from a pitcher.

"Most of the day. And I'll take the wine, my dear." He nodded toward a nearby decanter.

"It'll dehydrate you further," I scolded, handing him the cup of water. He scowled but drank it down eagerly. I watched him, still perplexed. "But why? You don't need the copper that badly."

"Perhaps not. But you do." He finished the water, and I gave him a refill. "Thank you. Waited on by a queen—truly the dream of many a man."

I pulled over a chair of my own. "You didn't need to do it," I protested. "You've practically killed yourself."

"Hardly. Give me and my stamina some credit."

"I still don't get it."

He finished this cup too and then gave me a look that was both exasperated and amused. "Eugenie, why do you keep having such a hard time believing I'd do things for you?"

There was earnestness in his voice, and I realized we kept having this conversation over and over. Out of everyone in my life lately, it seemed like he was the only reliable one. "I don't know why. I'm sorry. I just run into few people who give something for nothing. Mining isn't going to get me into your bed."

"Well," he said cheerfully, "nobody knows that

for sure, but even if not? It doesn't matter. You need it. It makes you happy. End of story."

I looked away. Dorian truly was my friend. "Thank you. It does make me happy. One less thing in a sea of problems today."

He handed me the cup. "Get me wine this time, and tell me what your problems are. You can even sit on my lap."

"No thanks," I said, but I did get him the wine.

"I saw you and the kitsune pass earlier, actually. Is that part of your problem?" He answered his own question. "Yes, yes. Of course it is."

I was a bit surprised to hear myself pouring my thoughts out to him again. I didn't even have the excuse of being drunk this time. "I saw the baby today."

"Cute?"

"Very. And it just made me feel . . . I don't know. Kiyo thinks it's jealousy, but it's more than that. I just can't explain it."

"Kind of a questioning of your own life and the choices—or lack thereof—before you?"

I looked up, startled, and met his eyes. They were unusually serious. "Yes, exactly." Dorian remained silent, and I found myself rambling more. "He's having a hard time getting all of it lately—the magic, the girls, the demons . . . he doesn't like me spending time over here. Neither does Roland." I couldn't help a smile. "Hell, neither do I. But . . . I have to. I have to put things right around here."

"I know you do," he said, face serious.

"Dorian . . . what would happen if I got a crown?"

This made him a smile a little. "It would make you look even more beautiful."

"No, I'm serious. Kiyo says it's a bad idea. That it would make all this real."

"It's already about as real as it's going to get, my dear."

"That's what I told him! But I don't get the big deal. You never wear a crown."

"Not often. But I have one, and I was crowned and all my people swore fealty to me. That's what a crown would lead to. You want one for ornamentation? Sure, that's easy. But put one on and walk out among your people—especially in a city like Highmore—and say, 'This is who I am, I am your queen . . .' Well, that's what the kitsune fears. You're already queen. No crown can affect that. But you accepting one and declaring your authority is when *you* truly believe you're a queen. And as far as Kiyo is concerned, that's where the danger is."

"Wow," I said, nearly as surprised to have such a thorough explanation from him as I was by the content itself. "Are you afraid of it?"

He snorted. "Hardly. I don't need a crown to know you're a queen. It radiates off of you. But I would like for *you* to know you're a queen."

If dealing with all the crap I had on my plate

didn't make me think I was a queen, then I didn't really know what else would. I let the crown issue go and instead recapped my latest intel about the bandits and Abigail. "I can't figure out her role here. You mentioned before that Art's motives would be . . . uh, understandable. But why her? Unless she's just enough of a pal to help him score some gentry action."

Dorian was still in his pensive mode. He'd poured himself yet another glass of wine and handed me one too that I sipped sparingly. "Let me ask you this. Why do men of the shining ones so often abduct your women?"

"Easy," I returned. "Because we're more fertile. You guys might have sex in public, but it doesn't usually result in anything. A guy who wants a kid has better luck with a human."

Dorian nodded. I had a feeling he'd already made some leap of logic and was prompting me here to figure it out myself. "And what about humans? Are you hoping for children each time you make love?"

I laughed, thinking of my stock of condoms and birth control pills. "Hardly. We go to a lot of trouble not to. Too easy for us."

He leaned toward me, green eyes shrewd. "Then think about it. You understand why we would want humans. Why would humans want us?"

I studied him, trying to catch up to what he'd already thought of. A few moments later, I got it.

"Because you'd fulfill the opposite need. A human could have sex with a gentry girl and not worry *too* much about her getting pregnant. Or getting a disease."

Gentry were healthier than us in that regard. It seemed to go along with them having such long life spans—

"Oh God. That would be part of it." The more I followed his logic, the clearer and clearer it became. "You guys live longer. Gentry girls would stay young and beautiful for a long time . . ."

The horror of it was setting in. Until that moment, I had thought there were few sexual crimes worse than gentry guys consistently trying to rape me to get me pregnant. As shocking as it seemed, I was wrong. If this were true . . . if this idea that Dorian was suggesting was true . . . well. That was worse. Gentry girls taken because they were the ideal sexual partners: young, disease resistant, hard to get pregnant—even with a human. I almost laughed. It was like Tim's poem about the maiden who'd come from another world, whose beauty and youth were so great that mortal men had coveted her.

The question was, how did the gentry girls feel about this role? A lot of girls wanting to get pregnant might wholeheartedly embrace human lovers—literally and figuratively. But Moria's traumatized state suggested her stint with Art hadn't been welcome . . .

I stood up and rubbed my eyes. "Oh God," I repeated. "The stuff . . . all the stuff . . ."

"What?" asked Dorian, understandably confused.

Dropping my hands, I looked back at him. "These shamans, Abigail and Art. They live well. They have more possessions . . . nicer things than they should for the jobs they have." Art's giant house in an upper-class neighborhood. The shiny SUV. Abigail's luxurious—albeit messy— apartment. Her extensive jewelry collection. "I don't know how, but they're making money off it. Off these girls." I slumped against the wall. "And I don't know what to do about it."

Dorian rose and came to stand by me. "You'll stop them."

I shook my head. "It's not that simple. Art was right—there's no shaman council. I can't report them to anyone, certainly not human authorities. There's no accountability, no laws that apply here."

"They're breaking *your* laws," he said, leaning toward me. "Therefore you have every right to stop them. Treat them as you would any other criminal in your land. Kill them."

"I can't!" I exclaimed. "I'd have to actually catch them *here*, and so far I haven't been able to. And I'm certainly not going to go to Texas and kill them there."

"Why not? If a murderer from my kingdom

killed someone in yours, I wouldn't bat an eye if you came to slay him."

"It's different. They're . . ."

"Human?"

I hated to admit, but yes, there it was. I had chased Otherworldly monsters from my world back to this one and never hesitated to kill them or banish them directly to the Underworld. But somehow, the thought of intentionally tracking humans and killing them . . .

I didn't need to voice my answer for Dorian to understand. Exasperation flared on his face, this time mixed with . . . anger.

"Damn it, Eugenie. You just told me you had to put things right! Which is it? Or does it only depend on what's easy at any given time? What your mood is? Who you like better that day?"

"It's not that easy!" I exclaimed. "You don't understand. You *can't* understand. I'm caught in two worlds here, with two sets of loyalties. I've spent my entire life being human—being part of that world. You can't expect me to throw all that away and betray my own kind."

He opened his mouth to retort and was interrupted by a faint roll of thunder. Whatever words he'd been about to utter disappeared, and he laughed. "Do you hear that? That's you, Eugenie. Your anger."

I shook my head. "I can't control thunder and lightning yet."

"Not control, no. But you can summon it unconsciously. Do you think there's anything in this land that isn't tied to you?" He gestured around us. "All these people here . . . all the people in this village looking at you with adoring eyes . . . *they* are your own kind too. This is what I meant when I said you're the only one who doesn't seem to realize you're a queen yet! All these people are looking to you to protect them and do what's right. If you can't do that, then you might as well back off and do what the kitsune and your stepfather want you to do."

"Dorian, I can't kill in cold blood!"

He gripped me by the arms, voice calm but infused with anger. "You can do whatever it is you have to do! You are a queen. Forget all this talk about Storm King's grandson. Right now, *you* are his heir. You are on the verge of becoming one of the most powerful rulers in this world, which means you don't have the luxury of being squeamish. You can rule with love, but you have to rule with ruthlessness too. You are going to go down in history, Eugenie, as one of the greatest monarchs we have ever seen. And it is going to start with *this*—this wrong that you're going to right. If you can't do it, if you can't stop those who are hurting your people, then you might as well stop the rest of this charade. Go out there and tell those people you can't do anything for them, that you can't feed them or protect them because

318

they aren't your kind and aren't worth bloodying your hands for!"

He was shouting now, breathing heavily. I stared at him, eyes wide, filled with a little of that fear I always got when his temper rose. Moments like these reminded me of just how powerful Dorian was physically and magically. His lazy, lean appearance was deceptive; I'd seen him fight. Between that and the power he wielded, I hoped there would never come a day when we were truly antagonists. Outside, I heard thunder again.

It took me several seconds to muster an answer, and when I spoke, my voice was very small.

"I can't," I said. "I can't tell them that."

"I know you can't," he whispered.

And then, still gripping me, he leaned down and kissed me. More astonishingly, I kissed him back. It seemed like all the emotions that had consumed me recently—all the rage and confusion—were poured into that kiss. My teeth bit against his lips, and when he shoved me against the wall, I welcomed the brief pain. Our hands were all over each other as we kissed, mine running the length of his body while his more aggressively hiked up the dress I'd earlier regretted wearing. In a matter of seconds, it was pushed over my hips, leaving my legs bare. With one hand still holding the skirt up, his other pushed between my thighs, slipping underneath the thong I'd put on this morning in the hopes of getting intimate with Kiyo.

Those clever fingers slid into me, stoking a wetness I hadn't thought could come on so fast. My small exclamation was muffled in his crushing kiss as he alternately thrust his fingers into me and pulled out to tease and dance with my clit. It was the latter he eventually settled on, circling and stroking as heat built between my legs and made all my muscles tense up. Then, the burning flood of sensation exploded, and I came with another cry that his kiss smothered, a cry that faded into a moan as my body trembled and spasmed from the shock waves of heat and electricity still shooting through me from his touch.

My orgasm created no pause in the action, though. The hand that had just brought me such pleasure moved from between my legs to his pants as he began to unfasten them. His mouth finally left mine, moving on to my neck, his kisses hot and fierce. He finally shoved his pants down, and I felt him against me, hard and ready as he pressed his hips to mine. My hands were tangled in his hair as I tilted my head back to receive his kisses, but his hands, busy as always, were prying off my underwear. The reality of what was happening sank in.

"Wait . . ." I murmured, lost as his mouth bit against my skin. "No, we can't . . . I can't . . ."

"You can," he breathed in my ear. "Let me . . . let me do it. Let me bury myself in you. Let me spread your legs and take you like I did before. We are gods in this world, Eugenie, with no other lovers who are our equals. No others who are worthy of this joining." The thong was on the ground now, and I could feel his erection pressed against my skin, so, so close to sliding in and doing all the things he promised. He rested his hands under my thighs and hoisted me up against the wall so that my legs wrapped around his hips.

"Dorian . . ." I gasped. "I'm with Kiyo . . ."

"So? You're a queen. Do you think you can't have as many lovers as you like?"

"It's . . . it's wrong. We can't . . ."

"We *can*," he said, voice low and full of promise. "And when we do, this land will be reborn . . ."

Afterward, I would never be entirely sure if I would have let him do it. I like to think I would have stopped him. I was in love with Kiyo, after all, and loyal to him. Surely I would have said no and shoved Dorian aside. I wasn't in love with him . . . or was I? In those moments before we'd kissed, I'd felt like he truly *got* me and understood the things in my head. I think I'd probably loved him since around the time we'd met; I certainly never lost the attraction. Still, that didn't make cheating on Kiyo right.

Whatever decision I would have made was taken from me when there was a knock at the door.

I jerked away from Dorian and hastily shoved

my skirt down. He more casually turned away to pull his pants back up, seeming in no particular hurry. The door opened, and the lead councilwoman stuck her head in. Even with Dorian's back to her and me dressed, it had to have been obvious what was going on—particularly with my underwear on the floor. If she found it shocking, though, she didn't show it, and I recalled how free the gentry were in public.

"Your majesties," she said politely, "there's a storm coming in, and the workers were wondering what the Oak King wanted to do."

Dorian, decent once more, turned around and gave her a laconic, charming smile. "A storm? Really? How truly unexpected. Well, tell them to bring as much of the ore as they can into storage before the rain and cover the rest up. I'll come check on it in a moment since I have a feeling the Thorn Queen is about to depart with some haste."

The woman gave a quick curtsey and shut the door once more. "You're right," I said, jerking my thong back on. "I'm leaving."

"Yes," he agreed, still smiling. "Because that's your normal course of action when something happens that you don't know how to process."

"That's the thing," I growled. "*Nothing* happened here, okay? None of this did."

His eyebrows rose. "Really? Because I could have sworn that something happened when my hand was between your—"

"No!" I would have approached him with clenched fists to drive home my threat but was afraid of what would happen if I was close to him again. "This didn't happen. This was anger and confusion and me in a weak place, okay? I appreciate what you've done here with the copper—really. And for the advice on the girls. But that's it."

I turned, not wanting to look into those green eyes or see that smirk anymore. I didn't want to admit that loving two men was just like the rest of my life, ripped into two worlds. I needed to get out of here and get back home—though I wasn't sure which home I meant. Dorian didn't try to stop me, but his voice rang out after me as I hurried out and rain began to fall outside.

"Don't forget what I said, Eugenie. Crown or not, you *are* a queen, so don't be afraid to do what you have to do. Love and ruthlessness. Those are the keys."

Chapter Nineteen

I returned to my castle in shock—and in a downpour. My control of water let me shift the rain away from me, but after a while, I didn't feel like wasting the mental effort on it. It felt kind of good after such a hot day, and besides, I had a few other things on my mind. Like if it was going to rain every time I got aroused. That was not cool. I guessed I could handle it so long as it rained other times as well. I didn't want the connection to be so obvious. *Hey, it's raining! The queen must have gotten laid. Ooh . . . is that hail? Must have been into some kinky shit today . . .*

I was also debating whether or not having a guy stick his hand up your skirt and get you off was technically cheating or not.

Okay, I supposed there wasn't much "technically" about it. I was getting caught up in gender stereotypes. If I'd gotten him off—say, like, by going down on him—there would have been no question of infidelity. So, this was no different. Fuck. How had it happened? One minute we'd been arguing ... the next? Grope central. There'd been emotion and magic, and it had all happened so fast. I shivered, thinking of all the warnings about using strong magic. Was that to blame? Or just my own weakness? And at the same time, I couldn't also help but think that strong magic could solve a few of my problems.

Excepting, of course, the problem of whether or not I should tell Kiyo what had happened between Dorian and me . . .

"Your majesty!"

Nia went crazy when she saw my drenched state. She had a hundred remedies for me, but all I wanted was a simple towel and the jeans and shirt I'd arrived in earlier. Waiting for the servants to draw hot baths around here took too much time and effort; I could get back to Tucson and into my own shower or sauna much more easily. And after still being unnerved by Dorian, I was particularly anxious to return to what I saw as safety. Though lately, I was starting to think no place was safe anymore.

Before leaving, I exchanged brief updates with Rurik and Shaya. I told Rurik that we had a date for demon hunting, and that Jasmine would indeed be going with us. His feelings on that were mixed. He knew her power was useful, but secretly—or, well, not so secretly—he was part of the camp that felt I should kill her. He seemed a little reassured about her, at least, because Girard had brought the custom cuffs as promised. They provided greater mobility for her but were even more limiting for magic. Judging from Jasmine's dismayed reaction, Rurik felt they'd been successful.

Well, that was something, I supposed. And from the look on Shaya's face, Dorian's help with the ore was a good thing too—even if it had come with strings attached.

"That was very kind of my lord," she said. Both Shaya and Rurik often used the honorific "my lord" when discussing Dorian, as though he were still their master. I considered their old loyalty endearing but wondered if they'd ever feel like they truly worked for me. "It's expedited things immensely. You can't imagine how quickly things will move once the ore is processed." She grinned, eyes gleaming as all sorts of plans and organizational thoughts swirled in her mind. "You must have been very pleased at what my lord did for you."

Well, "pleased" was one way of looking at, I supposed.

Oh, and I was happy about the expedited ore too.

A strange feeling settled over me, that same one I got each time Dorian did something nice for me—sexual gratification aside. I had no idea what his role in my life was anymore, save that he was helping me a lot. Judging from Shaya's face, this was a big favor he'd done for me. An idea for repayment came to me.

"Shaya . . . is Girard still here?"

She nodded. "I gave him a room for the night, so that he wouldn't have to travel in the rain. Is that all right?"

"Yeah, yeah. I just want to talk to him for a sec."

She led me to his room, and like before, he was overjoyed and overeager to see me. Seeing him reminded me of Leith, which gave me a small pang of regret. I still felt badly about what had happened with the Rowan prince, but there was nothing to be done about it. I couldn't return his feelings. Girard, fortunately, was a different matter. He wanted prestige and position for his talents, and I was more than willing to give that after explaining to him the project I wanted to commission.

"Yes, your majesty. I can most certainly do that. Why, I can start sketching right now."

No doubt he was happy to work on something that wasn't part of Katrice's woodland animal collection. I left him to it, gushing with praise and how much it would mean to me. Girard was a nice guy, despite his ambition, and I decided I'd rather surround myself in those wanting job promotion over getting me into bed.

I returned to Tucson at last, grateful to find the house quiet. Tim was out, but he'd left me macaroni and cheese—the good homemade kind with bread-crumbs on top—and a note:

Bitch receptionist called and wants to make sure you don't forget your job tomorrow.

I hadn't forgotten the job tomorrow, but the reminder was a good one with as much as had been going on lately. One of the cats rubbed against my leg as I microwaved my dinner, and I absent-mindedly scratched her on the head, wishing it was actually Kiyo's fox form circling my ankles. I didn't like the way he and I had left things, even if they'd ostensibly been friendly. There was still tension between us, and I couldn't shake the feeling that he just wasn't understanding me lately . . . and that Dorian was.

Argh. Dorian.

As I tossed my clothes on the bathroom floor—including that damned thong—I couldn't help but think of him again. *Stop it, Eugenie. You're obsessing.* Surely . . . surely I would have said no if we hadn't been interrupted earlier, right?

Right?

And Kiyo, Kiyo . . . what was I going to tell Kiyo? Just because we were having friction in our relationship, it didn't mean I had license to do what I'd done today. I had no respect for lies or any other subtle dishonesty. I didn't like that behavior in others. I didn't like it in myself.

But after standing in scalding water for twenty minutes, no real answers about anything came to my mind. I finally emerged, my skin sufficiently plump and pink, and toweled off. After that, it was into comfy pajamas: blue and gray flannel shorts and a white cotton tank top. It might have been raining in the Thorn Land, but here it was dry and hot. Night had cooled the air somewhat, and I'd opened all the windows to air out the house. As a light breeze blew in, it took everything in me not to start tinkering around with the air. I could sense every particle, and the thought of controlling them sent a shiver through me. *No*, I scolded myself. I'd done enough today. I needed to have a no-magic-in-Tucson rule, I decided.

Establishing that magic and men were issues that were not going to be solved tonight, I set out to work on another. It wasn't quite ten yet, which meant Roland would be up. Sprawling on the couch in front of the breezy patio screen door, I dialed him on my phone.

"Eugenie," he said with delight. "We've been wondering what happened to you. You haven't been returning calls. Your mother was worried, but I told her you were probably just busy."

I smiled. It was nice to have Roland in my life, someone who understood the ups and downs of this job. "I have been. Really busy." I almost started to offer him the overflow of jobs I'd had Lara turn down for me and stopped myself at the last minute. If he knew I wasn't keeping up with my work, it would only trigger an alarm for him and subject me to questions I wasn't ready to answer.

"Did you ever talk to Art and Abigail?" he asked.

"Yeah," I said, "and that's actually why I was calling you. I think . . . well, I think they're trafficking in gentry girls or something."

There were several moments of silence.

"Trafficking? What does that mean, exactly?"

"It means I think they're abducting girls and . . . I don't know. Either pimping them out or selling them or something equally disgusting. It's like a fairy sex trade." One of the cats, a calico, came and made herself comfortable on my stomach.

"Eugenie . . . I've known Art for almost ten years. I've known Abigail longer. What you're saying is absurd. You have to be getting bad information."

"They've both been sighted in the Otherworld, right around where their gate opens! I even talked to one girl who all but identified Art! She was totally traumatized, Roland. And both Art and Abigail live better than they should be . . ."

"That's not evidence," he said. "They're probably doing good business."

"In a town that size? Even with a gate like that, they can't have enough work to afford the stuff they have. You and I have a ton more jobs than they do, and we don't live that well."

"It's a moot point. This whole thing is far-fetched, and your evidence is sketchy. I mean, have you seen gentry girls tied up in his house?"

"No," I admitted. "Largely because he won't ever let me inside. Which is also suspicious."

"No, Eugenie, it's really not." Roland sounded tired. "Look, it sounds like all you've got is circumstantial gentry evidence. And you know how they are."

"I know that their people are being taken against their will and possibly having horrible things done to them."

"Key words: *their people*."

"Are you saying it's okay for girls to be sold into a sex trade? After what happened to Mom?"

"How can you ask me that?" he exclaimed. "But this isn't the same thing. We're not police who work both worlds. We protect humans. There must be someone over there whose job it is to protect them."

There is, I thought. *Me*.

"Can you at least talk to Art?" I asked.

"And what? Ask him if he's kidnapping gentry girls?"

"Well . . . maybe you could pose it a bit more delicately." I squelched a yowl of pain as the cat leapt up off me and onto the back of the couch. Her hair puffed up, and she twitched her tail in agitation. Not surprising. Both dogs had just entered the room.

"I can't ask him that," said Roland. "And what if he says yes? Then what are you going to do?"

Dorian's words came back to me. *Kill them.*

"Look, I don't know yet, but I just need to find out if—"

I heard a low growl from one of the dogs and was about to yell at them to knock it off. The cats and dogs didn't usually fight, but every once in a while, there would be a brawl. I couldn't see the dogs, though, and the bristling calico's attention seemed to be on the screen door, not the floor. I sat up and saw the dogs sitting right in front of the door, staring out into the night as well.

"Eugenie? Are you still there?"

"Yeah, hang on a sec."

Balancing the phone on my shoulder, I stood up and instinctively reached for my weapons, which were on the coffee table. I shoved the wand and my silver athame under the elastic waistband of my shorts and took the gun and iron athame with my hands. One of the dogs growled again, and I slowly approached them at the door.

"Eugenie? What's going on?" Roland's voice was worried now.

"I'm going to have to call you back."

I managed to disconnect the phone and drop it on the floor without losing the athame. Outside, the night was still, the only noises coming from the wind in the trees and the faint sounds of traffic on the far side of my quiet neighborhood. I closed my eyes a moment, reaching out to search for anything that didn't feel right in this world. Some shamans had this ability, but not many. The more time I spent in the Otherworld and among gentry, the more developed my senses became.

Finally, I caught it. The sense of something Otherworldly. The animals, God love them, had noticed before me. Whatever this interloper was, it was keeping to the farthest edges of the house's property. It had apparently been lurking for a while, which seemed odd.

"Ah," I realized with a soft chuckle. "Stopped by the wards, huh, you son of a bitch?" I'd had a witch lay protective lines and spells all around the house when the attacks on me first started. It was kind of a magical home-security system. It wouldn't keep out everything, but it definitely thinned out a lot of my nuisances.

I could have simply ignored whatever was out there, but the idea of Otherworldly creatures loose in my neighborhood didn't sit well with me. Sliding open the door, I slipped outside, every nerve in my body on high alert. I walked the perimeter of my backyard, keeping inside the ward's lines. My house was on a cul-de-sac, backing up to a small stretch of open, scrubby land before giving way to the next neighborhood over. I doubted whatever this was would be out in the front of the house, where it would be in sight of neighbors.

Ah, no—not an *it*. They. I could sense more than one. Standing on tiptoe to peer over the wooden fence, I nearly missed his eyes on my first sweep. A rock elemental—that is, one of the gentry who lacked the strength to travel to my world in his full form. He was blocky and unwieldy looking, his stone body mottled black and white. I had only a second to make my assessment before he charged. His weight and strength cracked the wooden fence, and then—he hit the ward. It was like an invisible wall that bounced him back.

His disorientation gave me what I needed. I dropped the gun and reached for my wand. Silver bullets weren't as effective against gentry as steel ones anyway, and I certainly wasn't going to fire off shots and possibly get the police called if I could help it. I channeled my will into the wand, ripping open a path to the Otherworld. My snake tattoo burned on my arm as I summoned the power of Hecate. I recited the incantation to finish the ritual. The elemental felt the magic of the banishing seize him but couldn't fight it. He was too weak. In a moment, he dissolved from this world, sent back to his own, leaving only a pile of rubble behind.

Another shape appeared beside where he'd been, and I saw the dim lighting shine off water.

Another gentry who hadn't been able to cross in his true body. He'd appeared as a water elemental, a man-shaped body of liquid that dripped and sloshed with each step.

Stupid, stupid, I thought. Whoever he was should have known better. I didn't need a wand for this. My own magic would rip him apart—

A hand suddenly jerked me backward, and I felt a knife at my throat. The hand gripping it was solid and flesh but tingling with magic. A powerful gentry, then. One with enough power to cross my wards and come over in body. Without hesitation, I kicked backward, dodging out of his grasp skillfully enough that the blade only nicked me. I turned to face him, glad I'd held on to the iron athame. He was no one I knew, young and good-looking, even with a scar on his cheek. He was well-muscled from physical activity, and the leather armor he wore over his red tunic suggested a possible military or guarding profession back in the Otherworld.

In a weird flash, Jasmine's words came back to me. *I know the difference between a bunch of gross beggars and trained soldiers.*

A coincidence, I decided. Any gentry brave enough to come seek me in my own world would likely have to be a good fighter. We circled, and there was a small smile on his face as he waited for an opening. I wasn't afraid. One-on-one combat I could handle, and I had long since developed the ability to banish while fighting. It was tricky but hardly impossible. Of course, as he lunged and I ducked, I realized I didn't need anything so complicated.

Almost like an inhalation of breath, I sucked the air from around us, creating a miniwhirlwind that pulled the dust and sand from within my yard. I blasted it forward at him. He cried out as the sand blinded his eyes and immediately started rubbing them—which wouldn't do him any favors. I was about to start the banishing when I faintly heard the sound of chanting and a tingle of shamanic magic. Startled, I turned to find the source and instead saw the water elemental come charging through the opening in the fence his friend had made. Someone had broken the wards.

I held out my iron athame to block him, though I knew it would only give me a few seconds. That was all I needed as I began to work the water magic that would tear him apart. A blow to my back suddenly shoved me forward, straight into him. Despite being made of water, he was solid, and his hands instantly grabbed hold of me. I twisted my head back and saw that the other gentry had recovered himself enough to come striding forward, though I could see tears streaking his face from where the sand had stung his eyes.

I tried breaking free of the elemental's grip but couldn't match that physical force. Again, I summoned water magic and heard him groan in pain as his substance began to rip apart. Then, the other gentry was on me, punching me again and breaking my concentration. He started to reach around me once more with the copper blade, and then I heard a startled cry of pain from him as he was pulled away from me.

I didn't look back to see what had happened but instead completed the magic on the water elemental. He exploded in a downpour that soaked me—great, twice in one day—and I immediately turned to see what else had happened. The other gentry was distracted, squaring off with someone else: Roland.

Roland's own athame was out in his left hand, and he was simply relying on the strength of his other fist—which was considerable—to sock the gentry in the face. The gentry was strong, though, and got a few good blows in on Roland. Seeing my stepfather take those punches kindled an anger in me. Rather than begin a banishing, I called to the air again, sucking it from around the gentry just as I had Ysabel. Eyes widening, he dropped the blade, his hands going to his throat in an instinctive gesture to draw breath. There was none to be had, though. I leapt on him, knocking him to the ground and delivering a solid punch to the face in exchange for what he'd done to Roland.

Around us, I felt the tingling of a banishing. Roland was opening up a hole to the Otherworld.

He chanted the words and then snapped, "Eugenie, get away!"

I did, jerking backward lest I get sucked in with the choking gentry. Power crackled around him, and a moment later, he disappeared, shoved back to his own world.

Silence fell. I was sitting on the now-muddy ground, soaking wet with my heart pounding. Roland walked over and extended his hand to help me up. "What are you doing here?" I asked.

He snorted. "You can't end a call like that and not expect me to show up."

"True," I said. I was weak and woozy from the combat and the magic, and my bare legs were skinned up from the fight. I'd need some soap and antiseptic. "Thanks."

Roland shrugged, not needing my thanks. Even in the dimness, I could see the angry look in his eyes. "What the hell did you think you were doing?"

Seeing as I'd just done several things, I wasn't entirely sure which he was referring to. "What do you mean?"

"That." He pointed to the spot where we'd banished the gentry. "You were . . . you were using magic to choke him!"

"I was keeping him subdued while you banished him," I growled, unwilling to admit I was kind of freaked out myself. It had all happened so fast. My only impulse had been to incapacitate the gentry. The means had just sort of happened. Realizing what I'd done—again—gave me a sick feeling. I'd sworn I'd never do it.

"Pinning him with the athame would have worked! Where the hell did you learn to do that?"

"I've picked up a few things here and there."

Roland's face was a mask of fury. "You have no business using that kind of magic, Eugenie. *None*."

My own anger was growing. "In case you've forgotten, that magic is in my blood."

"No," he said softly. "I haven't forgotten. Which is why it's so important you don't use it. What else can you do? How long have been using this kind of power?"

"It's not important. I can do a few things— things that have kept me alive when assholes like this come try to rape me—and it's not a problem. I can control it."

"You need to stop this. You need to stay away from the gentry. You're getting too involved with their world, with their magic . . ."

"It's part of who I am. You can't change that. And if you didn't want me taking drastic steps, then why'd you break the wards?"

Roland frowned. "I didn't. I thought that gentry had."

"No, he crossed them, but his buddies were locked out—for a while, at least. Then I heard someone undoing them. It was our kind of magic. I thought it was you."

"Why on earth would I do that?"

"Then some other shaman did." The accusing tone in my voice provided no need for elaboration.

"Stop this. Art and Abigail aren't out doing what you think. They certainly wouldn't break the wards so gentry could attack you. You think they're out in your neighborhood right now? One of the gentry must have done it. You were probably distracted."

"Have you lost all faith in me? All you keep saying tonight is that I'm wrong, that I'm mistaken. Roland, I *know* what shamanic magic feels like. Just like I know what gentry magic feels like, especially considering—as you keep pointing out—I use it all the time."

I'm not sure which part of my tirade did it, but I could tell he was done with the conversation. There was something weary in his face that made him look older than he was. "I'm not going to stand out here in the dark and argue with you, Eugenie. All I can ask is that if you can't control yourself for my sake, then think of your mother. Otherwise, do what you want."

"Roland . . ."

But he was already walking away into the night, and as I watched the man I'd always regarded as my father leave, I uneasily wondered whose daughter I truly was.

Chapter Twenty

Tim surfaced the next morning after some liaison or another, and I decided not to mention that our wards had been broken. He handled my array of paranormal activities fairly good-naturedly, but that was largely because they usually didn't follow me home. So, I called the witch who'd originally laid them and asked her to come back and discretely redo them, scheduling a time when I knew Tim would be out.

After that it was off to the first shamanic job I'd had in a while, fighting a nixie who'd taken up residence in some poor family's swimming pool. The ease with which I dispatched her was a bit alarming. Earlier in the year, Dorian and I had fought off a group of them that Jasmine had sent. Dorian had done the fighting, and at the time, they'd seemed overwhelming. Now, with my magic becoming more and more instinctual, fighting a water creature like this was ridiculously simple. Admittedly, I still banished her the old-fashioned way, not wanting to rely on magic more than I had to. I didn't agree with Roland about its use—though my fight with him still stung—but it was exhilarating recalling how easily I'd fought the water elemental. If I could only summon water creatures like Jasmine could, my life would be easier still.

And speaking of Jasmine, I summoned Volusian away from her later that evening. I was going to the Thorn Land shortly and felt confident that she wouldn't get knocked up before then. Well, I hoped so, at least.

Volusian appeared in the darkest corner of my bedroom, scaring off one of the cats that had been sleeping on my bed. "My mistress calls," he said in his monotone.

"I have a job for you."

"Of course."

"I need you to go to Yellow River and check out the house of a shaman there. Do not let him see you—or sense you, if you can help it." My vibe from Art was that while he could fight Otherworldly creatures, he didn't possess the same sensitivity I did.

"And what would my mistress like me to do once I am there?"

"Look around. Tell me if there's anything suspicious going on—particularly in regard to any gentry girls. Make sense?"

Volusian's look was scathing. "Certainly it makes sense. Do not confuse me with the other underlings who serve you."

Once he had the address, he disappeared in that way of his, and I sighed. It might be worth enslaving another minion destined for the Underworld. It was easy enough for me, particularly if I got one who wasn't too strong. I didn't have a huge amount of respect for Volusian, but he'd been right about one thing. He was so powerful that his skills were better suited to protection and battle. A lesser spirit would suffice for all these errands I seemed to be sending him on lately.

That was a thought for another day. For now, it was back to the Thorn Land. I planned on spending the night there since I wanted to get an early start on our demon hunting. Kiyo had said he'd come at sunrise, and I didn't want to miss a moment of being with him.

When I arrived at my castle, I was a bit surprised to see a party going on. Well, not a true party, but Shaya, Rurik, and a few of the other head servants were hanging out in one of the parlors, drinking wine and laughing. Girard was still around and had joined them. Even Ysabel was there, looking happy for a change. None of them seemed to have expected me that night and most leapt up like naughty children. Shaya started to stammer something like an apology, but I silenced her with a gesture.

"No, no. Keep having fun." I somehow always thought of them as utilitarian fixtures around here, but of course, they were only human—well, figuratively speaking—and entitled to their downtime.

After a few uneasy moments, they settled back down, and Rurik offered me a glass of wine. I shook my head. "You know," he said, "that your minion disappeared."

"Yeah, I know. I sent him on a task."

"I doubled the guards on her when I heard."

"Good. Let's hope she's managed to keep her clothes on in this short of time."

"You should have killed her," Ysabel noted darkly.

I ignored that and turned away, leaving them to their party. "I'm going to check on her myself."

The bedroom Shaya had assigned Jasmine was one floor up and very cleverly chosen—not that I'd expect any less from Shaya. It was spacious and furnished but not so large that the guards within couldn't see her most of the time—the bathroom excluded. The room's one window was only a tiny slit, too small for anyone to get out of. Four guards stood on duty outside and four within. To my relief, Jasmine simply lay on her bed, reading one of the books I'd sent. Girard's new cuffs had a longer, thinner chain that gave her much more range of motion but was packed with iron. Those blue-gray eyes looked up at my approach, but the rest of her didn't move.

"Oh. You."

I sat down on a narrow wicker bench and sent the guards outside with a curt nod. "I came to check on you."

"Right. Because you care so much."

"I do. Well, kind of."

"The only things you care about are having the heir yourself and forcing me to get rid of your monsters."

"Demons," I corrected. "And believe me, the last thing I want is to have the heir."

"I heard the guards talking. They said you've been hanging out with Dorian a lot. Why else would you do that? No one else would rather have our father's grandson. Well, except Aeson." A grimace fell over her face at the mention of her old lover.

"Dorian's just my friend, something you'll understand when you're older." *Oh, Eugenie, you are such a hypocrite.* "And you're better off without Aeson."

Her eyes returned to her book. "I loved Aeson. You have no idea what love is."

"Oh, I do. I know that it's the best high and the worst hurt all at the same time—not to mention confusing as hell."

Jasmine looked back at me, still sullen but with a new sort of consideration. "What do you want? Are you just here to babysit me until that fucking imp comes back? God, I hate him."

I started to tell her to watch her language and

then decided there was no point. "I came to tell you we're going to take out those demons tomorrow."

"At gunpoint."

"I don't have a choice. They're terrorizing people. How can you not understand how serious that is?"

She shrugged with her typical apathy and pushed some of that long blond hair out of her face. "Your problem. Not mine." Self-centered brat. She frowned for a moment, though. "Are they still taking girls?" She sounded almost concerned. Almost.

"I don't know," I admitted. "I don't know if this group's connected or not. I actually think there are humans involved."

The book slipped to her lap, forgotten. "Why would they do that? That doesn't make any sense."

"I'll tell you when you're older," I said dryly, which was silly considering all that she'd been through. "And you're certain . . . you're certain the group chasing you wasn't human?"

"Yes, for like the hundredth time. They were shining ones."

"You said they were soldiers . . ." A startling thought came to me. "Leather armor? Red shirts?"

"That's how soldiers dress, isn't it? Well, maybe not the red shirt. Depends on who they work for, I guess. I don't remember the color."

"Does it happen a lot?" I asked, recalling past thoughts about the similarities between the two of us. "Are guys coming after you a lot to . . . you know . . ."

"Get me pregnant? Yeah, sometimes." There was a sad look in her eyes, a very vulnerable one.

"But . . . you don't always give in . . ."

"Jesus Christ, Eugenie. I won't sleep with *anyone*. What kind of a slut do you think I am?"

A considerable one, actually. But I didn't say so, and I wondered if she'd ever been raped. "Sorry. You just seem so anxious to have that baby."

"Yeah, well, not with just anyone. And certainly not through rape." She held her head up, a fierce look in her eyes. "*No one* does that to Storm King's daughter. It's an insult to our father's awesomeness." Try as she might to deny her heritage, only the human part of her could have pulled up "awesomeness" to refer to a tyrannical fairy warlord.

"You know I don't quite share the same regard for him that you do."

"I know," she said. "Which is why you have such bad taste in men. You wouldn't catch me sleeping with a kitsune. I need someone worthy . . . like Aeson."

I started to argue again that Aeson had been a despotic asshole but knew logic and love rarely worked together—particularly if my own life was any indication. I was saved from further

347

commentary when a coldness settled into the room and Volusian appeared.

"Fuck," said Jasmine. Man, did she have a mouth on her.

I stood up, crossing my arms and trying to look imposing. It was a common attitude I kept around Volusian so there would be no question of my control. "Did you go to Art's house?"

"Yes, mistress."

"And? Did you find anything?"

"No, mistress. I could not enter."

"What do you mean? Did he invite you out back for beer too?"

Volusian didn't blink. "The house was warded."

"The house was warded," I repeatedly flatly. "And *you* couldn't cross it?"

"They'd have to be some serious wards if he couldn't," said Jasmine.

"Thanks, Little Miss Stating the Obvious." I racked my brain, thinking of the local witch network. I didn't know them well enough, not like I knew the shamans. "Where the hell would he find someone that strong?"

"The wards were not the usual type found in the human world. They were laced with magic from this world as well," continued Volusian.

"What? How would Art get gentry help to lay wards—especially if he's abducting them?"

"Maybe he put a gun to their head," said

Jasmine, in a fair imitation of my own dry tone. Another family trait, perhaps.

"I've got to get into that house," I muttered. "I guess that's gotta wait like everything else, though. Well, thanks for trying, Volusian."

"I neither require nor desire your gratitude, mistress. I want nothing in these worlds save your death."

Jasmine laughed.

"Well, I'm sure you guys'll have a great time together." I opened the door and beckoned the guards back in. With Volusian back, only two needed to be inside. "I'll see you both in the morning for demon hunting."

After that, I considered joining the others for their impromptu party but decided that would be the same as a boss crashing her employees' happy hour. Instead, I made my way to my own room but was intercepted by Girard.

"Your majesty." He swept me a bow in that flourish-filled way of his, making his cloak flare out dramatically. "I've made considerable progress on the project you requested."

"Already?" I knew he had magic for this kind of thing, but still.

He smiled. "The queen asks, and I obey."

From within the folds of his cloak, he produced a rolled-up piece of parchment, which he opened up for me. On it was a detailed diagram of a sword, and scrawled all around it were assorted technical notes about weight and composition. Those meant little to me. Mostly I noticed the sword's beauty, particularly its hilt.

"This is lovely," I said.

"I should hope so. Fit for a king."

In spite of myself, I smiled back. Dorian had left me in a miasma of emotions, but I'd been trying hard not to let that interfere with the honest favors he'd done me. And when he'd mentioned needing a new sword, I'd gotten the idea yesterday to have Girard make one. By all accounts, there were few more skilled, and his ability to touch iron made him particularly gifted.

Girard traced the line of the sword's blade and tapped the end. "I can work iron into the tip here, and it shouldn't harm the Oak King so long as he's holding the hilt. It also shouldn't affect his ability to control the rest of the blade." As a master of the earth and its contents, Dorian could infuse copper and sometimes bronze blades with magical heat.

"But the tip will be deadly to his enemies," I said. The idea to work iron into it had been mine.

"Considerably. I can begin production right away, but I'll need to get an understanding of his current sword's balance before I can finalize this one."

"He'll be here tomorrow. You can talk to him then." Dorian too had offered to help oust my demons.

"Excellent. And Mistress Shaya tells me you

have the materials here that I could use, if I have your permission to do so. Otherwise, I can return to my workshop in the Rowan Land."

I shook my head. "No, no. Use whatever you need here."

His lips twitched in a wry smile. "That's probably just as well. Were I to return home . . . well, I suspect my lord prince would spend days asking me about you."

I sighed. "Is he still upset about that?"

"He was, forgive me, quite heartbroken over your rejection of the gift and of him."

"I didn't want that. I liked him—still do. I just wanted us to be friends."

"In my experience, your majesty, men and women often have difficulty with that. It's not impossible—but not always easy."

I thought about Dorian. "That's for damned sure. Well, thank you for this, and let me know if there's anything I can do to help with it. But seriously—don't go work on it now. Go back to that party. Drink up. Flirt with Shaya. She could use a good guy."

Girard erupted into laughter. It was a rich, honey-filled sound. "I treasure my neck too much to risk the captain of your guards wringing it."

It took me a moment to catch on. "Who, Rurik? He doesn't like Shaya . . . not that way, at least. She's too, I don't know, refined. He only goes after trashy kitchen girls."

Girard merely shrugged.

"I'm serious!" I wasn't sure why this astounded me so much. "They might seem close, but it's because they work together. They're just friends."

Girard flashed another grin. "Didn't you just hear what I said about men and women being friends?" He dared a wink and bowed again. "Until tomorrow, your majesty."

I watched him go, that flamboyant red cape swirling around him. I was still in disbelief. Shaya and Rurik? No, it was ridiculous. I was certain she had no interest in him, and if he did want her, it was only for the same cheap reasons he wanted any woman. She was too smart for that.

"You give my lord gifts yet still claim no interest."

I turned and saw Ysabel standing near a corner in the hall. She'd apparently overheard my conversation with Girard. Did this woman have nothing to do except lurk in halls and wait for me? "He's done a lot of favors for me lately. It's the only way I can really repay him."

"No doubt there are other ways you could repay him," she said snidely.

I started to give the "friends" line but had already had enough of that with Girard. "Please, I don't want to go through this same old song and dance. And you know, we both fulfilled our side of the deal with Dorian. I let you teach me. You're free. He's coming here tomorrow to help with the demon problem. Go home with him afterward."

Those big blue eyes widened in surprise. "Why?"

"Why what?"

"Why would you let me go?"

"Because you don't want to be here. You gave me the foundation of what I need to know, and I've been building on it pretty quickly." With a shiver, I recalled how I'd nearly suffocated that gentry in my yard. That had been intentional. I had no accident excuses as I'd had with her. It was probably something I shouldn't mention to her quite yet. As it was, she looked troubled enough.

"Yes . . . you have learned quickly. The magic burns so strongly in you, I don't think it needs much of an excuse to burst out. You really are like Storm King."

"Did you know him?" I asked curiously. I was always conflicted on hearing about him. Part of me wanted nothing to do with him, yet the other part longed to know more.

"I wouldn't say 'know,'" she mused. "My father was one of his bodyguards, so I saw Storm King a few times. He was . . . terrifying. Terrifying and awe-inspiring." She tried to hide her fear but shuddered anyway.

"From what I hear, that's the reaction most people have." Kiyo too had seen Storm King in his youth, and I'd once had a flashback of my own brief meeting with my father.

"The power you try to summon . . . he was able to bring it about in a heartbeat. He had only to think about a storm and the world would tremble with its force."

"Well, I guess everyone can rest easy. I'm a long ways from that."

"Do you know why?" she asked.

"Practice?"

She shook her head and pursed her lips. "Because for all your titles and regard and impressive use of magic so far . . . you are still *human* in your heart." *Human*, by her tone, was a very ugly thing to be.

"Not according to my stepfather." It didn't seem like I'd ever fit anyone's expectations.

"You think like one. You want to divide everything up logically. The way you approach magic, it's very . . . scientific." Not a word gentry used very often. "You treat it coldly. You parcel up each fragment of air and categorize it. Magic requires control, yes, but at its heart, it is tied to your emotions. You said you'd summoned lightning accidentally. What was going on?"

"I was scared." It had also happened, I realized, when I was aroused. "And, um, excited."

"You were lost in your emotions, and the power seized you. But you'll never be able to do that regularly, never by choice. You repress your emotions. You don't give in to them." Her smile turned triumphant. "And that is why my lord will never love you like he does me."

Of course. I should have known there was a barb waiting at the end of this lesson. I wondered what she'd think if she knew her lord had been pretty willing to love me up yesterday.

"Well, thanks for the pep talk, but I'm going to my room now. I meant what I said. Go with Dorian tomorrow and love him as much as you want. I'll carry on without you somehow." No point in hiding the sarcasm I felt.

Ysabel gave me a sickeningly sweet smile. "You're presuming you'll come back."

I jerked around and gave her a sharp look. "Are you threatening me?"

"Certainly not. I have nothing to do with your adventure tomorrow. But you're going to face demons. Anything can happen. And if you don't return, I won't weep."

Great. Nothing like a good omen to go into battle with.

Chapter Twenty-One

Iwoke up the next morning, lying on top of my covers, with sunlight streaming in through the eastern windows. It was barely sunrise, but already the air was warming up. It was, as the saying went, going to be a hot one. If I truly was connected with the land, I wondered what a heat wave said about my mood. Was it indicative of my preparedness for battle?

I squinted up at the play of sunlight on the stone ceiling, unsure of that question, just like so many lately. With a sigh, knowing I needed to get up, I rolled over and came face-to-face to Kiyo. I yelped in surprise.

His dark chocolate eyes were open, wide awake. I think he'd been watching me while I slept. He smiled that sexy, smoky smile of his, eyes crinkling slightly. He was bare-chested, clad only in navy blue boxers.

"When did you get here?" I asked. "I didn't notice a thing."

"I know," he said. "You were sleeping pretty

heavy. Didn't even budge when I slid into bed."
He rested a hand on my hip and slid it along my
bare leg. I'd fallen asleep in a T-shirt.

Seeing his eyes and feeling his hand on my skin
warmed something in me. Surely all would be
right in the world—worlds, even—so long as I had
Kiyo. There was just something so over-
whelmingly strong and secure about him, a
steadiness in the midst of that dangerous sex
appeal. I reached out and touched the side of his
face, a bit surprised at just how happy I was to
have him here with me.

"I didn't know for sure that you'd come," I
admitted.

"Eugenie, how can you think that?" He
continued stroking my leg, but his other arm
pulled me close. "I said I would. I won't let you go
into danger alone."

"I know you don't approve of some of the
things I do. Roland doesn't. We had a huge fight."

Kiyo kissed my forehead, then my nose, and
then my lips. "He's worried about you. I am too.
But I understand what you have to do here and
why you want to help these people."

I looked at him and felt something lighten up
within me, some lonely and aching part that so
desperately needed someone to *get* me. Before, I'd
felt like Dorian could. I prayed Kiyo was able to
as well. "You do?"

"Yes." He kissed me again, his mouth warm

and searching. The hand that had been on my leg moved up to my breast. "I know what it's like to live in two worlds. You're brave and do what you think is right, and I'm not going to let anything happen to you," he breathed in my ear. "Neither are any of the people gathered downstairs."

He moved his mouth back to mine, but I wiggled out. "Wai—what? Who's gathered?"

He gave a half shrug, hands still roving over my body. "Everyone. Rurik's got the guards there. Jasmine's up and cuffed. Even Dorian's here."

I sat up. "Kiyo! We have to get downstairs then. We can't—ah."

He'd moved one hand up my inner thigh—up, up, and up. "We've got time."

"No . . . we . . . don't," I managed as his fingers moved in and out of me. For a moment, I thought of how Dorian had done almost exactly the same thing, but then I shoved the memory away. "They're waiting . . ."

"Five minutes, Eugenie," Kiyo murmured. His other hand shoved up my shirt, and he leaned down to kiss one of my breasts, slowly moving on to suck the nipple, harder and harder. I flinched slightly at the feel of his teeth, and he lifted his face up. "I've missed you, Eugenie, no matter what else you think. I've missed you and I love you." He slid his fingers out of me, and I whimpered at their loss. He smiled. "And I think . . . I think maybe you missed me too . . ."

And with no other preamble, he rolled me over to my knees and moved up behind me. I don't know when his boxers came off, but suddenly, he was in me, hard and swollen and grunting with each thrust. I gripped the sheets with my fists, keeping my body arched for him so that he could take me even deeper. His hands clutched my hips, letting him bury himself as far as he could go. I moaned and tipped my head back, my body wanting to take more and more of him into me.

Leaning his body over mine, he reached forward and managed to cup my breasts without breaking his rhythm. His fingers caressed them, thumbs rubbing against the erect nipples. The sensations in my body were dizzying, every piece of me feeling like it was on fire. At last he shifted back to his kneeling position and returned his hands to my hips, giving him the best position to fully take me. His strokes grew even harder and faster, shoving himself into me with such force that I could hear our bodies hitting each other. With a great groan, his nails dug into my hips and his whole body jerked as he came. Hands still tight on my hips, he held himself there for several moments, taking his full release.

Finally, he pulled away and collapsed onto the bed. Flipping over, I sprawled beside him. "Okay," I gasped. "Now I think I'm ready to fight some demons."

* * *

I don't think anyone really noticed that Kiyo and I had just had sex when we came downstairs. Mercifully, it didn't even rain. If anyone suspected anything, it was Dorian, with that uncanny way he had of reading people. The guards were drawn up in formation outside, but Dorian was in the parlor sipping tea with Shaya while Ysabel all but sprawled on his lap. Girard was there as well, testing the weight of Dorian's old sword while Dorian himself studied the drawing of the new sword.

"Eugenie," said Dorian, arching an eyebrow. "Don't you look radiant this morning. Why, you're positively glowing." Ysabel scowled at his praise.

"It's the leather," I said, tugging self-consciously at my shirt. I'd argued against needing armor, but Shaya had nonetheless obtained a sleeveless top for me made of lightweight leather, good for deflecting blades. It wasn't porn-star leather or anything, but it wasn't something I was used to.

"And this," Dorian continued, pointing to the drawing, "is exquisite. Thank you."

"What is it?" asked Kiyo.

"A sword from legends. One to slay evildoers everywhere. Eugenie's having it made for me."

Kiyo gave me a wordless look that was nonetheless full of questions. "It's a thank-you gift. Dorian's done me a lot of favors lately," I explained.

"I assure you," said Dorian straight-faced. "I

360

take as much joy in the giving as you do in the receiving."

"Okay," I said hastily. "Are we good to go? I saw the guards out there. I'd like this done sooner rather than later."

The biggest impediment turned out to be Ysabel, who threw her arms around Dorian and begged him to be careful. He patted her hastily on the shoulder, assuring her he'd be fine. His eyes were impatient, though, and he didn't look back when he strode out with the rest of us. Poor Ysabel. I was almost starting to feel bad for her, despite her hopes that *I* wouldn't come back. She really was nothing more than a bed warmer to Dorian, and while most of his women knew that, she just couldn't accept it.

Jasmine was ready as well, still bound and looking angry. Volusian was with us, and he had standing orders to subdue her if she tried anything—which I felt pretty sure she would. Unfortunately, I also needed Volusian to fight demons, which meant he couldn't watch her all the time. None of us could, and I was going to have to do some tricky maneuvering to keep the gun on her while still attempting banishing.

Kiyo frowned disapprovingly when he saw her, more so when she had to be helped on to her horse. "This is wrong, Eugenie," he said softly, once we were all riding. He was going in human form today.

"Which part? Bringing her or keeping her prisoner?"

"I don't like any of it."

"What happened to you saying you understood the choices I have to make?" I hissed. "Was that just to score sex?"

Dorian had ridden up on my other side. I had no doubt he'd heard the sex comment, but he didn't acknowledge it. "How would you suggest she handle it then? Let the girl go?"

"No," Kiyo said, giving Dorian a dark glance. "But there are more humane ways of dealing with her."

"I gave Jasmine her own room and got her better cuffs! What else can I do?" I asked.

"I don't know," admitted Kiyo.

"Then don't criticize if you can't offer a solution," said Dorian. "It's easy to want peace and love in hypothetical situations—then reality sets in, and sometimes we have to do what's ugly."

"I don't recall asking for your input here," snapped Kiyo.

"As it is, Eugenie, you've got a hard choice ahead." Dorian was speaking like Kiyo wasn't even there. "What are you going to do when you've finally taken care of this rabble? What will you do with the prisoners?"

I shrugged. "Send them off to work details."

"Even their leader, Cowan? The one who summons these demons? Surely you don't want him out and about, even if it is digging ditches."

"Don't listen to him," said Kiyo. "He's baiting you. There are prisons, even in the Otherworld. You can send him there if he survives."

"A charming act of mercy, no doubt," mused Dorian. "One that will terrify future enemies."

"I'm not going to kill everyone who gets in my way," I exclaimed. "I'm not my father, no matter how much you want me to be."

"I wouldn't quite say that's what I want," chuckled Dorian. "But as a leader, you need to make examples sometimes."

"Mercy's not a horrible thing," I argued.

"Storm King never showed any," said Kiyo.

"Indeed," agreed Dorian. "And I just want to make sure his daughter doesn't show too much. You aren't the only one who protects her, master kitsune. We all just do it in different ways."

"Enough," I ordered. Rurik was drawing the group to a halt up front, meaning it was time to go on foot. I was grateful, seeing as I was getting sick of listening to Kiyo and Dorian's pissing contest.

Just like before, we went on foot, the whole experience giving me a strange sense of déjà vu, even though the bandits had changed location. I also had odd recollections of the time I'd defeated Aeson. Dorian and Kiyo had been with me then, about as thrilled to be with each other as they were now. Shaya had been there too, but Rurik had nearly had a fit when she offered today, and I couldn't help but recall Girard's words.

I certainly hadn't had an army at my back when we'd gone after Aeson. Rurik sent men with a knack for moving stealthily to scope out the camp and dispatch any enemy scouts. The waiting made me restless, and a tense silence settled over everyone. I glanced at Jasmine, still bound. I wouldn't uncuff her until the last possible moment and still didn't trust her.

"You know what you have to do?" I asked her.

She'd been staring off thoughtfully at the guards ahead, taking in the sloped land and scattered pines. Probably planning her escape, I thought ruefully. Like before, these brigands had chosen the best cover they could find in this barren land. She turned to me, immediately putting on her standard scowl.

"Yes."

"And you know what'll happen if you try anything?"

"Yes." Pure malice looked at me from her eyes.

"Good," I said, shifting my hold on the gun. Her eyes flicked briefly to it, and if it scared her, she made a good show of still looking defiant.

"I hope you hold true to your word," murmured Dorian, walking up to me.

"Stop poisoning her," growled Kiyo.

"And both of you let me make my own decisions," I said.

The scouts returned shortly thereafter, giving us

the all-clear. We headed toward the encampment, circling it and descending in full force. Thankfully, no one announced our presence, and we had a brief element of surprise before the bandits mobilized. I unfastened Jasmine's cuffs, hoping I wasn't making a mistake. My right hand firmly held the gun against her back—holding it to her head had seemed a little too cruel—while the left held my wand poised and ready. Kiyo and the other fighters were going in for the hand-to-hand combat while the other magic users and I stayed back and waited—not that I intended to use magic today. I was strictly in shamanic banishing mode.

And there they were. A deep swell of magic permeated the air, and fiery forms materialized on the far side of the camp. I saw Rurik's gaze travel to the spot they'd come from, his attention not on the demons but on what was potentially the demons' summoner. Circling around, he headed toward that area. The demons were my job. I nudged Jasmine with the gun. "Do your thing. Volusian—attack."

I held my breath, wondering what Jasmine would do. A moment later, I felt magic well up in her, a magic similar to my own but with a slightly different feel. Some part of my brain tried to grasp it, hoping I could learn it for later. The rest of me watched as there was a ripple in the air—an opening to the Underworld. Two forms stepped out from the slash in our world. Much like the water elemental from the other night, these two demons were composed of water, sloshing with each step yet maintaining a solid form. They were bigger than the elemental, though, adorned with horns and glowing yellow eyes.

"Only two?" I exclaimed. "There are five of the others!" Jasmine didn't respond but held up her hand like a conductor drawing a powerful note from her musicians. For a heartbeat, I wondered if the water demons would come charging toward us. They didn't. Their attention turned to the fire demons, their ancient enemy from the Underworld.

Nearby, Dorian was wielding magic of his own, ripping up the earth from underneath the fire demons so that they stumbled and sank into great holes, making them easy prey. "Demons aren't that easy to summon," he said in her defense, eyes on his handiwork. "In fact, this will be it for the fire demons. There's no way that man can summon any more. I'd be surprised if he's still conscious."

Well, that was something. Jasmine's servants had two of the fire demons in a deadlock, which meant none of them were going after my people. Volusian was making good work on one of the demons as well, though the other two were rampaging forward. It was time for me to step up.

I drew up the human power I'd used my entire life, the power that was based on will and not emotion like gentry magic. My wand focused it, and I sent it out toward one of the loose fire demons, encircling him and summoning up the strength of Persephone to open up a way to the Underworld and suck him back. He sensed the banishment happening, and I felt his power surge as he tried to fight it. I steeled up my own strength, and what seemed like a land mine suddenly went off near him, showering him in dirt and rock as he stumbled. *Thank you, Dorian.* The Underworld opened up, and the demon dissolved back to his domain, unable to fight my strength.

And like the last time I'd fought these guys, the power required for that banishing took a lot out of me. Surveying the rest of the battle, I saw with pleasant surprise that one of Jasmine's water demons had defeated a fire demon. That water demon had then joined his partner, and it appeared as though they would make quick work of their target. Kiyo and the other soldiers were doing a good job of killing or subduing the rest of the bandits. I turned back to the fire demons, assessing my next strategy.

One was unengaged and starting to move toward my soldiers. This banishment was going to be harsh. I drew up all my strength and repeated the process, calling out to Persephone and reciting the words to send the demon back to the Underworld. It distracted him from my soldiers, and he started lumbering toward me. Fuck.

"He. Is. Coming," said Jasmine stiffly. I couldn't see her face with my gun to her back but got the impression she was as strained as I was.

"Yeah, I kind of noticed."

He was pushing back at me with his own strength of will. I clenched my teeth. *No, no. I am stronger. I am Storm King's daughter.* I needed another distraction to slip him up, but everyone else was busy. Dorian's attention was on the demon that Volusian battled. That demon was moderately stronger than my minion, but seeing that Volusian couldn't really die . . . well, it made it hard to destroy him. So, neither was gaining ground until Dorian used some of his magic to attack the demon with a nearby chunk of rock, letting Volusian move in for the kill.

My demon was still approaching, and I needed a distraction of my own. Iron didn't dampen my powers anywhere near as much as it did Jasmine's, but it could sometimes affect me a little. I could still work my gentry powers while in contact with it, but it was easier without. In an act I was certain I'd regret, I dropped the gun and immediately called upon my storm magic. I would have given anything to blast this demon with lightning, but that was still beyond my control. Instead, I reached up toward the sky, calling on water and air. To my astonishment, I was able to bind them together. Thick, leaden clouds formed, whirling into a weak funnel cloud that descended on the demon. It was the most powerful force of weather I'd ever—consciously—summoned, and it knocked the demon over. I couldn't maintain my hold on it, and the ministorm dissipated instantly. It was enough, though, and I sent out the banishing before he could respond. It felt like my insides were being ripped out, but I managed it, kicking him out of this world.

Gasping and woozy, I looked around, realizing there were no more demons left—well, no fire demons at least. The water demons, victorious, were still there—and they were charging toward us. *Shit*. I realized then what I'd potentially unleashed. I cuffed Jasmine on the shoulder, nearly knocking her over, and reached for my gun.

"I warned you not to try anything," I cried, pointing the gun at her. "Send them away!"

"It's not me," she exclaimed back. "I can't control them!"

Stepping forward, I got a good look at her face. She was covered in sweat, skin pale. Dorian had said demon summoning was hard, and the full weight of what I'd done hit me. She'd summoned them but no longer had the power to control them. I had no more strength left for banishing, but I could feel Jasmine still trying to work her magic, weak as it now was. It was impossible to sense every part of what someone else was doing with her magic, but I got a strong feel for hers. These creatures were bound to water.

They were part of my domain. Doing my best to mimic her, I joined my strength to hers, sending commands through my magic, willing them to leave this world.

They were nearly on us, and I almost laughed at the irony as my own death approached. Then, suddenly, I felt my magic sync up perfectly with Jasmine's. Control of the demons slipped into place, and they froze. Together, she and I ordered them back, and there was a tear in the fabric of space, an opening to the Underworld. It was almost like a banishing, but not quite. The demons were willingly—well, with our urging—returning, and our magic helped them with the passage. A moment later, they dissolved from our world.

After that, I felt like I'd run a marathon. Every part of me ached and was wearied. Yet, as bad as I was, Jasmine was worse. "I guess blood really is thicker than water," she whispered in a very bad attempt at a joke. She swayed on her feet, eyes rolling back in her head, and then she collapsed. I barely managed to catch her in my own weakened state, but then stronger arms took hold. Kiyo.

He barely had a scratch, and relief poured through me. "Thanks."

He lifted her easily into his arms. "Are you okay?"

"Fine," I said, looking down at my sister—who hadn't betrayed me after all. "She's bad, though. Get her to a healer."

Kiyo hesitated, not wanting to leave me. Then, he gave a quick nod and loped off in that way that was half-human and half-wild animal. Looking around, I saw that the others were rounding up the remaining rabble. My losses looked light. Rurik was leading a man who seemed to be in the same shape as Jasmine. The demon summoner. Dorian was with Rurik and gave me a quick glance. I knew what was in the look. Kill the summoner or not? I gave a sharp shake of my head. Dorian grimaced and then turned back to help Rurik with his prisoner.

No one seemed to notice or need me, and I sank gratefully to the ground, waiting for my strength to return. I wondered if I'd be able to call up the magic again that I had used with Jasmine. Trying to piece it together seemed like too much work now, and I contented myself with watching my people work.

Then, out of my peripheral vision, I saw movement. I stood up and looked far to my side, toward a stony bluff covered in cacti. A face peered out at me and then ducked back. I knew the face. It was the scarred gentry who'd come to my house the other night. With no further thought, I started to hurry after him. Then, to my astonishment, I paused and did what Rurik would have wanted. A couple of my soldiers were lingering nearby. "Hey, come here," I called, gesturing. They immediately followed as I set off at a brisk pace, moving as fast as I could to reach the bluff. When I turned around the side of it, I saw no sign of the gentry warrior I sought.

The ground rose sharply here, beginning to turn into foothills reminiscent of the ones near my house in Tucson. The vegetation was thicker, though still a far cry from a true forest. It was mostly cacti, shrubs, and scraggly trees. Going up the small hill was a narrow path, and on impulse, I headed up it in search of my prey. The footsteps of my soldiers sounded behind me, their boots crunching in the gravel.

Who was that guy? And why was he here now? Was he one of the bandits? I hadn't seen him in the fight. Was he some sort of spy, perhaps, which was why he'd come to my house and—

Snick. Snick. Two arrows came out of nowhere as we reached the crest of a hill. Each one hit one of my soldiers in the chest, dropping them to the ground. I came to a screeching halt, waiting for my arrow, peering around the trees for the mystery gentry to reveal himself.

But he didn't.

Art did.

He smiled, stepping forward. "Eugenie, nice to see you again. You've been very busy around here, I hear." He waved vaguely toward where I'd come from, though my people were nowhere in sight. *Eugenie*, I thought, *you are a fucking moron.* Beyond Art, I saw the gentry I'd chased emerge from the cover, along with two others—all wearing leather armor like Jasmine had described. They carried bows and wore red shirts under the armor.

"Roland called me last night and nearly bit my head off about getting you involved in gentry politics." Art shook his head, amused. "I wonder what he'd say if he only knew just how involved you were—your majesty."

I was exhausted as hell and devoid of magic. But—I was still human and not without human implements. The gun was still in my hand, and I jerked it up toward him. I needed to distract him until some of my own people came. Fuck. I shouldn't have come rushing up this hill, even if I had had the sense to bring some backup. The question now was, would the rest of my people notice I was gone? Usually, I could hardly step outside the castle's door without a dozen people in tow.

Art tsked me. "Would you really do it? Would you really kill one of your own kind? Or are we even your own kind?"

Magic suddenly filled the air—familiar magic. Shamanic magic. It encircled me like fog, thick and heavy. Forgetting Art, I turned abruptly around, toward the sound of words being chanted—words I knew by heart. Abigail was standing there, wand in hand.

And so help me, *she was banishing me.*

I felt her will shove up against mine, just as I'd grappled with the demons. The world around me began to tear open as a vortex started to pull my essence apart. I fought it, fought it with every ounce of strength I had—but there was just none left to give.

When it came to traveling the worlds, cross-roads and gateways were the way to go. They made for a smooth transition. Or, one could travel like I often did, journeying to some item imbued with your essence, an item that couldn't help but draw your soul to it.

And rarely, if you had the strength, you could tear open a gateway by force and shove your way into another world. That wasn't recommended. It hurt like hell. And essentially, that's what a banishing was—only it wasn't your choice. It was someone ripping you out of the world and shoving you into another.

I felt the fabric of this world open up, felt the unstoppable pull of another. I couldn't fight it. I tried. I kicked, I screamed, but I was too weak. I felt like I was shattering into a million pieces, sucked into a whirlwind . . .

. . . and then, I was gone.

Chapter Twenty-Two

I woke up with a headache even worse than the one I'd gotten shooting tequila on the night of Luisa's birth. Pain thudded to a steady drumbeat in my head, though at the same time, my senses felt foggy as a boring plaster ceiling slowly came into focus above me. Nausea welled up in my stomach, and I worried I was going to get sick. It had happened the last time I'd come crashing through the worlds.

And speaking of the worlds . . . where was I? Easy enough to figure out, my groggy brain quickly realized. I'd been pulled out from the Otherworld, which meant I could either have been sent to the Underworld or the human world. The fact that I was still alive indicated I'd gone onto the latter. Why on earth would Abigail summon me to—fuck. There it was: the nausea again. I bit my lip and tried to sit up, not wanting to choke on my own vomit.

Only, when I tried to rise, I didn't get very far. My hands were stretched above my head, tied to the headboard of the bed I lay on. No, not tied—cuffed. Cuffed with heavy steel, industrial-strength handcuffs. Bound or no, I did manage some semblance of sitting, just as my stomach betrayed me. A bowl got shoved under my face right at that moment, and I was grateful to spare the bedding and my clothes. I threw up twice before my benefactor gently asked, "Any more?"

"I don't think so."

I squinted up and found myself looking into the face of a young girl, heavily freckled and brown-haired, with a nose a bit too small for the rest of her facial features. She was still cute enough, though, and—she was a gentry. For a moment, I wondered if I'd gotten confused about the banishment. Was I still in the Otherworld? No. This was definitely the human world. I could sense it. There was a way that magic hung in the air—or, rather, didn't hang in the air around here.

The girl took the bowl away and returned with a damp cloth. She wiped my face with it and then my mouth. A moment later, she returned with a glass of water, which I drank gratefully. All of her movements were gentle and graceful.

"What's your name?" I asked.

"Cariena."

"That's really pretty. Where am I, Cariena?" I asked, tugging at the handcuffs. Those things weren't going to budge.

The girl sat down on a chair in the corner. "In the world of the humans."

"I know that." I tried hard not to let my tone get harsh. My leather from the fight was gone; I wore a T-shirt and underwear. "But where? What is this place?"

She glanced around, as though the room might offer some secret insight. The walls were painted pale gray and matched the bedspread, a pattern of purple and grayish blue flowers. There was a small dresser in the corner, along with her chair, as well as the narrow twin bed I lay in. There wasn't a lot of space here—and no windows at all.

"The Red Snake Man's house."

"The Red Snake—son of a bitch. Art."

My mind was still fuzzy, and I had a hard time grasping all the details of what had happened. I remembered bits and pieces of the fight. I remembered chasing the soldier and then Abigail banishing me . . .

But it was all still disjointed, and I had no recollection of how I'd gotten here. It was possible that was simply from the trauma of tearing through the worlds. Someone could have smacked me upside the head too, but the pain throbbing in my skull wasn't that type. As I'd noted earlier, it was more like the hangover type. Only worse.

"Where is he now?" I asked.

Cariena shook her head. "I don't know. He doesn't explain his activities to us."

"Us? Are there . . ." Again, my addled brain tried to remember what I already knew. Why

377

couldn't I line up my thoughts? It was like I had both the buzz and the hangover from drinking, all wrapped up into one. Us. Art. Red Snake Man. "Are there . . . others like you here? Other girls?"

She nodded.

"How many?"

"Five—no, four. They took Fara yesterday. Isanna's next."

"They who?"

"One of the men. They come sometimes. They look at us. Sometimes they just . . ." She looked away, unwilling to meet my eyes. "Sometimes they just . . . visit. But sometimes they make a deal with the Red Snake Man to take one of us."

"Art," I murmured. "His name is Art. Red Snake Man seems to give him some semblance of respect." I started to rub my eyes and then realized I couldn't with the cuffs. "Are the other girls chained up too?"

"Only the ones who resist."

"Well, yeah, I guess that would include me. I take it you're not one?"

"Not anymore."

"Why don't you leave? You must have some magic . . . even a little."

Cariena held up her hands. She didn't have handcuffs like me, but snug iron bracelets hugged each wrist, each with a tiny lock. The skin was red and swollen where the iron touched.

"Jesus . . . so you're blocked from your magic.

But, I mean, can't you just walk out the door?"

"There's iron . . . iron everywhere. The windows, the doors. They're all bound with iron and spells. And locks. Besides . . ." Her blue eyes widened slightly. "I don't know where I would go . . . not in this world . . ."

"Home," I said fiercely. "You'll go home. I'll take you there."

She shook her head, face sad. "There's no escape from here. Not even for you."

I eyed her curiously. "Do you know who I am?"

"You are the Thorn Queen. Storm King's daughter. You are my sovereign." She gave a deferential nod of respect. "And I know you are a great warrior and magic user. But if the Red Snake Man caught even you, then there's no hope for any of us. Moria tried to escape, and she died out there."

"Moria *did* escape. She didn't die, and—" I stopped.

Why was my brain such mush? Why was I thinking so slowly? *A great warrior and magic user.* I didn't need my hands to get out of here. I had my magic. The iron and steel that stunted Cariena's magic had hardly any effect on me, and I would have had enough time by now to rebuild my stores of power. I reached into myself and then to the world around, seeking water and air, though not certain what I'd do with them. Blow the headboard apart? Oxidize the handcuffs? The decision turned out not to matter.

Nothing happened.

I felt nothing. I felt . . . well, human. I felt as I had for years, long before I'd had any clue I could touch any sort of Otherworldly magic. I was cut off. My mind touched only empty space.

"What's wrong with me?" I asked, true panic starting to unravel in me. "My magic's gone. The steel shouldn't affect me . . ."

"It's not the steel," a voice suddenly said. "It's the nightshade. And I think you're overdue."

Art strolled into the room, looking as dashing as ever with his tanned skin and movie-star smile. I had nothing but contempt for him and instinctually tried to break the cuffs. Nightshade . . . nightshade. Where had I heard that before? Rurik, I realized. He'd advised something called a tincture of nightshade to completely cut off Jasmine from her magic. Was that what I'd been given? He'd said it was the most effective . . . but that it made those with human blood feel dazed and sick. All of a sudden, I knew this fuzzy hang-over feeling didn't have anything to do with me being banished.

There was no real purpose in discussing nightshade with Art, so I got right to the point. "I'm going to kill you."

Art laughed that hearty, deep laugh I'd once found endearing. "Forgive me if I'm not scared." He turned to Cariena. "Go get some more nightshade for Eugenie. And make sure Isanna is dressed and ready to go when Abigail returns."

Cariena was practically out of the room before he finished speaking. "I can't believe it," I said. "It's really true. When I first started putting together this fairy sex-trade theory, I thought it was as crazy as Roland thought it was. But it's really true. Where's this Isanna going? Is Abigail taking her to her new owner?"

He leaned back and crossed his legs. "I suppose you could say that. I like to think of it as her new loving home. The man who bought her is very eager to welcome her."

"You're a fucking bastard," I growled. "Selling them like they're property."

"Might as well be. And if it makes you feel better, I don't sell all of them. Cariena there . . . hmm, well, she's not pretty enough to get a good price. Easier to keep her around for house calls."

"House calls." I started to feel sick again, and it had nothing to do with the nightshade. "Basically, you're whoring her out. You sell sex slaves *and* run a brothel—and yet, all the while, you play hero shaman like you're doing the world a good deed. Roland couldn't say enough nice things about you."

Art straightened up, feet hitting the floor as a flash of anger shone in his eyes. "I am doing the world a good deed—this world. Those girls? They're nothing. They aren't human. And you . . ." He shook his head. "You're one to talk about image. You play hero shaman too, when in reality you're off commanding gentry armies. Does Roland know? Does he know what you really are? I'm sure he has to know you're a half-breed mongrel, but does he really know the extent of it?"

White-hot rage burned within the drug-induced haze of my mind. "I think you forgot the part where I'm going to kill you."

"And you forgot the part where I said I'm not worried."

Cariena returned holding a coffee mug. I eyed it warily.

"What are you going to do with me?" I demanded. "You would have killed me already if you could, yet you probably aren't going to let me go now that I know your dirty secret. Are you going to sell me off too? Keep me for yourself since you don't like gentry?"

Art shook his head and approached my bed. "Eugenie, you couldn't pay me enough to keep you around. I'd take one of these idiot girls any day. Turn on the microwave, and they're so scared that they'll stay docile for weeks."

He gestured Cariena to his side and reached down to hold my head in place. I realized what he was going to do and began thrashing. With one hand he tried to keep me still, and with the other he partially held my mouth open.

"Do it," he said. Obediently, Cariena poured the liquid from the mug into my half-open mouth. As she did, she mouthed, *I'm sorry.* The stuff tasted horrible, and I gagged on it. I tried to spit it out, but Art promptly covered my mouth until I had to swallow. That bitterness flowed down my throat, and I could feel a new wave of numbness start to sweep over me.

"Yes," said Art, almost cheerfully. "You're trouble. I don't want you. I don't know any human who would. But fortunately, we got an offer from someone who isn't."

I think he was smiling that stupid smile again, but I could never say for sure. The force of the nightshade flooded through me, pulling me into fuzziness, then darkness, and then sleep.

I immediately noticed two things when I came to later. One was that Art was still in the room, though I think he'd just returned and hadn't been watching me sleep.

The other thing I noticed was that I was uncuffed.

I didn't waste any time. I promptly leapt out of the bed and charged him. Unfortunately, I didn't really make it off the bed so well. The nightshade was chugging along in my system, and my limbs barely had the energy to stay upright. I fell off the bed and collapsed into an ungraceful pile on the floor. Cariena was there too, holding a bundle of clothing, and started to come help me. Art shook his head, and she froze.

"Looks like you won't be killing me today," he said.

"You fucking bastard," I said, tossing one arm on the bed and attempting to pull myself up. "How long was I out?"

"Oh, an hour or so. That's usually the worst part of it for humans. Now that you're bright-eyed and bushy-tailed, Cariena's going to help you look respectable."

I glared at him. I didn't know who'd stripped me down to this T-shirt and underwear, but if it had been him, he'd die extra slow. The scathing look he gave me suggested, however, that he found as little pleasure in me as I did in him.

"You can't keep me here," I warned, managing at last to sit back on the bed. "Someone's going to come looking for me."

"Who?" he asked. "You were the idiot who wandered off from your people. None of them saw you taken. None of them saw me or any of my companions—well, except for your two meager guards, and they won't say anything to anyone ever again."

With a sinking feeling, I knew he was right. Nobody knew what had happened to me. I'd mentioned the Yellow River theory off and on to a few of my friends, but none of them had any reason to suspect that was connected to my post-battle disappearance. If anything, they'd probably think there'd been another demon on the loose.

"Who the hell were your companions anyway?" I demanded, recalling the trained fighters. "Did you hire a mercenary army or something?"

Art only smiled. "Cariena, get her dressed." To me, he said, "Co-operate, or she'll be the one who suffers for your disobedience."

He left, shutting the door behind him. I heard the snick of a lock. Across the room, Cariena watched me with big, terrified eyes. She feared both me and Art. I sighed. "It's okay. I'll get dressed. I don't want to run around in my underwear anyway."

Visibly relieved, she stepped forward and unfurled what she held: a dress. A gentry-style dress.

"You have got to be kidding me," I said. "Isn't there something else?"

Cariena cringed. "It's all he gave me."

I eyed the bedspread, almost wondering if I could go all Scarlett O'Hara and make something for myself. Then, seeing Cariena's pale face, I yielded again. I wouldn't let Art beat her or give her to some guy because of me. I took the dress from her but discovered I couldn't put it on without help, not with my weak muscles and groggy motor control. Being in that state infuriated me. I hated being helpless. More up-setting still was that I was essentially free, unbound and able to move about . . . but I had no means to fight or defend myself. I could barely even stand. I was a prisoner in my own body.

The dress was a mix of lavender and pale blue. I guess you'd call it periwinkle, which I'd always thought was a dorky name. It was made of smooth, clingy velvet that hugged my body and laced up the back corset-style. The sleeves were long and form-fitting, and the scoop neckline was much lower than my usual style. I'd only wear something that showed that much cleavage if I was going on a date with Kiyo—or trying to coax a favor from Dorian.

Kiyo and Dorian. It sounded pathetic and all damsel-in-distress, but I would have given anything to have them here right now.

Cariena clasped her hands and studied me almost adoringly. "You look beautiful, your majesty. I see now why you have so many suitors back in our world."

Our world. "Well, I don't think my beauty plays quite as much a role as you think."

She produced a brush and undid the knotted ponytail in my hair. "I don't know if I want to be beautiful or not. I used to think I did. But since I'm not, no one will take me from here." She sounded grateful.

"You *are* beautiful," I said sharply, angry at

what Art had said. "And someone is going to take you from here—me."

Cariena gave me a small, sad smile, but for the first time, I thought there might be something like hope in her eyes. A knock at the door startled her back into timid mode as she leapt up from where she'd sat beside me. "Oh! He's here."

"Who?" I asked. Surely Art wouldn't have knocked.

The lock clicked, and the door opened. Leith walked in.

"Leith!" I exclaimed. He looked as I'd seen him before, clad in a red and white silk shirt, dark hair glossy and swept from his face in a ponytail. I wanted to jump up but knew I'd fall to the floor again. "Thank God." Someone did know I was here. I wasn't lost forever. I wanted to tell Cariena we were on the verge of freedom, but she was already scurrying out of the room and hastily shutting the door.

"Eugenie," breathed Leith, striding toward me. He knelt on the ground and caught hold of my hands where I sat. "You are stunning . . . as beautiful as I remember. No, more so. You can't imagine how I've missed you."

A chill crept along my spine. Something was very, very wrong here.

"Leith . . . we have to get out of here. You have to help me—and these girls. There are horrible things going on here."

"We can leave," he said. "But not quite yet. Not until everything's settled."

I tested his hand to see if I could free mine. I couldn't. "Until what's settled?"

"Until then," he continued, as though I hadn't spoken, "you'll have to stay here where no one can find you. But I promise I'll visit you every day."

"I can't stay here! I have to get back to . . . anywhere that's not here. Tucson. The Thorn Land. Anywhere! Leith, what the hell is going on? Why are you here?"

"Because you are. Because Art got you for me."

That chill down my spine spread to the rest of my body until I felt cold all over. I tried jerking my hand away again but didn't possess the strength. "How do you know Art? Oh God. Please tell me you aren't working with him."

He shrugged. "It's a mutually beneficial relationship. I help him collect girls in our—in the Otherworld."

"Girls from my kingdom," I said, the realization coming suddenly. "That's why none of yours were ever taken."

Leith had the grace to look sheepish. "I don't take important ones, Eugenie. Just peasants. No one notices they're missing."

"Their parents do."

"Look, it doesn't matter. My soldiers help round them up, and I bring them to Art and

Abigail to do what it is they do." *My soldiers*. The soldiers who always wore red, just like Leith did now. Normally, red shirts made me think of *Star Trek* extras, but in this case, it was in tribute to the Rowan Land's flag and emblem. The soldiers Jasmine and others had seen weren't Aeson's deserters. They'd been sent by Leith to help Art and Abigail with their abductions.

"They sell them, Leith! How can you stand by and enable that? They sell those girls to horny guys against their will. What can you possibly get out of it to justify having that on your conscience?"

"This." He gestured around. "Art and Abigail share things with me . . . their knowledge from this world. I take it back to mine."

I stared in disbelief. "And then you pass it off as your own. That's why everyone thinks you're such a technological genius. Did you really devise those irrigation plans for me yourself?"

"No," he admitted. "I had help. But does it really matter? Look, you don't know what it's like. You're strong. Your magic grows more powerful every day. But me? I'm a joke. I can't inherit. Proving myself with my 'genius' was the only way to get any respect . . . and even that wouldn't be good enough to let me inherit. Until I met you."

"Leith—"

"I know what you said, but my feelings haven't changed. I love you. And I know if you just spend a little more time with me, you'll love me too. We connect. There's something between us. It's more than just about power."

I leaned back. It was the only way I could put distance between us. "I'm not so sure about that. You think I'm your meal ticket to holding on to the Rowan Land."

"Not just that land, but all the lands! This world too. Eugenie, when you bear my son, you'll see that I'm right." There was a zealous glow in his eyes, and I couldn't decide if he was crazy or just really, really believed these things would be true if he said them. Maybe there wasn't a difference. "I can make you happy—and I know you can make me happy. You're so beautiful . . ."

He moved up to sit beside me on the bed and ran one hand along my velvet covered leg. "Leith . . . don't . . ."

"I just need to get you pregnant," he said earnestly. "Don't you understand? If I bring you back to our world carrying my child, everything will be solved. Art told me . . . he told me how you stop yourself from conceiving. How you take some potion every day." His hand moved up to my hip while his other touched my face and stroked my hair. I tried to back away, but his grip was too strong in my addled state. "He said if you're away from it long enough that you'll be able to have a baby . . ."

I swallowed. My heart was threatening to

pound out of my chest. "No . . . it won't work. You can't get me pregnant—because I already am."

His caresses froze. "What?"

"You were right before about me being involved with Dorian. Kiyo was a cover. He's not worthy—he's no one I'd want to father my child. Dorian and I have been lovers for a long time now in secret. We were afraid of what his enemies would do if they found out. I've been pregnant for . . ." What wouldn't show? ". . . two months. It's too late for you, Leith."

He had gone perfectly still, save for his eyes, which were searching my face thoroughly. "I don't believe you. You're lying. Everyone knows how you bicker with the Oak King. You aren't lovers."

"We are. He'll kill you when he finds out."

Leith shook his head and slid his hand from my hip to my stomach. "There's nothing here. Not yet."

Panic flooded me, and for a moment I couldn't breathe. Every other time I'd come close to being raped flashed through my mind—and there had been far more of those times than I would have liked. And every time, I had escaped the situation. Yet that never made the next time any less terrifying. This was no exception.

"Leith, please don't do this."

His hand moved fumblingly to my breast, and then he pushed me back against the bed. "It's

391

okay," he said, speaking as one would to a child. "It'll be okay. You'll like it. I promise."

"Don't do this!"

His mouth was on my neck, and lovesick boy or no, there was definitely a man's sexual need there. I struggled against him, trying desperately to free myself, but I might as well have truly been a child. With that fucking drug in me, both my body and brain were a mess. My body had none of its ability to fight him or stop him from pushing up my skirt. My brain had no clever ways to talk him out of this. And as he took off his own clothes and laid his body on top of mine, pressing me down, I realized he needed no handcuffs to keep me subdued. The strength of his hands pinning my wrists was more than enough.

Chapter Twenty-Three

There is no real way to describe rape.

Sex with Kiyo or Dorian, the men I loved . . . well, I could have described that for hours in exquisite detail. I could have elaborated on the way they stroked my hair or the way their lips touched my skin. Even with Dean—my cheating bastard ex—sex had still had its share of affection and joy, back when things had been good between us.

There was none of that with Leith.

Well, not on my part, at least. And I think that's what made it especially bad. For him, with his crazy infatuation, it really was an act of love. He visited me often over the next few days, and each time he took me against my will, he'd tell me he loved me and attempt some sort of gentleness and affection. The horrible part was, I couldn't even resist that. It barely required any force on his part to make me submit. Honestly, I wished it had been violent. I wish he'd been cruel and brutal. I'd spent my life in fights, dealing with pain and blows.

There would have been something comfortingly familiar about that, like it was just another battle for me. The twisted love he showed for me during each act of rape, however . . . well, that made it harder to bear.

In that time, I only saw Art once. Abigail checked on me a number of times, and I learned that it was she who mixed the nightshade, though Leith had taught her the recipe. Cariena was the one I saw the most. She seemed to have been installed as the live-in maid and occasional sex toy for visiting guys. When I arrived, there had been three others gentry girls, but Isanna—the one I'd heard mentioned that first day—left shortly. She was very pretty, and Abigail seemed particularly happy at the price she'd gotten for her.

The other two were stunning as well, and they seemed to glumly accept that their time would come. They faced it without much emotion or protest, like condemned criminals going to the gallows. Mostly, their faces were like pieces of a dream. I was kept so heavily drugged that my moments of clarity were few—though the drugs never made me forget what Leith did. None of the other girls had to be drugged; the iron was enough for them. Cariena told me, however, that when other women had required the nightshade, they hadn't taken nearly as much as me. Art and Abigail were too afraid of me getting loose, so they gave it to me more frequently than usual.

"When will you know?" Leith demanded one day. He had just arrived and stood outside my room, arguing with Abigail. The door was ajar. "I thought you people had the ability to tell this kind of thing."

"We can," snapped Abigail. "But not this soon. You've probably got to wait at least two weeks. Besides, you don't seem to mind passing the time that much." The sneer in her voice came through loud and clear. I made a mental note to choke the life out of that bitch.

Leith, however, didn't sound so happy. "Two weeks is a long time. I need to bring her back pregnant before anyone finds her! They're looking for her. She has powerful allies. Her people are loyal, and both the Oak King and the Willow Queen have taken up the search."

Dorian's dedication didn't surprise me, and knowing he was working to find me gave me the first hope I'd had in a while. But Maiwenn, too? Had that been Kiyo's doing? Or truly her own kindness?

"I don't care about your tree-based monarchs," said Abigail impatiently. "Nobody would think to look for her here."

"She suspected before. She told others. Someone could scry for her."

"They won't find her. Scrying won't work. Not with the wards here. Now why don't you stop whining and just get in there and do your business

395

so this won't be a problem. She's almost due for her next dose."

I decided wringing her neck wasn't slow and painful enough. Yet, their words had given me a lot to think about. There was a search on, enough of one that Leith feared discovery. Her mentioning the wards had reminded me of when I'd sent Volusian here. Volusian . . . there was an option I hadn't considered yet. I could summon Volusian to me and have him warn the others. The wards were a problem. He couldn't break them on his own, but if I was calling him, the ties that bound us would be enough to pull him through. *If* I could muster the energy to do it. The iron and nightshade affected the gentry part of my magic. My shamanic powers, the ones I'd used for years, were tied into my strength and will—which I didn't have a lot of lately.

That being said, I felt more coherent now than I had in a while—which was still pretty addled. Abigail had said it was almost time for my next dose. I had to imagine the further from the dose I got, the more its effects would dim. Cariena had said most people didn't take as much, which probably meant the nightshade would still stay in my system awhile. But if I could reach a point when its effects were lessened . . .

My brainstorming was halted as Leith entered. Consternation from his argument with Abigail showed on his face, but it soon transformed to a smile when he saw me. "Eugenie . . . you look so pretty today."

Yes, yes, I'd heard it all before. I was so beautiful, so amazing, a jewel among women that he loved so much. His words irritated me as much as insults would have. I'd been put in an ivory damask dress today, which gave me sickening bridal associations.

He looked me over, and his admiration again changed to a frown. I was lying on the bed, one hand cuffed to the headboard. "What's this?" he asked. "Why did they do that?"

"I was a smartass to Abigail. This was her punishment."

His face darkened further as he sat on the bed. "I don't like that . . . don't like her doing that. But, Eugenie, you have to admit you bring it on yourself . . ."

Oh, Leith. He was so lucky I could barely lift my free arm, or I would have punched that pretty face of his.

He peered at me intently. "You have to get pregnant soon."

"It's not something I can really control," I said. Well, I could have controlled *not* getting pregnant if I was still on the pill. I hadn't taken it in . . . how many days? Three? Four? I wasn't sure how long I'd been here. I knew all the stats, though, about women who'd gotten pregnant from just missing one pill . . .

He sighed and began unlacing the bodice of my dress. "We'll just have to keep trying then. If we just wait a little while afterward, I can do it twice today."

Oh, how fucking lovely. I wanted to explain that it wouldn't matter how many times he did it, not if I wasn't ovulating. That kind of science was lost on him, I knew, alleged genius or no. As far as most gentry were concerned, sex equaled babies, end of story.

"Once it's done, we can go home. We'll get married, and you won't have to be restrained like this anymore. You can move freely and use your magic."

I decided not to mention that if we did that, the first thing I'd do with my magic was make sure I was a widow.

"Things'll be good then," he said, moving his body over mine. "I promise. I love you so much . . ."

I didn't need any nightshade to make me feel numb after Leith left. He'd held good to his word to have sex twice, and I was slowly reaching that point where it just didn't matter. I couldn't feel anything. My body wasn't even attached to my consciousness. It was like my mind existed elsewhere, dreaming or, occasionally, plotting my revenge through the drugged haze. I thought of anything I could—anything that wasn't the violation of my body—while he was on top of me. Usually, I imagined it was happening to someone else and not me. That made it easier to bear until after he left, when the ache inside reminded me that it had indeed been me.

Cariena and another girl arrived shortly thereafter to give me my next dose of nightshade. I couldn't recall the other girl's name, though not for lack of caring. It was just the way my brain worked lately. She was extremely pretty, with curly black hair and sky blue eyes that reminded me of Ysabel's.

Abigail occasionally let the girls administer the nightshade, confident enough in her hold over them to do it. And her confidence was well-founded. I'd tried before to talk them out of it, but their fear of her was too great. This time, I merely attempted a delay.

"Wait," I said, as they leaned over. It looked like the black-haired girl was going to hold me down while Cariena poured. "Let me just talk to you for a minute."

Cariena immediately grew nervous. "Your majesty, we can't . . ." Sometimes I found her use of my title endearing. Other times, I thought it was a joke, considering my present situation.

"Just a minute. That's all."

"Let her," said the other girl.

I flashed her a grateful smile. "What's your name again?"

"Markelle."

It sounded familiar. *Markelle*. I would remember this time. I wanted to treat her as a person, not an object. "Look, I just want to know about the nightshade. How often do I take it?"

"Every six hours," said Cariena, still clearly worried about this delay.

"That's twice as often as they usually give it," added Markelle. And with those words, I saw the slightest flash of bitterness in her eyes, the first I'd seen in any girl. I wondered then if she was one of the other "difficult" ones that Cariena had described, one who had to be drugged as well and eventually subdued.

"Is there any way . . . is there any way you guys could, like, dilute it?" There it was, the big question.

Cariena gasped, but Markelle readily answered. "No, your majesty. Abigail makes it herself and makes sure we come straight here. There's no opportunity."

"Where? Where does she make it?"

"In the kitchen. She has the ingredients set aside and makes a fresh batch every day."

"What else is in it? Aside from the nightshade?"

Markelle looked at Cariena expectantly. Cariena gulped, and it took her several seconds to answer. She rattled off a list of herbs, some of which I knew, some of which were unfamiliar.

They probably had different names in the Otherworld.

"Do Abigail and Art ever eat here? Like, do they cook? Is their kitchen stocked?"

Markelle nodded. "But we never prepare the food—it's always them." She was quick-minded; she'd probably thought I was going to suggest poison. Not a bad idea, really.

"Are there any ingredients in the nightshade mix that look like other herbs they might have in the kitchen?"

Both girls looked confused. "I've seen no other herbs," said Cariena.

"You have freedom of the house." I knew most girls stayed in the basement, though. "The next time they're not around, go through the cupboards. If their kitchen's stocked, they must have a spice rack."

A knock sounded at the door. "What's taking so long?" Abigail called.

"See if any spices look like the ones in the potion," I hissed as the doorknob turned. "Swap them."

Abigail entered just as Markelle held me down. Cariena poured while Abigail watched with a critical eye. "You're too slow," snapped the shaman. "She needs this regularly."

Both girls groveled, bowing their heads deferentially. "Forgive us," said Cariena. I knew her contrition wasn't faked. "It won't happen again."

Abigail rolled her eyes. "Stupid girls. I'll have to do it myself next time."

The instant effect that damned potion always had began to run through me. The familiar blackness swept over me, and I slept.

Another day went by. Leith "visited," and the girls apparently hadn't taken my advice on the nightshade because my six-hour cycle repeated as usual. Abigail usually came with one of the girls now, apparently not trusting them anymore. Art came once as well, and a few caustic comments from me earned me another cuffed hand.

I began to understand the roles they played. Both participated in the brokering and sale of the girls. Art helped Leith's men catch the girls and offered his home—the one I'd once thought too large for a guy like him—as their prison. Abigail seemed to handle the day-to-day affairs of taking care of the girls, and it occurred to me one day that those handcuffs at her place hadn't been part of anything kinky. They'd been part of her arsenal for this hell-hole, and I suspected the trip to see her "sister" that day had probably been to deliver some poor girl to her new owner. I cringed at what that car ride must have been like. For a gentry to be surrounded in all that metal and technology . . . it would have been awful for her.

Leith was getting dressed after one of his conjugal visits one day. I was close enough to my next nightshade dose that I was able to shoot him looks of contempt—ones he didn't notice. He seemed particularly excited.

"It's been a week," he said. "One more week, and Abigail says we can test to see if you're carrying my child." He pressed a kiss to my forehead. "I can feel it, Eugenie. I know we've done it."

There was no "we" in sexual assault, but again, I found it easier just to remain silent lately. It usually made him leave that much more quickly, which then left me alone with my thoughts and my aching body. Sometimes after he visited, my body would feel so violated and dirty that I'd hate it. Then I'd remember that none of this was the fault of my body or me. It was Leith.

Shortly after his departure that day, Abigail and Markelle came in with my next dose. I'd heard talk that Markelle had a buyer. Her days really were numbered now, and I felt bad for her, this girl who'd once fought back against her captors. I was so used to the nightshade by now that they almost didn't need to hold me down anymore to force me to take it. It was a bit disheartening that I felt that way now and wondered if I too was on my way to that sad resignation everyone else had.

The two of them left, and I lay there, waiting for the unconsciousness that always followed. It usually lasted an hour or so before I came to and lived in my fuzzy state until the next dose. Sure enough, I started to feel a little tingly . . . but no sleepiness followed. I lay there, scarcely daring to breathe. After falling drearily into a strict regimen, any sort of change was a shock to my system. I waited and waited. No unconsciousness.

My blurry, addled state didn't disappear, but it didn't get any worse than when I was due for my next dose. Holy shit. One of them had done it. One of those girls had swapped out the nightshade tincture's ingredients. Who? I would have wagered money on Markelle over timid Cariena. Markelle occasionally had that rebellious spark in her eyes, despite her docile behavior, and her impending sale would be serious motivation. She was from the Thorn Land too—my subject. Sometimes I got the feeling that she truly believed her queen could get her out of this.

But did I? I still didn't know if I could get myself out of this. My weapons were long since gone, and I didn't think I had the strength to launch a physical attack on Abigail or Art. My door was kept locked, so there was no prowling for me. Gingerly, I sat up. The world shifted as usual, but again, not like it normally would have post-potion.

What to do with this freedom? I had no guarantees my next dose wouldn't be the usual stuff. That gave me six hours, and the further that time progressed, the better shape I'd be in. I would have given anything for a clock or even a glimpse of the sun. I needed to track the time, waiting until the last possible moment for my strength to be at its peak. It looked like I'd have to wing it and hope my guess was right.

For a moment, panic washed over me. There seemed no obvious options, and I didn't know how fast the potion would let up. Anyone could walk right in at any time. Leith could come in. Leith . . . With some of that fuzziness gone from my head, the memories of what he'd done to me came through more sharply, and my fear grew—

No! I swiftly ordered myself not to think about any of that. Not Leith. Not overwhelming odds. I needed to think only of escape, and for that, I needed to start with small details.

I'd been good today—no bindings. And with the nightshade, no one felt the need to give me iron bracelets like the girls. That meant no blocking of my magic, short of the potion. Somehow, I doubted I'd have the power in six hours to blow this place up with a mini-hurricane. What did that leave me? Hopefully physical stamina . . . and with it . . . my shamanic powers?

Now the countdown began. The minutes were agony, particularly since I had no way to count them. At first, I just attempted general counting in my head, but that grew tedious. I had nothing to do but wait and gauge my own body's recovery.

And recover it did. Oh, I was a long way from being able to kick anyone's ass, but my wits grew a little clearer. Standing and moving didn't hurt much either. Finally, I decided it was now or never. I had to take my gamble. Maybe it was well before the six hours, but I couldn't risk going over.

It would have been easier with my wand, candles, and other accoutrements. What I had to do wasn't impossible, though. I turned off the lights, plunging me into darkness, and sat on the bed cross-legged.

"Volusian," I said softly. "By the ties that bind, I summon you to come to me and obey my commands."

Weak as I was, I felt my will go out, stretching beyond the worlds to my minion. At first, I thought it was useless—then, I felt it. The slightest twitching of our bond. I gritted my teeth, drawing all the strength I could. "I summon you," I growled. "Obey me and come."

For a moment, I thought I'd failed. Then, a coldness filled the room, and red eyes burned before me. Seeing them in the blackness was too scary, and I stumbled up to turn the lights back on.

"My mistress returns," he said. "Or rather, I return to my mistress."

I didn't need to see the slight curling of the spirit's lips to know my hold on him was tenuous. It was like a fragile string of silk, ready to snap at any moment. Bringing him here, through those worlds, had sapped more of me than I thought imaginable. I still held him, but for the first time in the years I'd enslaved him, the full realization of just how powerful—and dangerous—he was hit me.

"I have tasks for you," I said sternly. I could show no weakness.

He took a few steps toward me. "My mistress is bold to say so. You can barely maintain the bond between us as it is."

"I can hold this bond until the end of time. Now, you will obey me."

And almost before I saw what was happening, his clawed hands were around my neck—cold, cold. So cold that they burned.

"I have waited for this for so long," he hissed. "So long for you to weaken so that I may finally kill you and make you suffer the way you have tormented me these years, enslaving me and sending me to do your menial errands."

I couldn't even manage a scream, not with the way his hands were cutting off my air. I could only manage something that was half-grunt and half-gasp. Desperately, desperately, I fought him mentally. I was one of the most powerful shamans in the world. I could control wayward spirits. I could enslave them easily. I'd once had a host of them. I *could* fight this.

"You will feel pain like you have never dreamed possible," he continued. "You will beg for death, beg for dismemberment . . . for even that would be easier than the agony I will inflict on you."

Everyone had warned me so many times about

keeping Volusian. *What if your control slips?* they had all asked. Dorian had even offered to help banish him to the Underworld for good. I had laughed the worries off. I was strong. Even after a battle like I'd had with the fire demons, maintaining that link to Volusian was practically subconscious. But now . . . now, this was different.

"You are losing it—the bonds are nearly broken. In a few heartbeats, your control will be gone . . ."

No! I couldn't speak a response, but the words in my mind burned. I would not lose this. I would not lose control of him. Wrenching up the last scraps of my strength was like ripping my own heart out. *You will obey me! Back off!*

The world startled to sparkle as my air grew less and less, and then—he did back off.

His eyes blazed with malice. He'd been so, so close, and we both knew it. My control now was still a tenuous thing, and I had to hope I would recover my strength soon and solidify my grasp.

"You will obey me," I said in a thin voice. "You will not harm me."

"As my mistress commands." But I could tell from his voice that he didn't believe this would last, that he was biding his time.

Meanwhile, I was running out of time to decide what to do, not only because I didn't know if he'd break free again but also because Abigail could be here at any moment. My initial instinct was to tell him to simply get me out of here. But if that command took the last of my strength, he could easily kill me once we were out. And even if I made it out, what about the girls? I couldn't rescue them on my own. How long until Markelle disappeared?

No, I needed to kick Volusian out of the house. If I didn't summon him back, those wards would keep me safe. I needed to send him for help, and that choice had to be a wise one.

"Leave this house. Go to Dorian," I said. I drew upon that fleeting strength of mine to enforce the order. "I command you. Go to Dorian and tell him where I'm at. Exactly where I'm at."

I could have sent him to Kiyo. Kiyo knew where this house was. But if the effort of these commands was enough to finally shatter my hold on Volusian, Dorian might be able to bind him back. It would be better than Volusian running loose. That, of course, depended on whether my order was strong enough to even get Volusian to Dorian to deliver the message. My first command had been to get Volusian out of the house and keep me behind the wards. If that was all I could manage, Volusian would no longer be bound to obey. *He has to*, I thought desperately. *He has to get to Dorian . . .*

"Go!" I ordered harshly.

"As you command."

Volusian vanished, eyes narrowed, confident

our bond was about to break. As soon as he was gone, I fell onto the bed, nearly ready to pass out. Would it work? Or had I just broken the last fragments of our bond? I was too afraid to reach out and test the link. I didn't have the strength.

The door suddenly unlocked. Nightshade time. With a sickening thought, I realized that if it was the original kind, I would almost certainly lose that control of Volusian. If it was Markelle's decoy, I could hold onto my strength.

Abigail entered, a cup in hand and Markelle in her wake. The gentry girl's eyes were down, her whole posture meek. I bit my lip at their approach, waiting to see what my future held.

Chapter Twenty-Four

It tasted as bitter as always, but as I drank, Markelle lifted her eyes. There was nothing obvious in them, no wink, no expectation. Yet, somehow, I knew. I *knew*. It was the fake again.

Satisfied that I'd swallowed it all, Abigail gave me a withering glance. "We need you cleaned up. That fool is coming for you again later tonight, and he did a number on that dress last time. He wants you looking good, though, so . . ." She gave a half-hearted shrug. Naturally, I couldn't tell her that my dress's rumpled and slightly torn state had nothing to do with Leith's sexual aggression, but, rather, an angry spirit bent on killing me.

Markelle's eyes were downcast once more. "Should I get her a new dress?"

"No. You've got to clean up too. Art's going to be here in a little while for you."

The girl flinched, but Abigail didn't seem to notice. But then, why would she? She didn't noticed any of these girls, not really. And I knew what those words meant. Markelle's time had come. "I'll send in that freckled one, once she wakes up again."

I realized that *she* was me and that I should allegedly be going under. I sank back against the covers, blinking like I was trying to stay awake. The two of them left, Markelle giving me one last fleeting glance. There were a lot of things in her wide eyes as she looked at me. Fear. Hope. Anxiety.

I exhaled once they were gone and sat up. Plan time. My muscles were still weak, but they reminded me more of what you'd feel after a hard run. What had Markelle said before? twelve hours was the normal dose? I was at that point. The nightshade had to be significantly wearing off. Theoretically, my magic should be returning too and—

"Why, hello," I murmured. I'd sent my mind out into the room and had just barely—*barely*—felt the tingle of air and water. I wasn't going to be blowing anyone apart soon, but the magic was coming back. And when it did, these assholes were fucked.

But I needed to wait this out. I wasn't going to jump the gun like I had with Volusian. Every minute brought the magic and my strength back. I had to use this downtime to assess the situation. Abigail was in the house still. Art and Leith were eventually coming back—together or apart, I didn't know. The one thing I felt confident of was that I did not want to face all of them at the same time. That meant Abigail had to be taken out first, but I was going to need help.

In what must have been a little over an hour, Cariena slipped in with a pink silk dress. It reminded me of something Maiwenn would wear. Apparently, no one had gotten the memo that redheads don't wear pink. I stood up and took the dress from Cariena, promptly tossing it on the bed. She looked aghast that I'd gotten up without falling over. Considering all that had happened recently, I couldn't blame her.

"Your m-majesty, what—"

"Cariena, we're getting out of here."

"We can't!"

"Oh, we can, and we are. Where's Markelle?" I had a feeling I was going to need an accomplice with a bit more boldness. "And Raina?" I rarely saw the third gentry girl around here and had no clue to her attitude, but she needed to be accounted for.

"Raina's in her room. She was—disrespectful. And Markelle is preparing herself."

Preparing herself for a lifetime as a sex slave. I grimaced. "And Abigail?"

"She's upstairs. Watching . . ." Cariena groped for the unfamiliar word. ". . . the television."

"Okay, okay." My mind was spinning now. It seemed to be recovering faster than my body. "Here's the deal. I need a weapon. Is there anything you've seen that would work as one?"

"We can't do this. We can't—"

"We *can*," I ordered, making my voice hard and fierce. This girl had been beaten into weakness, and if those shamans scared her, I would make sure that I—her queen—scared her more. "And you will obey me. You're my subject. You'll get out of this alive—I swear it. You'll see your family."

She was still scared out of her mind, but she gave a weak nod. "I see Abigail and the Red Snake Man carry weapons, but there are none around. I couldn't touch them anyway."

"All right. We'll make do with . . . hey, is the garage attached to the house?"

"Garage?"

"Another building. One where they keep cars." I recalled the garage but didn't know if it connected directly to the house. Surely she knew what a car was.

She nodded. "Yes. They go in and out of it sometimes. It's attached to the kitchen."

"When you come down here, whose room do you pass first out there in the hall? Mine or Markelle's?"

"Yours . . ." Cariena was clearly puzzled now.

"Perfect. I know what we're going to do. Take me to Markelle."

There was a moment's hesitation, and I knew this was the turning point of whether she could help or not. The door was unlocked; I didn't need her. But if I didn't have her assistance, I'd have

414

to knock her out to keep her out of the way.

"This way," she said at last.

Markelle nearly threw herself into my arms when we walked into her room.

"Your majesty! I knew you'd do it. I knew you could . . ."

She wore a strappy little red sundress and had been applying makeup. Funny. I got dressed up like gentry royalty, and the girls here were dressed like human whores.

"Shh," I said. "We're not out of here yet."

I hastily whispered my plan to them. Markelle understood instantly, and although Cariena still seemed terrified, she also appeared determined. I returned to my room, body tensed for action as I waited for my plan to unfold. Pressing my ear to the closed door, I listened as Cariena's feet thudded up the stairs. Presumably she spoke to Abigail, but I couldn't hear anything. A few moments later, two sets of feet came downstairs, walked past my room, and went to Markelle's.

I opened my door a crack to make sure the hall was empty. Next door, I could hear Markelle having the nervous breakdown we'd planned—saying she was afraid to leave, afraid to meet this man, didn't know what to wear . . . Abigail, clearly irritated, began to scold her, much as she had responded to Leith's whining. I waited to hear no more and turned in the opposite direction, heading for the stairs.

When I reached the main floor, I did a double take. The house was beautiful, all new construction and designer decorating as befitted the neighborhood Art lived in. The gentry sex dungeon below us kind of detracted from the maple cupboards and crown molding, though. All the curtains were closed, the windows covered with iron grating, and outside I could just barely make out the Sleeping Beauty hedges blocking the windows too. Art's lawn maintenance had been about more than aesthetics. The patio drapes I'd so admired weren't laced with silver thread. It was iron.

The garage was adjacent to the kitchen, just as Cariena had said. The top half of the door leading out to it had a window covered with more iron grating. I turned the doorknob. Locked. There were no signs of keys anywhere, which meant I'd have to do it the hard way. First, I double-checked the kitchen and living room, looking for any other weapon options. On a good day, I could have taken Abigail with my own fists. This was not a good day. Kitchen drawers revealed butter knives, nothing sharper.

With a sigh, I returned to the garage door. This was it. The grating was loosely bolted, enough to keep it up and prevent the girls from touching it. Hoping I'd gained enough strength, I gripped the sides of it and tried to jerk it off. For a moment, nothing happened. Then, in one movement, it ripped from the wood. I froze, waiting to see if anyone downstairs had heard, but the deed appeared to have been performed fairly silently.

The next part, I knew, would not be so quiet. I dragged a chair up to the door and then grabbed a smaller stool used to get into high cupboards. It was metal and had some heft to it. Would it be enough? I stood on the chair and swung the stool forward into the door's window. Yup. Enough heft. More than half of the glass broke. One more swing got the rest of it out, and I climbed through the hole into the garage. The whole maneuver was a bit awkward on my part; I wasn't in that good of shape yet. But, I made it through, incurring only a few cuts on my arms and legs.

I knew, however, I was seconds away from Abigail's arrival. There was no way that breaking glass had gone unnoticed. Small patches of light streamed into the darkened garage from narrow windows as I peered around. Yes, it was a normal garage—albeit it one with a Jaguar in it. I guessed that was why Art had to keep the SUV in the driveway. Part of me wanted to go kick in the car's door, but there was no time. I had to assess the garage's other contents. Scattered tools. Bags of fertilizer. Art's gardening equipment. A heavy metal wrench held my attention for a moment, but then I decided I needed more leverage with my weakened state. I selected a shovel from Art's gardening stash, its scoop heavy metal and wooden handle sturdy.

From inside the house, I could hear shouting. It wasn't going to take Abigail long to figure out where I'd gone when she saw the glass. Grateful for the darkness, I darted over to the side of the door that led into the house, pressing myself as flat as I could against the wall. There was a click as the door from the kitchen opened, but no one came out right away. I could picture Abigail standing there, looking around for any sign of me.

After several heavy seconds, I saw a hand holding a blade—an athame—come out the door first, defensively positioned in case I came charging at her. That wasn't my intent, though. I wanted to get her from behind. She took one step out, still cautious and slow, looking around everywhere. I had to give her credit for that. She didn't just barrel forward; she knew I might be waiting by the door. And in fact, when she looked in my direction, that's exactly what I was doing. My shovel hit her in the side of the head before she could react.

She crumpled to the ground, athame clattering against the concrete floor as it fell from her hands. I knelt down and immediately scooped it up and left the shovel. There was a bloody mark where I'd struck her, and her eyes were only half-open. My hand checked her pulse and found she wasn't dead yet. She was going to have a hell of a headache or concussion when she woke up—which wasn't something I could allow to happen any time soon.

I left her lying there on the garage floor and

stepped back into the kitchen. I opened a few cupboards and found what I'd hoped I would: the household's stash of medicine. Tylenol, multivitamins, et cetera. Behind them were a couple of prescription bottles. One I didn't recognize, but I thought it was some sort of heart medication. The other was Ambien, and I smiled. Just like me, a lot of shamans were insomniacs.

I popped a pill out of the bottle, reconsidered, and grabbed a second. I then propped up Abigail and managed to shove the pills down her throat, with the help of a glass of water and some acrobatics with my fingers. "Payback's a bitch," I said when her reflexes kicked in and she swallowed the pills the rest of the way. She wouldn't be waking up any time soon.

I stepped back into the kitchen and saw all three gentry girls standing there and staring at me. Cariena and Raina looked afraid. Markelle, though she bore a red slap mark on her face from the confrontation earlier with Abigail, looked excited and defiant. I ordered them to carry Abigail downstairs and lock her in one of the rooms. I didn't know which way Art would enter the house and couldn't risk him finding her on the garage floor. Of course, if he did come in through the garage, the shattered glass was going to be a dead giveaway that something was up.

Before they took Abigail away, I frisked her, hoping to find another weapon. Nope. Just the athame I'd already taken. I did, however, discover something nearly as useful: a set of keys. On the ring were several tiny keys, the ones that opened up the iron cuffs and bracelets the girls wore. Once they'd stashed Abigail away, I removed all the iron. Relief flooded the girls' faces, and I scowled when I saw the welts and bruises left from where iron reacted with gentry skin.

"You should have your magic back," I said, reaching for the phone. "We can use it when we get out of here. What can you guys do?"

I was dialing Roland's cellphone, and the girls described their magic to me as the line rang. Cariena had a knack for helping plants grow, kind of like Shaya. Raina had some healing ability. Markelle could summon beams and balls of light. I disconnected when I got Roland's voice mail and promptly dialed Kiyo.

"Son of a bitch," I muttered. None of the girls' powers were going to help us. And honestly? It wasn't a surprise. If I were Leith and had wanted to catch girls who would make docile servants, I too would have picked ones with little or no offensive magic.

Kiyo's phone rang only once before going to voice mail, meaning it was off or he was in the Otherworld. I hung up and prepared to dial my parents' home number. If Roland hadn't answered his cell, he likely wasn't home either, but I had to try. Before I could punch in the numbers, I heard the sound of keys at the front door on the far side of the house. I turned to the girls.

"Downstairs!" I hissed. "Now!"

Markelle looked like she would have stayed, but a stern glance from me sent her scurrying down with the others. Meanwhile, Art's voice rang through the house.

"Abigail?"

I'm not sure how he knew something was wrong. For all he knew, Abigail could have just been downstairs. Maybe it was just some sixth sense, but I heard him hurrying down the hall toward the kitchen, footsteps fast on the hardwood floor. I had a split second to react, no chance to find a hiding spot as I had with Abigail. Surprise was my greatest weapon now. As soon as he entered the room, I leapt on him with the athame.

The thing that gave me a fighting chance was that he'd armed himself too well in his wariness, a gun in one hand and an athame of his own in the other. Full hands prevented him from fully deflecting my attack, though in many ways, the strength of his arms were more than good enough to block the worst of it. I got a swipe in on his face, however, gaining a fair amount of satisfaction in seeing the blood it produced.

"You bitch," he said, circling with me in the kitchen as we each sized each other up for an attack. "Where's Abigail?"

"Taking a nap," I said. I gave him a wicked

421

smile, hoping I sounded stronger than I felt. With that one shove alone, I'd been painfully reminded that I was not in peak condition quite yet. I couldn't let him know how weak I was. "Don't worry. You can join her."

"I knew I shouldn't have let him keep you here," Art growled. "I should have made him drag you back by your hair to your own fucking world like a caveman. But he was too afraid they'd find you."

"It's too late. They know I'm here already. See the phone? I got a call in just before you arrived."

A lie, but an effective one as it turned out. Art's eyes flicked to the portable phone lying on the kitchen floor. It had come open when I dropped it, and the battery lay nearby. With that slight distraction, I tried again, lunging toward him. I got a kick in—not as strong as one of my usual ones, particularly since I was still in that fucking gentry dress—but enough to throw him off-balance. He was still stronger and faster, though. He'd dropped the athame earlier and grabbed me with that free hand, wrenching my arm painfully to get me to drop my athame. In his other hand, he held the gun but seemed hesitant to use it.

At last, his hand was too strong, and my fingers unclenched, releasing the blade and leaving me defenseless. Triumphant, Art slammed me back against the cupboard and tried to turn me around, probably to bind my hands. I'd noticed a glitter near his pocket earlier and suspected he had handcuffs on him. I fought him the whole time, refusing to turn around, and with only one hand free, he had a bit of difficulty in maneuvering me.

"Stop struggling, or I'll blow your head off," he yelled. "No one's coming, and you know it. Play nice, or there's nothing that Leith can offer me to keep you alive."

"I doubt that. Your whoring operation seems to bring in a lot of money. Are you going to give that up so easily?"

"There are other ways to get gentry girls," he grunted, still trying to shove me around and subdue me. The unfortunate thing was, he was getting closer. My strength was rapidly fading. "Other people will make deals. I don't need Leith or his half-breed whore to—ah!"

I saw the chair before I saw Markelle. It was the one I'd used to climb through the garage door. Abigail had shoved it aside when she went outside, and now Markelle had snuck up and clobbered Art with it from behind. It was hardly a blow to render him unconscious, but it caused him to release me and stagger back. Markelle immediately scrambled away, but Art's attention wasn't on her. His eyes were back on me. Weak or not, I knew I had to use that opening to take him down. I surged forward again, fists ready and—

He shot me.

So help me, that bastard shot me. The bullet took me in the right shoulder, and I flew back against the cupboards, sinking down to the floor as my left hand instinctively flew to the wound to stop the blood. Art walked swiftly toward me, gun pointed down. "The next one goes through your heart," he said. "Now turn around and put your hands behind your back."

"I'm kind of fucking bleeding here," I snapped back. My shoulder was on fire, and I couldn't even really move my arm. "How much more incapacitated could I get?"

His smile was bitter. "Eugenie, you won't be incapacitated enough until you're dead."

I saw Markelle come up behind him again. Her chair was gone, but her fists were out as she pounded him on the back, desperately trying to get him away from me. It was noble and tugged at my heart, but I wanted to yell at her to get the hell out of here. She was no more than a mosquito to him. With ease, he turned around and backhanded her, and I swear, she hit the floor harder than I had when I was shot.

In those fleeting seconds, I snaked one of my feet out as hard as I could manage and hit Art in the shin. He stumbled, leg buckling, but didn't fall. The gun, however, did fall from his hands. It hit the floor with a clatter and slid far out of my reach— but not out of Cariena's. She'd apparently been standing on the far side of the kitchen this entire time. When the gun slid up to her, the timid girl didn't hesitate. She picked it up—screaming as her fingers made contact with the metal and poly-mers—and slid it back across the floor to me.

I grabbed it. All the while, Art's eyes had been following the gun's journey, so when it came to my hand, he was facing me. I had the gun aimed in a flash, and while I wasn't a great shot with my left hand, I wasn't horrible either. No hesitation: I fired. The bullet bit into his chest, and he fell back-ward, blood immediately pouring from the wound. I'd hit the mark.

Markelle and Cariena ran up to me, Raina following moments later. "Are you all right?" exclaimed Markelle.

"Me?" I asked incredulously. "He smacked you across the room."

She shrugged. "They've done worse since I've been here."

Between the three of them, they managed to help me to my feet without putting too much pressure on the wounded shoulder. Raina attempted some of her healing magic—maybe I'd been too quick to dismiss their powers after all—and we found ban-dages to wrap the wound. Her power only lessened the pain; she could do nothing more extensive.

"It's made of iron," she said apologetically. Of course it was. Art would have had it loaded for wayward gentry.

"It's okay. I'm fine." We were back in the kitchen, and I was leaning against the counter, attempting to straighten the bandage. We were all kind of trying to ignore Art's body. "Okay. I can try to call for help again, but I think we need to get out of here on foot. I know where the gateway is, and it's kind of a long ways, but we should be able to—"

"Eugenie? What's going on?"

I'd set the gun on the counter while tugging my bandages straight, but in the blink of an eye, the revolver was back in my left hand, pointed toward the new addition in the kitchen. I knew the voice before I saw the face. How could I not? I'd been listening to that voice over and over this whole week, both sleeping and awake. A voice that was a contradiction because it promised love and devotion while only delivering pain and humiliation.

I'd numbed out the worst of it with sheer will and the nightshade's effects. But now, pumped full of adrenaline, on the verge of escape and in control of my senses, the true magnitude of it all slammed into me. The horror. The terror. The helplessness. Emotion after emotion burned through me, but in the space of a breath, my mind immediately dispatched any feelings that wouldn't help me right now. That left only the dark ones. Rage. Fury. Malice.

I tightened my hold on the gun and narrowed my eyes at the man I hated most in the world.

"Hello, Leith."

Chapter Twenty-Five

Leith stood there, frozen, eyes on the gun. Finally, swallowing, he slowly lifted his gaze to my face. He was pale, so pale that he could have been on the verge of passing out.

"Eugenie . . . you're hurt . . . are you okay? There's blood on your bandage . . ."

I didn't doubt it and didn't bother to check. "Stop it. Just stop your fucking concerned act. I don't want to hear it."

In the corners of my eyes, I saw the gentry girls edge their way toward me like some sort of honor guard. I started to tell them to back off, but Leith had no real magic, and I was the one with the gun.

"What are you . . . ? It—it's not an act, I swear it. I care about you. I love you."

"Love me?" I snarled. "People in love don't fucking drug and rape other people!"

"It wasn't rape. Did I ever hurt you? Did I beat you?"

For a moment, I was so stunned that I couldn't even speak. "You . . . you're serious, aren't you?

You really believe that? You really believe you didn't do anything wrong!"

"It was the only way I could convince you . . . the only way I could convince you that we're meant to be together. Normal courtship didn't work. Neither did Mother's attempt to just capture you and bring you to the Rowan—"

"Her attempt to what?"

"She used her magic to bind the power of several animals together and—"

"Jesus Christ! That was her?" Katrice had sent Smokey to bring me back for Leith. Lovely. Girard had mentioned her love of woodland animals but not her ability to control them.

"Look," Leith rambled desperately. "We'd be a great team—you know we would. We'd have two kingdoms. You saw what I was able to do to help yours! With your power and my ingenuity—"

"Ingenuity?" I cried. I would have laughed it wasn't all so horrible. "You have none! You've got a tiny bit more technological know-how than the average gentry, but everything else you stole from humans. You traded it in exchange for these girls' self-respect. You didn't even have the balls to kidnap from your own people!"

Again, much like when he'd raped me, I wished he'd be more belligerent. This idyllic, faux love was worse. It made everything he'd done to me worse. I could feel my temper surging, anger racing through me. I could hardly see because of my fury. Or maybe it was the blood loss. Odder still was a strange shift in the air, a cooling off. It had been humid and stuffy before, but it was definitely cooler now. Not in the way that heralded Volusian appearance but something different altogether that I couldn't quite put my finger on.

"I won't do it again, I swear. If that's what you want, if that's what'll make you happy and let us be together . . ."

He took a step toward me, and I fired a warning shot that just cleared his arm and hit the cupboard behind him. He promptly stopped moving, face going paler still.

"Don't move!" I screamed. "Don't even think about touching me."

I still couldn't believe it, still couldn't believe he was going on like this. I kept thinking about what it had been like in bed with him, that forcing and total violation of my body. Once more, there was a slight shift in the air, and I realized what it was. The barometric pressure. I didn't know how I knew, but I did. It was dropping. Rapidly. Ozone wafted through the air.

"I love you," he said in a small voice.

"You are a self-centered, fucking asshole rapist," I replied evenly. "And I—*I* am the Thorn Queen." As the words left my mouth, I suddenly understood what Dorian had meant about me needing to believe I was queen. In that moment, I did. And a person like Leith did not do something like that to someone like me.

"I'm the Thorn Queen," I repeated. Now the air stirred, around us, causing the curtains to flutter and a few things to fall off the counter. "And you are going to pay for what you've done."

"Eugenie, stop. Put the gun down."

I lifted my eyes from Leith's cringing form, and this time, I did laugh—but it was more of a choking sound. Kiyo, Dorian, and Roland stood in the entrance to the kitchen. My saviors. After leaving that front door open when Art had come home, it was like anyone could just traipse right in.

"Jesus Christ," I said. "You guys are a little too late."

It was Kiyo who had spoken, his face tense and worried. "Everyone needs to calm down. You got him, Eugenie. It's over. Put the gun away now."

Roland was tense too, his face unreadable as he stood with his own gun. Beside him, Dorian didn't seem overly worried, but there was none of that usual laughter on his face.

"You don't know what he's done," I growled. "You keep talking about mercy, but at some point it has to end. He needs to die." The wind grew stronger. Some of my hair whipped in my face, but I had no free hand to brush it aside.

"I didn't do anything!" exclaimed Leith. He looked to the other men, face desperate and pleading. "I won her fairly. You know how it is. Back in the old days, that's how it was. The man who caught the queen became king. If she's pregnant, she's my common-law wife."

I saw disgust on Roland's face, his hand tightening on the gun. He started to lift it, but Kiyo, still apparently the spokesperson, made a small motion that caused my stepfather to lower the gun back down. Slightly. "That tradition is like a thousand years old," Kiyo told Lieth. "It means nothing anymore. She's not yours."

"Besides," I said, my gaze back on Leith. "Do you really think I'd have your baby if I didn't want to? If I'm pregnant, it's an easy problem to fix."

His mouth dropped open. "You wouldn't . . . that's blasphemous . . ."

And indeed it was among the child-hungry gentry. Abortion was nothing I relished either, but there was no way on this earth I would bear a child born of such brutality. A gust of wind suddenly picked up considerably, nearly knocking me over. The kitchen window shattered.

Kiyo was still unmoved. "Eugenie, stop it. Stop the magic. Put the gun down. We'll take him and the girls back. We'll deal with him in the Otherworld."

"How can you say that?" I shouted. "You heard him! How can you let him walk after all this? You don't know what he's done!"

"He doesn't necessarily have to go free," argued Kiyo. "There are other ways."

A blinding flash suddenly burst in the kitchen, leaving me dazzled and unable to see for a moment. At the same instance, there was a crackling roar, so loud that I thought my eardrums would burst. And like that, the means to control lightning clicked in my brain. I understood the patterns, what I needed to summon it—and how to work my emotion into it as Ysabel had said.

I set the gun on the counter. "I don't need this," I told Leith. The wind was roaring around us now, knocking objects everywhere, blowing my hair like a cloud of fire. I was the center of the storm. A very, very faint roll of thunder—nowhere near as loud as the last one—sounded around us. I turned my gaze to Leith, wondering if my violet eyes had darkened the way Storm King's had when angry. "I'm going to suck the air from you and then blast you out of existence with lightning."

Leith sank to his knees. "Please . . . please don't do this . . ." The same words I'd uttered to him the first time he'd assaulted me.

The storm raged more strongly around me. "I'm the Storm Queen," I said in a low voice. "And you will pay for what you've done to me."

Kiyo took a step forward. I knew him well enough to guess his thoughts. He was considering attacking me but too greatly feared what I could do with the magic as it grew stronger and stronger. He made one last desperate plea.

"If you care anything about your people—about those girls—you won't do this. He's a prince. You kill him, and his mother will declare war on you. You think the drought was bad? Imagine armies sweeping in and devastating your land. Villages burned. Innocent people killed. Is that what you want? Can you do that to them?"

Around us, the storm raged, and within me, my hate for Leith was a storm of its own, a poison running through my veins. I wanted him to suffer. I wanted him blighted. I wanted him dead. He could not be allowed to be free of his sins. And yet . . . somewhere in all that hate, all that fury, Kiyo's words penetrated. *Is that what you want? Can you do that to them?*

I stared at Leith for several more heavy seconds. And then, bit by bit, the storm began to recede. No more lightning. The wind faded. Clouds vaporized. The pressure rose to levels similar to those outside. Leith sagged in relief, and I noticed how ragged my breathing was from the exertion of such power.

"No," I said softly, feeling all the energy run out of me. I was tired. So, so tired. "I don't want a war. I . . . I can't unleash something like that."

Then, for the first time so far, Dorian spoke.

"I can," he said.

And before anyone really realized what was happening, he strode across the kitchen. His sword came out from its sheath, brilliant and deadly in the light, and he plunged it straight into Leith's body. The Rowan Prince stiffened, eyes going wide, as Dorian pushed the blade further into Leith's stomach.

Time stood still for all of us. I don't think anyone—well, except for Dorian—really believed it had happened. A moment later, Dorian jerked the sword out in one swift, harsh motion. Leith's body fell to the ground. Dorian had used the new sword, I realized, the iron-laced one Girard had made. Blood poured out from where it had impaled Leith, as well as from his lips. It was a hundred times worse than the mess Art had left, and as that deep red liquid pooled and pooled, a bizarre image of blooming roses floated across my mind. I wondered if I was going to pass out.

Kiyo surged forward, like he might save Leith, but we all knew it was too late. The prince was already dead. Kiyo turned to Dorian in rage. "What have you done?"

Dorian's face was calm, voice smooth as he slid the sword—blood and all—back into its sheath. "What you should have done."

Kiyo stared at Dorian, who returned the gaze squarely. Kiyo's face was a mixture of many things: outrage, shock, fear. "You have no idea what you've done . . . what you've unleashed . . . what you've unleashed on *her* . . ."

Dorian glanced down at Leith's body, then Art's, and then back to Leith. The look of contempt on his face clearly showed just how beneath his acknowledgment they were. They were not even worth his notice, not even worth regarding as people as far as Dorian was concerned. He looked back up at Kiyo.

"I know what I've done. And do you think I'd really abandon her to the consequences? Leave her alone to them? Besides . . ." A wry smirk crossed Dorian's face. "I'm the one who did it. I'm the one Katrice will come after."

Kiyo shook his head. "No. She'll come after both of you. You shouldn't have done it."

After what felt like an eternity, my voice had finally come back to me. I wet my lips, trying to speak. "Maybe," I whispered. "Maybe he should have . . ."

Silence fell over us all, thick and heavy. Kiyo gave me a look . . . I couldn't fully interpret it. "You're in shock. You don't what you're saying. We'll get you and the girls back to the Otherworld. Art's records might show us how to track the others."

I looked back and forth between his and Dorian's faces. I wouldn't go so far as to say I hated all men, exactly, but suddenly, I just couldn't be with either of them, even though I loved them both. Plus, at the moment, I didn't want anything to do with the Otherworld. I shook my head.

"No. Take the girls . . . I'm not going."

Dorian arched an eyebrow. "What will you do?"

I turned toward Roland for the first time in a while. He still had his gun, but it was lowered now. He'd been ready to attack the whole time but had been content to let the other two men take the lead in this. Later, I would have to find out how this motley crew had banded together. Right now . . . right now I was more concerned with the look on Roland's face. He was regarding me like he didn't know me. I felt a piece of my heart break.

"I want . . ." And to my shame, I felt tears burn in my eyes, which was just stupid. Throughout this entire week, I'd never cried. I'd taken it all straight-faced. I'd fought and killed today without remorse. Now . . . now it was like a lifetime of sorrow was coming out of me. "I want to go home," I said. The tears escaped, running down my cheeks. "I want to see my mom."

For a second, I thought Roland was going to turn away, condemn me as the half-gentry he'd always feared I would turn into, the one who'd lied to him about her involvement in the Otherworld. I think if he had turned away, I would have died then and there. Instead, he held out his hand. I couldn't actually bring myself to take it. I didn't think I could let anyone touch me right now. I loved all the men here, but right now, I was inexplicably afraid of them.

Still, I felt safe leaving with Roland. Roland was my father. Understanding my feelings, he lowered his hand and simply beckoned. I approached him, stepping over the bodies in the kitchen.

"Okay," Roland said softly, his own eyes shining with tears. "Let's go home."

Chapter Twenty-Six

It was no secret: my mother hated Otherworldly things. Her feelings weren't that hard to understand, considering that she'd been a prisoner there, serving as Storm King's forced mistress—not unlike my own experiences now. Just as she tried to ignore what Roland and I did for a living, she also tried to ignore the gentry blood in me, treating me as though I were fully human and often refusing to hear otherwise.

Therefore, I was a bit surprised that she took everything better than Roland did when we got back to Tucson. I knew they had discussions when I wasn't around. He filled her in on what had happened in Yellow River, how I'd been practicing magic on the sly, and how I was now the reigning monarch of a fairy kingdom. He told her about Leith too. If she was shocked by any of it, if she was repulsed by it and hated me for what I'd become . . . well, she never let on. She was just . . . well, my mother.

She set me up in my old bedroom. It hadn't

changed much over the years and even still had the same glow-in-the-dark stars I'd stuck to the ceiling. When I'd put them there in my youth, she had fretted that they'd never come off without ripping out part of the paint. So, I guess she'd never bothered in all these years.

Roland knew someone who knew someone who came and did a field surgery on my shoulder, removing the bullet and leaving me with pain meds and antibiotics. That was about all I saw of Roland in those initial days of recovery. It was my mom who stayed with me the most, talking about anything that wasn't Otherworldly and making sure I had entertainment in the form of books and TV. I could pay little attention to those diversions, though, not when my mind was on so many other things. I would turn the events of the previous weeks over and over in my head until I grew too weary to string any coherent thoughts together. When I reached that exhausted point, I would usually just let my mind go blank for a while. It was oddly soothing, particularly since I so often woke up from nightmares about Leith. An empty mind was sometimes welcome.

And it was my mother I went to when my period came. She'd already bought a pregnancy test too, just for peace of mind. When it came out negative, I stared sobbing. My mom held me in bed and rocked me the whole time, saying, "I know, baby, I know." It was odd because *I* didn't even know why I was crying. The negative test was a good thing, and I was glad there were no loose ends with Leith. As she held me—the first time I'd really let anyone touch me since Art's house—I suddenly wondered how she had felt when she was pregnant with me. Had she been repulsed by the thought of the half-gentry child forced on her? Had she wanted to get rid of me but been unable to in the Otherworld? I shuddered, not wanting to ponder that too much. Thinking I was cold, she went and got me a sweater.

It was a few days later that Roland and I finally talked. I was more mobile then and had come downstairs to make a bowl of cereal in the kitchen. He strolled in and joined me, sitting at the table with his coffee. His face seemed to have more lines than the last time I'd seen him. My fault, no doubt.

"I'm sorry," I said when the silence grew too hard to bear. "I . . . I should have told you."

He looked up from his cup. "Which part exactly?"

"All of it. Everything. I . . ." I sighed. "You were always so mad that I was spending time in the Otherworld at all. I thought you'd be upset if you knew the rest."

"Oh, believe me, I'm much more upset to hear it *now* than I would have been then."

"I'm sorry," I said again, not knowing what else

to say. "It all just happened so fast. There was that fight with Aeson—"

"I know, I know. Kiyo gave me the details of that, though he too was a bit surprised to find out you can conjure up hurricanes worthy of Storm King now."

I shook my head. "I'm a long way from that. And once I started learning the magic . . . I just can't stop."

Now Roland sighed. "He's been by a couple of times."

It took me a moment to realize he meant Kiyo, not Storm King. "I'm not ready to see him."

"I know." There was a pause, and I think it took a lot for Roland to say his next words. "He's not so bad. Relatively speaking."

I gave him a sad half-smile. "Yeah, he's great." And I meant it . . . but something was bothering me about Kiyo, something that kept nudging me in the back of my head. I continued to ignore it.

"So what happens now?" Roland asked. "What are you going to do?"

I stared in surprise. "Well . . . what else would I do? The same thing I've been doing."

"What, running back and forth between the worlds, trying to act like you have some semblance of a normal life?"

The tone of his voice hurt me. "What do you expect me to do? And it's not like our lives have ever been normal."

He shook his head. "This is different. You can't do this. You can't literally live in two worlds."

I munched on my cereal for a moment to give me a chance to think. "I don't really see that I have a choice. That land is bound to me. If I neglect it, it dies."

Roland said nothing.

"Oh, come on! You think I should do that? Abandon it and let all those people suffer? You're as bad as Art." The mystery of what had happened to Art's body and to Abigail was ... well, a mystery. No one had told me exactly, save that it had "been taken care of."

Roland's eyes flashed with anger. "No, I'm nothing like him. Don't ever make that mistake. But the gentry aren't our people. They aren't your people."

"They are now," I said, surprising myself.

He stood up, his entire posture weary and defeated. "I don't know what to think anymore. I don't know what to think of you. I don't even feel like I know you."

In all these years together, he'd never raised a hand to me. But in that moment, it was like he'd slapped me. "What does that mean?" I asked. I meant to sound defiant. Instead, my words came out very small and very scared, much like a pleading child's. I remembered how grateful I'd been to see him at Art's. My father. My protector. "Do you not ... do you not love me anymore?"

He'd started to walk away but paused to look back. His blue eyes took me in for several moments. "Of course. I will always love you. You're my daughter. But . . . I'm not sure if things can ever be the same."

Roland walked out of the kitchen, and that's when I realized it was time for me to leave.

Tim nearly knocked me over when I got back to my own house. My mom had called him to tell him I was okay when I'd first come to her place, but between my recovery week and the week at Art's with no contact, Tim had done a fair amount of freaking out.

"What happened? Are you okay? I dealt with Lara while you were gone. You would have been proud." I smiled, more pleased that he'd called her by her first name instead of "bitch secretary." "Do you want me to make you something?"

"You sound like my mom," I teased. "Always wanting to feed me."

He shrugged. "You're too skinny. And I don't say that lightly, considering the kinds of girls I go after."

He was right both about me and his choice in women. They'd fed me at Art's, but I'd hardly eaten any of it. I'd lost a lot of weight, and while part of me wanted to bulk back up by tapping the bag of Milky Way candy bars in my pantry, I knew I should probably be delving into some serious nutrition for a change. So, I dispatched Tim to cook up some steak stir-fry, a request he was more than eager to accomodate.

I spent the rest of the day restless and bored, unsure of what to do with myself. I did some laundry, despite Tim's protests that he could do it, and scarfed down lots of his stir-fry. The animals were all there, which led me to believe Kiyo was still staying there too. After I'd refused to see him at my parents', I half-expected him to have moved out.

Honestly, I wasn't sure what to do now. I didn't plan on going to the Otherworld anytime soon, and there was no way—as I told Lara later on the phone—that I could take any new jobs for a while. This made both Tim and her nervous about my accounting, but I knew my savings account was at least temporarily secure.

My magic I left completely alone. I wasn't going near that, even though there were times the air and the water vapor around me would call to me like a siren's song, and I'd burn to touch them. The one bit of magic I did use was shamanic: I tried to summon Volusian. He didn't come. I wasn't sure what to think of that.

I was almost grateful for nightfall so that I could go to bed and stop trying to figure out things to pass the time. I wondered if this apathy was just a natural consequence of the trauma I'd been through, some kind of numbed state. TV, my puzzles, even Tim's cheery chatter . . . none of it could hold my attention. I wasn't bored, exactly. I just wasn't very engaged with the world.

That night, just as I used to do, I dreamed of the Thorn Land. The dream was so vivid and real. It was like I'd stepped outside my own home to go walking in the foothills, like my soul was traveling on without my body. The air was sharp and clean, filled with the fragrance of desert flowers. The sun was warm and merciless—yet comforting in its familiarity. And the colors . . . the colors made my dream self want to weep. Peaches and greens and all the colors of the cacti flowers looking up at the clear blue, blue of the sky. For the first time since my capture and rape, I felt at peace. I felt whole and healed in the dream.

I woke up with a longing in my chest, like there was a piece of me missing. The sharpness of it startled me—and scared me a little. Tossing on a robe, I made my way out to the kitchen, hoping coffee and breakfast would shake of that all-consuming desire to run to the Otherworld.

"Kiyo," I exclaimed. He sat at the table with coffee, both dogs at his feet. I had a weird déjà vu from coffee with Roland yesterday and suspected there was "a talk" in store for me.

"Eugenie," he said, looking up from the paper. His eyes were warm and chocolate-brown, filled with so much love. He rose from his chair and approached me, arms open. I started to go into his embrace but something made me shrink back, some protective instinct of my body's to keep itself

safe. I knew he wasn't Leith. I knew Kiyo loved me
. . . but there was just something within me that
was afraid to touch anyone else. My mother was
the only one I'd allowed to hug me so far.

Sadness and hurt flashed through Kiyo's eyes at
my rejection, but he seemed to understand.
Awkwardly, he simply gave me a soft touch on the
arm, which I allowed with only a slight flinch. We
both sat down—after I'd fetched coffee—and he
drank me in with those intense eyes, like he hadn't
seen me in years. Of course, these last two weeks
or so had certainly felt like years to me, so perhaps
that wasn't such a bad comparison.

"How are you?" he asked. "I've missed you so
much. I've been so worried."

"I'm okay. I was in good hands."

"How's your shoulder?"

I gave it a slight shrug. "Stiff. But mending. I
could probably go over to the Otherworld and get
someone to patch it right up."

His face instantly darkened. "I think you need
to stay away from there for a while."

"Jesus Christ. Not you too. I'm that land's ruler.
I have to go back." A flash of the dream came
back to me. It was more than some subconscious
musing, I knew. The Thorn Land and I were tied.
We couldn't stay apart. I had known that being
away from it would cause it to die, and now I was
realizing that I might die without it as well.

"There has to be a way. I was talking to

Maiwenn, and she's going to look into it. Surely, somewhere in the pages of their history, someone gave up their kingdom without dying."

"Is that a good idea?" I asked. "Me giving it up?"

"Of course," he said, shocked. "You've never wanted it. You've said so a hundred times. It'd be better for everyone. The next person bound to the land probably wouldn't transform it into a desert. You'd be free, able to go on with your life here, free of the magic . . ."

I narrowed my eyes. "I'll never be free of that either."

"Yeah," he agreed, stiffness in his voice, "but there'll be less temptation outside of the Otherworld. Why the hell didn't you tell me you were learning all that stuff?"

"I did tell you! I told you about Dorian sending Ysabel."

"What I saw you do in there . . . that was nothing like what you said she taught you."

"It happened fast . . . I didn't realize it half the time myself, and I didn't want to upset you."

"No one learns that fast," he muttered. I remembered Shaya's words. *Storm King did.*

"Well, I'm apparently not all-powerful. I lost hold of Volusian during that ordeal. He didn't come when I called."

"Oh. I thought you knew."

"Knew what?"

"He's bound to Dorian now."

I stared for several seconds. "Oh my God. I thought that might happen . . ."

Kiyo stared back. "You did? Then why the hell did you send him to Dorian? Why not send him to warn me?"

"For exactly that reason! If Volusian broke from my control, I knew Dorian could probably bind him."

"I suppose. But I feel like you've just given Dorian a nuclear warhead."

I didn't say it, but I had a feeling Kiyo was more upset that it was Dorian I'd contacted for help and not him.

"And that's how you found me, right? Volusian told Dorian, who then told you and Roland?" I'd heard it from Roland but wanted to hear it again.

Kiyo nodded. "We'd been looking for you as soon as you disappeared after the battle. None of us had a clue what had happened. We got Roland involved a few days later to help with a hunt in this world, but none of us . . ." He shook his head. "None of us had any idea that that's what had happened to you."

Awkward silence fell, each of us thinking about the things neither of us would give voice to. My imprisonment. My rape. I lowered my eyes, playing with the edge of the coffee cup. The memories were like a rollercoaster. Sometimes they'd sink way down low into the bottom of my mind. Other times, they'd flare up sharply,

447

pushing to the forefront of my mind and unleashing all the dizzying, horrible feelings of fear, violation, and helplessness that ordeal had caused.

I suddenly looked up sharply and met Kiyo square in the eyes. "Why didn't you let me kill Leith when I had the chance?" With a shiver, I remembered the vengeance burning within me and the storm swirling around me.

The question clearly caught Kiyo off-guard. "What? You know why. Because of the political fallout . . . because you're not the kind of person given to revenge . . ."

"Aren't I?" I demanded. I was suddenly angry at him, and it occurred to me right then that I'd been suppressing a lot of it this whole week. "You have no right to talk about when revenge is right. You didn't go through what I did."

"I know," he said, trying to be gentle. "I don't doubt he deserved a horrible punishment. I can only imagine how it was for you—"

"No. There is no *way* you can imagine."

"It's more than just revenge, though. Do you know what's happened in the wake of this? Katrice is massing her armies, Eugenie. The monarchs haven't had an all-out war in ages. This could get very bad. People are going to die. I wanted to save you from that . . . wanted to save you from being her target."

"All right. Then why didn't *you* kill him?"

Dead silence.

"*What?*" Kiyo exclaimed at last.

I never lowered my gaze, astonished at the coldness in my voice. "You said he deserved a horrible punishment."

"Yeah, imprisonment or—"

"Imprisonment? Are you crazy? He's a prince. We couldn't have kept him without the same 'political fallout.' He would have walked."

"Going to war is worse, believe it or not."

"Then you still should have killed him," I repeated. "Everyone keeps going on about how you're 'just' a kitsune. You aren't technically aligned with anyone. Maybe she would have put a hit out on you, but she wouldn't have gone to war against you alone."

Kiyo's eyes were wide. "Are you listening to yourself? This is insane! You're condemning me for not killing a man that was on his knees."

"That man did horrible, awful things. He didn't deserve to walk away unpunished."

Kiyo's shock had given away to anger. "I can't believe you're holding me responsible for this. And you know what? This is the magic talking. The more of it you use, the more it changes you. This is why you need to stay away from the Otherworld! For your own protection. Before you turn into someone you don't want to be."

"Oh, now you want to protect me! Look, you of all people should understand. I can't stay away

449

from the Otherworld. I can't stay away from this world. I don't belong anywhere! And yet . . . I belong everywhere. There's no good fit for me. I'm split, Kiyo. I thought you'd get that. You told me before that you did. You're the same."

"It . . . it's different somehow."

"That's not good enough. You're being a hypocrite," I exclaimed. "You make decisions for both of us based on what's convenient at any given time. You think you can handle it one way but that I can't. That's not fair. You can't make different rules for each of us."

"I'm trying to protect you," he repeated.

"You don't think I'm strong enough to handle the things you can?"

He held up his hands. "I don't know. Maybe I'm the one who isn't strong enough to make the tough decisions."

"Dorian is." It was out before I could stop it.

Dead silence, round two, descended on us.

Kiyo finished his coffee. "I see. So that's what this is really about." He stared around, taking in the house and the cats sprawled everywhere. "Maybe . . . maybe it's time I pack up my things."

I crossed my arms. "I think that's a good idea."

"It might take me a day or two to collect these guys, though."

"That's fine." I kept perfect control in my voice, focusing all my energy on sounding flat. If I slipped up, I might start crying or begging him to stay. I might apologize for being so harsh and holding him responsible for not letting me kill Leith. It wasn't fair for me to blame Kiyo and laud Dorian . . .

. . . and yet I did.

Kiyo stood up, saying he'd come back to do a thorough packing when I wasn't around since that might be easier on both of us. I agreed. Tension engulfed us as he moved toward the door. I'd hurt him; I knew it. And truthfully, I didn't fully know if I was making the worst mistake of my life here in breaking up with Kiyo. True, we had been fighting a lot, with him not understanding the choices I'd been having to make. The heart of it was, though, that I felt he'd had the opportunity to protect me . . . and hadn't.

"Eugenie," he said, hovering near the back door. "I know you were hurt. I know you suffered—and still do. And I guess I can see why you think what Dorian did was noble. But it's not. There are big consequences to this, and someday—probably soon—you're going to regret what he did."

I shook my head, still obstinate. "I don't know. Maybe."

"No matter what you think of me, it's not too late. You can make amends with Katrice. You can stop this." There was a desperate, pleading look in his eyes, and I wondered if it was because of his desire for peace or the agony of leaving me. My own hurt over him leaving was steadily growing, but something in his words halted it.

"Make amends? What's that mean?"

"I don't know . . . apologize . . . blame it on Dorian. Maiwenn might negotiate . . ."

My anger spun back up. "I *am* not going to grovel to the woman whose son raped me. And I'm not going to let Dorian get punished for something I should have done myself." Maiwenn didn't even deserve mentioning. "I'll face the consequences, Kiyo. I'm the Thorn Queen."

He gave me a small, sad smile. "Are you sure? Or are you the Storm Queen?"

I frowned. "What?"

"That's what you told Leith. Back in the kitchen."

"No." So much of those memories were fragmented, but I was certain I'd recall that. "I told him I was the Thorn Queen a few times—but good God. Not Storm Queen."

"I heard you. Once you said Storm Queen."

I shook my head, anger returning. "You made a mistake. They sound alike. Easy to mishear."

His smile twitched; his sadness grew. "Not with my hearing."

Kiyo left after that—to where, I didn't know. It didn't matter. My heart was broken, and thinking about him too much was only going to make things worse. Instead, I knew I had to leave too. I had to get out of here—and I knew exactly where I had to go.

I had to go to my kingdom.

Chapter Twenty-Seven

When I crossed over to the castle in the Thorn Land, I was surprised to find Nia sitting on the floor beside my rabbit paperweight. Her knees were drawn up, and her face—which appeared tear-streaked—rested on her knees. Yet, when she saw me, her face lit up like the sun bursting from behind clouds.

"Your majesty!" she cried, springing up. "Some of them said . . . they said you wouldn't come back. But I knew. I knew you would."

The devotion in the girl's eyes was startling. Nia had been another servant passed from Dorian, and it had never occurred to me that she would serve me out of such love.

"Of course I came back," I said softly. "Why wouldn't I?"

She averted her eyes. "After everything that happened, and . . . well, because of Queen Katrice. There are those who assumed you'd abandon us and stay in the world of the humans."

I didn't bother pointing out that abandoning

this land would kill me. I was too shocked by something else. "They thought . . . they thought I'd just start a war and leave?"

"I knew you wouldn't," she said fervently. "I knew you wouldn't."

I gave her a small, comforting smile while a knot twisted in my stomach. "Take me to Shaya and Rurik."

The two of them were surprised by my arrival, but something told me they hadn't doubted I would return either. I could tell by the compassion on Shaya's face that what Leith had done to me was common knowledge. To my surprise, it was Rurik I took the most comfort from. He didn't question my appearance. He offered no sympathies. He simply jumped straight to business.

"We've gathered as many soldiers as we could while you've been gone," he said. "Some are camped outside, and Dorian's said he'll send reinforcements—his military's much larger. The majority of yours is in Highmore. We'll need to determine the best way to distribute them."

For a moment, I felt dizzy as he continued rattling off military strategy. What was going on? What was I doing? I was a girl from Tucson who'd grown up in a middle-class neighborhood. How on earth was I standing here, listening to a fairy soldier explain how to lead a war?

I held up a hand. "Wait . . . before you go any further. Is there . . . is there any way this can be avoided?" Kiyo's words came back to me, and I hated to say what I did next. "Is there any way to make peace?"

Rurik's eyes widened, and shock and anger filled his features. "Peace? After what—"

Shaya silenced him with a gesture of her own. "Yes, actually. Katrice sent a rather long letter about it."

"So . . . we could get her to understand that it . . ." Was an accident? Hardly. "I mean, could Katrice let all of this go, considering Leith started it?"

Shaya cleared her throat uncomfortably, and Rurik looked angry. "Well," she began, "not entirely. For Katrice not to go to war, she demands that we become her subject kingdom and has very specific details on the kinds of tribute and taxes she requires for that. She also . . . she also says that you must marry her nephew in place of her son and tie this kingdom to her through that branch of the family. My impression is she sent a similar list of demands to Dorian—aside from the nephew part—which he refused rather, ah, indelicately."

I stared, my mouth agape. That was not what I had in mind. How could Katrice demand those kinds of things after what Leith had done? How dare she act as though I had done something wrong? Yes, I could imagine her grief for her only son. I wasn't that heartless. Yet . . . what she was suggesting was ludicrous. And if she thought I would ever, ever let another member of her family lay a hand on me . . .

I turned back to Rurik as though the issue of peace with Katrice had never been mentioned. Later, I would ask Shaya to help me compose a formal response to Katrice's letter, something along the lines of *I am the Thorn Queen. Fuck off.*

"What should I do next?" I asked Rurik.

He smiled, a fierce delight in his eyes. "You should speak to the soldiers gathered here and make an official declaration of war. And then you should go to Highmore and speak to the ones there. They don't even know you as their queen yet, let alone the person sending them to fight. *And* you should practice up on your magic, both for battle and to show your own people that that Rowan bitch can't touch you."

I shivered at the feelings his words inspired in me. In Tucson, I'd been trying to hide from my magic, but now it was calling to me again. And with this threat from Katrice—no, this insult from Katrice—there was nothing I wanted more than to summon all the forces of nature and rip her apart.

"Dorian is coming here—today, I think," said Shaya, interrupting my murderous thoughts. "Follow his lead. He knows what to do."

I wasn't entirely sure what that meant. The only thing I felt certain of was that I wasn't quite ready to go over the maps Rurik had laid out and examine all the troop placements he had in mind. I'd always sucked at Risk and had a feeling this would be similar. Besides, I hadn't returned to the Thorn Land to make war—not right at this second, at least. I'd come because of the dream from last night, the dream where I'd felt at peace.

Because at the moment, I felt no peace. A gentry queen wanted to lead armies in and kill my people—and I was supposed to do the same to her. I'd just broken up with my boyfriend, someone I loved dearly, because I—possibly irrationally—held him responsible for not protecting me from an assailant. And as for that assailant . . . well, his face still flashed in my mind, and no matter how much time passed, I couldn't seem to rid myself of that dirty feeling within me or my repulsion at being touched.

I swore to Rurik that I'd talk to him later, that I needed some time to myself first, and left them both for one of the castle's enclosed gardens. It was the one I frequently meditated in, where Shaya was still attempting to grow grass and where Kiyo and I had made love. I sat down there cross-legged, taking in the sun on the orange rocks around me and relishing in the faint breeze that stirred the branches of the mesquite and smoke thorn trees. A tiny lizard scurried off behind a rock, and I heard what sounded like a humming-bird—or a big-ass bee—in a cluster of nearby flowers.

I cleared my mind and tried to communicate with and heal the land like I had before, but for whatever reason, the connection didn't come. Panic seized me. Had the events with Leith broken something within me? Had I lost my ability to revive the kingdom? I sat there sweating, wondering what would happen to the land if I couldn't connect to it. The heat eventually made me sleepy, and I lay down on the grass, my hands digging into the earth.

When I woke up, two things immediate became apparent. First, I felt . . . better. I felt strong and refreshed, and all around me, the colors and scents seemed stronger and more vivid. I still wasn't happy about the impending war, but that horrible feeling in me . . . the bitterness Leith had left . . . well, it had lessened. The air hummed around me, and for a disorienting second, I couldn't tell where I ended and the land began. It was then that I realized why my meditation hadn't worked. I had been in no condition to heal the land. It had had to heal me. I was energized now, ready to do anything. Ready to lead a war.

The other thing I noticed after waking was that Jasmine was sitting right beside me, gray eyes staring into mine. I bolted upright. "What the hell are you doing here?" I exclaimed. "You're not supposed to be loose."

Girard's cuffs were still upon her, and she jerked her head back toward the castle. "I'm not exactly loose."

I followed her motion and saw a dozen guards, all keeping a respectful distance, but all watching Jasmine closely. When Volusian had disappeared, Rurik had undoubtedly increased her security detail.

"Jasmine," I said, "I'm not really in the mood for your banter, okay? Save your whining and insults for a day when I don't have to worry about having caused a war."

Her face was perfectly calm. "I heard what happened to you."

I braced for smugness. "Yeah, I'm sure everyone has."

"I'll fight for you, you know."

"Look, I'm sure—wait. What did you say?" I stared at her, waiting to see that composure crack. It didn't. She was still serious and actually looked older than her age.

"He had no right. I told you before: no one does that to a daughter of Storm King. Not even to you."

I was speechless for a moment, still waiting for a punchline. "Jasmine . . . you hate me."

She nodded. "Yup. But that doesn't change what happened. No one does that to our father either and gets away without punishment. Dorian should stab Katrice too."

I decided not to mention that nothing had been done to our father technically, seeing as he had died years ago. "What will you do exactly?"

"Same thing you will. Fight. Use my magic. Summon monsters."

"But . . . I mean, even if you're trying to, um, protect our family honor, you realize you're still helping me in the process, right? I thought you wanted to destroy me and go have Dad's world-conquering grandson."

"Oh," she said sweetly, "I still do. And I will. But we're going to deal with Katrice first. Our father's heir *cannot* be born from rape. I told you before—only someone worthy. That bastard wasn't, and his mother has to pay for it. Once she's done . . . well, then I'll deal with you. Besides, someone's got to take her kingdom when we kill her. Might as well be me."

Whoa. There were so many parts of Jasmine's logic that were flawed that I didn't even know where to start. I didn't entirely know the story of her own conception, but my mother had been raped. God knew how many other women Storm King had taken advantage of; I found it hypocritical of Jasmine to take such a high moral ground about his heir in light of that. Still, I couldn't deny the fact that she would be useful, and if that was the reasoning it took for her to help me, so be it. It would also be handy to not have her trying to kill me.

"Well, then, thanks," I said at last. I decided not to mention just then that there was no way in hell I would ever let her rule the Rowan Land. Details, details.

Jasmine looked supremely pleased. "So I can go free then, right?"

I scoffed. "Not a chance."

"But I'm helping you!"

"Yeah, and in the same breath, you talked about how you want to usurp me. Look . . ." I glanced back at her guardians. I would have to consult with Rurik about those least likely to try to knock her up, now that Volusian was missing. Some of my soldiers were female. "You can wander the castle more—under guard, of course. And I'll see about . . ." I frowned, suddenly recalling my helpers at Art's house. They were close to Jasmine's age, relatively speaking, and for Markelle at least, I had no doubts whatsoever of her loyalty. I wondered if she might have the makings of a bodyguard/friend. "I'll see about getting someone your own age to hang out with you."

Jasmine scowled. "That's not what I had in mind."

"Yeah, well, your cell in the dungeon is still available."

She gave me her trademark sullen glare and then stormed off back inside. Nonetheless, I felt like she really would help me, and frankly, I was going to need everyone I could find to get me out of this mess. Kiyo had implied that Katrice might call in some allies, and if this became about multiple kingdoms squaring off . . .

I stood up, suddenly feeling ill about it all once more. The flames of passion and initiative that had flared in me earlier began to flicker uneasily. I couldn't do this. I couldn't lead an army. I couldn't go to war. What was I thinking?

Trying to shake off my building panic attack, I headed back toward the castle, wanting to hide in my room for a while. I passed Rurik along the way. He'd apparently been seeking me, hoping I'd go talk to the gathered soldiers and inspire them—particularly since word had come that Dorian was almost here. I nodded quickly, promising anything, so long as I could get a moment to compose myself and summon my earlier confidence. All of this was overwhelming me. I needed to be alone, lest I start crying.

Only, I was apparently still a ways from being left alone. Ysabel was standing outside my bedroom, arms crossed. Apparently, my earlier suspicions had been right. She really did hang out in the hall waiting for me.

"No magic lessons," I told her.

"Magic lessons?" she exclaimed, straightening up. She was as immaculate as ever, her red hair twisted into myriad braids. "I'm never teaching you anything again. My lord is sending me away—and all because of you!"

The land might have healed me, but there were only so many weird revelations I could handle today. Jasmine becoming my ally currently held the lion's share. "What are you talking about?"

"My lord is on his way," she hissed. "And he sent word that I was to pack up my things and be prepared to leave. He has a small group of guards ready to escort me away."

"So?" I shrugged, eyeing my door longingly. "Isn't that what you wanted?"

She took a step toward me. "He's not sending me back to the castle. He's sending me back to my village—back to my children. Don't you understand? He's through with me! He's casting me aside because of you!"

The anger and hate on her face made me guess she'd forgotten I could suffocate her. As it was, she was in my personal space so much that I feared she might actually attempt physical blows. I wanted to tell her that Dorian casting her aside had little to do with me. That was just Dorian's way. Shaya had said Ysabel was one in a string of mistresses who resembled me. He'd grown tired of her, just like the rest, but that wasn't my fault.

Telling her that wouldn't help, though. "I'm sorry. But, I mean, won't you be glad to see your kids?"

"Glad?" she cried. "What do I have to give them? What do I have to show for my time at court? I have nothing. I came to Dorian's court to improve my children's lives—to bring us wealth. Now I have to return empty-handed, tossed aside to our backwoods village."

Ouch. I didn't know what to say, didn't know whether to laud a mother's attempts to improve her kids' lives or look down on someone who'd tried to do it via sleeping with a king.

"I'm sorry," I said wearily. "I'm sure you'll figure out something."

I started to turn away, and to my astonishment, she grabbed my shoulder and spun me toward her. I think she'd been about to hurl an insult, but I gave her no chance. I still wasn't ready to be touched, and she'd caught me off guard. With no second thoughts, my instincts summoned up magic, the air shoving her away from me and slamming her—hard—into a wall. She stood there, dazed, and I gasped, horrified at what I'd brutally done without even thinking. I really was turning into my father's daughter.

"Are you okay?" I asked, stepping toward her when she didn't move.

She jerked away from me, which I hoped meant no concussion. "This isn't over. I will never forgive you for taking him from me! I'll make you pay. He's mine. Do you understand? *Mine*."

This was followed by a whole tirade of ranting and insults about how much she hated me and would see me destroyed. She kept her distance, though, so apparently my brief lapse into violence had done some good. After a while, I had no patience for it and simply went into my bedroom, leaving her out there. I locked the door but could still hear her going on and on.

Remembering Rurik saying that I should go out and talk to the people who could possibly be dying for me, I tried to distract myself from Ysabel by looking through the room's closet. I figured I should probably wear something gentry, and Nia had kept me well-stocked. The spark was re-kindling in me, that need to take revenge against Leith and show Katrice we couldn't be pushed around. I would prove a strong leader for those out there. I was pulling out a silvery blue silk dress that looked suitable when Ysabel's shouting finally stopped. With a sigh of relief, I started to drape the dress over a chair—and caught a glimpse out the small window.

There was an army out there.

I immediately backed away, trying to block out the sea of faces encamped outside. I dropped the dress, feeling dizzy. The reality of it all hit me, and I again felt helpless and out of my league. A sharp knock sounded on the door, momentarily breaking through my panic. Anger was an easier emotion to deal with, and I hurried over, yanking the door open.

"Look, I told you there's nothing I can do about—"

I stopped. It wasn't Ysabel outside my door.

It was Dorian.

Chapter Twenty-Eight

"Oh," I said lamely, stepping aside so that he could enter. "I thought you were someone else."

"Someone in a velvet dress shrieking at the top of her lungs?" he asked. He moved past me in that graceful way of his, and I noticed he was careful to keep a healthy distance between us without being asked, as though he suspected my aversion to touch.

"Something like that." I shut the door.

He shrugged and immediately found the room's wine. "She won't bother you anymore," he said, pouring a cup. "I'm sending her away."

"Yeah, she told me. You know, I feel kind of bad for her."

"Stop," he ordered. "She's none of your concern. She should have had no expectations about her relationship with me."

"Yeah, well, she kind of did."

"Again, one angry person is none of your concern—not with everything else going on."

I grimaced. "I suppose not, though it sure seems like a lot of people are angry at me—oh. God. I nearly forgot. Do you have Volusian?"

Dorian was setting his sword and cloak down. He didn't look happy at the reference. "Yes . . . I enslaved him to me."

"Can I . . . can I have him back?"

He eyed me. "Are you sure that's what you want? It'd be better if we banished him together."

I hesitated, recalling Volusian's hands on my throat and knowing what would happen if I ever lost control again. I wouldn't, though. I would stay strong, and I needed him for what was to come. "Yes," I said firmly. "I want him back."

Dorian shrugged. "Then I'll summon him later. Let's not ruin the moment just yet. He's quite depressing, you know." Dorian strolled toward the window and bent over, picking up the dress I'd dropped. "This is lovely."

"I was going to put it on, but . . . but . . ." I swallowed and nodded toward the window. "There's a, um, army out there."

He neatly laid the dress on the chair and glanced out the window. "Yes. Yes, there is. Yours and mine. Well, part of them."

"I can't believe this happened."

"Hiding from them won't make them go away."

"I kind of hoped it would."

He said nothing but gave me an expectant look. Something about it drew me out, and steeling myself up, I approached the window again, staring out at the wide, sandy stretch in the back of the castle.

There were so many more than I'd expected— and this was only allegedly a portion of the soldiers that would be fighting Katrice. My small army in their mismatched attire stood to formation on one side. Dorian's "reserves" stood beside them, much more sharply dressed in deep green shirts under their leather armor and golden oak emblems. So many . . . and again, still not the whole force. More of his soldiers would join up, and then my numbers would grow when the call went out throughout the land when I went to Highmore—if I went there.

"All of this," I murmured, "all of this because of a chain of decisions. Me refusing Leith, him kidnapping me, you . . ." I couldn't finish the words, but Dorian and I both knew what I'd been about to say.

"Do you regret it?" he asked. "What I did?" He sounded as cool and confident as ever, but I could have sworn there was a tiny note of fear in his voice—fear that he'd done something I hadn't wanted.

Kiyo's words about how I would regret all this came back to me, and I kept wondering if it was really worth it, all these men and women who might die . . . for what? For my honor? My revenge? I could still respond to Katrice's message, tell her I'd marry her nephew and make peace . . .

A knot formed in my stomach, and I knew that wasn't an option. I could never be with anyone in that family, not without thinking of Leith, of his hands and his body. I could never let her or anyone else think I or my people could be pushed around. After all, Leith hadn't just taken advantage of me. Those girls had suffered too. I was the protector of my people. I was the Thorn Queen and the Thorn Land both.

An image of Dorian running his sword through Leith returned to my mind. Probably I should have found it gruesome. Instead, it brought me . . . peace.

"No." I turned and looked straight into Dorian's eyes. "I don't regret it. I . . . I'm glad you did it." My voice wavered a little. "I'm so glad you did it."

His face transformed somewhat, filled with a type of wonder. I think he'd grown so accustomed to my usual style, my human way of being rational and merciful . . . Well, I think he'd been long bracing himself for my wrath. My earlier suspicion about the worry in his voice had been correct. He'd probably expected a reaction similar to when he'd given me the Thorn Land.

The look on his face made me flustered and confused. I turned back to the window and admitted, "But I . . . I'm scared. I don't want to wage a war. I certainly don't know how to."

Dorian came to stand beside me, still careful to maintain a buffer between us. "It's in your blood," he said. "Storm King was the greatest tactician in centuries."

"I'm not him. I don't want to be like him." A nasty voice spoke in my head: *But you called yourself Storm Queen, according to Kiyo.*

"You can inherit his genius without his cruelty," said Dorian.

"I suppose, but still . . . I still don't know what to do. Will you help me?"

We turned to look at each other, and again, his face seemed to be lit from within. "Of course. You're not the only one Katrice is after. I'm the one who killed the poor bastard, remember?" The light faded from his face a bit at the reference to Leith. He leaned toward me, eyes intense. "I'd do it a thousand times over, if I could. War or not."

That earnestness in voice, that fierceness—it sent a shiver down my spine. "You only say that because we haven't gone to war yet. You don't know what's going to happen."

"Ah, Eugenie. I know. We will be victorious, you and me. We're the strongest monarchs in this world. Katrice knows this but is blinded by her grief and rage. You and I will lead this army, and we will conquer the Rowan Land. We'll split it between us, adding on to our own kingdoms . . . and from there, we can go anywhere. We could rule half this world together—all of this world—

you and me. Kingdom after kingdom would fall to us . . ."

I stared him, almost caught up in his vision. The apprehension I'd been holding began to lift as I imagined us destroying her forces and me summoning up storms that made the world tremble. I laughed uneasily, alarmed at the way my thoughts had gone. "One kingdom's enough," I said, the human part of me bringing me back to earth.

"You say that now, but I tell you, it's in your blood." He looked down at me intently, and those rapture-filled eyes seemed to be every shade of green and gold in the world. I fell into them. I felt beautiful in them. Like a goddess. "Eugenie, you're going to be a warrior queen the likes of which no one has ever seen. Your name will live on when Storm King's has faded to dust. You will lead your armies on—powerful, fearless, and beautiful. Katrice's 'war' is but a skirmish you'll stamp out underneath your boot."

I had a disorienting moment then, recalling a vision I'd had in the Underworld. My soul had been seeking Kiyo's, but it was Dorian I'd seen in a dream-like state, with the two of us standing on a cliff before armies, both of us radiant and majestic. There'd been a baby in my arms and a crown on my head.

I'd never told anyone about that. It had been a test, not a vision of the future. Trying to keep things light with Dorian, I asked, "And where will you be in all of this? Somehow I don't think you'll be lurking in the shadows."

"My sweet Eugenie," he said, back to his flippant, gallant self, "there you go, always suspecting ulterior motives." He straightened up, affecting a dignified air. "I, of course, shall be by your side."

I laughed. Dorian would always be Dorian. "Sharing in that glory and power, no doubt."

"A little, certainly." His mirth vanished, and he grew serious once more. "But also there to keep you safe. Whatever battles you engage in, whether you choose to conquer this world or simply go back to exorcising ghosts . . . what happened with Leith will never, *never* happen again. Not while I live. I swear it. I will always keep you safe." He moved forward but was still careful not to touch me. The vehemence in his voice was so strong, however, that it was practically tangible. "*Always.*"

My smile was gone. I studied him for a long time and realized I believed him. Kiyo had failed me. Dorian would not.

And I realized then that I'd been an idiot to keep trying to push Dorian away. Did I entirely trust his motives? No. I did trust him to protect me, though. I'd realized just before my capture that I loved both him and Kiyo, loved them just as my blood and soul were also split in two. The two halves of my nature would always war with each other. And right now, I didn't need the cautious human half that would rationally seek peace. I needed the part of me that wasn't afraid to unleash all the power I had, to charge forward with no restraints. I needed Dorian right now. It was his love that was going to allow me to be strong and unafraid of what was to come.

Slowly, hesitantly, I reached out and caught hold of his hand. It was monumental. I think he knew it was, too. I hadn't been able to stand anyone except my mother touching me these last couple of weeks. I certainly hadn't been able to handle any man doing it. His eyes widened slightly at my contact, and I realized he was holding his breath, afraid for me.

I held his hand, feeling its warmth and the long, smooth fingers. There was so much power in connecting with another person, in having physical closeness. With just as much care as I'd used to touch it, I moved his hand to rest on my hip and stepped forward. Dorian swallowed, and for the first time since I'd known him, he looked timid.

"Eugenie—"

I pressed a finger to his lips and then stood on tiptoe to kiss him. His mouth opened instantly to mine, warm and eager. I pushed myself closer to him, but when I put his other arm around me, he pulled back slightly. I could feel and see the desire all over him, but he shook his head.

"No, no . . . it's too soon . . ."

"I'm the one who says when it's too soon." I kissed him again, harder, and was surprised at how quickly the lust burned through my body. Despite what I'd just said, I had believed until this moment that I would never want another man. But being near Dorian, feeling that electricity and power crackle between us . . . it brought forth all the old desire I'd been fighting recently, the desire that had nearly made me give in to him in that little village, back when I'd still been committed to Kiyo . . .

But I had no such commitments now.

He returned my kiss with equal intensity, his hands running along my hips. The passion was seizing him, he was starting to lose himself in it. Then, like before, some reasonable part of him slapped him to attention one more time. I think the world would have been shocked to know the Oak King had such a conscience. He broke away again, but this time, I didn't let him speak.

"Do you want my most recent time to be with *him*?" I demanded. "Do you want Leith to be the memory I carry with me of the last time I had sex?"

My fingers moved to the buttons of my short-sleeved cotton shirt and unfastened them all. Catching hold of his hands, I brought them toward my chest, spreading the shirt apart and making him touch my breasts. I'd gone braless today, and his hands felt warm where they stroked my bare skin.

"Make *this* my memory," I said huskily, with a bit more command in my voice than I'd intended. "Make it good. Make this be what I think of when I think of sex. Finish what you started that day . . ."

His hands no longer needed my urging. He cupped my breasts, fingers dancing around my nipples. At the same time, he pushed me toward the bed, laying me out on my back. His mouth crushed me with its kiss, and then his lips moved down my neck and to my breasts, taking one of my nipples in his mouth. He sucked gently at first, tongue darting back and forth, but then his lips grew more urgent. His teeth nipped at me while his hands deftly slid my jeans off. After they were on the floor, he sat up a moment, surveying me and all the bare skin before him.

Not having him touch me was agony, and I reached up, unfastening the bejeweled belt and his pants. He backed off the bed, standing up so that he could push his pants down the rest of the way. His shirt came off next, and then he stood there naked before me for my inspection, the perfect, marble god he'd been once before. Looking over the leanness of his muscles, how strong and hard he was, I felt my own body respond urgently. I'd complained to Kiyo before about foreplay, but right now, I wanted none with Dorian—though I had no doubt he would have given me hours of it, armies be damned.

"Don't wait," I begged him as I pushed my panties down over my hips. "Don't wait."

He caught hold of the panties and pulled them the rest of the way. I thought he'd join me on the bed, but instead he remained standing. He caught hold of my ankles and pulled me toward him until my ass just rested on the bed's edge. Still holding my ankles, he brought my legs up so they were nearly straight in the air, almost leaning on his shoulders. Then he leaned forward and pushed into me, moaning at the warmth and wetness he found there.

I threw my hands over my head, arching my body up and watching as he thrust back and forth. His eyes were on me too, taking in every part of me. There was something special about sex in the daylight, particularly with him standing over me like that so we could both fully see each other. There was no hiding. Everything was exposed. Vulnerable. It's easy to feel insecure in such moments, but I didn't, not with the way he looked at me, not with just lust—but with awe and adoration too.

He buried himself in me over and over, hard and forceful without being painful. It was such a lifetime away from what had taken place at Art's house that I realized nothing there could even be considered sex. Having Dorian in me felt good and right. My body was brimming with need, and he felt like fire where he moved between my thighs. That heat intensified within me, and I felt a spark of aching pleasure grow stronger and stronger, fueled with each thrust. I cried out, feeling my body on the verge of orgasm, and when it came, it was like an explosion of me, of the world . . . pure ecstasy and elation bursting from between my thighs to the tips of my fingers and toes.

He set my legs back flat on the bed and then lay on top of me, never breaking stride. If anything, he pumped more forcefully, nearing his own climax. That glorious hair rained down on my face, and I wrapped my arms around his neck, tangling my fingers in the silken strands. His own arms wrapped around my body, encircling me like a cocoon as his hips moved harder and harder.

Then, he exclaimed loudly, words that had no real form, and pressed his face against my neck as he came, his body spilling into mine. I held him close as he breathed heavily against my neck, his heart racing. Minutes passed, and his body finally calmed, though I continued to hold him. Finally, without breaking from my embrace, he lifted his head and brushed the hair from my face.

"I told you, Eugenie. I told you the world would be reborn when we were together. It will be reborn, and we will conquer it all . . ."

I brushed his lips with my fingers. "Don't get

carried away. We're just settling a grudge here."

The look in his eyes told me he believed a lot more would come of that, but he wisely said nothing. Rolling over, he settled beside me on the covers, and we both lay there, our fingers interlaced.

"I suppose," I said at last, "I should go talk to all those people out there, seeing as they're going to risk their lives for my honor."

"It's more than just your honor," he said. "It's the land's too. You are the land, and when they see you, they will gladly fight for you."

I sat up, my eyes falling on the silk dress. "I guess I've got to play the part. Too bad there's no crown."

Dorian sat up as well. "Isn't there?"

He walked over to the table he'd set his sword and cloak upon when entering. I'd been too distraught to notice at the time, but there was a small cloth-wrapped bundle there too. He brought it over to me, and I found myself holding my breath. I suddenly knew what it was, and I was afraid.

"What's wrong?" he asked when he held it out to me and I didn't take it.

"I . . . I had a dream . . ."

I couldn't explain that vision from the Underworld to him, that one where we'd stood on the hill together. When we had, I'd accepted Storm King's crown—or, well, a feminine version of it—

and that's when I'd found myself looking down upon all those soldiers waiting to fight for me.

"What kind of dream?"

"It's hard to explain."

Not waiting for me, Dorian unwrapped the bundle himself. My heart lurched as I braced myself to see it again, an elaborate work of platinum, laden with diamonds and amethysts . . .

But it wasn't.

The crown he held was gold and very, very delicate. I hesitantly took it and studied the fine details of it. There were little roses etched into it—roses with lots of thorns. Tiny emeralds—nothing too overwhelming—were scattered amongst the golden leaves. It didn't resemble Storm King's crown at all.

"This is Girard's work," I said with certainty.

"It is," Dorian agreed, running a finger down my bare arm. He seemed relieved that I had taken the crown. "You aren't the only one who can commission projects."

"But he works for Katrice."

"Not anymore. Remember that day you met him? I told you then he was an opportunist. He's rolled the dice and decided we're the side to align with—which, of course, we are. He'll come in very handy for weapons, I think."

My eyes were still on the crown and its beauty. I couldn't explain how relieved I was that it was nothing like the crown from the vision. Hesitantly,

I lifted it and rested it on top of my head. I looked to Dorian for confirmation. "What do you think?"

He smiled, reaching out to straighten it and arrange my hair slightly. "Go see for yourself."

Climbing out of bed, I walked over to the full-length mirror and surveyed myself. I was still naked, all that pale skin contrasting with the red of my hair and the glitter of the crown. My hair didn't have the blond that Jasmine's did, but it had the occasional gold highlight, and the crown made those locks gleam as they rested just past my shoulders. The emeralds were subtle, not gaudy, but vivid enough to further set off my hair and eyes.

"So what do you think?" Dorian asked.

I glanced over at him, still sprawled on the bed and watching me with amusement. I turned back to the mirror, studying my naked, crowned self. I smiled.

"I think it looks good on me."